RAWHIDE
JAKE

WESTWARD HO!

RAWHIDE JAKE

—————— • · • · • ——————

WESTWARD HO!

THE LIFE AND TIMES OF DETECTIVE
JONAS V. BRIGHTON BOOK III

JD ARNOLD

HAT CREEK

HAT CREEK

an imprint of
Roan & Weatherford Publishing Associates, LLC
Bentonville, Arkansas
www.roanweatherford.com

Library of Congress Cataloging-in-Publication Data
Names: Arnold, Jeffrey D, author
Title: Rawide Jake: Westward Ho!/JD Arnold |
The Life and Times of Detective Jonas V. Brighton #3
Description: Second Edition. | Bentonville: Hat Creek, 2023.
Identifiers: LCCN: 2023931641 | ISBN: 978-1-63373-813-3 (hardcover)
ISBN: 978-1-63373-814-0 (trade paperback) | ISBN: 978-1-63373-815-7 (eBook)
Subjects: | BISAC: FICTION/Westerns | Mystery & Detective/Historical
FICTION/Biographical
LC record available at: https://lccn.loc.gov/2023931641

Hat Creek trade paperback edition March, 2024

Cover Design by Casey W. Cowan
Interior Design by George "Clay" Mitchell
Editing by Amy Cowan

*Dedicated to all my grandchildren
and to the memory of Jack Becker.*

ACKNOWLEDGMENTS

POSTHUMOUS THANKS TO Jack Becker who meticulously researched and compiled the colorful history of Round Valley, Arizona. Also, I am indebted to Rita K.W. Ackerman for her information on Brighton in her book, *O.K. Corral Postscript: The Death of Ike Clanton* and to Harold L. Edwards for his research, and the composition of his article "The Man Who Killed Ike Clanton," published in the October 1991 issue of *True West* magazine, and gift of his material to the Arizona Historical Society. Much thanks as well to Marshall Trimble, Arizona State Historian and Contributing Editor of *True West* magazine, and Mark Boardman, Features Editor of *True West* and Editor of *The Tombstone Epitaph*. And whereas this edition is the product of Casey Cowan and Dennis Doty and their crew at Hat Creek, to whom I am most grateful, I am likewise grateful to Tiffany Schofield and her crew at Five Star Publishing for their endeavor in Books One and Two of this series. Of immense value and much use as needed in the trilogy are the Arizona, Kansas, Missouri and Texas state historical societies and, of course, Wikipedia.

ONE
ADIÓS AMIGOS • 1883

IT WAS CHRISTMASTIME 1884. Jonas Valentine Brighton—aka Rawhide Jake—brought his new wife of seven months, Mary Jane, to Independence, Kansas, to meet his two sons, who were in the care of his former sister-in-law, Mary, and her husband, Johnathan. Six years back Mary was married to Brighton's brother, who'd taken his sons under his wing because Jonas's wife and daughter were killed by a tornado while he was an inmate at the Kansas State Penitentiary in Lansing, later doing detective work and out riding the range. His brother, William, died suddenly three years past, and Mary remarried. Now that Jonas was married to a fine woman who was willing to be a mother to his boys, he thought it time to bring them to live with him and Mary Jane.

Jake tossed their bags off the passenger car landing, then clamped his hat on his head with one hand and pushed his muscular frame against the wind. He carefully navigated the icy steps of the train car down to the platform where he turned and held out his hand to Mary Jane. The wind blew her full-length coat every which way, and the valise she held in the crook of her elbow bounced against her side. She had to hold on to her hat with her free gloved hand while turning her face away from the stinging wind-driven snow.

"Welcome to Independence," Jake said with his dark gray eyes squinting nearly shut and a crooked smile etched on his face. He wrapped her in his arms and hustled them into the depot where heat radiated from the large potbelly stove in the center of the waiting room. As soon as he forced the door shut behind him, he turned to see Johnathan Gorham, who saw him at the same time. They moved to each other and shook hands. Since Jake was of average height, and Johnathan was tall and thin, Jake had to look up a little at him, which didn't matter one way or the other to Jake.

"Good to see you, Jonas," Gorham said.

"And you too, Johnathan. This is Mary Jane, my wife."

"Pleased to meet you, ma'am," Gorham said as he doffed his hat. "Hope the train ride wasn't too awful in this weather."

"Oh, I'm used to it. Take more than this little blow to bother a old Texian like me." She smiled up at him her gracious and beautiful smile that Jake loved. As always, she smelled deliciously of lavender. Under her hat, she wore her thick and shiny auburn hair swept up to the top of her head, with frizzled bangs over her forehead. Adorning her slim figure was a handsome dark-green traveling dress over which she wore her coat which she had unbuttoned. Her deep-blue eyes gleamed against her fair complexion with good cheer over full lips set in a little mischievous smile. Jake chuckled inwardly. He wasn't sure but that Johnathan wasn't smitten, like he had been the first time he saw Mary Jane.

"Good. I brought the rural mail delivery wagon to ride to the house. No seats, but it is closed on all sides, top and bottom. Keep you out of the wind." He beamed at Mary Jane.

"How considerate of you, Mister Gorham. Thank you." For once Mary Jane was serious and did not appear to be flirting.

"Please. Call me Johnathan. After all, we are family."

"Of course we are. Thank you, Johnathan." She smiled at him, and Jake watched Johnathan melt.

"All right," Jake said. "Let's get on board that mail wagon and head for the barn."

Later, at the supper table, Jake said to his sister-in-law, "That was delicious, Mary. Best pot roast I've had in a long time. Second only to yours, dear." Jonas winked at Mary Jane as he wiped his mustache and mouth clean with a white napkin.

"Jonas, would you like some coffee with your berry cobbler? I have one of those newfangled percolators, and a fresh pot is about ready," Mary said with a gracious smile as she rose from the table and started gathering up dirty dishes. "Alice, you can help with the dishes," she said to her twelve-year-old daughter.

"Yes, that would be excellent," Jake said.

"Me, too, hon," Johnathan said.

"Here let me help clean up, too," Mary Jane said as she stood.

"No, no. Alice and I will be just fine."

"Please. After all, we are all family." Mary Jane glanced quickly at both Jake and Johnathan and graced Mary with a beseeching expression on her face.

"Oh. All right. You are right. Besides, we have a lot to talk about which we can do while we clean up. But first, let me serve that coffee and cobbler while you and Alice finish clearing the table."

"I'd like a cup of coffee, too, Ma," piped up Harry, Jake's oldest, and the oldest of the five children at the Gorham house. He looked a little sheepish and adventurous at the same time.

"Oh, so now that you are a big fifteen-year-old, you think you are all done growing and a little coffee won't stunt your growth. Or are you just testing me, young man, now that your pa is here?" Everyone could see she was holding back a smile.

"Well, it would be all right with me, but you better listen to your Aunt Mary and do as she says." It was not lost on Jake that Harry called his aunt, "Ma." True enough, Harry and his brother had lived with Mary for over six years, and she had been a ma to the boys, but now Mary Jane was ready to step in. It was going to be a delicate situation, to say the least.

"Well, boys, looks like you growed about a foot since Christmas before last. Sorry I couldn't make it last Christmas. I was laid up. But just like year before last, we'll go down to the dry goods store, and you can have your pick of anythin'—within reason, of course." Jake grinned big at his two sons.

"Thanks, Pa," Harry said with a big grin splashed across his face. "We were kind of hoping you were gonna say that. Weren't we, Edgar?"

"You betcha. Yeah, thanks a heap, Pa. I still got my paint set from the year before last. Use it a lot, too." Edgar said the last with a serious expression.

"Well, I'd like to see some of your paintings. Might have a young

Rembrandt here. Maybe the cousins want to come along, eh, Johnathan? What a yer say?"

"Well, I am sure they would, but we already got their presents under the tree, and since you only got three days before Christmas, I think the time would be better spent with your boys and Mary Jane."

"Yeah. You're probably right. Well, it was just a thought."

Later that night, Jake and Mary Jane whispered in bed. "The boys seem to be very attached to the Gorham family," she said.

"Yeah. I noticed that too. I suppose it's only natural after all these years. Seems like my niece and nephews have taken to Johnathan too. All together, they seem like one big happy family. I don't know, Mary Jane. Do you think it's such a good idea to separate the boys from the rest of them? Oh, I know you are ready to take them in and be a ma to them, and a good ma you'd be too. And if we head for Arizona, that means they would be goin' to a strange land, to boot. I don't know."

"Let's give it a few days before we discuss it with the Gorhams. See how it goes."

"Yeah. That's a good idea."

The next morning, Jake held open the door to the dry goods side of Baden's store for Mary Jane and the boys. They trooped in and immediately started looking around at all the displayed merchandise. Jake kicked some snow aside and started to shut the door when a large clean-shaven man with a wild shag of black hair, no hat, and sheathed in a long black overcoat barged in through the door and gave Jake a nasty look. Jake glanced at Mary Jane and the boys and held back his temper. From his six-foot-plus height, the man stared down at Jake in an obvious challenge for Jake to say something. Jake averted his dark-gray eyes to the floor and said timidly, "Excuse me, sir, but I would like to shut the door." At the same time Jake sized up the feller and thought he might be a wrestler or something. He reminded him of Teasley, who Jake killed in prison—big and burly, mean without conscience, a bad man. While continuing to stare down at Jake, the man slowly moved to the inside and Jake shut the door. By this time Jake was aware that everyone in the store was watching them, so he slipped around behind the granite block of a man and went to stand by Mary Jane. He acted as if he were inspecting the goods she was holding while he kept an eye on the feller. The boys, a couple of tables over, went back to testing the slingshots they were examining.

"Boss needs a roastin' pan," the man said in a loud and gruff voice to the clerk. "Needs it to fix his Christmas goose. Show me whacha got." He ordered the clerk around like he was some kind of military sergeant, and Jake didn't like it. Didn't like him. He was just like Teasley.

"Right over there on that shelf." The clerk seemed reluctant to leave his post behind the counter by the cash register and pointed at the shelf where the pots and pans were displayed. The man swiveled his head and stepped off in the direction of the pointed finger. Half the distance to the shelf was where the boys were standing. They stepped aside as the man approached them. As he went by, he swatted them with a backhand that sent them both reeling against a table, which they bounced off of, and fell to their knees on the floor.

While the boys were floundering on the floor, the big, broad man took one more step, and Jake was on his back like a lion on an antelope. He wrapped one strong arm around the brute's thick neck, locked it in the crotch of his elbow and squeezed like an anaconda. That cut off the blood supply to the man's brain. Then he pulled the neck and upper body of the mini-giant hard toward him and brought his knee up and into the feller's groin. With that, the big man wilted, and Jake dropped him to the floor. The moans and groans of the injured man were loud and grotesque, but he was recovering. Jake saw that, so he dropped a knee into the man's broad midsection right at his solar plexus. That did it. The feller's eyes rolled in his head and he passed out. Jake grabbed the man's coat at the shoulders and dragged him over to the door, rolled him out onto the boardwalk and into the snow on the street. Jake went back inside the store and shut the dual-doors behind him.

"You know what you just done?" the clerk exclaimed with his mouth hanging wide open. "That there is Big Jack Horne. He's the bouncer over at Dalton's Saloon and Dance Parlor. He's killed men with his bare hands. The devil's henchman, he is, and he'll be after you. Won't stop till he kills you."

"He had no call to shove my boys."

"He don't need no call. He pretty much does what he wants."

"Uh-huh. I knew one of those kind before. He ain't walkin' this earth now."

Mary Jane had gathered up the boys and urged them to the door away from the fracas, but Jake held up his hand for her to stay back. "That Big Jack is still out there," Jake said as he glanced out the window and back to Mary Jane. "Best stay in the back there."

"Who are you anyway, mister?" the clerk said.

Jake stared at the clerk for a long minute. He decided he better get it out now rather than later. Besides, maybe the bouncer would be deterred from trying for revenge. "Rawhide Jake Brighton, range detective from Texas aka Jonas V. Brighton, detective from Nodaway County, Missourah," Jake said matter-of-factly.

"Rawhide Jake Brighton! Yeah. I heard a you. I used to clerk in Wichita Falls. You and Wes Wilson single-handedly cleared three, four counties in northwest Texas of all the rustlers. Killed most of 'em. Yessir, I heard a you. Maybe you can handle Big Jack Horne after all."

Jake glanced over at the boys whose eyes were open as wide as wide could be. Mary Jane tugged the boys to the back, but she couldn't plug their ears. When they heard all that was said by their pa, and about their pa, they zeroed in like eagles on the hunt.

From the window beside the doors Jake watched the big walrus regain consciousness and roll around in the snow holding his midsection and crotch until he got his head clear and had his bearings. Jake watched the black cloud of rage come over the bouncer's face as he stood up and swayed a bit in the street. As he regained his balance, Jake got ready. He tore off his coat and tossed it away to the floor off to his side. Horne roared and charged headfirst toward the doors to the store. Jake waited and just before the bouncer collided with the doors, he threw them open, caught the man by his coat front, balled up his body with his shoes in the bouncer's stomach, leaned way back, pulling the bouncer down almost on top of him, did a back roll somersault and thrust his legs upward, which sent the bouncer into a flip, crashing him to the floor against a display counter. Jake scrambled to his feet, and before the bouncer could stand up, kicked him hard in the head but his kick glanced off the blockhead. An evil, murderous grin and killer, demonic eyes came to the bouncer's face as he stood up, towering over Jake who lashed a wicked kick at Big Jack's right knee. A sickening crack of tendons separating rang out. Another kick to the left knee made the same gut-wrenching crack. The giant crashed to the floor in a roar of pain. He tried and failed to stand. He had no leg support, and the pain must have been excruciating. But his rage only increased as he tried to pull himself by scratching his hands and arms across the floor to get to Jake. He bellowed and mucous flowed from his nose and mouth as he reached with grasping hands to clench Jake's ankles.

It was hopeless. This man would not relent and would always be on Jake's trail. And who knew what he might do with Jake's family. Sooner or later there would be another showdown. Jake chose to make it sooner.

He let the monster grab his left ankle and pull him down to the floor. As he went down, in a blur Jake brought his right leg in a roundhouse kick that landed square on the big man's temple, and with a thud, bounced his head off one of the stout wooden table legs. In a whispering sigh of escaping air, Big Jack Horne went limp and breathed his last.

Mary Jane tried to hustle the boys out the front door, but they pulled away from her and stood gawking at the whole scene.

Jake glared hard and cold at the bouncer. "Shouldn't a shoved my boys and tried to kill me. It got you kilt and ruined our Christmas."

Everyone except Jake stood stark still in near disbelief of what they had just witnessed. Their eyes went from the bouncer to Jake and back again.

Jake sat heavily on a barrel and hung his head, slowly turning it from side to side. "Mary Jane, can you go with the boys back to the house? I'll stay here until the marshal comes. We'll finish our shopping tomorrow, boys." He said the last with a weak smile.

Again, his temper flare at bully abuse and other injustices probably was going to get him in trouble. He wasn't sorry for what he did. He could not abide bad men, and this bully was obviously a bad man. Swatting around young boys like that and, well, he got what he had coming to him, especially since he was also trying to kill Jake. And he absolutely could not let himself be killed in front of his boys. So, he had to slay the giant. He was sorry that his boys had to witness it and now maybe he might be spending Christmas in jail. The more he thought about it, the madder he became. And he was stewing about it like that when the marshal came in.

"What in tarnation is goin' on here, Harley?" the marshal boomed as he marched in through the doors. "Angus Carter said Jack Horne was rollin' around in the snow out front. That him there?" The marshal nodded toward the fallen bouncer. "Is he drunk or what?" Then he stooped down and rolled Horne over on to his back. "He's dead!" he exclaimed. He stood and in a quiet voice said, "Harley, what happened here?" And he looked over at Jake and stared at him for a long minute.

"Well, tell you the truth, Grover, looked to me like that big ox, Jack Horne, finally tried to push around the wrong person. Marshal Grover Nelson, meet Rawhide Jake Brighton outa Texas," Harley said as he held his hand out toward Jake as if he were introducing a vaudeville act. Marshal Nelson shrugged.

"Don't recognize the name."

Jake started to speak, but Harley beat him to it. "He's one a them stock detectives working for a cattlemen's association around Wichita Falls, Texas. Him and another detective cleaned all the rustlers outta four counties. Killed most of 'em. You remember I just came over from Wichita Falls a few month's back?"

"Uh-huh. Pleased, I'm sure," Marshal Nelson said as he tipped his hat to Jake. "But what exactly happened to Big Jack Horne here?"

"Well, Horne came bustin' in here like he busts in everywhere he goes, and says he needs a roastin' pan. So, I points to where they are over there, and he heads for them. Well, Jake's young boys are in the aisle there lookin' at the slingshots. They step aside for Horne, but that ain't good enough for him. He backhands 'em and knocks 'em to the floor." He swung his hand and arm in a backslapping motion and stared hard at Nelson. "Like that. Even draws a little blood in the mouth of one of the boys. Then Jake here goes over to him and says, angrily a course, 'What're you think you're doin'? You apologize to these boys.' A course you know Big Jack Horne, black-hearted as he is, he ain't gonna apologize for nothin'." Harley made a sour face. "He grabs Jake by his coat lapels and tries to shake him. That was his first mistake. Jake kicked him hard in the crotch, and that sent the bastard to the floor. Then Jake pounced on him with a knee to the gut, and Big Jack Horne went out like a light. He got some of his own medicine." Harley folded his arms across his chest and nodded his head up and down.

"So, how was he rollin' in the snow out in the street, if he was knocked out in here?"

"Well, Jake drug him out and tossed him in the street."

Nelson looked over at Jake and studied him for a long few seconds as if to appraise anew this Texas fellow. Jake looked away so as not to show any sign of challenge. Besides, Harley was doing just fine telling the story and embellishing it all by himself. "How'd he get back in here?"

"That was his second mistake. I guess he came to out there and came charging to the doors. Jake swung the doors open at the last moment and flipped that big bear up in the air and over on his back. Horne stood up, and Jake broke both his knees with vicious kicks." Harley demonstrated with his own kicking motion.

Again, Marshal Nelson looked over at Jake, who was looking more and more remorseful with each passing minute.

"Well, that did it for the Big Jack. He couldn't even stand. But you know how crazy he is, Grover. He's roarin' like a wounded bear, and he's crawlin' toward Jake." Harley made pulling motions with his arms like he was crawling and twisted his face up ugly. "He gets a hold of one a Jake's ankle and pulls him down, but, on the way down, Jake

kicks him in the head with a kick so fast and powerful, I could hardly see it. Well, that did it. Jake must of caught him in the temple or
somethin'. But I tell you, Grover, if Jake hadn't a done that, he would
be dead right now instead of that devil there."

"Uh-huh. Any other witnesses?"

"Just my family, Marshal. I sent them back to my sister-in-law's
house. We're visitin' them and my two boys for Christmas," Jake said.

"Who's your sister-in-law?"

"Mary Gorham."

"Oh! You're the Brighton brother of Bill, the blacksmith, with the
two boys he, before he passed, and Mary were carin' for while you
were in prison. Now she and Johnathan are carin' for 'em. Yeah, that's
right. What's your name again? Your real name?"

"Jonas V. Brighton."

"Yeah. Bill spoke highly of you. Said you were in prison because
you got mixed up with a couple a horse thieves, and they did you
wrong. Is that right?"

"Pretty much. Yes, sir."

"All right. I guess you agree with all that Harley described about
this here incident. Would that be correct?"

"Yes."

"Okay. Harley, I'll send the caretaker over. Both a you need to be
at the courthouse at nine in the morning tomorrow for the coroner's
inquest. You hear? All right. Good day."

After the marshal left, Jake stepped over closer to Harley and held
out his hand for a shake. "Thank you, mister, uh—" Jake said.

"Mulvane. Harley Mulvane. Glad to make your acquaintance,
Rawhide. Just call me Harley. What're you thankin' me for?" he said
as he shook Jake's hand.

"Well, for addin' on to the story like you did. Made it sound like I
was bein' more reasonable."

"You mean when I said you told Horne to apologize?"

"Yeah. And the other thing you said. He grabbed me and was gonna shake me. Makes it look more like self-defense. I am much obliged."

"Well, you're welcome, but you don't need to thank me. I'll tell the same story at the coroner inquest. The way I look at it, he was a bad feller and had it comin' to him. My first week here he roughed me up, and I ain't ever forgot. So, reckon he's paid up now. We're even." Harley slashed his hand across the air in front of him as if he were cutting off something, and his face held the countenance of a judge.

AT THE SUPPER table, the clanking of utensils on dinner plates seemed like it was amplified in the awkward silence. Finally, Jake spoke up. "Mary, Johnathan, I am sorry this happened. And particularly at this time of year. But there was nothin' I could do about it."

"You killed a man, Jonas," Mary said in a purely disgusted tone.

Jake pierced her through with a hard stare from his dark-gray eyes. "He slapped my boys, and when I protested, he tried to kill me. If he hadn't done that, he'd be alive today. That's how it is, Mary, in a world I am sure you know little or nothing about and aim to stay clear of. I heard he had a reputation around town for killing men with his bare hands. What was I to do? It was just fate. That's all. He did the wrong thing at the wrong time. At first, I just taught him a lesson with a little beatin'. But he came charging back with murder in his eyes. I wasn't of a mind to get kilt. That's the long and the short of it." Jonas held his gaze steady on his sister-in-law. "Do you understand?"

Mary glared back at him with unflinching steadiness. "Yes, I believe I do. And I will pray for you."

"Thank you. And while we are discussing unpleasant matters, I might as well tell you, now that I am married, I intend to take the boys back to Texas with me. Mary Jane has offered to help me and be their new ma."

Mary's facial skin tightened noticeably, her body went near rigid, and her eyes burned bright with seething fire. "We appreciate Mary Jane's offer, but we don't think that would be a good idea," she said through clenched teeth. "Children, you may all leave the table and go to your rooms. Don't be sneaking back to try and eavesdrop." The Brighton boys did not even glance at Jake. They, along with the other three children, obeyed without question. Jake took note of that.

"Well, now that I am able, I think it's about high time that I started doing my duty to raise up the boys. Don't misunderstand me. You and Johnathan have done a darn good job with those boys, and I am truly obliged. But the time has come for them to be with their real pa and his wife, who will be a ma to them just like you were. Listen, though, tomorrow is Christmas Eve Day, and I promised the boys I would take them back to the store for the presents. Why don't we put off discussin' this until after Christmas?" Jake smiled affably at Mary and Johnathan.

"Fine. But I suggest you take them to Covell's on Main. The boys said they don't want to go back to Baden's. Probably hear tomorrow anyway that Henry Baden doesn't want you back in his store. He is a devout Lutheran."

"What's bein' a Lutheran got to do with it?"

"Killing. Like us Catholics they don't cotton to killing."

Jake, dismayed, looked away. Then he said, "I told you. There was nothin' I could do about that."

"Yes. And since you couldn't control yourself, we have to live with the stigma. You'll leave in a couple of days, and we still have to live in this town. This town is growin', too. Natural gas discovery and all. Johnathan's the postmaster for God's sake." Jake glanced at Johnathan. He continued to stare out the window as he had the whole time. Mary Jane twisted her napkin, but they both kept quiet.

"How many men have you killed, Jonas?"

Jake stared at her and she at him, defiantly. "What's that got to do with anything? Don't seem like that is any concern a yours," he said tersely.

"It is my concern. I am the surrogate ma to your boys, and that information will influence my decision, if you persist, on whether I file an injunction or not. How many, Jonas?"

He remained silent for a minute. In a quiet but stern voice, he said, "I told you. None of your business."

Mary scraped her chair back, stood with her fists clenched at her sides and screamed, "How many!?"

Jake threw his chair back and it tumbled against the wall as he stood up. "You want to know. I'll tell you," he shouted. "Nine. And all of them but one were in the line of duty—usually self-defense. Maybe more. How do you like that, miss high-and-mighty?" He fairly shook with anger, and his eyes burned with rage.

Mary's hands automatically went to cover her gaping mouth as she dropped back down into her chair.

"I think we all just better calm down," Johnathan said, like he was in charge. He stood and put an arm around Mary, who now sat weeping quietly.

Jake sneered to show he was not impressed and said, "I *am* a stock detective, you know. Come on, Mary Jane. Let's go for a walk."

The clouds were parting, having just sent a thick flurry of soft snow to the earth. All sound was muffled by the blanket of white all around that twinkled in the light of a full moon glowing between the clouds. Except for a sporadic squeak from the soles of their boots, it was still and quiet. Even their footsteps made no sound in the new snow. Jake jammed his hands in his coat pockets and stalked his own shadow in the moonlight. Mary Jane kept up with him by wrapping her arms around his arm and interlocking her fingers.

"Well, I guess that took care of that," Jake breathed out. "She'll fight me every step of the way to keep those boys. From the sounds of it, they don't want to be with me, anyway."

"Why do you say that?"

"Well, they're so squeamish they asked not to go back to Baden's because, because what? Because they saw a man killed there? I wasn't but a year and a half older than Harry when I saw my first man killed and a whole bunch more—all in the war. Nah, she's got them brought up in her way. If they came with us, I'm afraid we would just butt heads all the time, and that ain't good for them or for us. Nah. Probly better just to let it be. What do ya think?"

"Yes. I think you are right. I see a lot of oil and water there. Not that I am trying to slip out of caring for them, mind you. Cuz I'm not. Let me, see? How to say this."

"Just say it."

"Well, I think they are city boys and would have a lot of trouble in Texas and Arizona. We are just a few years past the Indian Wars, you know. And I hear there is still trouble with the Apaches in the Arizona Territory. Those boys probably don't have the stomach for that kind a stuff. That means, like you said, you'd be butting heads. You'd always be trying to teach them, and we both know you ain't a patient man except when you're stalking a rustler." She tittered.

Jake squeezed her arm, turned his head to look into her eyes, and said tenderly with an affectionate smile, "I love you, Mary Jane."

"And I love you very much." She gave his lips a quick peck.

"Well, let's get back and break the news. See if we can salvage anything of this Christmas." He led her around in an arc in the snow to turn back the way they came, and they giggled together.

Halfway there, Jake said, "You know, Mary Jane, I don't think I like being Rawhide Jake much anymore. Seems to get me more into trouble than not. If we go to Arizona, I think I'll just go back to being plain old Jonas V. Brighton. That way there ain't no reputation to go ahead a me or follow me. Mary's right. They got to live in this town and so do the boys. They'll probably be pestered to death about what I done. Maybe even challenged. Might be good for them to stand up to it, though. But, even still. If it wasn't for losin' my temper at the sight of bad men doin' bad things, it pro'bly would be better for the boys and for Johnathan and Mary."

"Oh, I think that is a bit overestimated. After all, that fellow had a real bad reputation around town, and folks are probably glad he ain't around anymore."

"Yeah. They probably are, but they won't say it. After all, he was of the crowd in the saloon district across the tracks, and they don't like to reckon such a place like that in their town. But you would think they didn't like that feller crossin' the tracks neither." Jake kicked a small snow pile and said, "Well, I'll make up to Mary. Got the coroner's inquest tomorrow. Shopping with the boys," Jake turned his face to Mary Jane and rolled his eyes. "At Covell's. Maybe, hopefully, have a Christmas filled with peace and joy." He made a little ironic smile at Mary Jane. "Even though Harry and Edgar won't be coming with us. I wonder if they'll even talk to me."

Back at the house, Jake and Mary Jane arrived to find that everyone was in their bedrooms. Jake tapped lightly on Mary and Johnathan's door. Johnathan opened the door a little way and said, "Yes. What is it, Jonas?"

"Well. I just wanted to tell Mary that we decided to leave the boys here with ya'll."

Johnathan opened the door wider, and Mary came up beside him. She said in a voice that was a little hoarse, "Jonas, I am sorry for being cross with you. I—"

"Me, too, Mary. I guess I was just a little too touchy. But Mary Jane and I decided that it probly ain't, as you said, a good idea to up-root the boys and have all of us learn each other's ways. And, besides, my line a work don't help, plus it ain't a sure thing, but we might be movin' to Arizona Territory."

Mary smiled pleasantly and said, "Yes, I think that is the right decision. Let's talk more about it in the morning."

TWO WEEKS LATER, Jake and Mary Jane were back at the settlement and their apartment in the big house of Xavier Calhoun, owner of the huge spread of the Flying XC, headquartered at Comanche Creek. They lived in the back of the house where Mary Jane cooked and kept house for the Calhouns. Another two weeks later, Jake's range detective partner, Wes Wilson, was at their house for supper.

"I heared yer got yerself another notch in yer pistol grip 'cept yer didn't use no pistol," Wes said to Jake as he glanced back and forth at Jake in the looking glass with a sly smile and eyes full of jollity. He carefully pulled the straight-edge razor across his chin and around his big, yellow handlebar mustache. He was stripped down to his union suit but still wore his boots and spurs.

Jake responded, "And I see yer ain't been to the barber shop since I left. Didn't even get a haircut for Christmas. Red-headed wild man sittin' so tall in the saddle like you was king of the range detectives. What kind a heathen are yer, anyway?"

"Wal, I reckon the worst kind, but at least I didn't kilt nobody at Christmastime, and I ain't sittin' the saddle right now. And this mirror must be the worst one in the house." Wes tucked his head down as if to dodge any missile Jake might throw at him. He laughed his regular rolling laugh.

"If yer weren't so tall you'd be able to see in that glass just fine. Just be glad Mary Jane had it. How'd yer hear 'bout that, anyhow?"

"The boss told me. I told yer he tells me everthin'. Yer did right by reportin' it to Jim. And he had to tell me so's I could keep my eye on yer." Wes grinned and ducked again.

"Yeah, well. What's he got planned for us now?"

"Same 'ol thing. Ride the range. See if we pick up any sign a rustlin'. Talk with the cow bosses and range bosses at all the brands. See how they's all doin'. Lot a 'em got all they's critters in close for feed and water cuz a the drought. Talkin' to the hands. Keepin' our ears open at the saloons. Just doin' our job." He grinned in the mirror. "But he wants us to go back out to Seymour and work all the spreads thereabouts."

"Uh-huh. Wal, hurry up. I smell vittles cookin'. Mary Jane'll be callin' us for supper any minute now."

Wes took a towel and wiped the excess shaving cream off his face and said, "I'll be right there as soon as I change my underwear and put on some clean duds."

At the table over coffee after dessert, Jake looked seriously at Wes over his cup as he sipped the hot brew. Wes stretched out his lanky frame on the chair with his boots crossed with one muscular arm and sun-bronzed, gnarled hand laid out on the table to tend his coffee mug and the other draped across the back of the chair that was filled with his broad shoulders and chest. He smiled pleasantly as if he was well-satisfied with the meal.

"Told Loving yet?" Wes asked.

"No. I ain't ready to go off the payroll just yet. And yer said he wants us down to Seymour. So, at least for a few more months, that's where we'll be. Probly stay at Madison House. What 'bout yer?"

"Yeah. Wal, we cleaned that Conroy crew out a the Hashknife last year and yer and Jimmie Roberts jailed Sour Billy Connell's outfit that was rustlin' the XC and L Bar. We knocked out that crew that was hittin' the MC, and we got a few more along the line. Fencin' war is all over. We may end up just sittin' back with our feet against the fire for the rest of this winter." He smiled again at Mary Jane.

"Yer seen Loving's new office yet?" Jake said

"In Jacksboro? Nope. We ought ta head on down there and pay him a visit."

"When I'm ready," Jake said with a firm look over the rim of his coffee mug.

"Yeah. Wal, it's 'bout seventy-five mile from Seymour to Jacksboro, and I sure ain't bouncin' around in no stagecoach all that way. So, have to ride it. Two days. Or there's the train from Wichita Falls to Decatur. Bring the boys and ride back to Jacksboro from Decatur. Me and Noble ain't never been on a fancy train before. Bet Jasper ain't neither." He grinned his big devil-may-care grin at them.

Jake started laughing, and Mary Jane joined in. "Yer are a silver-tongued devil, yer are. I knowed yer could always talk a blue streak. But didn't never think yer was the persuadin' type. Cuz yer just made me think. Okay, it's comin' up on February, and Vandervert says even though they ain't got a signed deal, they's roundin' up a herd on their Pecos spread to deliver to Aztec. So, they must think a deal is gonna be made. Reckon, sometime or other, me and Jasper'll be in a train."

Wes shrugged his shoulders. Mary Jane got up and brought a bottle of Overholt and two glasses to the table, then started washing the dishes.

Jake continued, "Wal, I was thinkin' it might be good for Jasper to ride a train to Decatur and get used to it before the long haul to Arizona. But what if he don't like it. You know how he can be. Then he'd be ruined, and I never get him on a train."

"Have to blindfold him," Wes said matter-of-factly.

Jake filled their glasses and studied Wes's face without seeing him. He was thinking. "It's 'bout four or five hours by train to Decatur. Um, I don't know." They both sat silently and sipped their whiskeys. After a couple of minutes, Jake said, "All right. We'll give it a whirl. See how he does. He's gonna have to have his own stall. Yer know how he hates to be in a herd."

"Yeah. He thinks he's the prince, all right."

"Wal, if we're headin' out for Seymour sooner than later, I better get on over to Comanche Creek and say adiós to Walt and Jimmie."

"Yeah, Walt'll probably have trouble runnin' the Flyin' XC if yer're gone, and now Jimmie'll have to ride the whole fence instead of just half it." Wes frowned his concern for a minute, followed by a smile.

"Just showin' my respect by stopping by. Probably ride over tomorrow." Jake ignored Wes's joke. "I did work two years undercover for Walt, yer know. And saved his life pro'bly twice. And Millie, that's his wife, did give me and Mary Jane a little wedding reception. And me and Jimmie rode together and faced down killers and all that. So don't yer think I should at least say goodbye?"

"Wal, I think 'ol Walt and Jimmie oughten ride over here and pay their respects to yer." Wes clucked his tongue and took a sip of whiskey. He watched Jake over the rim of his glass.

"That ain't likely to happen. If Walt was the feller leavin' he'd probably do that. But he ain't. So, he expects me to show up at his place."

"Oh, a course. I was just joshin' yer." He grinned again and tapped Jake's shoulder with his fist.

———————

A WEEK LATER they stood on the loading platform and watched

as the wranglers pushed Wes's bay gelding, Noble, into the stock car. He turned around, and they tied off his bridle. Then they locked the stall-side fence into place so Noble couldn't move sideways. Next, it was Jasper's turn.

"Maybe, I better load him," Jake said.

"And get yer dandy new duds all dirty? He'll be fine," Wes smiled assurance as he looked Jake up and down. They both wore brand new jeans and shirts, had polished their boots and brushed their hats. 'Course a body couldn't see their new duds because of the heavy fleece-lined full-length gray ulster coats they wore.

As one wrangler led the big feller distinguished by large tobiano black and white splotches of color and a golden tail and mane, Jake smiled in admiration. His boy stood about sixteen and a half hands and he was well muscled with a mind of his own. When Jasper approached the ramp up to the platform, he crow-hopped and started backing down the ramp. Jake hurried over next to him and caught his bridle, caressed his neck and spoke sweet-nothings into his ear. He got him heading back toward the platform, then took from his pocket a couple of pieces of hard candy, held them in front of Jasper's nose as he led him up the ramp and into the stock car. Then he turned him around and gave him one piece of candy. Once he was tied off and wedged in to his stall, Jake let him nibble the other piece of candy out of his hand. He dusted his hands together as he came out of the car and said to Wes, "See. Nothin' to it."

Wes turned his head from side to side and said, "Yer spoilt that hoss, sure." And they made the train ride on down to Decatur with no trouble. They were enjoying the scenery from the smoking car where they sat with their cigars and whiskies. Halfway along Jake pulled a sack from his saddlebag, and they dined on ham sandwiches Mary Jane had packed for them.

"Wal, so this is how the civilizees get by, huh? Must be tough," Wes said and bit a hunk off his sandwich. Jake just grinned. He was thinking about what he was going to say to Jim Loving, the president of the Stock-Raisers' Association of North-West Texas. It was

Jim who gave him the nickname Jake, hired him to be a range detective for the association when he didn't know a thing about cows, brands, and cowboying, and he also got a murder charge against him dismissed. Jake owed him a lot. Then he glanced sideways at Wes and smiled to himself. It was Wes who gave him the handle Rawhide Jake. Guess he owed him, too.

It was dark when they rode into Jacksboro. They got the boys fed, watered, and settled in at the livery. Carrying their saddlebags and rifles, they made for the hotel to check into their rooms. Next stop was a saloon, then supper at a café, and back to their rooms.

In the morning they crossed the threshold of the association office, and Jim Loving happened to be there to greet them. "Wal, now, look what the cat drug in," he said with a big smile under his big mustache and stepped forward to shake hands with Wes and Jake. "What brings ya'll down here to HQ? Ya'll ain't both gonna quit, are you?"

"No, boss. Not us both. Just Jake," Wes said as Loving stood in front of them as tall as Wes and still sturdy for his age but not as muscular as either Jake or Wes.

Jake snapped his head around to glare at Wes and said, "Sheeze, Wes. Have some respect. I could a told him in my own time."

"Aw, yer beat around the bush too long. Best to jest git it out right away."

"Says yer," Jake said, clearly annoyed.

"Well, let's sit down, and ya'll can tell me all about it. I'd offer ya'll a whiskey, but it's a tad early. How about some coffee?"

Jake told him the plan and watched anxiously while Loving contemplated his coffee mug.

"Yeah, I know most a those boys," he said. "Bill Hughes, Henry Warren, John Simpson, his brother Jim, Charlie Buster. Don't know that Kinsley feller, though. He's a Easterner. Guess he brought in the eastern investors to capitalize Aztec. Of course, Simpson tells me all about it every time I see him. His brother, Jim, is gonna go on out to Arizona. Warren's goin' into Aztec pretty heavy. Well, no matter. Got yerself married, huh?"

"Yes, sir."

"Well, you know about my policy on family men. Probably for the best that you want to quit the posse now." He smiled so as to show he meant no offense.

"That's what I was thinkin'. Sorry. Couldn't help it. She's a beauty. Ain't she, Wes?"

"Yep."

"Well, you did a real fine job for us while you were with us."

"I ain't quittin' yet, boss."

Loving raised his eyebrows and said, "I thought that's the reason ya'll are down here. Turn in Jasper, saddle, tack, and all."

"No, sir. Just came to give you notice and, if the price is right, I'll buy 'ol Jasper and all from you."

Loving sipped his coffee, swallowed and said. "Well, that's mighty fine a you. Give me a chance to hire and break in your replacement. Know anybody, Wes?"

"Jake can't be replaced." For a few seconds the room was silent. Wes grinned to which they all laughed. "Wal. Hard to replace, anyhow," he said with a wink at Jake.

"I agree. And just to show you I mean it, I'm givin' Jasper and the saddle and tack to you."

"Aw, no. You don't have to do that, boss. Honest now."

"I know I don't have to, but I want to. And I'll give you a letter of recommendation too."

"Wal, thanks a heap. But you don't have to." Jake swallowed hard and stared at the floor. His chest heaved slightly when he looked up and said in a choked voice, "You're the best boss I ever had."

Loving said, "Oh, go on now," and waved him off. "Let's see. Simpson told me he expects the Aztec deal to be signed in a couple a months. So that gives me until April or so before you leave. You wouldn't mind if I partnered you with your replacement for a month or so?"

"Absolutely not."

"All right, then. I guess that's it, then. I'll send the letter to Seymour. You be at the Madison?" Jake nodded yes. "Wal, all right, ya'll gonna ride on out to Seymour?"

"Yep. Reckon we better git goin'," Wes said as he set his coffee mug on the table and stood up.

"You boys keep up the good work," Loving said while he lightly slapped their backs as they walked to the door. "The association appreciates it a heap. You had breakfast yet? No? Well, come on I'll buy down at the café."

After breakfast the detectives said their goodbyes and within the half hour were riding out of town on the road west to Seymour. Wes turned in his saddle and said to Jake, "How come yer waitin' fer the Aztec to sign the deal afore yer go to Arizona?"

"Yer know. I don't know. I think at first I thought about hirin' on with 'em. But I don't know. Just carried over that a way, I guess. 'Sides, it gives Jim time to replace me. Yer got any ideers on a replacement?"

Wes grinned at Jake. "No. All joshin' aside," Wes said. "Wal, there is Jimmie Roberts and anuther feller I know outta Vernon. Maybe. Hard to say."

THE DEAL BETWEEN Continental and Aztec was signed on April 20, 1885, for the Continental's Pecos ranch cattle and horses and outfit to be counted and delivered to Henry Warren on Aztec's Pecos Spread. That meant that from that date the hard work of counting and preparing the herds to trail to Holbrook, Arizona Territory, commenced. And it meant Jake and Mary Jane could move on out to Arizona ahead of them and, hopefully be settled in by the time the first Aztec herd arrived. But they had decided to roll the dice and he had no idea what he would do for income. Maybe something with the Hashknife brand or something else.

Jake brought Mary Jane down to Seymour by buggy from the Calhoun settlement two weeks past. Everything was ready to go. Jake had the Conestoga wagon he and Wes owned for the fencing business and the team of draft horses holed up at the livery. The wagon was partially loaded with the Brightons' goods they were bringing along, and Jake had his teamster, Chenglei, of the fencing crew, rig up a canopy to shade Mary Jane. It was a one-day haul to the Hashknife at Miller Creek, where they would stop overnight. Then another two days on to Abilene to board the train. They were planning to leave in the morning, so Jake, Mary Jane, and Wes decided to have a last supper together at the Brazos Saloon.

The three of them stepped into the saloon through the double doors, one of which Wes held open for Mary Jane, while he smiled broadly at her and Jake as honored guests, and so did everybody else who would look at them. "Let's get a table over there in the dining area," Jake said.

There was one poker game going on the other side of the room. About five fellers were at the bar and there was no piano music playing. The low murmur of intertwining male conversation was all that could be heard.

Wes pulled the chair out for Mary Jane and seated her proper, still smiling. "What're yer, the butler or somethin'?" Jake said sarcastically.

"Just a proper gentleman," Wes answered as he pulled off his hat and dipped his head slightly. Then he hung his hat by the stampede string on the knob of his chair back, swung a leg over the seatback, like he was stepping into a saddle, and sat down.

"Wal, yer must be a civilizee, after all," Jake said with a feigned look of astonishment.

"Thas right. Yer ain't the only one, yer know."

"Yeah, but—"

"Boys," Mary Jane interrupted. "Let's do try and behave. Look, here comes the waitress."

Cherry, the New Orleans belle and soiled dove, who worked undercover for Jake, came to the table, walking elegantly. She smiled gracefully and under the pile of brunette hair atop her head her face shone with a friendly demeanor, highlighted by sparkling smokey gray eyes.

"Good evening, ya'll. Alex said I should wait on ya'll tonight. So here I am." She spread her arms as if to present herself to them.

"Wal, that's top shelf. Wouldn't want nobody else," Wes lavished her with the best adoring grin he could offer. Jake stared at him for a few seconds and shook his head.

"Mary Jane, this is Cherry LeClaire from New Orleans. She used to work for me."

"And that's all. Detective work and nothing else. Pleased to meet you." As she held out her hand, she gave Mary Jane a knowing woman-to-woman look that let it be known that she and Jake had never rolled in the hay.

Of course, that was a bit of a stretch since early on in their relationship they were intimate. Either Cherry had forgotten or was protecting Jake.

Mary Jane got the message and said with a pleasant smile, "Likewise, I am sure."

"Watch out for that Mex, Desi, though. She could care less about a man's wife. If you get my drift."

"Okay, Cherry, I think we got the idea. Is Desi here tonight?" Jake said as he glanced around the room.

"I haven't seen her, but that doesn't mean anything. You know how she can sneak up on you." Cherry grinned at Jake, and he turned a little red. Wes was still mooning over Cherry, and she noticed it, so she gave him a cute and slightly lascivious smile as if to say, *later.* "And what do you mean by 'used to work for me?'"

"This is our last night in town. We're headin' for Arizona."

"Arizona? Don't they have Indians on the warpath out there?"

"Nah. They's all on the reservation down the south. We will be up north."

"That ain't what the paper says," Alex, the owner/bartender, said as he sauntered up to the table holding a newspaper in his hands. He took a drag off his cigarette, blew the curling blue smoke away from him, and said, "Look at this."

He held the front page up for everyone to see the banner headline.

GERONIMO BREAKS OUT AGAIN
Arizonans In A Panic.

Jake stared at the newspaper for a few seconds, glanced at Wes, who shrugged, and looked inquiringly at Mary Jane.

"We Texans beat the Comanches. I guess we can handle a few renegade Apaches," Mary Jane said in response to Jake's inquiring eyes. "Are there any specials on the menu tonight?"

"Sorry. Alex doesn't put on specials. Ya'll have a choice of beef steak or ham steak. They both come with mashed potatoes and green beans. I think he has a strawberry pie tonight. Don't you?" she said to him.

"Sure do. Fresh today from Lorna's." He made a circle with his thumb and index finger to signal excellence.

"Well, Alex fixes up a real good beef steak. Ages his meat even after he gets it from the butcher. That's what I recommend," Jake said.

"That's right. I do. So tender it'll melt in your mouth," Alex said as he held his head high.

"I'll have one, too," Wes chimed in.

"Well, might as well make it three," Mary Jane said.

"And if yer ain't tapped that barrel of Overholt I know yer keep hid in the back," Wes said with a scowl at Alex, "then crack it open and bring us three tall glasses."

"How'd you know about that?" Alex looked peeved.

"See this here nose?" Wes said as he put a finger to the tip of his nose. "It gits inside a hunnert feet of good rye whiskey and it starts to itch real bad. Happens evertime. That's how I know." He grinned and his eyes danced with delight.

"Well, I only sell it on special occasions, so I guess I can spare some. It'll cost you, though."

"Ain't worried 'bout that. Yer just bring it on out here."

"Back in a jiffy."

Alex and Cherry departed to retrieve the orders, and Jake leaned in and said to Wes in a low voice, "Does yer nose really do that?"

Wes's grin widened, and his eyes seemed like they would dance right out of his head. Then he looked at Mary Jane, who was staring at him scornfully in a playful way. That sort of soured Wes's glee, and the grin vanished to be replaced by a serious expression. "'Course not," he said. "What're yer think I am? Some kind a drunk?"

"No. For a minute, though, I did think yer might be a civilizee, hah, hah, hah. Detectin' good whiskey and all." The joke brought laughs all around.

"Cherry told me 'bout it one time when I was hankerin' for a good whiskey. She snuck me some." He smiled like he was one so persuasive.

Cherry brought the whiskies and set them around in front of the three. Wes smiled broadly at her, plucked his glass from the table, held it up and said, "Here's how!"

"Here's how!" Mary Jane and Jake said as they clinked glasses with Wes.

Mary Jane took a sip of her whiskey and said, "Well, Wes, when you gonna get yourself hitched?"

"Oh, I 'spect that'll be a long time comin'. I like it out there on the range. I like rangerin' and Jim. Wal, he don't like his men bein' in a family way what with the danger and all. So...." He grinned and took down some whiskey. "Mighty fine," he said as he admired the glass of amber liquor. "Kind a reminds me a the time we was at the Circle Bar B and had that fancy white lightnin'. 'Member that? What'd they call it?"

"Vodka."

"Yeah. Vodka. That's it. This Overholt is better, though."

They chatted on about nothing important when presently Cherry brought the food and served it all around. Wes and she exchanged love-looks, and after she departed, he said, "'Course ol' Jim may have to change his rules if I start sparkin' that Cherry beauty. I don't think I'd mind bein' hitched to her." He grinned.

They had finished supper, and the men smoked their cigars and drank more Overholt whiskey while Mary Jane amused herself listening to their banter and stories. When she looked up, she saw a pretty petite Mexican girl in a flashy red dress hustling directly for their table. She came right up and stood between Mary Jane and Jake with her hands on her hips. She glared down at Mary Jane with hot Latin eyes and pouting lips.

"I see this is the woman who stole my Jake away from me, eh?"

Mary Jane stood up and said, "I am Mary Jane Brighton, and who might you be?"

"I am Desi. I was Jake's lover until you got your hooks into him. I don't like that. So, take this, *gringa.*"

Desi wound up to land a roundhouse punch to Mary Jane's jaw. She swung her fist viciously, and the punch was but ten inches away from Mary Jane's face when Jake jumped to his feet to grab Desi and was too late. But Mary Jane parried the punch away with her forearm, sunk her gripping hands into Desi's shoulders, and threw her to floor with a heave of her body against the lesser weight of Desi's little body. Desi hit the floor with a thud, and the breath escaped from her mouth in a great gush. She was dazed and could not catch her breath. Jake made a move toward her to help her and was bumped away by Wes who said, "Let me handle this bronc." He bent down over her and lifted her backside slightly off the floor to try and relieve the shock to her abdomen so she could breathe. Slowly, she came around, and Wes lifted her up and tossed her over his shoulder. "I'll take care of her," he said and headed for the stairs to the second floor carrying her on his shoulder like a sack of grain.

Halfway up the stairs, Desi came to and started screaming in Spanish. Wes covered her mouth with his hand and continued to climb. Cherry hurried up after him. They got to the top, and Cherry said, "Over here. In this room." She pointed down through the yellow cast of the wall-mounted lamps of the dim passageway. She opened the door, Wes went through with his cargo, and tossed her on the bed.

"You stinkin' bastard *gringo.* Who are you? Nobody. And nobody treats Desi like this." She screamed it so loud the room seemed to vibrate. She started flailing about while trying to bite a chunk out of Wes's arm. She tried to scratch his face and kick him in the head with her flying feet. Through it all Wes just grinned at her and dodged all her attempts to injure him while he held her down against the mattress with one hand pressed into her chest.

Meanwhile, Jake and Mary Jane sat at the table talking in a bemused way.

"Well, now you've met Desi," Jake said with a smirk.

"Were you one of her customers?" Mary Jane was not smiling, and Jake faltered.

"Well, yeah. But not since I proposed to you."

"You better not ever touch her again," Mary Jane said with a very stern glare at Jake. Then she grinned wryly and said, "At least, don't let me catch you."

"Whew." Jake let out a big breath of relief. "You had me goin' there." He laughed. "I ain't ever touchin' anyone one but yer, my love." He smiled affectionately and tipped his glass to her. "Besides, after I seen the way you tumbled Desi, I don't think I would chance you comin' after me." He grinned and sipped his whiskey.

"Yeah, she wasn't much fight at all. Not strong. 'Course, what a you expect from someone who spends all her time on her back?" She grinned and sipped her tea. "Sure is making a hell of a racket up there. Wonder what Wes is doing to her."

"He's probably just trying to dodge that rattler's fangs." Jake sneered.

And, sure enough, Desi got her teeth into Wes' arm. He had to grab her hair and yank hard to break her grip. "That does it, little *senorita*. Yer're gonna get it now," he growled as his grin immediately changed to a clenched-teeth grimace. He reached over her and pulled the bedsheet over the top of her and wrapped her up like a mummy. Holding her flailing legs down with his knee, he tied the corners of the sheet over her head and around her feet. "There, that should hold yer until yer fire goes out. Cherry, yer got a key for the lock on that door?"

"Yes. I'll fetch it."

"There. Guess we're safe now," Wes said with his infectious grin as he turned the key in the lock and turned to gaze upon Cherry.

"Let me see that arm where she bit you. A body can get a bad infection from a human bite." He rolled up the sleeve of his shirt, and

Cherry took his arm in her hand and turned it over and back. "Didn't break the skin. Only a deep bruise."

"Pro'bly couldn't get through my canvas shirt, huh?"

"Probably."

"Want to go back downstairs?"

She let her lips part in a seductive smile. "No. Let's go to my room."

Downstairs, Jake strode over to the bar with Mary Jane on his arm, motioned Alex over, held out his hand and said, "Well, guess this is it, Alex. You've been a big help to me, and I want to thank you proper before we leave."

Alex took his hand, gripped it, and shook it friendly-like. "It's been my pleasure, Jake. Hope to see you again down the road. Nice meetin' you, Missus Brighton." He beamed smiles, but when the banging noise came from upstairs, he quickly looked annoyed and said, "Guess I better go up and straighten out that hot chili pepper. Jake, could I impose on you to watch the bar for me while I take care of this?"

"Absolutely. We'll be right here."

Alex flew upstairs taking the steps two at a time. The banging was caused by Desi kicking the door she was locked up behind. She apparently had loosed herself from the sheet Wes tied around her. The key to the door lock was on the floor in the hall in front of the door. Desi's kicking the door had shook it loose. Alex picked it up, unlocked the door, kicked it open, and shoved Desi back on the bed. He pulled a deadly-looking throwing knife from inside his shirt at the back of his neck where it was hidden in a slick scabbard. His eyes were fierce, and he bared his teeth like a snarling dog.

"You know what I can do with this, Desi. Don't make me use it on you," he said low and quiet while he held her fixed in a near trance as he glared at her. Her eyes were large, she shook, perspiration appeared on her forehead and dripped to her already sweat-stained bodice.

"I— I— I. They, they—" she stuttered.

"There is no excuse. You get out a here and go home. Don't come back until you got control of yourself. And you will get control if you want to work here. Do you want to work here?"

She nodded her head yes and said, *"Sí, jefe.* Sorry I lose my temper. I'll be good girl."

"Alright. That's good. And you leave those folks alone, including Wes and Cherry. You hear me?"

"Sí." She dropped her eyes and stared at the corner of the bed sheet she was twisting.

"Okay. Go on. Get out a here."

"No more work tonight?"

"No." She stood and with her head hanging shuffled out the door. "Go out down the back stairs," Alex ordered. She looked back at him with a little fire starting to brew in her eyes from the apparent insult. "Just so the customers don't get to talking, is all." She tossed her hair and walked down the hall with her nose in the sir. Alex, re-sheathed his knife, straightened his collar, and went back downstairs.

"No orders," Jake said with a wry smile. "Everything okay up there?"

"Yep. Thanks, Jake."

"Well, let's head for the barn, my love," Jake said to Mary Jane.

"Shouldn't we wait for Wes?"

"Oh, I think he'll be a while yet."

JUST BEFORE SUNUP it was still chilly for a spring day in the middle of May, when Jake stepped off the Madison House steps and onto the dirt street. He pulled his coat collar up around his neck and hurried over to the livery where by lantern light Jake's wagon driver, Chenglei, was harnessing the horses for hitching to the Conestoga wagon they used in the fencing business. He was seventeen years old now and had been driving the wagon for Jake and Wes for two years as part of the Chinese labor crew they employed to install barbed-wire fence throughout the four counties. At this time, the crew was working on fencing farm pastures not far from Seymour.

The horses Chenglei was harnessing were a matched pair of big dapple-white geldings, at least eighteen hands tall, big-boned and as stocky as an ox. Their undercoats were creamy white splashed with light blueish-gray with creamy dapples spread over the gray. They would have been white if not for the patches of light gray. Their faces were white with pink and blue-gray noses and their manes, tails, and stockings were white. They were a handsome pair of matched Shires.

"Mornin', Chenglei," Jake said as he came up to the horses and stroked their necks.

The young Chinese man stopped what he was doing, bowed slightly, and said, "Good morning, *zhǔ rén*."

Then a cackling laugh came from the dark depth of the barn, followed by a short and lean man who appeared saying, "Chew en. Chew en. What's that mean? Some kind a tabaccy?"

"Howdy, Quincy. Reckon it don't make no difference since yer won't be seein' me no more. What do I owe yer for stablin'?"

"What a yer mean? Where yer goin'?"

"Arizona."

"Arizona? Well, if that don't beat all. What ya gonna do out there?"

"Don't rightly know yet."

Quincy scratched his bald head. "Never figgered yer for somethin' like that. Missus goin' with yer?"

"Yep."

"Wal, even though we done had our ups and downs, I wish you all the best." He stared at the dirt floor and traced a circle with the toe of his boot. Then he popped his head up and said in a challenge, "But yer ain't gettin' away without payin'. Be three bucks for ever'thing." He stuck out his lower lip, spread his feet, and put his hands on his hips.

Jake stared at him until he started fidgeting. "Already asked yer what I owed."

"Wal, now yer know."

"What a ya'll jawin' 'bout?" Wes said as he walked in through the barn door.

"Settlin' up. What are yer doin' here?" Jake queried.

"Reckon I'll mosey along with yer on down to the Hashknife just so's yer don't git in any trouble yer cain't git yerself outta." He grinned and Quincy cackled. "Howdy, Chenglei," Wes said.

Chenglei bowed slightly and said, "Good morning, *zhǔ rén.*"

"Yer a chew en, too? Heh, heh, heh." Quincy said in singsong way. Jake and Wes glared at him. He looked away, went around and hid beside one of the horses, but he couldn't stop his low giggling.

"Yer had breakfast?" Jake said to Wes.

"Not yet. Ain't even had any coffee yet."

"Let's go over to the café. I'll buy yer breakfast. Chenglei, you want some breakfast?"

"No, thank you, *zhǔ rén.* Finish job here. Eat later."

Jake looked inquiringly at Quincy who came back around in front of the horses. "Aw, nah. Thanks. Already et, and I got coffee on the stove in the office," he said with a wave of dismissal.

"All right. Let's go. We'll be ready to pull out in about an hour, Quincy." Jake got a wave back from the livery owner.

The ranger partners finished their breakfast, and Jake asked if he could take some biscuits and coffee to Mary Jane. The waitress made up a little bundle and poured a tin of coffee. "Thank you," he said. "I'll be sure to bring it back directly," Jake assured her.

As for Mary Jane, she gave Jake a big wet kiss on the cheek and said, "You are so thoughtful." Her eyes glistened with admiration for her husband.

"Yeah, well. Better get it down. We gotta get goin'."

"Ain't real romantic, though."

Jake came up to her and wrapped her up in his arms and said, "Got the trail on my mind, is all. I'll make it up to you later." He grinned knowingly.

She returned Jake's grin with an impish look of her own as she slowly and suggestively munched a biscuit. She sipped some coffee and Jake said, "These bags ready?"

Mary Jane shook her head yes. She turned away with a swish of her skirt as she finished her biscuit and coffee.

After returning the coffee tin to the café, they walked to the livery and found Wes leaning against the barn wall with one leg crooked at the knee and his boot heel pressed to the wall. He casually smoked a cigar and tipped his hat to Mary Jane. The team and wagon were off to the side of the barn. The horses fidgeted with their bits, swished their tails, and stomped a hoof to the ground every so often to shake off flies. "Mornin', Missus Brighton," Wes drawled with a big smile.

"Mornin' to you, sir." She dipped her head. Jake started into the barn.

"Where yer goin'?" Wes said.

"Saddle up ol' Jasper."

"Already done."

Jake stood still for a few seconds and stared at Wes. Then he broke a little smile and said, "Chenglei take care a him?"

Wes dropped his crooked leg, stood straight, clamped his cigar in his teeth, and said long and drawn out, "No."

"Oh. Wal, Quincy wouldn't a done it unless I paid him, so that must mean—why yer did it, pard?" Wes turned his head and scowled at nothing down the street. Jake walked over to him and punched him lightly on the shoulder. "Thanks, pard. Yer saddle Noble, too?"

"'Course. The boys are all ready to go. Wouldn't saddle one and not ta other."

"All right. Wal let's move 'em out."

Jake and Wes helped Mary Jane up into the wagon, Jake threw up their bags onto the bed, slammed the tailgate shut, mounted Jasper next to Wes who sat on Noble, glanced at Wes and simultaneously they tapped their spurs to the boys. Chenglei slapped the reins to the backs of the Shires and called out, "Yee Joe. Yee Jeb." The big horses stepped out and the wagon lurched behind them, jostling Mary Jane. The whole little troupe was moving, and Jake turned in the saddle to look behind him. Quincy stood in the barn door opening. He raised his hand in a wave goodbye. Jake waved and turned back to the front. The troupe rumbled in front of the Brazos Saloon where Alex, Cherry, and Pinky, the piano player, stood on the boardwalk. They waved and called out their goodbyes to Jake and Mary Jane. Farther down the street at the end of town, they turned left on Hackberry.

Jake dropped back a half a length and looked behind him kitty-corner to a low, brown adobe house across the street. Desi leaned against the jamb of the open door. She raised her hand to her shoulder in a hesitant wave. Jake tipped his hat, stared at her for a long minute, smiled, then looked away and pulled up even with Wes. A tear leaked from Desi's eye and trailed down her cheek. She abruptly wiped it away and turned to disappear into the house. Jake did not look back.

───────────

THEY MADE IT to the Hashknife without incident and bunked there on the first night. In the morning they were ready to move on. Jake and Wes lounged beside the wagon while they waited for Mary Jane to come out. "Yer think yer gonna be okay all by yourself out there on the range with no one to help in case a trouble?" Wes stared at Jake with an overexaggerated serious look.

Jake stared back with a hard look and said, "Yer joshin', ain't yer? Ain't like I never been alone on the range."

Wes smiled, dropped his gaze, and returned it to Jake's face. "Wal, I know yer kin take care a yerself. But yer got some baggage this time."

"That's what them two cowboys over there are for." Jake nodded toward two cowboys who were waiting by the barn corral with their saddled horses. "They's ridin' along with us to Abilene."

Wes turned his head to take a gander at them and looked back at Jake. "See, I knew yer had ever'thing under control." He grinned and slapped Jake on the back. Jake smiled and shook his head.

Sadie Vandervert came out of the house with Mary Jane. They said their goodbyes and Wes helped her up to the wagon where she took up her comfy spot. Then he picked up Noble's reins and led him over toward the side where Jake and Jasper were standing. "Yer go on ahead, Chenglei. I'll catch up directly," Jake shouted as the wagon moved out.

With Noble trailing behind him, Wes, dragging his boots in the dirt, came up slowly to Jake and Jasper. Jake looked Wes in the eye and said, "Well, pard, looks like we are at the end a the trail."

Wes heaved a big sigh and said in a thick voice, "Wal, someday mebbe our trails'll cross and we'll ride again, eh?" His eyes were damp. Jake's eyes were damp. The boys nickered nervously. They let them nose each other.

"Ain't no sense in wallowing in it," Jake said as he stepped up into the saddle.

Wes mounted up. "No, it ain't." He held out his hand. They shook.

Jake said, "See yer when I see yer," and smiled big.

Wes grinned and said, "See yer when I see yer."

Jake spurred Jasper after the wagon. Noble started to move in the same direction, and Wes reined him back. Noble whinnied mournfully. Jasper stopped, turned, reared, and whinnied. Jake reined him around and spurred him away.

TWO

CHANGING HORSES • 1885

THE ATLANTIC & PACIFIC chugged into the station at Holbrook with little fanfare. A few toots of the whistle and a clanging bell to announce the arrival of the westbound train out of Gallup, New Mexico, was the extent of the intrusion into the otherwise lazy afternoon of the warm day. Sleeping dogs and a dirt street absent people with hodgepodge adobe, brown and whitewashed box and strip buildings packed in a straight line on one side of the street with a boardwalk, was about it. Far on the other side of the street the tracks ran parallel. The cast of the shadows leaned to the east, and only a few people were lounging around waiting to greet disembarking passengers when the train arrived at what Jake took to be the station house.

"Doesn't look like we're expected," Jake said with a wry smile as he pulled his watch from his vest pocket and flipped open the lid.

Mary Jane leaned across him and looked out the window. "Guess not." She smiled hesitantly.

"Just about suppertime," he said and closed his watch. "Guess we better get off and see about our crates and trunks. Make sure they made it here."

The conductor remained in his caboose, and only one porter jumped down to set a step stool in the dirt right next to the gravel ballast of the tracks for Mary Jane and the other lady passengers. There was no platform to step onto. He held out a hand for Mary Jane, and she took it as she descended the steps of the stool to the dirt.

"Thank you, my good man," Jonas said with a tip of his hat. "Can you direct us to the horse-loading ramp and the freight office?"

"Yas, sir, right yonder. See that feller comin' out with the big hand truck in that building? Thas where for freight." He pointed to a building behind them that had a track siding next to a dock that surrounded the brown box and strip building. Jake studied it for a long minute. "Right on down a little more is the horse ramp. See it yonder? Ya got trunks and sech?"

"Uh. Yes," Jake answered with a perplexed look on his face.

"The engineer'll back up the train and take on water from that tower yonder. Needs just a leetle more to make it to Winslow. Then he'll pull it onto that siding so's your trunks'll be unloaded at the freight dock there, and the stock car'll be lined up with the ramp."

"I see. So, we should stay on the train instead of walking in the dirt back to the freight office. Is that right?"

"Yas, sir. Ya'll should stay in your seat. I'll put a stool out for you when we pulls up to the dock. Dock's too high for the Pullmans."

"Okay. Thank you. Here you go." Jake smiled and pulled a silver quarter from his vest pocket and handed it to the porter. "Oh. What is the best hotel in town?"

"Thas the Holbrook House, for sure, yas sir. And if you wants good food, you go over to Mister Harvey's in those boxcars on that siding yonder." Both Jake and Mary Jane looked off in the direction the porter pointed to five dilapidated boxcars. "They ain't much on the outside but on the inside, whoa boy, they's top shelf."

"All right. Thanks. Can you direct us to the Holbrook House?"

"Yas, sir. Down thataway. Jest stay on the boardwalk 'til it ends and look to your right. You'll see a building with a porch and a balcony on top and a big sign that says Hotel Holbrook. You caint miss it." Again he pointed back up the track to the east.

"Okay. Thanks again."

As soon as the train stopped on the siding, Jake hopped off and hurried back to the stock car. Wranglers were already starting to bring Jasper out of the car onto the ramp that fortunately had high siderails on it or Jasper might have bolted. But he came down quietly and when he saw Jake he nickered and whinnied and bounced around like a yearling colt. A wrangler held Jasper's halter, and Jake said to him, "Hand me his bridle. I'll put it on." As soon as the wrangler turned his back to them Jake slipped Jasper a piece of hard candy.

When he turned back the wrangler looked curiously at the munching Jasper and smiled. Jake got the bridle on and tossed a rein under and over Jasper's neck, held both reins in his one hand, grabbed a hunk of mane in his other hand, vaulted onto Jasper's bare back, pulled back the reins and Jasper reared up. Jake let out a Texas-sized *whoop,* and the wrangler let out a whoop as horse and rider galloped off to the freight dock. Jake ran Jasper headlong and just as they came close to the dock, he sat him on his haunches, and they came to a sliding stop in a cloud of dust whereupon Jake vaulted off Jasper's back to the ground.

Mary Jane sat on a trunk on the freight dock by a stack of their trunks and crates. She grinned as she watched Jake's antics. The agent was standing just inside the door and shook his head. "He don't look like no Texas cowboy in that three-piece suit and tie and all," he said as he stepped across the dock.

"Oh, he's Texan, all right," she said admiringly. "Even got some notches on his pistol grip." She watched for the agent's reaction.

He remained poker-faced and just said, "Figgers. Tell him to come into the office."

Mary Jane added, "But that big black-and-white paint is more Texan than us all. Pure cow horse." The agent was already inside the office.

Jake came out of the office folding some papers while he held his rifle cradled in the crook of his right arm. "Agent says we can store the crates and trunks in the back for a week or two. Guess you might as well head on down to the hotel and check us in while I get Jasper settled in." He squinted and pulled his hat brim down to block the sun. "You be all right?"

Mary Jane smiled and said, "'Course I will. I'll freshen up and by the time you finish with Jasper I'll be ready to go over to that Harvey House for supper." She grasped one of their cases by the handle and pulled it from the stack.

He pulled his thirty-two from his vest pocket and handed it to Mary Jane. "Here, take this with you just in case. I hear this is a pretty rough town."

She took it, grinned, and winked at him. "Not rough enough to bother an old Texan like me."

"You ain't that old. That's what bothers me."

"I'll be all right. Don't worry."

Jake leaned over, grabbed his saddle by the horn, and hefted it onto his shoulder. Then he bounded down the steps off the dock and dropped the saddle in the dirt next to Jasper. He pulled a brush from his saddlebag, brushed down Jasper's back, threw the saddle blanket over, smoothed it, and tossed up the saddle, cinched it down, mounted and rode off to the livery.

Later, as the sun was on its last leg for the day but still spreading light, they stepped out of the hotel and walked across to the boxcars. The paint on the cars was faded and peeling, and the trucks and wheels were all rusted up. There was a little wooden platform set up with steps and handrails to a regular-sized door cut into the boxcar wall. Over the door was a sign fastened to the wall. Large letters with much larger capitalized first letters read *"FRED HARVEY MEALS"*

Jake and Mary Jane stomped the dust off their shoes and stepped through the door. They were greeted by a matronly looking woman with a pleasant smile and affable nature. She wore a white blouse with a small black bowtie, puff shoulders and long sleeves and a full-length black skirt. Other younger ladies dressed in all black full-length dresses, tight around the neck with a white "Elsie" collar and starched white half-aprons around their waists glided between tables covered in white linen and set with sparkling crystal stemware, white china, and silver utensils. The smiling young ladies waited on diners sitting at the tables in two of the boxcars that were decorated in the style of an exclusive St. Louis restaurant. The patron conversation was subdued, and it was easy for one to forget one was in a boxcar in Holbrook and not in a fine hotel dining room in St. Louis. The supper hour was in full swing, and the dining room was packed with people in various stages of their meals.

"Good evening. Welcome to the Harvey House," said the cheery matron, who apparently was the hostess or at least the hostess in charge.

"Good evening," Jake said with a courteous smile. "I see you seem to be full up this evening."

"Yes. However, there *is* a gentleman sitting alone at a four-person table who said he would be willing to accept company at his table. Would you care to join him?" Discreetly, she nodded in the direction of the party in question. Mary Jane and Jake followed her line of sight and saw a fairly normal-looking fellow with a large white serviette tucked into his collar and draped down his chest. He was busy with his meal. Jake looked at Mary Jane; she looked at him and gave a slight shrug of her shoulders.

"I suppose that will be fine," Jake said with a slight smile.

"Hello, sir. May these fine folks join you?" the hostess said as they arrived at his tableside. The fellow scraped his chair back, stood, pulled the serviette from his collar, quickly wiped his mustache left and right, smiled and said, "A course. Please," and gestured to the empty chairs. He stood at least six feet tall and looked to be about Jake's age, late thirties or early forties, clean-shaven except for a black mustache in the popular imperial style, although it was in need of barbering, black short-cropped hair with receding hairline, calm gray eyes.

Jake held the chair for Mary Jane as she sat down, then he sat after her. The fellow held his hand across the table for a shake and said, "Ben Irby's my handle."

"Howdy. This is my wife, Mary Jane, and I am J.V. Brighton."

They shook hands around and Irby said, "Ya'll are Texans? Ya got that drawl. I hail from Pecos myself. Shackleford and Throckmorton counties afore that. What about you?"

Jake and Mary Jane smiled and Jake said, "Baylor and Wichita counties." Then they turned to study the menu. In but a couple of minutes Jake put down the meu and said, "What you doin' in Holbrook? You with the Hashknife?"

"As a matter of fact, I am. Getting ready to receive the first Aztec herd from the Pecos spread. You know about the Hashknife?"

"Yes, sir, I do. You know Bill Vandervert?"

A pretty young waitress came to the table and took their order. Irby waited while they finished.

"Yeah. Bill's at the Miller Creek spread up in Baylor County. He's getting the Miller herd ready to ship to Montana. Brighton, huh? Sounds familiar."

"You might want to put a 'Rawhide Jake' in front of it," Mary Jane said with an ironic smile and a coy look at Irby. He stopped chewing and stared for a long quarter minute at Jake who gave Mary Jane a little kick in the ankle under the table.

"You're Rawhide Jake Brighton?"

"Unfortunately, I am."

"Why do you say unfortunately? If I recall correctly, you and Wes Wilson got rid a lot a rustlers in northwest Texas."

"We did. But I am changin' occupations and lookin' for opportunities. I'm a blacksmith and a wagon maker too. A course if there's a stockman's association around these parts, I can always fall back on detective work." He grinned.

"Apache County Stock Growers Association. Run by a feller named Alfred Clark. From back east but he is a hard-drivin' cattleman. Owns the La Cienega Ranch south a St. Johns. Runs a LC brand." He forked a hunk of meatloaf and mashed potato and held it momentarily. "Sorry. Ya'll mind if I eat my chuck while it's hot?"

"No. Please go right ahead," the Brightons chimed together.

"St. John's is the county seat. A two-day ride southeast a here on the Little Colorado River. Another day's walkin' ride due south close to the river is Springerville." He took another bite. "I hear tell a blacksmith shop in Springerville's up for sale. Don't know for sure. Don't get down that way much. Hashknife headquarters is south a here at Obed Meadow. Half a day ride. Spread is mostly south and west." He forked in the last of his food, took another drink of coffee, pushed his plate away, wiped his mustache, and said, "Then there's Show Low on the Rim and Heber, and northeast of there is Taylor and Snowflake. That's about all there is 'sides Holbrook and Winslow, unless you're interested in goin' over the Rim, south to Pleasant Valley. I wouldn't recommend it, though. It ain't very pleasant." He smiled wittily. "Been a lot a shootin' goin' on down there. And a course there's Flagstaff 'bout a hunnert miles further west."

"The Rim?"

"Mogollon Rim. 'Bout fifty miles south a here. Runs east and west for a couple hundred miles goin' as high as two, three thousand feet. Tonto Basin below it is where Pleasant Valley sits. Whewee. Talked more this evening than I have in a week. Well, if ya'll don't mind, I'll be takin' my leave. Got a git back to the outfit." He stood and shook hands again saying, "Good luck to you. Let me know if I can help you in anything. I'm usually on the range or at the Hashknife headquarters." He put on his hat, tipped it to them with his hand, and sauntered out.

Jake and Mary Jane finished their supper and sat lingering over coffee. "I thought you wanted me out a the detective business," he said with a little smile and gleam in his eye. "Why'd you tell him about Rawhide Jake?"

She smiled at him with a curious look in her own eye and said, "I've heard of Ben Irby. Well-respected Texas cowman. Pretty well-known in northwest Texas before he went west to Pecos. He's probably the cow boss here at the Arizona spread. 'Course, they don't call them that here. I think I heard on the train they say superintendent. Anyway, maybe I was just a little jealous and had to let him know you are famous too." She leaned in close and kissed him on the cheek.

In the evening dusk they strolled arm in arm back toward the Holbrook House. As they came abreast of a dark alley between two buildings, a masked man jumped out and brandished a knife. "Good evening, folks. You, sir, hand over your wallet, and you, ma'am, your bag there," he said in a low threatening voice. Jake maneuvered Mary Jane behind him so that he was between the man and her. He reached to his vest for his pocket pistol, but there was no pistol there and he instantly remembered he'd given it to Mary Jane for her protection. No sooner had he remembered than she stepped to his side and pointed the pistol right at the robber's head.

"You want what's in my bag, mister. Here it is, and its gonna put a hole right between your eyes unless you skedaddle real fast out of my sight." She sounded full of confidence and looked like she knew what she was doing. The man turned lickety-split and disappeared up the alley. "Shall we chase him?" she said to Jake. He fell into rolling laughter and hustled her to the hotel. They laughed all the way there and opened a bottle of whiskey when they were back in their room.

"You are the prettiest Wild West Texas whirlwind I ever met," Jake said as he tossed her onto the bed.

IN THE MORNING they sat at their table in the Harvey House after breakfast and slowly finished their coffee. Mary Jane stared curiously at Jake and said, "I've been meaning to ask. You introduced yourself as J.V. Brighton to Irby. How come?"

He gazed out the window for a half-minute, then turned to look directly into her eyes. "Like I told you in Independence. I am tired of being Rawhide Jake. I think if Rawhide Jake does any work around here it will be way down undercover, and nobody will know it is him because he is now J.V. Brighton." He smiled with a little ironic look. "I aim to ride on down to that Springerville and investigate that blacksmith shop. I think I will just be J.V. Brighton, blacksmith. It's a pretty good living, and we got money besides. What a ya think a that?"

"I think anything you do that ain't out on the range is just fine."

"Wal, I might start missin' it." He smiled more. "But, probably not. And there might be other opportunities in that town. It ain't been there very long, ya know. Ya gonna be all right while I'm gone? Be over a week. Three-day ride down. Three days back plus investigatin' time."

"Yeah, sure," she frowned. "I got my little friend in here." She raised her bag and shook it a little. "And I'm gonna see if I can help out here in the kitchen. Just to keep busy. Maybe, if you decide to buy the shop, you might look up a house down there, too, if they got any." She smiled coyly.

At dawn the next day Jake was in the livery barn saddling Jasper while he munched on oats he nibbled out of a bucket Jake had set on a stool for him. Jake tied on his saddlebags, bedroll, tarp, and slicker. Then he slid his rifle into the scabbard. He wore his usual range duds of a nutria-colored Stetson Big Four with its wide brim and high crown, blue bandanna, tan leather vest, beige canvas pants, scuffed brown boots and spurs, and cross-draw double-action Colt Army revolver with an additional cartridge belt. From the looks of the lay of the land, he didn't think he needed his chaps, but he rolled them up and tied them on the back of his saddle.

As the sun beamed its rays in a fan across the eastern horizon, he rode out of the barn headed southeast and in short order was into the gama and galleta grass still in their spring green on the vast Colorado Plateau, spotted here and there with purple sage. He rode along a tableland of rolling hills and around low mesas that sported sumac, manzanita, and other evergreen shrubs. Mostly, though, it was a fairly constant prairie of grass dotted by head-high juniper shrubs. He walked and trotted Jasper along the two-rut stage road that ran straight on a course more or less parallel to the west bank of the Little Colorado River. By midday he came up to the halfway point way station. Jasper was a hardy Texas stock horse and could have made it all the way to St. Johns before sundown. But he hadn't had much exercise in the last few weeks and was probably out of shape. Jake decided to let him rest up the last half of the day.

The next day he took a leisurely ride on in to St. Johns, stabled Jasper, and got a room for the night, ate supper, walked around smoking his cigar for a while, and went to bed. In the morning he was on the road to Springerville. He took most of the day to get to his destination because he wanted to give the country a good look-over. Arriving in late afternoon, he came to the town proper where the wide dirt road on a curve was sparsely populated by houses and businesses. There were some pretty long, board fences along the road in front of the houses on both sides and trees here and there. He saw a mercantile store, some houses, one pretty good size, another mercantile, a billiard parlor, and the post office among some other buildings. He ignored the stares coming his way as he rode down the middle of the road. He passed an intersection with another road to the south and heard what he was listening for—the ringing hammer of a smithy. He pulled up Jasper and turned down the road. Of note was a saloon he passed and a little farther south he spotted what he thought was the blacksmith shop. He had a thousand dollars cash on his person, and he intended to make a deal.

"Howdy," Jake said as he walked into the shop. "J.V. Brighton." He held out his hand for a shake.

The feller looked to be older than Jake and about the same stocky size. He had a big head of salt-and-pepper hair, a full beard that was stained with tobacco juice all down the chin whiskers, and wore a pair of bib overalls, denim shirt, and leather apron. He set down his hammer, dipped his hands in the water tub, and dried them off with a rag. He had a twinkle in his hazel eyes as he smiled and said, "Howdy, yerself. Henry Shaw's my name. Proprietor."

"Nice to meet yer. Yer're just the man I aim to see," Jake said as they shook hands.

"How's that?"

"Wal, I hear tell yer might be lookin' to sell out."

"Where'd yer hear that?"

"Oh, up in Holbrook. Just talkin' to a feller who said that's what he heard."

"Wal. S'pose so. Broke my swingin' arm last December. Thought I'd come back to work when it healed," he dropped his gaze to the hard-packed dirt floor, "but it ain't workin' out. Takes me twice as long to shape anythin' and I git real tired real fast. Too old to train my left arm to swing, so I figgered I'd just sell out and do somethin' else."

"How much you askin'?"

"Wal, I ain't lookin' to get rich. Just git back what I got sunk into the shop. That forge is just two years old. Best yer kin git. See how heavy it is? So, that'd be thirty-seven dollars, anvil is six, vice and tools anuther twenty. So, I reckon yer could by the basic outfit fer what's that, sixty-three bucks. I'd throw in the cedar tub and pump for anuther four and ten fer everthin' else. Say seventy-five fer the whole shop. I own the land and the building so if'n yer wanted to stay here, I'd charge rent of eight dollars a month."

"Uh-huh. You a farrier?"

"No. He comes down from St. Johns every Monday on a circuit on up to Show Low and down to Taylor and Snowflake, then back to St. Johns. Stops at ranches along the way. Makes a big circle. I shape the shoes for him so he don't have to set up his little forge."

"Uh-huh. If yer don't mind me askin', what's yer monthly revenue?"

"Yer mean, how much do I make?"

"Yeah." Jake held his gaze with his steady dark-gray eyes challenging, almost daring him to lie.

"Wal, a good month's thirty bucks. Usually 'bout twenty a month."

"What about expenses?"

"It depends. Mostly I can add that back into the cost of a job. So, every month I'd say 'bout five to ten."

"Any competition?"

"Wal, there's Peter Thompson up on Papago Street. He's the onliest one. Been here long time. Since near the beginning. Came in seventy-nine, I think. He's Mormon. Gets all the Mormon farmers' work. He's gittin' kinda old now. But he still swings a mean hammer."

"Uh-huh." Jake softened his stare and said, "Wal, listen, I'll buy the shop at seventy-five cash. How much for the building and land?" Then he grinned winningly.

"Wal, uh, pretty dang good I guess for the shop. Uh, hadn't thought about sellin' the building and land." Shaw looked a bit bewildered.

"Okay. Well, why don't you think about it and give me a price tomorrow? In the meantime, I need a tool, equipment, and stock inventory and a looksee at yer books before we can shake on it. You got books?"

"Yer mean ledgers? No. I cain't read or write."

"All right, then. We'll do the inventory together. I'll write it, and you can have someone yer trust read it to yer. Then I'll draw up a bill a sale and a deed, and we can sign them and have them notarized. You got a notary here in town?"

He shook his head yes and said, "What's a inventoree?"

Jake smiled and said, "That's a list of all the tools, equipment, and stuff yer got on the shelf, like horseshoe blanks and sech."

"Oh. All right. Let's git started."

It took about two hours to finish. Jake signed it, and Shaw made his mark. Then they shook hands and Jake said as he checked his watch, "It's a few minutes before five. Too close to suppertime. I'll draw up the paperwork tonight and have it ready to sign in the mornin'. We can plug in the land and building price then. That all right?"

"Sure enough, by doggie."

"All right, then. I saw a saloon up the road aways. Can I buy yer a drink to celebrate?"

"Wal, I thank yer fer the offer, but I'm convertin' to Mormon, and we don't drink liquor."

"Beer?"

"Thanks. I could, but I don't like it. I got some lemonade in the cooler if you'd like."

"All right. Lemonade, it is. You get it, and I'll be right back."

Jake hurried out to his saddlebag and pulled out his flagon of "medicine" he kept to treat wounds and such. He stuffed the flask in his back pocket and hurried back into the shop with but ten seconds to spare before Shaw returned with two glasses of lemonade.

Jake took a taste and said, "Uh, could I trouble yer for some sugar?"

"Oh, sure. I'll get it. Not sweet enough fer yer, huh?"

While Shaw was out of sight Jake pulled the cork on the flask and spiked his lemonade with a couple shots of rot gut whiskey.

"Here yer go. Don't mind my dirty hand. It don't rub off. Ground in," he said with a smile as he held out his hand with three cubes of sugar in his palm.

Jake dropped a lump of sugar in his lemonade, stirred it with his finger, took a drink and said, "Ah. Just right. Thanks. Wal, here's how." He held his glass up.

"Huh?"

"It's a toast we say in Texas."

"Oh. I see."

"Celebrating our deal," Jake said with a nod of his head in the way of explanation.

"Yeah. Congratulations. Say. I never asked. You are a smithy, ain't yer? I wouldn't want all my customers go over to Thompson."

"Yes, sir. Kansas and Missourah."

"Good. Cuz we got a lot a farmers here abouts and theys always needn' work. Breakin' things and all."

"Many Mormons around these parts?"

"Oh, yeah. Mostly farmers. Some ranchers and dairies."

"Why you convertin'?"

"Don't rightly know. Just a feelin', I guess."

"Wouldn't have anything to do with business, would it?" Jake laid his challenging look on Shaw, who in turn arched his back and looked indignantly down his nose.

Then he cracked a little smile and said, "Maybe. But, they's got a likin' for bein' together and helpin' each other out, and I like that."

Jake smiled, nodded his head, downed his drink, and said, "Wal, I better head on out. I'll see yer in the mornin'." They shook hands, and Jake left. He stopped at the saloon, tied off Jasper at the hitching rail, walked in the door and stepped to the side while he let his eyes adjust to the darker environment. As he did, he looked around casually. It wasn't much of a saloon. Barrel and board bar with spittoons lined up and down the floor in front of it. The floor in a ring around each spittoon was stained with tobacco juice. No mirror. Four poker tables and no piano that he could see. The floor was dusty and there were dirt clods scattered around. Probably hadn't been swept for a week or more. The place was empty except for a lone bartender behind the bar. It smelled more dank and dirty than many saloons he had been in. Didn't look like there was any food available, and since it was suppertime, that could explain the absence of patrons.

"What'll you have, mister?" the bartender asked as Jake stepped up to the bar.

"Whiskey. What kind yer got?"

"We got Kessler for two bits a shot and regular old red-eye for a dime. If you want more Kentucky bourbons, you have to go over to Charley Kinnear's billiard parlor on Main Street. Take your choice."

"Kessler. Two." Jake put two quarters on the bar and said, "I take it yer don't have any chuck here."

"No. Just whiskey and beer."

The bartender set Jake's glass in front of him and he took down half of the whiskey, smiled, and said, "Where's a body git some supper in this town and a room for the night?"

"Wal, Mrs. Baca'd probably feed you and put you up. You can ask at Baca's Mercantile up on Main Street."

Next morning Jake got his business with Shaw done. They agreed Jake would take possession of the shop no later than two weeks hence, and he and Mary Jane would be Arizona property owners. That gave Jake time to run back up to Holbrook and pick up Mary Jane and return to Springerville. But, in the meantime he spent the rest of the day looking around the town and surrounding area.

On the way back to Holbrook the next day he stopped briefly at the St. John's Courthouse and recorded the bill of sale and transfer deeds. Jasper was feeling his oats so Jake made the ride back to Holbrook in two days while taking care to rest Jasper along the way. They came into Holbrook just before sundown on the second day. He put up Jasper in the livery, then dropped his gear at the hotel where Mary Jane was not in so he walked over to the Harvey House. He asked for Mary Jane and she came out from the kitchen drying her hands on a towel. They embraced briefly with a peck or two on their cheeks and moved off to the side of the room where Jake told her all the news of his trip.

"So, what time will you be done here?" Jake asked.

"Right now. I'm just fill-in. No clock for me. I told ' 'em I'd help out for fifty cents a day if they could use me," she answered as she untied the strings to her apron, pulled it off, and tossed it on a table. Then she smoothed her hair and said, "Let's have some supper."

They chatted up plans and things for the move while Jake kept coming back to the shop buy. "It was all I could do to keep from falling over when he told me the price. He never included anything for the value of his business, his reputation, and customer goodwill. I was ready to pay two hundred and got it for seventy-five. And the real estate for another one-fifty." He leaned back in his chair and smiled broadly. When the dessert and more coffee came, Jake finished the pie, pushed the plate aside, sat back and lit a cigar. "Tomorrow, first thing, I'll have to find a wagon and a driver."

"What do you need a driver for?"

"Well, to drive to Springerville and bring the wagon back to Holbrook. I doubt whoever I rent from will want me to leave it in Springerville."

"Why rent? Why not just buy it and sell it in Springerville?"

"Who's gonna drive it?"

"Me." Jake looked at her evenly; astonished but not showing it. Then slowly a smile came across his face, then a grin and he chuckled. "You?"

"Yes, me." She stared at him with no smile and appeared perturbed. "I have you know I've driven plenty a wagon mile in my day. Mules and horses."

Jake stopped laughing and appraised her anew. "So, you're not kidding?" She shook her head no. "Well, I guess it would probably be the least complicated, except maybe for the team. See if we can buy a team of mules. Farmers down there'd probably buy the team and the wagon."

"Sounds good to me. It'll be fine." She reached across and put her hand on the back of his hand. "Happen to see any houses?"

He smiled and said, "Yep. I did. Got one all picked out for you."

SINCE THE ROAD was just two wagon tracks worn into the grass and only wide enough for one wagon at a time to pass, Jake mostly rode off the road alongside of the wagon. Twice they were met by oncoming wagons and once gave way and once remained on the road. But when the stage came rolling along behind them, Mary Jane pulled off the road and let it pass, although it amounted to not much of anything as the stage was just a buckboard pulled by a team of horses at a trot. There was a driver and two passengers on the seats. Everyone waved as they passed. Mary Jane pulled off her broad brim hat and waved it at them. Then she wiped the sleeve of the man's white shirt she wore across her forehead and slapped at the flies that had immediately attacked her when she stopped the wagon.

At last, the Brightons arrived at the point in the road where it started a slight descent to the river crossing. Jake held them up so Mary Jane could gaze out over the terrain and see Springerville not more than a mile off in the distance. "There she is," Jake said as he swung his hand slowly in a flat plane in front of him, left to right. "Your new home."

Mary Jane stood in the box and rubbed her back. As she looked out over the land she said, "Well let's get on down there. My back's about to break."

"Looks like over there is where theys crossin'," Jake called out as he pointed off to their left. "See the wagon tracks?"

"I see 'em. I'll drive on over that a way. Giddy up, mules," Mary Jane yelled as she slapped the reins to their backs. "Woah! Slow now! Take her easy, boys!"

Jake held Jasper alongside the mules to help watch for rocks and debris, not that it did much good as the river was pretty muddy. "Not very high for this time of year," Jake said up to Mary Jane as they eased into the water. She did not answer as she was concentrating on her mule skinning. The water was now up to their hocks and seemed to stay at that level. The bottom was fairly smooth, but there were small boulders here and there that jarred the wagon as it rolled over them. The mules were careful and felt their way along so they did not stumble, but about halfway across they were jerked to a stop as the left front wheel of the wagon dropped into a hole. The sudden stop ripped Mary Jane from her seat, and she nearly went head over heels into the rumps of the mules. Had she not caught herself on the brake handle, she would have gone over.

"What the hell!" she screamed. "What happened?"

"You hit a hole. Back the team up and see if you can git out of it," he hollered.

Mary Jane got herself rearranged on the seat, braced herself in the box with her legs, and pulled back on the reins. The mules tried but couldn't move, and the wagon did not budge. Jake jumped down and inspected the problem. The wheel was fully submerged. That meant it was a pretty deep hole, and since they couldn't move the wagon at all, it probably had vertical sides of hard rock. Only thing to do was put more horsepower to the pull. So, in front of the mules, he hitched Jasper up to the wagon tongue with a rope to the saddle horn and untied his drover's whip from the saddle skirt. He held it up for Mary Jane to see. "You know how to use one a these?"

"'Course I do," she said as she stood in the box with her hands on her hips.

He tossed the whip up to her and said, "All right, then. I'll go around to the back to push. On the count a three, yer snap that whip and get everbody pullin' as hard as they can. See what happens. If it don't work, we're gonna have to unload this wagon, and I don't want a do that."

"Me, neither."

"When it comes out, turn those mules hard to the left so the rear wheel don't fall in—okay?"

"Got it."

Jake went around to the rear of the wagon and put his back to it. "Ready?" he shouted.

"Yep." She yelled back.

"One, two, three," he hollered and groaned as he pushed his back against the wagon with his legs.

Mary Jane was standing and snapping the whip and slapping the reins and yelling, "Pull! Pull! Pull, boys!" The wagon started to come up, then stalled and fell back.

"Try it again. One, two, three! Aweee!"

Twice more they tried it and were getting nowhere. Jake climbed up and sat heavily on the wagon seat. In between his heavy breathing he said, "Ain't movin'. I hate wagons." Mary Jane sat with her head in her hands. Sweat popped out on Jake's forehead and the flies were buzzing around his head and Mary Jane's. They both jumped at the sound of a horse snorting slightly behind them off to their right side.

Then a man's voice, *"Whoa,* girls!" Jake stood up with his gun hand close to his pistol butt. A team of big black Belgians stood next to the wagon, swishing their tails and mouthing their bits.

"Looks like you fell into the devil's hole," the feller said as he stared up at them. He looked like a farmer.

Jake shaded the sun from his eyes with the flat of his hand and said, "That what they call it? Well, the dern thing has us caught."

"Good Lord is smilin' down on you today. I was just takin' my team across to neighbor Butler's field to do some hay loading. Reckon these big girls can pull you out a that hole."

"Much obliged. J.V. Brighton's the name. New blacksmith in town. This is my wife, Mary Jane."

"Pleased, I'm sure, ma'am," he said and tipped his hat.

"Likewise." Mary Jane said as she stood in the box next to Jake.

"We bought Shaw's shop. You get us out a this hole, and your next job is no charge at the shop, long as it ain't no great big job, uh, mister?"

"Robert T. Brown. Just call me Bob."

"Okay, Bob. It's a deal."

"You got anything extra heavy in that wagon?"

"No, sir," Jake said as he jumped down from the box and splashed into the brown water. "Just the usual household goods."

"All right. Let's just unhook that double tree and pull your mules away. I'll hitch the tree I got on the girls to your wagon and pull you right out a that hole. You better come down from there, missus. Probably gonna be a pretty big jarring." Mary Jane hesitated. She did not want to jump into the river and get her shoes and skirt all wet. But it was better than an injury of some sort. Of course, with a scream she slipped and fell into the water so that she was soaked from head to foot. Neither Jake nor Bob said a word as she came up fuming, but Jake could not hold it back, so he turned away from her and chuckled his heart out. Finally, he turned back and said, You all right?"

"Yes," she grumbled as she shot daggered looks at him, lifted her skirts, and waded across to the opposite side.

With what looked like easy work, the Belgians flexed their huge muscles, dug in, and pulled the wagon right out of the devil's hole, even with the back wheel dropping in and yanked out, stopping only when the wagon was on dry land on the other side. As Brown was unhitching his tree from the wagon, Jake brought up the mules, and Mary Jane caught Jasper and led him up next to them. Brown said, "Wal you're new here, but now you know to stay on the downriver side a this crossin'," he chortled with a grin. "We tried to fill that hole in twice when the river was dry, but soon as the rains and spring melt come, it washes right out agin. That's why we call it the devil's hole."

"Yes, sir, I can see that. And thanks again."

"Yes. Thank you very much," Mary Jane said,

"You're welcome. Good day now." He tipped his hat and called out, "Let's go, girls."

"Don't forget my promise," Jake called out. "Well, that was mighty neighborly of him."

"Sure was. If most folks are like him, I think I just might like it here. Now you want to get those mules hitched up so I can hurry up and get a bath." She looked down at Jake from the box and grinned.

"Looks like you already had one. But you did real good, Mary Jane." He beamed a loving smile up at her. She waved her arm as if to dismiss the incident.

As they lumbered into town, she appeared to have forgotten her humiliation and looked about at the various businesses, sparse though they were. Jake on Jasper was in front and when they passed the post office, he turned left onto a street made so by the many passages of various wagons, buggies, and horses. On up a little way, he turned right onto the intersecting street of the same sort, except that this one disappeared into a group of houses that were set in line with wide spaces between them. There were no trees, and the structures were completely exposed to the elements as if they had fallen out of the sky and landed there in the middle of empty range land that happened to have a town right next door to the houses. In the un-demarcated backyards were outbuildings, chicken coops, outhouses, and vegetable gardens, but there were no fences. Neighbors could stand on their front stoops and wave to each other fifty yards away. Jake stopped in front of the second in line of these houses.

It was a weathered gabled frame house with exterior walls of tan adobe bricks. The roof was sheeted with cedar shingles with two stubby chimneys protruding from it, evenly spaced from each end of the house. The gables were sheeted with wood planks painted a beige color. There was a double sash window framed in white set in the gable end and another in front toward the other end of the house from the door. The beige single front door was placed toward the other end. Plain old brown dirt surrounded the house.

"Well, here it is. One of your finer Springerville houses," Jake said as he sat on Jasper alongside the driver box of the wagon where Mary Jane stood with her hands on her hips. "Stable in the back with a corral for Jasper. Two bedrooms. And it can be ours for a hundred and fifty dollars." He beamed at her as if he had made a very profound statement. "Includes a coal-burning cookstove and a Great Western cast iron parlor stove in the sittin' room. What do you think?"

"Well, it ain't the Calhoun house, but I ain't never owned a house before, so I'll take it." She leaned over and wrapped her arms around Jake, leaned back, and smiled big at him.

He pointed to one of the other houses. "That's the Rudd house over there, and that one is the Johnsons. All nice folks. I met them the other day."

"That's good, cuz I am the neighborly type. Where's the shop?"

"Oh, it's less than a quarter mile back to the southwest there on the Eagar road across Main. Easy walk."

"Well, when can we unload?"

"Reckon as soon as I get the bill of sale signed and the money paid out. Julius Becker at the mercantile is acting as agent for the owner. I'll go on over there and be back directly."

Jake returned within the half hour. He found Mary Jane out back exploring the outbuildings. "Well, that's done," Jake said as he came up to her. "Now we can move in, and as soon as we get the deed from the recorder, it'll all be official. Our first house." He smiled lovingly.

'Course, I guess we're gonna have to sleep on the floor until we get some furniture. Soon as we're unloaded, I'll take care a Jasper and the mules, and you might as well get right on over to Becker's and order our furniture."

Well, they got themselves settled, and in two weeks their furniture arrived from Albuquerque. So they slept a little better. Mary Jane was busy with her baking and cooking and housekeeping. Jake got his shop set up to his liking and waited for the jobs to come in. Meanwhile, just to stay busy, he started fabricating a wrought-iron gate for a speculative sale. The jobs were coming in few and far between, but he kept swinging the hammer.

THREE

NEW TOWN, NEW BUSINESS • 1885

LONG ABOUT THE end of August Sheriff Hubbell rode into town and after whetting his whistle at Kinnear's he rode the little ways up to Jake's shop. As he walked in he was silhouetted in the doorway by the outside light. Jake caught the motion of the silhouette out of the corner of his eye from where he was bent over his anvil shaping a piece of red-hot metal. He looked up and saw the tin star on the man's chest and took note of the pistol on his hip. He set the piece aside and snatched up a rag to wipe his hands.

"Howdy," Jake said. "How can I help you?"

"Hello. J.L. Hubbell. Sheriff of Apache County." He held out his hand. Jake made a quick appraisal. He had a hint of a Spanish accent, was a little taller than Jake, appeared to be muscular, strong facial features, Roman nose, popular imperial mustache with a light touch of gray here and there, well barbered, close-cropped dark brown hair and intense brown eyes that looked out through rimless spectacles, all wrapped up in a stern, no-nonsense demeanor. He seemed to be all business.

Jake shook his hand and said, "J.V. Brighton."

"You a new blacksmith in town?"

"Yeah, I bought the shop from Shaw."

"Uh-huh. I heard he's turning Mormon. I don't get along very well with Mormons. Just got over a big legal scrape with them and the Texans. Where do you hail from?"

"Well... Texas." Jake stared steadily at him and knew that his usual challenging gaze was naturally coming out. Hubbell stared back and did not flinch. Jake continued, "Before that, Missourah and Kansas." It was going to be the usual snooping of the lawman that Jake would undergo, just like he himself had done to many persons.

"Well, welcome to Apache County. Always been a blacksmith?"

"Learned the trade right after the war."

"Uh-huh. So, you been swinging the hammer ever since?" He smiled ever so slightly.

"Well, uh... I spent the last two and a half years working for Jim Loving."

"Loving? That sounds familiar."

"He's secretary of the Stock-Raisers' Association of North-West Texas and the son of Oliver Loving. Both of them were partners with Charles Goodnight. You heard a him?"

"Yes. Believe I have. Cattleman out of Texas?"

"Yes."

"What did you do for Loving?"

Jake held his breath for a long few seconds. He was not at all sure how this fellow would take the information he was about to give. Some sheriffs supported range detectives, and others opposed them. "I was a stock detective."

Hubbell nodded his head slowly and stared directly into Jake's challenging eyes as if trying to read Jake's mind. "You quit that business and went back to blacksmithing, is that it?"

"Yes."

"I came over here 'cause my horse has a loose shoe. Can you fix that?"

"I ain't a farrier, but I'll look at for you."

"Thanks. Front left. Don't get down here much. I came down here to inspect Charley Kinnear's saloon," Hubbell said as they walked out to his horse. "You remember hearing about that robbery of the county safe last July when the thieves stole county warrants and books and burned them?" Jake nodded his head again. "Well, as you probably know, Sol Barth and Charley Kinnear are the suspects, and we got Charley in jail. So a fellow has to ask what happens to Kinnear's saloon if he goes to prison? I am watching that one close and may make a run at buying out his wife. There is a little hitch, though. I hear Tom Brady is making offers. He has a ranch west a here. He might beat me to it. I'm always looking for business opportunities.

"Another reason I am down this way is to find an applicant for Springerville Constable. It isn't a law enforcement job, not a town marshal or anything like that, but constables do have the authority of a sheriff when needed in the execution of their job. Do some prisoner-escorting too. Somebody with lawman experience who is a constable helps out a lot." He raised his boot and set it on a box, then bent forward a little and placed his elbow on his thigh and twilled a twig between his hands. He looked steadily at Jake and said, "This sheriff job I have is not my main business. I'm a trader and a businessman. Got a trading ranch up at Ganado and some other things too. I agreed to run for sheriff to do my civic duty and get to know more people around the county. Maybe you might want to think about doing the same thing." Again, he smiled that slight little smile.

"What's a trading ranch?"

"Most folks call them trading posts. I am an Indian trader."

Jake nodded his head in acknowledgement. "What's a constable do?"

"He works for the district court and the JP. Process server. Subpoenas, notices, complaints, warrants. Stuff like that. Hear tell that John Hogue had applied for the JP job."

"What's the pay?"

"Ten dollars a month plus expenses. Got the application right here." He pulled a form from his inside coat pocket and held it in his hand.

Jake reached for the form, and Hubbell handed it to him. He unfolded it and read it over, looked up at Hubbell and said, "All right. I'll do it. Help out with expenses here, if nothin' else."

"That's the way to look at it. Of course, you won't be very popular with the riffraff, but the good citizens of the community will appreciate it. You can diversify your business interests that way. Get my drift?"

Jake nodded his head as he sat down at his rolltop desk to fill in and sign the application form.

"Speaking of keeping your eyes open, you've seen the advertisements in the *Herald* by the Apache County Stock Growers Association? Two-hundred-and-fifty-dollar reward?"

"Yeah. I've seen them."

"We've got our share of rustlers around here, that's for sure. There's the Tewksburys and the Grahams down in Pleasant Valley. Always causing trouble and stealing from each other. But the worst of them all is the Clanton gang. You heard of them?"

"Nope."

The sheriff looked at Jake curiously as if to say, "How could you not have heard of them?". "Well, you heard of that big gunfight down in Tombstone a few years back."

"When was that?"

"I believe it was in the fall of eighty-one."

"Fall of eighty-one I was in Illinois. That's a long ways from here. But I think I heard it talked about once in Texas."

"Well, it was old man Clanton and his boys Phin, Ike, and Billy raising hell in Cochise County. They made up a gang and rustled cattle from Mexico to Clifton. The old man died, and Billy was killed in the gunfight with the Earps. Later, Morgan Earp was murdered, and Wyatt Earp went on a vendetta, killing any of the Cowboy gang he found. Phin and Ike ran for the hills and ended up in Nutriosa, just south a here. Their sister and her husband have a ranch there." He dragged his boot off the box, stood, and leaned against the doorjamb. Jake pulled up the horse's hoof and wiggled the loose shoe. Hubbell continued his story. "They made a claim on some land southeast a here on Coyote Creek. Run a Z Four brand, but they are not cattlemen. They are rustlers. They steal cattle in the north and in the south and bring them to their ranch, re-brand them and fatten them to sell in the south or to the Army. Lot a times they partner up with the Stanleys."

Jake stood and said, "If you know all this, why ain't you caught 'em?"

The sheriff stiffened and peered into Jake's eyes. He stood erect and took one step toward Jake, who did not move. Then he relaxed and said, "This is a huge county bordered on the east by New Mexico, on the north by Utah, south down to midway in the territory, and west clear to Yavapai County. The whole northeastern corner of the territory. I have one deputy. We can't be everywhere all the time. They slip through on us. That's one reason. The other is if I make an arrest, I can't get an indictment, on the Clantons anyway." He shrugged his shoulders indicating clearly without saying it that it was a waste of his time. "What we need is a stock detective working the range." He looked hard at Jake.

"My wife don't want me back out on the range." He grinned friendly-like.

"Well. All right, then. Guess I've bent your ear nearly completely off." And he grinned friendly-like. "What about that shoe?"

"I can put a couple of nails in it for you. But you need to get it fixed by a farrier."

"Okay. Thanks." Jake went back into the shop and came back out with a hammer and nails.

"I'll take this application right up to the Board of Supervisors in St. Johns. You should be hearing from them soon. What do I owe you?"

"Nothin'."

He gave Jake one last long look and said, "All right, then. Good day to you," turned and stepped up into the saddle.

At the supper table Mary Jane said, "So are people gonna want to shoot at you when you are serving papers on them?"

"I'm thinkin' maybe they might, cuz the sheriff said a constable has all the authority of a lawman when a constable is executin' his duties."

"Well, I don't like it, then."

"I don't think it's that common. And we need the money. It'll pay expenses in the shop until some jobs come in. Won't have to eat into our savings just to live. If it gets too dangerous, I promise I'll quit."

Mary Jane gave him a skeptical look with no smile and went to the stove to fetch the coffeepot. "What else did he say?"

"Well, he was tryin' to talk me into goin' back out on the range." He let that one lie for a minute to watch Mary Jane's reaction. She brought the coffee and poured without looking at him. Then she shot a defiant glare at him and said, "And?"

"Well, he says he knows who the rustlers are but he can't catch them because the county is too big for just him and his deputy to cover. I think he was kinda askin' for help. Or he's too busy with his other businesses to worry much about rustlers he can't catch, anyways." Jake sipped his coffee, pulled a drag on his cigar and blew the smoke across the room. "Says the big rustlers around here are the Clantons and the Stanleys, especially the Clantons. You heard of them?"

"Nope."

"Me, neither. You heard a the Earp brothers?"

"Nope."

"Me, neither. But I *did* hear once about a gunfight in Tombstone. I guess the Clantons were the outlaws, and the Earps the lawmen."

"And?"

"You know the association is payin' a two-hundred-fifty-dollar reward for the capture and conviction of any rustler." He looked up at her with a twinkle in his eye.

Mary Jane plopped down in the chair, put her elbows on the table and her forehead in her hands. "Money," she said. "I cannot compete with that harlot."

"Aw, I was just joshin' yer. I ain't gonna take no stock detective job. I got bigger plans than that."

She raised her head and looked lovingly for just a few seconds before she lashed out, "You better not play with my emotions like that. I might just have a fit."

"Aw, yer too tough for that." And he grabbed her and pulled her into his lap for a big slobbery kiss.

"Eek. Wipe your mouth," she squealed, and Jake rolled in laughter.

SEPTEMBER 19 JAKE was appointed Constable and John T. Hogue Justice of the Peace of the Springerville District by the Apache County Board of Supervisors. The notice was published in the September 24 edition of the *St. Johns Herald* newspaper. On Monday, October 5, in the morning, he was in the shop reading through the October 1 edition of the *Herald* over a cup of coffee. Elmar Van Arman, the farrier, was in front of the shop filing on a gray mare's hoof he had turned back into his apron and held between his legs.

"Want a cup of coffee, Elmer?" Jake called out to him.

"El—*mar!*"

"Sorry, Elmar."

"Yah. Maybe I do." He dropped the hoof, walked into the shop proper and took the cup Jake handed to him. He sipped and said, "Das goot. Cool, this morning, yah?"

"Yeah. Fall is here. Well, I'll be. Lookee here. Says that Charley Kinnear was bailed out a jail by Sol Barth and Antonio Gonzales." Jake shot a questioning look at Elmar. "You hear about that up in St. Johns?"

"Yah. I hear 'bout it."

"Never heard nuthin' down here. And look here. Next it says that Tom Brady left St. Johns last week to make his headquarters here in Springerville because he took over the lease and business of Charley's saloon." Jake looked a little incredulous. "You hear 'bout that too?"

"Nah. I don't."

"Wal, Hubbell was right. There's an opportunity gone. Proves out. Early bird gets the worm."

"Huh?"

"Never mind." Jake stepped through the wide shop door and tossed the dregs of his cup into the dirt off to the side. As he did, he looked up the road and saw four cowboys loping their horses around the corner and down the road toward his shop. They were riding proud like they were mustang stallions of the range in search of more mares to add to their herd. As they came closer Jake could see they were well armed with pistols, rifles, and knives. Not having a firearm on his person or nearby, he felt a little naked and exposed. He watched them closely and, sure enough, they skidded up in front of the shop all in a bunch, reining in their broncs so they stamped their hoofs and tossed their heads in a cloud of dust. Jake didn't move.

The obvious leader of the bunch reined his horse around, steadied him and hooked a leg over his saddlehorn. "Howdy," he said with a smile and furtive glances at Jake and Elmar. He was a lean man, obviously wanting for some good home-cooking. In fact, they all looked thin and hungry. "Name's Ike Clanton. Which one a yer is the hoss-shoerer?" His voice was gravelly and his manner gruff. His face was like sunburned leather, and he squinted his dark eyes as if he were daring them to lie. He spat a stream of tobacco to the ground, wiped his sandy mustache and pointy beard with the back of his sleeve, and said, "Wal?"

"It's me," Elmar said boldly.

"Wal, pleased to meet yer, uh?"

"Elmar Van Arman."

"Elmer Van Arman. Wooee. Hear that boys? We got a German prince here. Hah, hah. Wal Mister Van Arman, this here is my brother Phin, and this is Lee Renfro, and this is George West and we need our hossess re-shod." They all sat their horses and stared down absently at Jake and Elmar. "Can yer do that?"

"Yah. Be a quarter per hoof."

"All right. Four bucks for all four. That sounds fair." He dropped out of the saddle and the rest of the gang dismounted. "And who might yer be, friend?" He turned his attention to Jake, who had been covertly studying Clanton.

"J.V. Brighton. Blacksmith."

"Uh-huh. Good to know. Pleased to meet yer. Wal, we'll jest hitch these hosses right here and walk on over to Charley Kinnear's and play some billiards while yer shoein' them hosses. How long yer think yer'll be?"

"Rest of the morning, surely. Maybe by two o'clock."

Clanton raised an eyebrow but said nothing. Jake said, "Ain't Charley's place no more."

"Hell yer say?" He turned a sour look on Jake, and the rest of the gang whipped around to glare at Jake.

"Yeah. What're yer talkin' 'bout?" Phin Clanton demanded.

"Tom Brady owns the place now."

"Who tol' yer that?" Ike scowled at Jake and took a step closer to him. Jake did not move.

"Says right here," Jake said as he held up the newspaper for Clanton, who snatched the paper out of Jake's hand and tossed it to one of the men.

"What's it say, Westy?"

Jake stepped over next to West and said, "Right here and here," as he pointed out the two short notices which West took a minute to scan.

"Yep. That's what it says, boss. Says Charley's been bailed out too."

Clanton sneered, "All right, so we play billiards at Brady's," turned on his heel, stomped off in the direction back up the road with the gang falling in beside him. Once he looked back curiously at Jake who waved goodbye to him.

"Funny fellow, eh?" Jake said to Elmar.

"Funny? He is scary."

"Aw, no. He's all gurgle and no guts."

"Yah, wal, I better get this mare finished so I can get to their horses."

"Yeah. Probably best."

Jake helped Elmar shape the shoes to help speed up the process and so Elmar had all four horses completely re-shod by one thirty. He was anxious to get on the road to Show Low but was delayed because the Clanton bunch didn't show until four o'clock.

Jake saw that Elmar was annoyed and so he sidled up next to him and said, "Might want a let me ride point on this one, Elmar. They's probably pretty well liquored up." Jake patted the butt of his pistol he had strapped on.

Elmar's eyes widened as he looked down at Jake's six-shooter. "I don't want no trubble."

"Me neither." He watched the crew saunter down the middle of the road, laughing, guffawing, shouting back and forth like they were kings of the road. They were all grins when they came up to Elmar and Jake at the big door of the shop.

"Wal, here we are. Yer got them hosses done?" Ike blurted out as he squinted one-eyed at Elmar. He didn't seem to be too drunk, but he was definitely feeling it.

"Yah. They all ready. That be four dollars," Elmar answered.

"Four bucks? We said fifty cents a hoss. Didn't we boys?" The gang sort of nodded yes, and Phin stepped forward and said, "Yep. That's right. Heard it with my own ears."

"That's two bucks," Ike said and stuck his hand in his pants pocket to pull out some money.

Jake took two steps forward so that Elmar was a little behind him and to his side. "Ya'll might be a little muddled from the drink," Jake said with a kindly grin. "I heard four bucks for sure, and that is Elmar's all the time regular price, so he wouldn't charge any less. I heard you say that four bucks was fair. Yer might a forgot that. But, yer a man a yer word, ain't yer?" Jake continued to smile in a friendly way but stared hard and straight at Ike with challenge in his eyes.

The men of the gang shuffled around, put space between them and inched their hands toward their pistol butts. Jake didn't flinch, continued to hold Ike with his steady glare and never even glanced at the other men. Jake had his thumbs hooked in his pistol belt and stood relaxed in front of Clanton, who glanced down at Jake's pistol and back up at Jake. The breeze rustled the leaves in the cottonwoods beside the shop but, except for the twitching of the horses' ears, no one or anything else moved. The crew was focused on Jake, and he on Ike. Not a word was said for a whole long minute.

Then Ike grinned and chuckled. "Yeah, I'm a man a my word. Ain't I, boys? I must a forgot. Used to be fifty cents a hoss, weren't it? Wal, here yer go." He dug four silver dollars out of his pants pocket and held them toward Elmar. But he did it with a sly look in his eye, a wicked little smile, and a slip of his hand down to his pistol. Jake stepped forward and took the money with a pleasant smile and his glare still fastened on Ike.

"That's honorable a yer, Ike. Brings a man respect. I respect yer fer that." Jake changed the expression of challenge in his eyes to that of admiration. Ike looked confused.

"Wal, er, uh. Thanks." He looked side to side and behind him in quick turns of his head, shrugged his shoulders and said, "Wal, guess we better git on back to the ranch." He stepped over to unhitch his horse, and the rest of the crew followed. He vaulted into the saddle and reined around to look down at Jake. "Hear tell over at Kinnear's yer the new constable in town."

"Yeah. I am."

"Wal, welcome to town. Be seein' yer." He thumbed his hat, smiled big and spurred up the road with his gang.

Jake handed Elmar his money and said, "See. All gurgle. No guts."

"Yah. But he make a lot a trouble 'round here."

WELL INTO JANUARY there was six inches of snow on the ground and the temperature remained below freezing. It was ten degrees and dark outside, but Jake and Mary Jane were cozy in their chairs by the stove. Jake had the newspaper in his lap. Mary Jane was knitting.

"So, here's the whole story on the county treasury theft. On Sunday, December 27, the county safe was broke into at St. Johns, and there was a lot of finger pointin' goin' on over the eleven thousand dollars that was stole. Naturally, the Clanton bunch was blamed because the story was that five masked men, in the middle of the night, broke into Francisco Baca's house. You know he is the deputy treasurer for the county?" Mary Jane nodded yes. "They forced him over to the courthouse to open the safe. Then they took the money and hightailed out a there. Ike, Phin, Renfro, and Ebin Stanley swore they were innocent, but warrants were issued anyway. And Dionicio Baca of here in Springerville, filed a complaint, and a search warrant was served on the Clantons and Stanley by a specially appointed constable for Springerville named James T. Barron. The Clantons and Stanley turned themselves in. Barron searched and found nothing. Ebin Stanley then filed a complaint against Dionicio Baca for fallaciously procurin' a search warrant without probable cause. Barron searched Baca's residence also and found nothing. But Baca was charged with filin' a false report. Except for Baca's, no arrests were made and the whole thing has drifted into the background. What a ya think a that?"

"Those Clantons and Stanleys sure get themselves into a fair bit of trouble."

"Yeah. They do seem to."

"What a you think about them appointin' a special constable for the case instead of giving you the warrants to serve?"

"Aw, they's all from that crowd at St. Johns. Lopez issued the warrant. I work for Judge Hogue. So, I don't care. Less work and I still get paid." He smiled and winked at her to which Mary Jane smiled back as she glanced up from her knitting. "Reminds me, though. We need to have the Hogues over for supper soon."

IT WAS THE first of April when the buds on the apple trees were plump and ready to burst into bloom any day soon. There was still chill in the morning air, but Jake did not notice because he was busy over his forge. Sheriff Hubbell did, though, as he walked into the shop and held his hands out to the forge. "Aw. That feels good," he said.

"Howdy, Sheriff. Just get into town?"

"Yep. Thought I'd bring you a little news."

Jake set down the piece he was working on and looked up at Hubbell. "What's that?"

"Well, you have any coffee?"

"Sure. Here. I'll get yer a cup." Jake poured from the pot on the side of his forge and handed the cup to Hubbell. "So, what's on yer mind?"

Hubbell blew the steam off his cup and took a sip. Then he looked Jake right in the eye and said, "I guess we know who you are."

Jake tried to hold his indifferent expression and smiled. "What'd yer mean?"

"You acquainted with Ben Irby?" At the mention of Irby's name Jake felt his stomach flop a little.

"I couldn't say that. Only met him once. Last May."

"Uh-huh. Well, he knows about you—Rawhide Jake."

Jake dropped his gaze to the floor and stood with his shoulders hanging for a minute. "Don't change nuthin'," he said. Then he looked up and said, "Hope you can keep it to yerself, though."

"Oh, I can, but I don't know about the others. There was a meeting of the Stock Grower's Association a week ago Thursday. They elected their officers. Al Clark is president. Ben Irby, vice president, and Will Barnes, secretary treasurer. I ran into Irby and he told me they were having a glass of whiskey after the meeting and Clark was complaining about the rustling when Irby told him all about you." He gave Jake a knowing look and squinted his eyes. "Said Clark wants to talk to you. Said he could make you a real good offer. I don't get along with those Texans or I would of found out more."

Jake was annoyed and it showed. "I'm tryin' to live a peaceable life here. Gettin' to know folks 'round town. Doin' free work for the new Catholic church. Helpin' 'em out. Even gave 'em the gate I made. My wife likes it here. Last thing I need is for folks to find out my past. Not that it's all that bad, but I killed a few men in my day and folks generally don't like that. Been my experience. Reckon I better talk to Clark. Send a letter to Irby." He threw his gloves onto the vice. "I can count on you, Sheriff?"

"Came down here and gave you the news, didn't I? You better be sure to talk to Will Barnes. He's the blabbermouth. Kind of a gossip. Uh, are you a Catholic?"

"Yeah. Not a very good one, though."

"Me too." He smiled.

"Lost out on Kinnears', eh?"

"Yeah, it's all right. You win some. You lose some. Got a building up in Sanders. Gonna put a saloon in there also with a billiard table." He smiled and nodded his head in affirmation of what he said. "And come to think of it, after we were talking last year, me and my cousin Walter bought the St. Johns Saloon." He gave Jake a sure-enough serious look as one advising another.

"Square with me. Is there any money in the saloon business?" Jake said seriously.

Hubbell took a drink of his coffee, and seemed to be contemplating the dregs before he answered. "Most people think there is. There's always thirsty customers around, eh?"

Jake nodded his head yes. "But a saloon's gotta be run right to make money in most small towns. Mostly you got to make sure there are enough customers to go around if there is more than one saloon in town. Then watch your costs real close. That's the big thing. Don't invest too much right out the gate. Why? You thinking about something?"

"Just thinkin' and askin' questions. We got Kinnear's and Castillo's, Kinnear owns 'em both, and that dive down on the road to Eagar's."

"Yeah. So, you see there is competition. Well, I better get back on up to St. Johns before I am missed." He cracked a bigger smile and the crow's-feet at the corners of his eyes crinkled.

"Thanks for the information, Sheriff—all of it."

"Sure enough. Let me know if I can be of any help to you down the road. Good day to you."

"You, too."

Jake watched him ride away and lost himself in thought for a few minutes.

JAKE TROTTED JASPER up to the barn and lots of the La Cienega Ranch, north of Springerville. Off a little ways to the east, stood a brown adobe house with a deep porch across the whole length of the house. It was all brown scrub around the house except where there was bare dirt from horse or man traipsing across the ground. It was all by itself—no trees, no bushes, no green. A big man stepped from the barn into the sunlight to meet Jake. As he came closer, he took hold of Jasper's halter and stroked his neck. Jake said, "Howdy" and dismounted.

"Hello. Don't believe we've met." He looked to be well weathered and squinted his eyes as he looked at Jake and his holstered pistol and belts. His accent was decidedly Easterner.

"No, sir. J.V. Brighton's my name. Blacksmith in town. Likewise, I don't recall seein' you at the shop. Got any work you need done?" Jake grinned pleasantly. It was not returned.

"So, you are Rawhide Jake Brighton, eh?"

"You have me at the disadvantage, sir."

"Alfred Clark. I own this spread in partnership with a couple of other fellows and am president of the county cattlemen's association. I heard about you from Ben Irby." He held out his hand to Jake for a shake and said, "Why don't you come on in and we can have a glass of sweet tea on the porch? You want to sell him? Give you top dollar."

"Huh?"

"Your horse. You want to sell him? Looks like some fine horse flesh here." He smiled as he stroked Jasper's neck.

"Oh. Awe, nah. Couldn't do that. Me and him been through too much together."

"Aye. Thought so. Well, come on up to the porch for refreshment."

They walked up to the house with Jake trailing Jasper behind him. A strong gust of wind blew through and wound up a dust devil that danced across the lots. Jake had to clamp his hat down with his free hand, but he managed to tie Jasper off at the hitching rail without losing his hat. Then just as sudden like, it was calm. He followed Clark up the steps to the porch and sat in the chair indicated to him by Clark. "It usual for wind to gust like that around here?" Jake said.

Clark was about to answer, but just as they sat down, the screen door to the house swung open and a pleasant looking Mexican woman came out to the porch. *"Sí, Señor* Al," she said.

"Esmeralda, this is Mister J.V. Brighton," Clark said as he made proper introductions. "And this is Señora Esmeralda Perla de Tovar. She's a distant relative by marriage to the Tovar who came into this area with Coronado in the fifteen hundreds." He smiled at Jake.

"Pleased to meet you, Señor Brighton. Sweet tea, Señor Al?"

"Yes. Thank you." He turned to Jake, "To answer your question, yes, it often comes up suddenly and suddenly it's calm. Just like the rustlers plaguing us. They come in fast, gather up some beeves and head them south. In and out before we even suspect we've lost cattle."

"Any idea who they are?"

"Oh, we're pretty sure it's the Clantons and the Stanleys. Especially that good-for-nothing troublemaker, Ike Clanton. Can't prove anything. I've gone over to their range more than once looking for my brand. Once in a while I find a stray or two but nothing I can pin on them. They probably run the cattle down south as soon as they steal them. Or they rustle them from the south and trail them up here to fatten up and sell to Fort Apache." Esmeralda came out with a tray of sweet tea in a pitcher and two glasses. "Clantons ran a gang down in Cochise County. Stealing cattle and horses. Robbing stages. Shooting up towns. Killing people. Raising all kind of hell. And Ike Clanton was the ringleader and worst of them all. They hightailed it up our way when the Earps ran them out a Cochise County. Their kind attract ones just like them. And so now they're doing the same thing here in Apache County. We ranchers are losing money, and we don't like it at all. This Round Valley is about as lawless as a place can be. That's why I am very interested in what Ben told me about you. The association is paying two hundred fifty for any conviction, you know?" Esmeralda filled the two glasses from the pitcher and took her leave.

"Yeah. I know that," Jake said and drank a little tea.

"So, let me get right to the point. With your know-how and experience I would think you'd be after that reward like a bear to honey. And we could sure use the help."

Jake took another drink and looked off out to the lots. "You see, Mister Clark, there's a couple of problems here. From what I heard, you don't have any warrants. So that means a feller would have to ride the range and catch the rustlers in the act or trail 'em and catch 'em with stolen livestock. Then, he would have to arrest 'em and bring 'em in for trial. Just ridin' the range could take months before anything came up and a trial more months. Before you know it, a year is gone and there ain't been any pay. The other problem is my wife don't want me ridin' the range no more." He gave Clark a long hard look and fished a cigar and match out of his vest pocket. He snapped the match with his thumbnail and lit the cigar. He puffed the cigar tip into a red-hot glow and said, "See what I'm sayin'?"

Clark took a long drink of his sweet tea and said, "What if we were to bifurcate the reward money?"

"Huh?"

"Say, pay half upon arrest and half upon conviction."

"What if a feller brought 'em in dead?"

Clark studied Jake for a few seconds and a slight smile creased his lips as he said, "That's as good as a conviction, isn't it?"

Jake smiled and said, "Reckon so, except the court's gotta go along with it. A big part of why I got outta the stock detective business is because of a judge that threw me in jail for killin' a outlaw who was wanted dead or alive and who was gonna kill me! If I was to bring in a known suspected rustler tied facedown over the saddle, and there was no warrant out on him, I'd need to know I'd be paid, no questions asked." He paused and looked seriously at Clark, who in turn studied Jake. "But all that only solves problem one," Jake continued. "My wife still don't want me out on the range, and I want to keep her happy. That's why we moved here in the first place." A little ironic smile stretched across Jake's face.

"I see. Well, I can lead a horse to water but, as they say, I can't make him drink. I will talk to the board at the association and see if we can increase the reward. Would that help?"

"Maybe. But, let me make a suggestion. You know I am the district constable. I get around to a lot a folks, listen to 'em talk. Likewise, I got my shop and people comin' and goin', talkin'. I am gettin' ready to buy out a saloon, and people really get to talkin' after a few drinks. Gonna partner up with a feller who can supply a lot of information. So, I suggest that I keep my ears open, and when I hear anything worthwhile, then maybe we can get some warrants up and talk pricin'."

"Sounds fair enough. As it is, it doesn't seem like we have any other choice."

"What 'bout this feller Barnes? I hear he likes to shoot his mouth off quite a bit."

"I'll keep him under control."

They chewed the cud for a while longer, then Jake rode out. When he got back to the shop, George West was there waiting for him. West had his horse hitched out front and was inside the shop by the forge leaning back in a slat back chair with his boots up on the edge of the forge. Even as Jake walked in, he continued to draw the blade of his jackknife across one of Jake's whetstones. He was a man of average build, standing an inch or two taller than Jake, in his thirties, with the weathering of the range on his face and his hands. His hair and beard were a mass of thick brown hair. He had a ready smile that revealed a wide gap between his two front uppers, and his brown eyes were full of expression, depending on his mental state at the time. Usually, he was in a good mood but could be mean if riled.

"You might get a hotfoot off that forge," Jake said as he shoved his hat back and sat down in another chair.

"He say anything?" West said with a suspicious look at Jake who ignored it.

"Nope. They don't know nothin'. Can't prove it anyway."

"What a ya mean?"

"They know the Clantons and Stanleys been rustling their cattle, but they ain't got no proof."

"So what'd yer say?"

"I told 'em I'd keep pokin' around and see if I could find anything out. And if I do, I'll just steer 'em in the wrong direction." Jake smiled.

George returned his smile and said, "Wal, I still got this five hunnert burnin' a hole in my pocket. When we gonna seal the deal on the saloon?"

"I'm thinkin' in about a week. Meanwhile, let's talk 'bout it over supper. Sure, Mary Jane's got the chuck comin' outta the oven right about now."

GEORGE PUSHED BACK from the table and wiped his beard with his napkin and cleaned his fingers. "I declare," he said, "Next to my mama's, that is the best fried chickin I ever et, Mary Jane. I thought yer said yer was from Texas. Only a Southern belle can fix fried chickin like that. My mama was from Alabama."

"Well, truth be known, *my* mama taught me, and she was from Georgia." Mary Jane gave George a playful grin, and he guffawed.

"I know'd it," he laughed. "Ya'll tried to trick me."

Jake smiled. Didn't seem like it was all that funny. "How'd we trick yer, George?"

"Wal, uh, er. Cuz that was *Southern* fried chickin, after all, and not Texan." He showed a triumphant grin. Then he sort of melted into a cowed look as if he realized he had said something kind a dumb. Jake rescued him.

"Wal, yer caught us. But let's sit down and have a smoke and a whiskey. Talk some saloon business. That suit yer?" Jake broke into a big smile.

"Yeah. Okay. Sounds good."

After he left for the evening and the dishes were done and the kitchen cleaned up, Mary Jane came and sat in the chair next to Jake. She took up her knitting and said, "So next week we are saloon owners, eh?"

"Yep. Kinda funny. George coming and propositioning me like he did."

"You know why he did?"

"Said he was impressed with how I handled Ike Clanton when we first met down at the shop. He seems like a upright feller. 'Course, his association with the Clantons and Stanleys causes me to wonder."

"How much?" She spoke without looking up from her knitting.

"Five hunnert each. Got have a proper bar made with a backbar and mirror, buy a billiard table so we can compete with Brady's Kinnear's." He drew on the cigar and blew a smoke cloud to the ceiling. "Few more tables and stock the inventory with better whiskies and beer."

"And give that place a thorough muck-out. Stinks to high heaven," she said emphatically.

Jake glanced at her and chuckled. "What's so funny?" she demanded.

"Just like a woman. Got a have a clean house."

"Well, of course, and speaking of houses, I hope you got yours in order. You are playing a dangerous game ridin' both sides a the fence."

"You worried?"

"A little. Yes. Clantons ever find out. I think I'd be a widow."

"Don't worry. I got some life insurance."

"I know you do." She looked up from her knitting and stared him hard in the eyes. "That's not my concern, and you know it."

Jake waved away a cloud of smoke and stood up. "Yeah, I know it," he said and smiled lovingly at her. "With you at my side, though, I got the best pardner in the world. 'Sides, I told you I ain't gonna do anything too dangerous. Just gonna see what develops. We're gettin' a pretty good reputation here, and I don't want to bring you any embarrassment." He grinned. "And George is a good source of information on the Clanton doin's."

A few weeks later Mary Jane was at Becker's Mercantile for her weekly shopping. She was looking over the bolts of cotton dress material when Louisa Becker came alongside her and said, "Good morning, Mary Jane. How are you today?"

"Oh. Hello, Louisa. Just fine. How are you?"

"Well as could be expected, I suppose," she said as she patted her slightly rounded midsection. "Gustav says I have to go into confinement, but I am resisting." She smiled meekly and searched Mary Jane's face, apparently for sympathy.

"I don't blame you. Not until the last month or so, anyway."

"Yes, well. I hear you and Jonas are opening a saloon or buying one."

"Yes. He is. I am not involved. Thank God. I have enough to do as it is." She cast a glance to the ceiling with an expression of semi-mortification upon her face.

"I suppose such establishments are necessary to satisfy the more base desires of our menfolk. But I hope he is not planning to bring in any women of ill repute. That would be going too far. I am sure the upright citizens of the town would object." She talked and looked as if she was scolding Mary Jane, who in turn stared at her with a quizzical and somewhat amused look.

"Well, you can rest easy. I don't think he is."

"Good. Now what can I help you with on these fabrics?"

AROUND THE MIDDLE of May, Jake and West had their saloon all cleaned up, new bar with brass rail and backbar with mirror installed, and more tables and chairs. All that was missing was the billiard table that had yet to arrive from Albuquerque. The day before the grand opening Jake said to George, "What shall we call it? West and Brighton or Brighton and West?"

"What sounds best to yer, Mary Jane?" George said with a little bit of a leer.

"Oh, no you don't. I ain't gettin' involved in that." She dried her hands on a towel and brushed back a few strands of her hair.

"Yer been workin' hard. I figger yer got a say in it."

"Why don't you flip a coin?"

"That's a good idea," Jake said. "I got a silver dollar. Here you flip, Mary Jane." He tossed the coin over to her. "Go ahead and call it, George."

"Tails." He grinned big, thoroughly exposing the gap between his teeth. "Thought I was gonna say heads, didn't yer?"

Mary Jane tossed the coin into the air flipping it with her thumb. It landed on the floor with a clatter, and spun to rest tail side up. She blurted out a short scream of mixed excitement and disappointment.

"Tails!" George said loudly. "Hah, hah."

"So, what's it gonna be?" Jake said.

George stared shrewdly at Jake for a few seconds, grinned big and said, "Wal, I could say Brighton and West, but that don't sound good. I guess it has to be West and Brighton." He beamed like a politician and stuck his thumbs in his suspenders. Jake took two steps toward George, and he looked angry and dangerous. George's grin disappeared. He took a step back and felt for his pistol but it wasn't there. He forgot he took it off so he could work. He looked concerned and licked his lips as they were suddenly very dry. But, before he could do anything, Jake busted out laughing and said, "I just wanted to see how sure yer were 'bout that. Guess it's West and Brighton then. Shake on it." He held out his hand. George's grin returned and, apparently relieved, he shook Jake's hand, vigorously pumping it up and down.

"Yer ol' rattlesnake. Yer had me goin'."

All in all, the place looked pretty good and the next night Jake, Mary Jane, and George were all there in all the hubbub to greet customers at the grand opening of the West and Brighton Saloon just off Main Street on the road to the Eagar's. Mary Jane wore a modest burgundy waist with high standing collar and long sleeves and a navy-blue walking skirt. She moved in and out of the men milling around with drinks or beers in their hands and back and forth to the bar with their orders. More than once, Jake managed to discreetly disengage from his many conversations and catch her eye, wink at her and smile lovingly.

Most all the men from town and the close-by ranches were there. Noticeably not there were Ike and Phin Clanton. "Where's Ike?" Jake said to George.

"Dunno. I ain't seen him in a few days. Probably for the best. He just brings trouble, and I don't want no trouble on this our opening night, eh?" He held up his glass and Jake clinked his against it.

Then Jake said in a loud voice, "Gentlemen." He waited for the place to quiet down. He continued, "For our grand opening, we are offering Overholt at fifteen cents a shot, Kessler at a dime, and regular at a nickel." He raised his glass and continued, "Better get your orders in now because this'll be the last time you see those prices around here." And he flashed a big grin all around. There was a little cheer that went up and a decided movement toward the bar. Jake turned and grinned at George who returned the sentiment. Business was looking good.

BUT, SURE ENOUGH, on the night of May nineteenth, just before bedtime, there was a pounding on the door at Jake's house. He was startled out of his doze and jumped up out of his chair. Mary Jane was in the bedroom and came hurrying out. "Who the hell is that?" she cursed loudly. Jake pulled his pistol from the holster on the belt hanging on a wooden pin by the door. The pounding started up again and was so heavy it nearly rattled the door right off the hinges.

"Who's there?" Jake hollered.

"It's me. Ike. Open the dang door. I'm in a hurry," came the shout from outside.

Slowly, Jake swung the door and before it was halfway open, Clanton busted into the room. Jake held the pistol behind his leg and Mary Jane screamed and backed into the bedroom but stood so she could see what was going on.

"What the hell are yer doin', Ike?" Jake demanded.

"A Mexican almost got me. He shot at me and the ball splinters hit my leg here. See? Here's the gun. You take it and hold it. I got a hide out for awhile." He was taking in big gulps of air in between blurts and he was sweating.

"Why do you want me to keep his gun?"

"Wal, you're constable an' a man a yer word an' respected 'round here. I know yer won't give him his gun back to come and shoot me. 'Sides when the law comes, they'll want the gun."

"Uh-huh. Why don't yer sit down here and let's look at that leg. Mary Jane, maybe we can deal with this wound?"

"What?! I ain't no nurse."

"Nah. Don't you worry none 'bout it. Just a nick," Ike said with some bravado.

Jake jammed his pistol in his waistband and took the rifle out of Ike's hand, threw down the lever and an empty forty-four flew out of the breach. He smelled the open breach and determined that a round had been recently exploded in the gun. Then he looked at Ike and noticed there was a powder burn on the shirtsleeve of his left arm. "Tell me what happened."

"Wal, I was sittin' in Senon Castillo's saloon havin' a drink when Pablo Romero came in and started gettin' after me for a game of Casino. I didn't wanna play, but he kept hazin' me so I said okay. We got in an argument 'bout points, and I could see he was gittin' hot. So, I pulled out a cigar and went behind the bar for a match. 'Course, I knew my pistol was there by the match box and I wasn't takin' any chances, just in case." He made a cutting motion with the flat of his hand across the space in front of him. "Wal, don't yer know," he paused and turned the palm of his hand up and shrugged his shoulders, "soon as I struck that match, he grabbed his gun, that one right there. He raised it up and I saw him cock it so I knew he was meanin' business. He pointed it at me, and I brushed it away with my left hand. I grabbed my six-shooter at the same time, and we both started firin' and got all tangled up. But he wasn't stoppin' so I hit him over the head with my pistol and ran over here with his gun. That's it. Cisco Padilla was there. He saw the whole thing, too."

"Well, we better go on over there and see what's goin' on. Might have to arrest someone."

"Wal, it won't be me. That Mexican was tryin' to kill me. I had to defend myself."

"Mary Jane?" Jake called out. "We're goin' over to Castillo's. You wanna come?"

"I'm right here. You don't have to yell. And, yes, I'm comin'." She threw a black shawl over her shoulders and stepped out into the night behind them, shutting the door after her. They walked the hundred fifty yards down to the saloon and went in to see Castillo and two other men in a huddle at the end of the bar.

"Howdy, Senon," Jake said. "Heard you had a little fracas here. Where's Romero and Padilla?"

Castillo frowned and glared at Ike. "Yeah, we had a fracas, all right, and him right in the middle of it."

"Where are Romero and Padilla?" Jake stared hard at Castillo who could not return the look.

"Padilla took Romero to the doctor. He's been shot through the hip."

Jake turned his gaze on Ike with an accusative and inquisitive expression. Ike shrugged his shoulders and said, "I didn't know he got shot."

Castillo said loudly, "You shot him."

"He was shootin' at me. Look at that bullet hole in the door over there." He pointed at the double door entrance to the saloon. Jake walked over and inspected it. "I was facin' east, and Romero was facin' west. He's the only one who could have made that hole in the door on the west side. He was shootin'."

"Looks like a hole from a forty-four slug. Splintered on the outside so it had to come from the inside," Jake said. The two men from the end of the bar came over and looked at it.

"Howdy, Bill. Albert." Jake said.

"Sure looks that way," William Woods said.

"Yeah. Well, I couldn't tell who was shootin'. So can I please have the gun, Mister Brighton," Castillo said.

Jake handed him the rifle and said, "Guess that's it. I'm goin' home. C'mon, Mary Jane. See yer around, boys."

"You ain't gonna arrest him?" Castillo said clearly showing his shock.

"Not me." Jake said and started to walk out the door.

"You're in cahoots with him," Castillo shouted.

Jake stopped in midstride, turned around, and moved slowly and deliberately to Castillo. Mary Jane retreated off to the side against the wall, out of the line of fire. Jake still had his pistol in his waistband, and Castillo had the rifle in his hand at his side. Jake stopped in front of Castillo within eighteen inches of his face and scowled at him with cold eyes set in a granite hard face.

"I ain't in cahoots with *nobody*. Way I see it, there was a mutual combat here. So, nobody to arrest. You see it differently, you can file a complaint. Clanton's free to go, far as I can tell." Then Jake surprised everyone when his countenance turned happy and he grinned at Castillo, who still had the rifle, turned a one-eighty, put his arm out for Mary Jane to take and swaggered out the door.

Clanton fell in step and slapped Jake on the back. "Thanks, pard," he said with a big grin. "Guess I owe yer one now."

"Yer don't owe me nuthin'. Just doin' my job."

As for Mary Jane, she turned her head and looked back twice to make sure they weren't going to be shot in the back.

When they were back in the house, Mary Jane said, "You either got ice water in your veins or you're just plain stupid. What bothers me is

I know you ain't stupid. But your bravado is gonna get you killed one of these days." A tear leaked from the corner of her eye.

"Aw, honey, come here." He took her in his arms and hugged her tight. "That Castillo feller wasn't gonna shoot me. He ain't no killer and I knew it. I can tell killers. Like that feller John Dove. There was no doubt about him. He was a killer. It's more about figurin' right 'bout who you're dealin' with and takin' the right action." He grinned and held her at arm's length. "I was just play actin' to advertise for our saloon. Once word gets out, we'll get more business."

She gave him a soft punch to the chest, smiled and said, "Oh, you. You are *so* frustrating." Then she gave him a big kiss.

On the twenty-fourth of May, Jake, Clanton, Padilla, and Castillo were subpoenaed to appear in Judge Hogue's court at two p.m. to testify as witnesses in a criminal action brought against Ike Clanton. The action was in pursuance of a complaint filed by Senon Castillo. Judge Hogue found there to be insufficient evidence to remand Ike to higher court, and he was discharged without further action.

FOUR
MURDER GALORE • 1885

TOWARD THE END of July, it finally started raining. The whole year up until then had been a drought. On the thirtieth there was a break in the rain, and Jake decided to take Jasper out for some exercise. He rode out early in the morning and when he returned there was a crowd around the front of his house about fifty yards out. He stood in the stirrups to get a better look and saw a body lying in the mud. He spurred Jasper into a lope until he came close to everyone and reined him in. He searched the group of about twenty people for Mary Jane but didn't see her. At the front door to their house, he saw her leaning against the jamb watching all the goings on. She waved at him, and he waved back at her. He was about to rein Jasper over to her when Judge Hogue caught Jasper's bridle.

"There's been a killin' here, J.V." He was all lathered up, shouting, eyes bulging and his big gray mustache and mutton chops bounced up and down with every word. "I need a coroner's jury right now. Meet at your blacksmith shop, and I mean I want to see the jury there right now. Soon as you have the names of the jurors, I'll put 'em in the record. I'll be waitin' at your shop. Now git goin'." He slapped Jasper on the rump, and Jake scowled at him a murderous look while Jasper crow-hopped and would have run through the crowd if Jake had not reined him hard to the right. He got control of Jasper and trotted him over to Mary Jane.

"What the hell happened here?"

She shrugged her shoulders and said, "I got no idea. I was out picking up supplies at Becker's, remember?"

"Oh, yeah. I gotta round up a coroner's jury for Judge Hogue. He wants to meet down at the shop."

"Ours?"

"Yeah. You wanna come?"

"No thanks. I had enough with that Clanton debacle." And she waved her hand dismissively at the whole suggestion and went back into the house.

After he answered a thousand questions, Jake finally had eleven men designated with orders to report to the shop. By the time Jake got back to the judge with his list of names, the crowd had moved from Jake's house to Jake's shop. There were probably fifty men crammed into the shop. Good thing the forge was cold. There was a lot of talking going on and a lot of gawking at the deceased. The body was laid out on Jake's workbench that had been cleared of the tools and supplies. Jake came up and looked at the body. He was a little miffed that his bench was all messed up but forgot about it when he saw that the body was that of Charley Lewis who was about twenty years old and shot through the chest. Anthony Harris, a twenty-one-year-old, was off to the side with his hands tied behind his back and watched over by a feller with a pistol on his hip. Jake knew both Charley Lewis and Tony Harris. He also knew the brothers Charles and George Everett, who were friends of Charley Lewis. "What happened, Judge?" he said to Hogue.

"We're gonna find out." Then he bellowed, "All right. Come to order. I, John T. Hogue, Acting Coroner of the Springerville Precinct in and for the County of Apache in the Territory of Arizona, having hereby impaneled a jury of eleven citizens of said Precinct, do hereby open a Coroner's Jury Inquest upon the body identified by those who knew him as Charles Lewis."

"Aw, c'mon, Judge. Skip all that mumble-jumble. Let's git to the meat," a man from the back of the crowd called out.

The judge picked up one of Jake's hammers and banged it on the anvil. "Constable. Remove that person from these proceedings. This ain't no kangaroo court. Proper procedure will be followed." And he spat a stream of tobacco juice onto the ground next to Jake's forge at which Jake cringed.

He went to the man and pressed close to him. "Let's go, Clarence. You heard the judge."

"It's a free country. I got a right to be here. Git yer hands off me."

Jake spun him around and pinned one of his arms in a hammerlock up his back. "Clarence, don't git me mad. Now, you been ordered out." Jake forced him against the wall and shoved his face into the wood siding. "You gonna leave? Or am I gonna have to hurt you?"

"All right. All right. You're breakin' my arm. I'll go. Argh. Let go a my arm."

Jake watched him stumble into the road with his arm hanging limp at his side. He made sure Clarence kept moving on down the road before he went back inside the shop, where he saw the Coroner's Jury passing by the body in a single-file line. Then they moved off to one side and stood as a group.

The judge called George Everett as the first witness who testified that when he, Lewis, and Charles Everett were walking up to Brighton's to have a friendly talk with Harris, he saw Harris stick a rifle out the door of Brighton's house, and without provocation or warning, shoot Lewis. His brother's testimony was basically the same. They both said they went to Brighton's to give Ike Clanton a drink, but he wasn't there. Harris begged advice of counsel and was given one day to procure a lawyer.

The next day, Harris testified in his own defense by offering a written statement:

I shot Charles Lewis because I was told to look out that he was going to round me up, and he has rounded me up previous to the shooting, four times with his pistol, and cursing me and abusing me, and shooting in my presence where I was at work, with a six-shooter. That Brighton and Isaac Clanton, and others have warned me that Chas. Lewis would round me up, as much as to say that he would shoot me. Evertime [sic] Chas. Lewis met me he would try to pick a quarrel or fuss with his hand on his six-shooter, and dared me to fight. I supposed when he saw me going into Brighton's house, and him peeping around the corner of the School Master's Corral, with the two Everett boys with him, that they were walking toward Brighton's house where I was, and Lewis, the man I shot holding his hand on his pistol, and the larger Everett boy pulled his pistol around from the back of his pants to his side. And both men walked toward me holding their hands on their pistols. As they were walking toward me I stood in the front door of Brighton's house with my Windchester [sic] rifle lying by my side. I called to them and told them not to come any further. They kept coming and I fired. When Lewis fell, and the smaller of the Everett boys threw up his hands and said he was not on the war-path, and had nothing to do with the fight. The larger Everett boy stood still and looked around, holding his hand on his six-shooter. I told him not to do any thing, [sic] and then I walked away down to Marcilino Jaramillo's house where I was arrested.

Signed, Anthony W. Harris.

After all the testimony was complete the jury found that the murder of Charles Lewis was committed by Anthony Harris. The judge agreed and found there to be sufficient evidence to believe that Harris had committed the murder and be held to answer for the same. "Constable Brighton," he called out, "immediately transport forthwith the accused to the county jail in St. Johns."

Jake opened his mouth to protest or at least suggest the transfer be delayed until the morning but was cut short by the banging of the hammer on the anvil. "This inquest is adjourned." The judge said loudly.

Jake rounded up a good horse and saddle and got Harris mounted and tied to the saddle. He looked up at Harris with a death stare and said, "Yer try and escape and I'll kill yer. Yer don't wanna die, do yer?" Harris did not answer as he was in a full sulk. Then Jake stopped by the house and told Mary Jane he would stay the night in St. Johns. He led the horses around to the stable and fed them both a bag of oats. While the horses munched their oats, he sat on a wooden box and lit a cigar. "Why were you in my house?" Jake said to Harris.

"I was lookin' for Ike."

"Uh-huh. Don't yer know it ain't right to go in somebody's house when they ain't home?"

"Wal, I was just waitin' for you or Ike to come along."

"It still ain't right to go inside. Yer could wait outside."

"Didn't think a that. 'Sides, yer and the missus and Ike are always real friendly."

"Don't matter. You get out a this scrape, you don't go in my house without me. Understand?"

"I might not be in this fix if yer and Ike didn't keep talkin' to me about Lewis roundin' me up. I thought sure he was gonna shoot me, and I beat him to it."

"Me and Ike was half-kiddin' yer and tryin' to git yer to stand up for yerself."

"Well, guess I did."

"Yep, yer did that. But not very smart. Can't ambush a man in front of witnesses and 'spect to git away with it. Okay. Looks like the horses finished their oats. Go ahead and swing up into the saddle."

Jake pulled off the feed bags and while setting out the water he thought he heard something so he looked back at Harris who was quietly sobbing. Jake took up the reins of Harris's horse, vaulted into Jasper's saddle, brushed his spurs against the big paint's sides and they trotted away from Springerville.

It was after dark when they rode into St. Johns. Jake had to roust Deputy Sheriff Frank Hubbell out of the Monarch Saloon to come over and take charge of his prisoner. "You J.L.'s brother?" Jake asked as they walked up the street side by side to the jail. Jake trailed Jasper and the other horse behind him while Harris was still tied to the saddle.

"Sure am. And you are?"

"J.V. Brighton."

"Oh yeah, the constable down Springerville way. We don't get down there much. Too many Mormons and Texans."

"Yeah. I heard about the St. Johns Ring."

Hubbell looked askance at Jake and said, "Which side are you on?"

"I ain't on any side. I'm just a blacksmith and businessman trying to make a livin' is all."

"Yeah. Well, who you got here?"

"Anthony Harris. He's being held to stand trial for murder."

"Okay. Here we are."

In the morning it was raining steady and heavy. Jake had his breakfast at the hotel dining room. After he finished, he shrugged into his black slicker and trudged through the mud to the stables where he had put up Jasper for the night. When the big black-and-white paint saw Jake, he nickered and whinnied in anticipation of his morning treat and feed. Jake gave him his candy and forked hay into his crib, then rustled up a pair of brushes and gave him a good brushing all over. "Enjoy yerself now, big boy, cuz it ain't gonna be a nice ride home," he said quietly.

Not long after sunrise they were on the road back to Springerville. The rain never let up and when they got home Jake got Jasper put away in the stable and gave him a good rubdown with a pair of burlap sacks, filled his water bucket and filled his feed trough with hay. "There you go, boy. You warm up now."

He slogged over to the house, and when he opened the door, he was greeted with the aroma of baking bread and the warmth of the room. Clotheslines were strung across the room with Mary Jane's bloomers and Jake's union suits hanging from them. There were big buckets of water boiling on both the heating and the cooking stove. Mary Jane was at the sink and turned to greet Jake as he walked in. "Well, howdy, you old muskrat. You look about drowned." She grinned at Jake and continued. "I'd give you a big hug, but you got a get outta that slicker. But first, can you fill the coal hod? It's empty. Then—" she pulled the tin bathtub away from the wall— "I'll give you a nice bath to warm the chill outta your bones." She smiled in the seductive way she always did with a sparkle in her eye and flaunt of her body.

Jake threaded his way through the hanging laundry to give Mary Jane a kiss on the cheek. Then he went out and came back a few minutes later with a hod full of coal. "That should hold us for a while. At least until this rain stops, I hope."

"Here. Let me pull that slicker off you, and I'll pour the water while you undress."

Mary Jane scrubbed his back with a soaped-up sponge and finally got around to asking, "So what all happened yesterday? I heard Charles Lewis was killed."

"Yeah, Anthony Harris ambushed him from our front door."

"What?" she exclaimed. "From *our* front door? What do you mean?"

"I mean he was hiding in our house, and Lewis and the Everett brothers were coming to round him up. He pointed a rifle out the door and pulled the trigger. He hit Lewis in the chest and killed him."

"What the hell was he hiding in our house for?"

"Said he was waiting for me to come home or Ike Clanton to show up."

"Alright," she said angrily, pulling off her apron and throwing it in a chair, "I am sick and tired of our home being like a saloon. You let too many varmints in here to shoot the bull with, especially that no-account Ike Clanton, and I want it to stop."

"Wal—"

"Don't you well me, mister. I want it to stop."

"I was gonna say, I use this to get information. They feel comfortable here and let their guard down—"

"I don't care," she screamed. "This is my home and not your, your, your, whatever you call it, and I won't have it anymore. Do you hear me?" She stood over Jake with her hands on her hips and glared down at him with fired up hot eyes bugged out in a face as red as a tomato.

Jake stared up at her for a long minute and smiled. "You're almost as beautiful when you're mad as when you're full of laughter and fun."

"You answer me now, Jonas Brighton. What's it gonna be? Me or your cronies?"

"Don't even need to think 'bout that one. Always you, my love." And he grabbed her skirt and pulled her into the tub with him that sent a wave of water over the side. Mary Jane screamed and rotated to give Jake a big kiss.

FOR THE REST of the summer and well into fall, except for the bugle whistles from rutting bull elk, it was quiet in the Round Valley. The most noise around town came from Jake's hammer and the occasional rumble of a wagon and team of horses or mules passing through. Not so quiet, though, out southeast of town. Even though cattle were putting on weight and starting to get woolly as winter was coming on, and the sheep had a good enough growth after their spring shearing to get them started into winter, reckon some fellers just couldn't keep their pistols in their holsters and their fingers off the trigger.

Judge Hogue had another Coroner's Inquest in session, this time at the residence of Dr. W.N. Sherman. Jake took some time off from the shop to attend the hearing. It was a particularly cold fall as made evident by the ice that crunched under Jake's boots as he walked to the doc's residence. It froze overnight, and he didn't think it was going to thaw out that day. Didn't matter, though. Mostly what concerned Jake, other than Mary Jane and Jasper, was steady business at the shop and the saloon, so both of them do well.

The deceased was Isaac Ellinger, the brother of William Ellinger, who was a wealthy stockman from back east and, in addition to the three ranches he and Isaac owned in Socorro County, New Mexico, he owned land in Oklahoma and Texas. While Isaac resided on the ranches as manager, William remained in their native Baltimore and made frequent trips out west to inspect his holdings. Jake was aware of the brothers and was acquainted with Isaac but had never met William. Because he rarely rode more than ten miles out of town when he was exercising Jasper, and the Williams's three ranches, individually called Mangetia, Cow Springs, and Cottonwoods, were better than a day's ride east into New Mexico Territory, he had not been to them. But he knew the brand that all three used—IXL on the right side. Couldn't break the habit of brand inspecting from his days as a stock detective in Texas.

As he walked, his thoughts turned to consider the fate of things. Here Isaac Ellinger was a wealthy man, still young, as he recollected, and a recent member of the Apache County Stock Growers Association. He was gaining in influence in the county. He didn't know whether he was married or not and if there were any children. But now, he was dead. Cut down in his prime, as the saying goes. So, what did it matter if he was rich or influential? He wasn't here to enjoy it anymore. And if he did have a wife and children, now they were a widow with children. That thought sparked thoughts of his own boys. Harry was seventeen now and Edgar fifteen. He wondered how they were doing. When he was Harry's age, he was a soldier fighting in the war, already killing men or other boys like himself. But he didn't do much of that because he spent most of his time in the Army either in prisoner of war camps or on infirmary leave. Of course he wouldn't wish any of that on the boys. In the last letter he received from Mary, she still hadn't said anything about what the boys were thinking about doing. Four letters a year. Not much. But then he wasn't on the best of terms with his sister-in-law. And—

"Oh, sorry, Brighton. Thought you saw me," Gustav Becker said as they both arrived at the door to Doc Sherman's house at the same time.

"Sorry, Gustav. Wasn't payin' attention. Mind was somewhere else."

"Completely understandable under the circumstances. Nasty business this shooting business. Are you on the jury?"

"No, just a bystander. You?"

"Yes. The judge has reined me in again. Don't mind too much though. Civic duty and all." He beamed a smile at Jake.

"After you," Jake said with a return smile. Becker owned the local store and other businesses around the valley. Guess you could say he and Hubbell were competitors. Of course Hubbell had the Navajo trade sewed up, so he had an extra leg up. Why the heck was he thinking this stuff, and as he walked in, he saw the body stretched out on an exam table. That's why. There you are dead and for what has been all the work? He shuddered and shook his head clear of the line of thinking he had been on. No profit in it.

"All right. Let's come to order," Judge Hogue called out.

The first witness called was a fellow named Wilds P. Plummer who worked for Isaac Ellinger. He testified that together they had ridden to Cieniga Amarilla, which was the Phin Clanton ranch just a few miles west of the New Mexico Territory border near Coyote Creek. Isaac had business with Ike Clanton and wanted him to ride to Springerville with him. But Ike did not want to go in spite of several attempts to convince him by Ellinger. So, they decided to stay for dinner. They sat at the table and wolfed it down. Ike, Lee Renfro, and Ellinger finished first and went to the east of the building where the sitting room stood off by itself. Plummer said he heard a voice holler ho! ho! like someone excited, then a pistol shot. He met Lee Renfro at the door to the sitting room with a six-shooter in his hand, full cocked. Renfro ordered him to throw up his hands and unbuckle his belt, which he did not do. Renfro told Phin Clanton to take it off him and Plummer warned them not to make any moves at him and they backed off, but Renfro kept him covered with the six-shooter. Plummer found Ellinger shot and trying to stay standing. Ellinger said Renfro had killed him without cause. Phin and Ike told Bill Jackson, who was the other feller there, to fetch a horse for Renfro. Ellinger said for them to take Renfro in and don't let him get away. When asked by Plummer how Ike Clanton stood on the affair, he said Renfro was his friend and he stood with him. Renfro walked into the kitchen and stood with his pistol drawn and held down at his side. Plummer went outside, mounted up, and rode for Dr. Sherman's in Springerville.

Next to testify were T.W. Jones and Dr. Sherman. Jones said he arrived at Cieniga Amarilla about two hours after the shooting and stayed with Ellinger until he died. He said that Ellinger told him that he and Renfro were talking about Ellinger's Cottonwoods Ranch, and Renfro told Ellinger that he understood that he, Ellinger, would have made him, Renfro, run down the Canyon if he Renfro, had jumped the Cottonwoods Ranch. Ellinger said it would have been no difference to him whether or not he ran. Jones said Ellinger told him Renfro went for his pistol and tried to hit Ellinger with it first and then shot him. Jones said that Ellinger said Renfro shot him without any cause. Only he, Ike Canton, and Lee Renfro were in the room when the shooting occurred.

Dr. Sherman testified to the cause of death and the statements made to him by Ellinger before he died that Renfro had shot him without provocation in cold-blooded murder. The jury determined that Isaac Ellinger died by gunshot inflicted by Lee Renfro and adjourned.

———————————

"WHAT'RE THEY GONNA do?" Mary Jane said, forking a piece of pork steak into her mouth. She and Jake sat at their supper table and Jake was telling her about the Coroner's Inquest.

"Oh, he'll be indicted by the grand jury for murder, and there'll be a warrant out for his arrest. The new sheriff, Commodore Perry Owens, is his name. Pretty fancy, huh?"

"Goes with that long straggly hair he wears."

"Yeah. Well, I hear tell he is pretty tough and good with a gun, so he'll probably go after him unless Renfro ain't in the county no more. 'Course, he don't take office until January."

"Uh-huh. But I mean the Ellingers. What do you think they'll do?"

"Oh. I don't know. By the time his rich brother receives the news of Isaac's death the inquest will be long over and Isaac will be residing in the Springerville cemetery. Maybe he'll put up a reward for Renfro's capture and conviction." He bounced his eyebrows and grinned at Mary Jane.

"No, you don't. You got plenty to do right here with the shop and the saloon and your constable duties." Mary Jane glared at him with a frown on her brow. She rose to take her dish to the sink, and Jake reached for her but she danced away and grinned at him. "'Sides you're gettin' slow in your old age. Startin' to put on a paunch there. Can't even catch me anymore."

"Oh, yeah?" He stood, gazed at her lecherously, made a move toward her and banged his toe on the table leg. He was not wearing his boots and the pain shot up his leg and numbed his toe. He yelped and Mary Jane chuckled but came to his aid and helped him over to the sofa, where he flopped down and apparently lost all desire for further arduous activity.

———————————

THE NEXT WEEK, on the Saturday after Thanksgiving Day, Jake had the evening duty and was tending bar at the saloon when Ike and Phin Clinton and Bill Jackson came in and sauntered right up to the bar. "J.V.," Ike demanded, "give us a bottle of Kessler and three glasses, four if yer want one."

Jake finished pouring for another customer and brought the bottle and four glasses down the bar to Ike who lowered his voice in saying, "They get a warrant out on Lee?"

Jake glanced right and left as if he was about to reveal a state secret. Then he looked Ike in the eye, "I don't know," and poured the whiskies, including one for himself. He leaned in close to Ike across the bar and said, "What in tarnation happened out there?"

"Wal, me, and Ellinger and Lee were talkin' and Ellinger accused Milt Craig, yer know Milt." Jake nodded his head. "Accused him of jumping his Cottonwoods Ranch while he was gone back east. And that Lee probably got him up to do it. Wal, son-of-a-gun." Ike faked astonishment. "Lee didn't take too kindly to that and pulled his pistol to smack Isaac with it. But he missed, and I got in between 'em. Lee was hoppin' mad by then and pushed around me and he shot Isaac. Pratt and Phin and Bill came in and we sent Pratt off for the doc. That's the long and short of it."

"Pratt?"

"Wilds Plummer. That's his middle name. He goes by it. You probably never met him."

Jake refilled their glasses, skipping himself and said, "And where's Renfro now?"

"Oh, he's up in the mountains somewhere. We gave him a horse."

"Got him outta there, huh?" Jake grinned knowingly as he faked his collusion.

"Yeah. He's our friend."

"Wal, here's to our friend," Jake said as he held up his glass and they all grumbled their agreement.

ON THE MORNING of December sixteenth, Jake came in after caring for ol' Jasper, poured a cup of coffee from the pot on the stove, and took a seat at the table. He sipped his coffee while Mary Jane finished scrambling their eggs at the stove. "You know they exhumed Ellinger's body couple a weeks back?"

"Yes." She drew the word out long and with anticipation.

"Did you know William Ellinger sent a letter to the governor?"

"Suppose you're sniffin' around for a reward."

"Thought crossed my mind."

"You know what I said about that. You don't need to be out there on the range gettin' shot at. How much is the reward?"

"I hear tell six hundred."

"Six hundred?!"

"Yeah. And that's just from local folks. I hear William offered more to the governor—a lot more. Could go over a thousand, all told."

She smiled wickedly at Jake and said, "Maybe I can make an exception in this case. Just once."

Jake chuckled in his cup as he brought it to his lips for a sip. "Be a nice Christmas present." He might have to go out in pursuit of bad men, after all.

BUT THERE WERE other things brewing in Springerville for Christmas. There were many of the outlaw and cowboy types in town celebrating the holiday. That meant there was a lot of drinking, whooping, and hollering and shooting holes in the sky.

On Christmas Day Jake stood against the outside wall to the saloon by the door. It was a lot cooler outside than inside the saloon, where it was packed elbow to elbow even now at the noon hour. Mary Jane was inside helping with serving drinks to the crowd. She wore her red dress with white lacy trim and her usual pretty smile that brought her a lot of tips. She stepped out the door and up to Jake's side and rustled the pocket on her dress. "Hear that," she said with an impish smile. "More than egg money." And she grinned her cute girlish grin with sparking eyes then pirouetted away from him but not before he caught her on the fanny with a love swat. She looked back over her shoulder with that secret love you look they always shared.

Jake went back to wishing his patrons a merry Christmas as they came in and as they left. Day's work was done early and the smart ones were heading home to their families or friends or other places of repose. The not-so-smart or those without family stayed. Up the road Jake could see a group of five or six outlaw-looking fellows staggering down the road toward his saloon firing their pistols in the air, passing bottles of whiskey among themselves, trying to sing Christmas carols, laughing and generally whooping it up. There was a couple of inches of snow on the ground and they slipped and slid along, joshing each other with every near fall by one or the other. As they came closer, Jake recognized them generally, and one in particular who called himself Ace of Diamonds when he was drunk. Otherwise, he was J.W. Dimon, alias W.N. Timberline. Fact of the matter is nobody knew his real name. When sober he usually went by Diamond. And he was no diamond but was a distinct sort of human viper.

Jake looked the other way down the road to see if anyone coming might be a target for this bunch's abuse. There were two men walking together and a bunch of cowboy types just behind them. The cowboys were shooting and singing and slipping and sliding too. Of the two men he recognized James Hale, an older prominent Mormon. The other one he didn't know, but he was probably LDS, too. They came close to the bunch of outlaws and were surrounded by them. The outlaws started shoving the two of them, and the cowboys, apparently thinking it was all in fun, joined in with the outlaw bunch. Shots were fired in the air, whooping and hollering, jostling, men staggering. Through it all Jake, nevertheless, thought he saw Diamond yelling at Hale. Then his view was blocked by all the men jostling around and the outlaws and cowboys all clambered up the steps and into Jake's saloon. He was all smiles to them as they came through, and when he turned back to look at the road, he stiffened. Lying in the snow was James Hale with a red puddle around his chest and on his knees next to him was the other man.

Jake hurried down the steps and rolled Hale over. He was dead, shot through the chest. "What happened?" he demanded of the other man who looked like he had seen a ghost.

"I— I— I don't know. When that bunch quit shoving us around and went into the saloon there was James lying in the road."

"You see who did it?"

"No. I guess he got hit by a stray bullet."

"Let's get him up on the boardwalk and outta the road." Jake hefted the body by the arms, and the other fellow pulled up his ankles. Together they hauled it over on to the porch off to the side of the front doors. "You better run and get Judge Hogue. Tell him we got another dead man."

By the time the judge arrived there was a group hovering around the body, but they didn't seem all that concerned about the dead man as they passed bottles of whiskey between them and guffawed about this or that.

Jake went up to one fellow and said, "You already paid for that bottle, Marv?"

"Yes, sir, I did. You can check with George in there," Marv said with an indignant look on his face.

"You, too, Sam?"

"Absolutely. 'Sides, even if I didn't, yer know I'm good for it."

Jake gave him a slightly toothy smile and said, "I know yer are."

The ruffian group was inside, and things were starting to get a little argumentative between the cowboys and the outlaws, but when the judge came on up onto the boardwalk, the whispers and head nods in his direction started up and things quieted down. He took a long look at the deceased and said, "Jim Hale. He was a good man. Let's get him laid out on one of your tables, J.V., and then you can go round up a jury."

"But, Judge," Jake pled, "it's Christmas. I got a full house a customers. Can't this wait until mornin'? A body in the saloon'll kill the mood, and I got a stay and manage things."

The judge stared at Jake for a long few seconds until he said, "I said it once. I ain't in the habit a repeatin' myself."

Jake glared and said to Hale's friend. "C'mon. Let's drag him in and put him on a table." They dragged in the corpse and Jake said to the men at one of the tables who were drinking but not playing cards, "Here. Git outta the way. Judge wants this table for the corpse." Then the murmuring started up. A lot of the men were pestering Jake with questions so he called out, "I don't know what happened. We found this feller outside in the snow. Judge is here to conduct a inquest. I gotta go out and muster up a jury. You, Snow! I saw you out there. You are hereby summoned as the first juror. And you, Cooper. You are number two. Ya'll come before the judge and he'll swear yer in." Then he hurried behind the bar, pulled out his pistol belt with six-shooter and knife, strapped it on and went out the door. Sometimes folks were especially irritated at being summoned for jury duty and so he always went out armed when mustering a jury. But on this occasion there were no problems and it all went quite fast. Stores were still open so he went to them first. Soon as folks heard the deceased's name they were quickly on board. When Jake went into Becker's store and made the announcement, Gustav Becker himself came forward along with Elisha Everett, and just up the street at Baca's General Store, Justinano Baca and Tony Long put on their hats and coats and went to West and Brighton's Saloon. Jake rounded up two more and became impatient, so he assigned himself a spot.

Judge Hogue banged his fist on the tabletop at two p.m. and the room came to order. He went through all the formalities and listened to the testimony of the witnesses such as it was. Nobody knew nothin'. But then, as he leaned with his back to the bar, swaying a little, whiskey bottle hanging from his hand in a limp arm at his side, the Ace of Diamonds piped up. "I dunno how ol' Misser Hale got hisself shot, an' it don't make no never mind to me. Seems like what goes aroun' comes aroun'."

"Identify yourself, sir," Judge Hogue demanded.

"Why, ever'body knows me, the Ace of Diamonds."

"All right, Mister Diamonds, what exactly do you mean by what you said?"

The Ace waved his hand across the air in front of him and said, "Aw, I was just sayin' if a body does a body wrong it can come back to bite 'em." He grinned stupidly and turned his back to the judge and jury.

Jake kept facing the Ace and kept his eyes on his back but whispered just loud enough so that only Judge Hogue could hear and that no movement of his lips could be detected by anyone. "Don't look at me, judge, but just so's yer know, I seen the Ace of Diamonds in the bunch that was shootin' up the sky around Hale. That's all I saw. Him in the bunch."

"Mister Diamonds," Judge Hogue called out, "were you in the group of men who surrounded Mister Hale?"

The Ace turned back to face judge and jury. "Wal, I think I were. But I don't rightly remember for sure."

"Did you see Mister Hale get shot?"

"Like I said. Don't rightly remember. I drunk a lot a whiskey today, and the day ain't done yet." He grinned that stupid grin again.

While he was talking Jake noticed that J.R. Woolsey, who was a son-in-law of Hale's, was being constrained by his friends. He looked as if he wanted to attack Diamond, as his face was flushed red and screwed up in hate. Jake lightly poked the judge in the ribs with his elbow and nodded in Woolsey's direction.

"Mister Woolsey?" Judge Hogue queried loudly. "Do you have some testimony you want to present to this jury?"

"You bet I do. That skunk Diamonds killed James Hale, sure enough. You all know Mister Hale is... was... my father-in-law. I was there the other day when he and Diamonds had words. Diamonds accused Mister Hale of falsely accusing him of rustling Mister Hale's cattle. He would a killed him right there. Or tried to. But I threw down on him and ordered him to git far away from us."

Jake slowly pulled his pistol from its holster, cocked it, and held it down beside his leg. The Ace already had his hand on his gun butt and would have drawn if his friends didn't have a hold of his wrist so that he could not draw. The look in his eyes was of the cold-blooded killer. Jake recognized the look. And the look in Woolsey's eyes was of hateful vengeance. Jake recognized that one too. It was quiet and still in the room like on a dead calm sea and everyone's eyes flashed back and forth from Ace to Woolsey. The silence was broken by Judge Hogue. "Mister Diamond, did you have an argument with Mister Hale?"

"Wal, he said I stole his cows. An' I didn't."

"Did you shoot Mister Hale?"

"Yer mean on purpose?"

"Yes."

"Nah. I didn't."

"Liar!" Woolsey yelled. "P.H. Snow said he heard you say you shot Mister Hale just to see if a bullet would go through a Mormon."

"I never said no sech thing," Diamond said in loud protest and with a shocked look on his face as he looked around the crowd.

"Did you shoot him on accident?" the judge said.

"I don't think so."

"Bah!" Woolsey bellowed and walked out.

"All right. Let's proceed," Judge Hogue said as he shuffled his papers. "Let's examine the wound. Remove the deceased's coat, vest, and shirt and pull down the top of his union suit. Somebody! Thank you," he said as two men stepped up and did the judge's bidding. "J.V.," he said, "wipe the wound clean and report what you see."

Jake took a bar towel from the bartender, scrubbed the milk white skin of the deceased to clean away the dried blood, and exposed a bullet hole under the right nipple of the deceased's chest. "Looks like a forty-four right through the chest here," Jake said matter-of-factly.

"Any exit wound?"

Jake lifted and rolled the torso to the left and saw a lump just under the shoulder blade. "Looks like the bullet might a been stopped right here. It's under the skin."

"Cut it out."

Another man held the body while Jake pulled his knife, which of course was razor sharp and easily sliced the skin right over the top of the lump. A lead slug popped out like a bean from its husk and Jake caught it in his free hand. He held it up and examined it then said, "Forty-four, all right."

"Mister Diamond. What caliber of pistol do you carry?" Judge Hogue said like an inquisitor at a trial and glared at him maliciously.

Diamond straightened up, tossed down a whiskey, smiled slyly and said, "Forty-four."

"Mind if we examine that pistol?"

Diamond's smile grew in size and slyness. "Not a'tal," he said and whipped the pistol out of its holster in a fast draw and lifted it to point at the judge. Several audible gasps escaped from several mouths amid the sound of scraping of shuffling boots moving bodies out of the line of fire.

"Put the gun down," Jake said in a voice that dripped pure death made sure by the muzzle of his pistol he pressed against the Diamond's temple. While the judge was talking with Diamond, Jake stealthily slipped over, eased up behind the Ace and was able to get the drop on him like he did.

The eyes of the Ace of Diamonds opened in big circles that showed the whites for just a brief few seconds. "Aw, I was just joshin'. I was gonna spin this here six-shooter like this and hand it over." He rotated the pistol in his hand so the butt was facing forward and offered it to the judge. When Hogue took it from him, he slowly turned to see who it was that pressed a gun to his head. Jake met him eye to eye with a frosty stare that made him take a step back and turn his head away and back again. Then Jake smiled at him and holstered his weapon. The Ace said nothing but stared curiously up at Jake.

"Pistol is fully loaded. No empty cartridge," Judge Hogue said. "Okay, Mister Diamond. Thank you for your cooperation. I'll hold onto this pistol until the inquest is adjourned—if you don't mind," he said with a glance at Jake.

And with a glance at Jake the Ace said smiling, "I don' mind a'tal, judge. I'll just have me anuther whiskey while yer, what-a-they-call-it, carry on?"

"Proceed is the word you are looking for."

"Oh, yeah. Okay, proceed." He turned his back, faced the bar, and motioned for another bottle.

"Well, we've heard the testimony, such as it is, and examined the body of the deceased. Looks like death by gunshot from some person unknown. How say you. All in favor? Carried unanimously. I'll issue the certificate of death accordingly. This Inquest is adjourned." Not having anything else, he banged a beer mug on the tabletop. Gradually, the clientele began to drift out the door. Some men from the LDS church pulled up out front with a team and buckboard and carried James Hale's body away.

Mary Jane came up beside Jake. "Might as well close. Don't think there's gonna be much business after this." She looked long into his eyes.

"Yeah. Let me see what George wants to do. Guess he can stay here with the drunk outlaws and cowboys. Think we'll go home and celebrate Christmas right like. Might even go to church if there is a service or a Mass goin' on." He looked with endearing eyes into her loving eyes. "Why don't you head on home? I'll be along right directly."

"Okay. Just don't do anything to get killed."

"You mean by the likes of the Ace of Diamonds?"

"Exactly. He's probably a back-shooter and he's drunk as hell."

"Yeah. Hey, George," he called out and motioned for him to come over. "We're gonna head for the barn. You can keep the place open if yer want, but I'd druther it be closed."

"Wal, reckon I'll see if I can drain a few more pesos from these hombres' britches, and when they pass out, I'll carry 'em out to the porch and lock up. How's that sound?"

"Suit yerself. Ain't seen Ike or Phin today."

"They're movin' cows."

Jake gave him a curious look. So, he continued, "Movin' the whole herd down to the Blue by Eagle Creek. They's wanted me to help out, but," he winked, "figger I make more money here."

"Sure enough. That's a fact. I hate movin' cattle."

There were not any afternoon services or a Mass at the Catholic church, so Jake and Mary Jane sat down at the kitchen table and poured a couple of glasses of good Overholt whiskey. Jake lit a cigar, sat back and listened to Mary Jane read the Christmas story from the family Bible. When she finished reading, he said with true affection, "Merry Christmas, my love."

The very next day Woolsey filed a complaint against J.W. Dimon, alias W.N. Timberline, more commonly known as the Ace of Diamonds, for the intentional shooting by Dimon of James Hale resulting in Hale's death. A warrant for Dimon's arrest was issued and placed in the hands, of all people, J.R. Woolsey with authority to summon aid to make the arrest.

Later that evening at the supper table, Jake told Mary Jane what he had heard about the warrant. "That makes Woolsey a Special Constable," Mary Jane said with a modest tone of incredulity in her voice as she refilled Jake's coffee cup.

"Yeah. But like I said before, I don't care. I still get paid ten bucks a month plus expenses so it don't matter to me if someone else gets appointed for the job of riskin' gettin' shot by the Ace of Diamonds." He rolled his eyes and feigned importance in the name of the Ace. "I hear Woolsey has a posse of five men but can't find that weasel Diamond. He's probably cleared out by now or lying in some gully somewhere passed out."

Mary Jane sat down at the table and with adoring eyes fastened on Jake said, "I just admire you for keepin' your promise. You probably got the itch to go after that bad man, but you ain't doin' it. You're a good man, Jonas Valentine Brighton." She planted a wet one on his cheek and smiled big and lovingly at him.

"Aw, shucks, Mary Jane. You make a feller blush." He played like he was embarrassed.

Next morning Jake tied ol' Jasper off at the hitching rail in front of the shop as his intent as usual was to get the forage lit up then take Jasper out for a ride. His apprentice would be along directly. This morning, however, he stopped tying Jasper's reins to the rail when he heard the thunder of a group of mounted horses coming up the road. They were coming up the Eagar road from the south. The bunch of them galloped by Jake without even a look sideways at him. It was Woolsey and his posse. He untied Jasper, swung up into the saddle and took off after them. He caught them at the livery where they were dismounting. And just as Jake arrived, a horse and rider burst out of the livery barn at a full gallop. The rider was the Ace of Diamonds and his pistol was a blazing. But more ablaze were the pistols and rifles of the posse. In a matter of a few seconds, the Diamond's horse fell, shot dead. He jumped from the saddle and cleared the falling horse but hit the dirt with a scream and rolled over to reveal a growing patch of blood on his pants in his groin. He was shot good and just lay groaning in the dirt.

"Well, so much for that, eh Jasper?" Jake said as he patted Jasper's neck. "Let's go get that forge goin' then we can mosey down along the river for a ways."

In the afternoon Judge Hogue came by the shop. "Well, you hear the news," he said sarcastically as he leaned against a post.

"You mean the Diamond's arrest?"

"Yeah, that, too. But I'm referring specifically to the disappearance of all the evidentiary papers and the certificate of death of one James Hale." He stared at the floor and dug a divet in the dirt with the toe of his boot.

"What?" Jake exclaimed and turned away from the forage to face the judge. "What a yer talkin' 'bout?"

"Somebody stole the papers right off my office table while I was at supper last evening. That's what I'm talkin' 'bout." His anger showed.

"Somebody meanin' the Ace of Diamonds."

"Likely. Ain't got no way to prove it unless we find the papers. Probably burned 'em by now."

"Real sorry, judge. How will it affect the case?"

"Don't know. We adjourned until the twenty-ninth to give him time to procure counsel and medical aid. Guess we'll see then."

"Yep." Jake turned back to the forage and said, "Why yer tellin' me all this? Except for night before last, I don't think I've ever seen you in the shop here."

"Don't know. You are about the only one around here in Spring-erville who understands these things. Guess I just needed a shoulder to cry on." He smiled weakly, and said, "I won't trouble you no more," then he turned around and left.

"Be seein' yer, judge," Jake called out behind him. The judge waved his hand over his head. Jake watched him go until he was out of sight. For some reason he felt an anger rise up in him. Wasn't right for all these bad men to give a good man like Judge Hogue so much headache. Might be time to think 'bout doin' somethin' 'bout it.

FIVE

TIGHTENING THE NOOSE • 1887

IT WAS A Saturday night in late January. There was a foot of hard snow on the ground and—there ain't no other way to say it—it was freezing cold. The snow on the ground thawed during the day and froze at night making it slicker than a greased pole. Anybody trying to walk on it who didn't have their boots wrapped in burlap or heavy cloth risked a slip and fall that could break bones.

Jake and Mary Jane sat at a table in the saloon near the parlor stove. There were two fellers playing billiards and two more at the bar. Mary Jane usually helped out on Saturday nights, and that is why she was there. But on that particular night most everybody was hunkered down in their own houses instead of coming out to play. So, at about nine Mary Jane was talking about going home when the door swung open and their partner, George West, stood swaying on the threshold. "Have I got a deal fer yer!" he called out too loud to Jake and Mary Jane.

"Shut the door, George," Mary Jane said tersely. "You're lettin' in all the cold."

"Oh, yeah. Sorry." He navigated a crooked line to their table, sat down heavily in a chair, folded his arms on the tabletop, espied them with one eye open and the other half shut. He pushed his hat back, revealing a fresh cut with smeared blood on his forehead over his right eye and said, "I got a deal thas gonna make some good money. You want in on it? Willie, come on over here. Yer might want a hear this, too."

"What happened to your head?" Mary Jane asked sarcastically.

"Huh? Oh, that. Nuthin'. I slipped on the ice."

Willie Johnson set the glass he was polishing on the stack on the backbar and came over to the table. "Hi, George. How you doin'?"

"Ah'm doin' jus' fine. I got somethin' I want ya'll to see out back. C'mon. Put yer coats on an' come look see at these beauties I got."

Jake bent over in his chair and tightened the burlap wrapped around his boots. Then he stood up, pulled his coat off the back of his chair, put it on, glared at George, and said, "Yer been drinkin' all this time since I saw yer yesterday?"

"Yer could say that, I 'spose."

"You go ahead, Jake, and come back and tell me what you saw. I ain't goin' out in that cold except to go home," Mary Jane said as she shuffled a deck of cards.

"Yeah. I'll stay here and tend the bar. You can tell me too, J.V.," Willie said skeptically.

"All right. Let's go then, pardner." George threw his arm around Jake's shoulders and they went out the door to the corral behind the saloon. There, in the moonlight, next to the corral Jake saw three men on horseback, one saddled horse with no rider and three bareback horses on tether held by the three men. Even in the dim light of night he could easily see that two of the horses were well-muscled stallions.

"Wal, what we have here is some fine breeding stock we acquired and we are sellin' shares in 'em. Get a piece of ever'thing we make off their foals. Yer interested?"

Jake took a torch from its iron holder attached to the wall of the building, struck a match and ignited it. He acted as if he was inspecting the horses—two bay stallions and a sorrel mare—but what he was really doing was covertly identifying the three men on horseback. He got what he wanted and said, "Pretty good horseflesh there. You should do good with them. Maybe in New Mexico or Texas or somewhere far away from here. I ain't even gonna ask where yer got 'em cuz I got no intention a swingin' from the end of a rope." He gave George a hard look, plunged the torch in a snowbank to extinguish it, stuck it back in its holder, and walked away.

"Guess that means no," George said as he shrugged and vaulted into the saddle of his horse.

Jake came back in the saloon and said to Mary Jane, "C'mon. Let's go home." He held her coat for her to slip into, looked over at Willie and turned his head slowly one way and the other as if to say, *don't even go near it.* "Let's lock up, Willie," he said. "Just bag up the money and give it to me. We'll count up in the mornin'."

MARY JANE PUSHED with her behind into the door to shut it against the wind. A frigid wind it was that threatened to fast-freeze all the canned goods on the shelves of the Becker Store.

"That's a ice-cold north wind that chased you through the door. Glad you shut it fast," Louisa Becker said with half a smile as she held down the piece goods on one of the tables. "I been fightn' it all day. Trying to blow all my goods to kingdom come. What're you doin' out in this weather, anyhow?"

"Oh, this ain't nuthin' to a old Texian like me. Been in a lot worse than this. Cold and hot." She chuckled as she straightened out her skirt. "Gotta keep the house supplied."

"Well, as long as you have it, anyhow," Louisa said with a crooked little smile.

"What do you mean by that?" Mary Jane's chuckles ceased and her brow came down.

"You ain't read the paper this week yet? Came out today."

Mary Jane shook her head no and said with a foreboding sense of concern, "Why?"

"Delinquent tax list is out. You're on it."

"What? Let me see that." She stomped over to the newspaper stack and pulled the February third issue off the top. Right there on the front page on the bottom of the fourth column over from the left was the Brighton name. The house, the shop, the wagon and harness, and the furniture were all listed with taxes and penalty of $13.60 due. Her mouth dropped open.

"Don't see any Beckers on the list. Lot a *Bacas,*" Louisa said coyly.

Mary Jane's face turned crimson. She retrieved her coin purse from her bag, dug out a nickel, dropped it in the coffee can next to the rack, abruptly folded the newspaper in half, tucked it in her bag, and without another word stamped her way to the door, pulled it open and let it fly. She went through with her hand on top of her bonnet and did not bother to shut the door. She heard Louisa's screams but did not care. There was sleet in the air and even that didn't deter her as she ducked her head and marched over to the saloon. She threw the door open, slammed it shut, spied Jake sitting at a table reading the newspaper, angled right for him and ripped the paper out of his hands. She threw it down on the table with the front page facing up. Jake was too surprised to speak. "What is the meaning of this?" she said through clenched teeth.

"Meanin' a what?"

"Meaning a this right here." She pointed at their name.

Jake looked at it and said, "Oh, that. Ain't nuthin'."

"Ain't nuthin'? It's somethin' to me when I have to suffer humiliation at the hands of Louisa Becker. Pointing out that we are delinquent on our taxes and freeloaders. And that on top of bein' subpoenaed by the grand jury."

"She said that? And keep your voice down," Jake said as he looked to the bar to see if anyone overheard her.

"Well, no. But she implied it well enough."

"She can imply all she wants. Fact a the matter is that it ain't what she might think or gossip about. Plenty a good folks ain't paid their taxes yet. Look here." He pointed to a name. "Judge Hogue. And here's J.L. Hubbell. Hell, see this, even the city of Holbrook ain't paid their taxes yet."

Mary Jane's face softened, and she dropped into the chair across from Jake. "It's only thirteen dollars and sixty cents. Why don't you just pay it?"

"County owes me a lot more than that for expenses, and they ain't paid me. So, I ain't gonna pay them until they pay me."

"And maybe lose the house and the shop?"

"Oh, they ain't gonna do that any time soon. They gotta foreclose first, and I doubt they're gonna foreclose on the city of Holbrook. If they threaten foreclosure, I'll pay it. How's that sound?"

Mary Jane smiled weakly, nodded her head yes as she stared into her lap. Then she popped her head up and said, "I am going right back over to Becker's and tell that Louisa it's a matter of pride with us. We Texans don't just follow along like little puppy dogs. We got to have right what's right. Ain't that so?"

"You betcha, you Texas whirlwind. Go get her."

Mary Jane marched back the way she came and into the Becker Store. "Hello again, Louisa," she said to Mrs. Becker who was behind the counter. "Just wanted to let you know that I talked to my husband and he informed me that the county owes him money and the taxes are in dispute so he is not paying them. We Texans don't just follow along like little puppy dogs. We got to have right what's right." She looked down her nose at Louisa like Louisa had done to her and said, "Now, if you don't mind, I have a few things to pick up."

"Well, I declare." Louisa said with a half-smile.

Meanwhile, Jake, out of curiosity, looked in the newspaper for the Clanton delinquent taxes. The delinquency was under P.F. Clanton's name and the property listed for taxes was the ranch, seventy-five Mexican cattle, seventy-five young cattle, four horses and miscellaneous other property. Mexican cattle? That was interesting. How did the assessor know they were Mexican cattle unless Phin told him that to discourage him from looking closely at the brands? Probably took a running iron to a local brand. Would have been more accurately listed as stolen cattle.

Later at the evening supper table Jake finished his meatloaf, washed it down with some coffee, stood and took his plate to the sink. He came back to the table where Mary Jane sat, still eating her supper. Jake lit a cigar and sat down in his chair at the table. He got the cheroot going good and said. "Okay, let's make sure we got our stories straight. We can't say we don't know nuthin' cuz Willie Johnson was right there with us, and he knows I went out and looked at the horses that George, Evans, Sprague, and Powell sure as hell stole. Hard to believe that George would do that. He knows that if he goes to prison, he loses his interest in the saloon. Probably that snake Sprague talked him into it. Anyway, all we gotta do is tell the truth of what was said and what we saw. There ain't nothin' we can say that directly incriminates George, except he had the horses. Can't get around that one. Sprague probably figured he'd get some fast money to ride them horses outta the county and sell 'em somewhere, so he planted the scheme in poor ol' George's head." Jake shook his head in disgust and blew a cloud of blue cigar smoke to the ceiling. "I got you a good horse and a straddle saddle." He grinned. Mary Jane smiled.

"What's so funny?" she said.

"Oh, nuthin'. I was just thinkin' what all the fine Mormon folk in St. Johns will think when they see you ride into town straddlin' a hoss like a regular cowboy. Their women folk ain't allowed to do somethin' improper like that."

"Just being practical. And it is a lot more comfortable than riding a buckboard all the way."

"Yeah. I figure we leave at sunup and trot and lope most a the way. We'll be there before the one o'clock appearance time."

All four defendants were indicted and arrested. And lo and behold ten days later Deputy Snow walked slowly into the shop and Jake did not notice him. So, he said, "J.V.," upon which Jake turned and faced him. "Sorry to say, J.V., but I got a warrant for your arrest."

Jake was stunned silent for a long few seconds. "What for?"

"Accessory to Grand Larceny."

"Grand Larceny? What Grand Larceny?"

"I guess it's horse theft."

"Who's the affiant?"

"A course the warrant don't say, but I know it was Elisha Averett and William Eagar filing on the theft of Penn Wiltbank's two horses."

"Well don't that just beat all. I give the testimony that probably convicts the thieves and now they want to say I was an accessory." Jake shook his head in disgust and said, "Let me shut down the forge and lock up the shop. Then I got a tell Mary Jane 'bout it."

"Sure. We can do that."

"How much you think the bond'll be?"

"I don't know. Maybe five hunnert."

So again, Jake had to ride up to St. Johns, but this time to stand before the judge as an accused. Deputy Snow was good enough to not handcuff Jake. He asked Justice of the Peace Luther Martin for time to get counsel, bought a bond, and posted it. The case was scheduled for trial on February seventeenth.

———————————

JAKE SAT AT the defendant's table with his attorney when the jury filed in and took their seats. Right off, Jake saw that Al Clark was a member of the jury. That gave him a little comfort and when Clark winked at him, he felt even better. The judge came in and with one look at him, he felt worse.

After the formal rising and sitting, the judge motioned to the prosecutor who rose and requested that the case be dismissed. Judge Martin wasted no time, banged his gavel and said, "So ordered."

Jake looked to Clark sitting in the jury box. He was smiling ever so slightly and winked again at Jake.

Mary Jane was waiting outside the courthouse with Jasper when Jake came out, and he was fuming. He roughly untied his cravat and jerked off his collar and stuffed them into the pocket of his overcoat.

He came up to the hitching rail where she was and grumbled, "I have half a mind to sue that Eagar and Averett. Damn Mormons. They been ridin' me since I bought the shop and doin' more business than Peter Thompson."

"Well, since the case was dismissed, I wouldn't worry about it," Mary Jane said as she handed Jasper's reins to him.

"'S'pose not." He brightened and said, "Good part 'bout it is that to the outlaws I am lookin' more and more like one a them. 'Course, to the good folks a Springerville I'm lookin' more and more like a outlaw." He shook his head. "This business. Damned if you do, damned if you don't. Oh, well. It always comes out in the end."

"What business?"

"Detective work."

"Oh. I though you weren't doing that."

"Never said that. Just ain't out on the range." He grinned at her. "'Sides, I need to have you to keep bein' my number one assistant, and a good job you're doin'.'"

Mary Jane smiled at the compliment and said, "So that's what I been doin' at the kitchen sink?"

"No. Well, yes. You don't know it, but you provide my cover story, and I listen to your advice and other stuff you have to say."

"I see. I guess that's okay. Here's my advice now. Let's get going so we can get home before sundown so we don't freeze in the night." She grinned at him and stepped into her saddle. Jake returned her grin with a look of admiration and a loving smile and stepped up into his saddle. Together they rode off out of town in the face of the sun to the south.

On March nineteenth George West and two other prisoners broke out of the St. Johns jail. He was never again seen in Apache County.

Two days later, on Monday, Sheriff Owens rode into Springerville on a big buckskin gelding wearing two pearl-handled six-shooters holstered for a cross-draw. It was a cool day but sunny and Ike Clanton and his in-laws, the McLowerys, were sitting in the sun on the bench in front of Becker's Store, drinking beer. As the sheriff came closer to them, they started talking about him loud enough so he could hear. Ike was doing most of the talking. Jake was inside the store and stood back away from the door just far enough so as not to be seen but able to see the whole scene in front of him.

"What kind a feller wears his hair that long?" Ike called out.

"A damn sissy. That's what. A little ol' sissy," one of the McLowery boys said.

"That's right. Our sheriff is a sissy and probably slow as molasses on the draw since he has to draw across himself. Wonder how long it'll take us to run him outta the county, like we did the other sheriff."

"Yeah, let's run the skunk outta town." They all started talking even louder and calling Sheriff Owens every vile name they could think of. He, on the other hand, ignored them and rode closer. He acted like he didn't hear them at all. Then he dismounted and picked up a twelve-inch board that was lying in the road. It was about four feet long and he braced it on edge in the dirt. Then he took a piece of charcoal from his coat pocket and drew two circles, one at each end of the board, turned around and started to walk away. As he walked, he counted the paces out loud. The Clanton bunch was silent as they watched like curious little pups. When Sheriff Owens said "thirty," he spun and the two pistols seemed to leap into his hands. He fired both at the same time. The bullets hit the board simultaneously in the center of each circle and it fell over. He fired again, sending it flipping into the air. Then he holstered his weapons and stood waiting as he faced the Clanton bunch. Quietly and cautiously, they mounted their horses and rode out of town.

Jake came out of the store and walked up to Owens where he was tying off his horse at the rail. "Guess you speak a language those varmints understand," he said with a half-smile. The sheriff turned around and stared deadpan at Jake for an uncomfortable minute.

"What's your name?" he finally demanded.

"J.V. Brighton."

"Think I've heard a you."

"I'm the district constable."

"Now I know I heard. You own the blacksmith shop and a saloon in town, too."

"That's right. And I use a cross-draw, too." Jake remained congenial, steady, and unflinching, even though Owens verged on rudeness.

"Hear tell you got a few more skills too. We might need to call on you someday. Nice to meet you. Good day." He walked past Jake and into the store.

"What did he mean by that?" Jake mumbled to himself.

At supper Jake told Mary Jane all about the Sheriff Owens incident. After they finished the dishes and cleaned the kitchen they sat down in their regular chairs by the parlor stove, Mary Jane to her knitting and Jake to his cigar and newspaper. After a half hour or so, Jake slapped the paper down on his lap and said, "That just ain't right. A body ought never to disrespect a lawman like those Clantons and McLowerys did.

They's just raw. No manners. They's nothing but killers, rustlers, and horse thieves. I don't like 'em."

"I've been telling you that."

Jake stared at her for just a second or two, then stuck his nose back in his newspaper.

Even so, later that month on an afternoon that was threatening a late snow, Ike, Phin, Bill Jackson, and Ebin Stanley came in to the saloon. They shook the cold off, and Ike threw a leg over the back of a chair and sat down with his arms folded on the tabletop. The rest of them sat down, and he motioned for Jake to come over to their table. Jake came with a bottle of Kessler and five glasses. "Afternoon, boys. Ain't seen yer around for a long while now," Jake said as he started pouring drinks.

"We been busy movin' the herd down to the south. Down on the Blue afore it dumps into the San Francisco," Ike said as he snatched one of the glasses of whiskey.

Phin weighed in, "Got debts to pay off, so I'm a sellin' off the beeves down south and givin' the cows to my sister. She's married to Ebin here, yer know?" Jake nodded his head yes.

"We coulda kinda eased into this, yer know," Ike said with a little disgust in his tone.

"Don't make no never mind. We got business. Let's get her done. This ain't no social visit."

Ike gave Phin a sideways glance and shook his head slightly. "All right, then. Here's what we come for. Sit on down here, Jake," he said as he scraped a chair back away from the table for Jake, who looked skeptical.

"Am I gonna be likein' this?" Jake said as he sat down.

"You'll like it when you see the cash. Now the reason we took the herd south is cuz a all the minin' goin' on down at Joy's Camp and Clifton. Big companies comin' in with a lot a workers. Mexes, Chinks, and white men. Thousands a them." Ike's eyes were big and round and his hands were in constant motion as he spoke. "They gotta eat. We got a deal with a new meat-packer there. He's supplyin' all the butchers down there. Says he'll buy all the beef we can supply. Sooo...." he grinned from ear to ear. "Here we are and we need beef. Yer gonna help us? For a share a the profit, a course."

"How can I help yer?"

"Wal, like yer told ol' George there a while back. We can be operatin' in a certain area and you can slip the word to Clark and his pards that we're workin' in the opposite direction."

"You be rustlin' critters in the east and I tell Clark I heared ya'll talkin' 'bout workin' in the west. Is that it?"

Ike spread his arms wide and again grinned from ear to ear, "Xactly!" he exclaimed.

"That's aidin' and abettin' a rustler. I could go to prison for that." Jake took a shot of whiskey.

"Aw, no. We wouldn't let that happen. Would we, boys?" They all turned their heads side to side and back again.

"What's my cut?"

"Oh... say five percent. That's pretty good, too."

"Fifteen."

Ike's eyes narrowed and he stared at Jake as he sipped his whiskey and was silent for a long minute. "Ten," he said.

Jake tossed his head and looked at the floor. Then he raised his head, staring steadily at Ike he said, "I shouldn't do this," he paused a few seconds, "but, all right. Yer got a deal. Ten percent. When yer gonna start?"

"Tomorrow."

"Yer gonna work outta Cienega Amarilla?"

"Yep," Phin said with a challenging glare at Jake.

"How many head yer figure on procurin'?"

"Procurin'. Hah, hah." They all started laughing with Ike. "Yer usin' them big eastern words now. I 'spect that means grabbin', huh?"

Jake nodded his head slowly. Ike said, "At least a hunnert, 'round here. Maybe even cut a few head outta that Hashknife outfit. Then a bunch out a Socorro. An' then we'll go back to our ol' range in Mexico and Cochise County. Sky's the limit." He spread his arms and grinned.

"I expect to get a headcount a my own and see receipts for the cattle yer sell."

"Well, a course. We got a deal?"

"Reckon so. But, why don't yer start day after tomorrow so's I don't have to ride through the night in this weather to get to the La Cienega and tell my fable to Clark?"

Ike looked at Phin, and Phin looked back then shrugged his shoulders. Ike said, "Sounds right. Now, here's to yer." He held his glass up and they all clinked glasses.

IT WAS MIDMORNING under a bright sun in a clear, cold sky when Jake arrived at the La Cienega Ranch. Al Clark hustled him right away into the house and next to the fireplace. After accepting a cup of coffee from Esmeralda, Jake said, "Just so's yer know, I ain't no horse thief, and I ain't no accessory to hoss thievery."

"Didn't see how you could be."

"We have a rule in West Texas. If yer catch a horse thief—hang him right then and there."

"I like your rule."

"So, I been wonderin'... did yer say something to the district attorney? Is that why he dismissed the case without even putting the evidence in front of the jury."

"I talked to him and told him you were working undercover for us."

"Yer didn't—"

"Working for us as J.V. Brighton. *Not* Rawhide Jake. Far as I know, your secret is still safe."

Jake told him about Ike's plan. Then he said, "So I think if you circle around and come in from the east, it won't look so much like I might have spilled the beans on them. They'll be gatherin' from the west and drivin' 'em south to their ranch. They'll rest up there and push on down to the Blue."

"Why don't we just ambush them at the Cienega Amarilla?"

"Cuz I think that would show we knew they were comin'. Ruin my cover. Supposed to look like your crew just happened on 'em. If you chase 'em to the Cienega Amarilla, I think you can make some arrests. Should take Deputy Snow with yer. I don't know 'bout Mckinney. I think he's off with a posse chasing the jailbreakers Murphy, West, and the Browns."

"Yes. A good suggestion. What will you do?"

"I'm gonna ride on over to the Cienega Amarilla and see if I run into Ike or Phin. My story will be that you weren't home when I went to see you so I couldn't put out the bait. You never know what can happen, so that should keep my cover."

"Yes, that is good. Also, just so you are aware, William Ellinger withdrew his reward offer. Telegrammed the governor. We are talking with him about investing the reward money with us to incentivize fellows like you. He, of course, is most interested in finding Lee Renfro and bringing him to justice. But I think he realizes that there is a good chance we may run into Renfro in our hunt for rustlers. So, he may just do that. I will keep you informed."

"Thanks. Okay, so yer start gettin' your crew into position and come down on them tomorrow, I would say, when they have the critters under control and well on their way to the Cienega Amarilla. I'll ride out late in the day with my message for Ike and Phin."

"Sounds aces. Maybe I'll see you tomorrow."

JAKE LOPED JASPER off to the southeast, around the mesas, through juniper, sagebrush, and grassy plain. He wore his cross-draw, double-action forty-four and knife on two cartridge belts and his Winchester forty-four was tucked in its scabbard with the butt facing forward. There was a cutting wind in his face so he had his blue bandanna wrapped over his nose and mouth and tied off at the nape of his neck underneath the collar of his brown coat that was buttoned up tight. Likewise, he had the stampede string of his hat cinched up to keep it on his head even with the front brim bent backwards by the wind. They were steadily climbing with pine-covered and snowcapped mountain ridges all around them.

By late afternoon he arrived at Cienega Amarilla. He came up over a rise and looked down on the ranch house, outbuildings, and lots situated at the base of a hill heavily forested in juniper. The outfit was in the lee of the east wind, protected by the slope behind it, so the smoke from the chimney of the house rose slightly to the west. Jake gauged it to estimate wind speed and direction in case he got into any kind of shootout. There was a small bunch of cattle in one of the corrals, a few saddled horses at a rail in front of the house, and a flock of six buzzards circling a little ways off to the west.

Crouched over in the saddle, alert for any sign of movement, Jake walked Jasper down the slope toward the ranch house. He kept a keen eye out for any rifles poking out of any windows or doors. Things seemed too quiet, but he kept a steady pace. When he got to what he figured was just outside average rifle range, he reined in Jasper and hollered, "Hello, the house. Anybody home?" He was about to call out again when a feller came out onto the covered porch. When the feller stepped into the sunlight, Jake could see that it was Ike.

"Howdy, J.V. Come on down here and set a spell," Ike called back.

When Jake came up on the porch Ike was already sitting in a straight-backed chair and scratching his ribs. He threw on a coat and Jake took note that Ike was not armed.

"How'd yer know it was me?" Jake asked.

Ike cocked his head to the side, made a toothy smile, gave him a wily look and said, "Shucks, J.V. Ever'body knows that big ol' paint yer ride." He widened his smile and scratched his head. "Whatch yer doin' out here? Making yer first headcount already?" He chuckled.

"Wal, yeah. That too. But, first off, I came out to warn yer."

The smile left Ike's face and he said, "Warn me 'bout what?"

"I never got to see Al Clark yesterday. He weren't home. He could have riders out on his east range and you'd never know it." Jake sat down in a chair off to Ike's left.

"Wal, we made a raid and didn't never see a soul out on the range. C'mon. Yer kin make yer count." Ike led Jake to the corral where there were twenty-three head a steers milling around. All of them were branded with a LC on their left ribs.

Jake counted them out and Ike nodded his head. "Was gonna run the brand out to a Circle Flying LC, but I think now I better get these critters down south right away. Phin'll go over Socorro way and gather up a few more head."

Jake walked a little ways upwind of the bunch of steers and leaned up against the fence rails with his arms draped over the top rail. Ike followed him. "What a yer think yer can git for these steers?"

"Oh, I'd say we let 'em go for thirty-five bucks a head. That meat-packer ain't gonna get 'em any cheaper, and he needs the beef. Anyways, yer gonna stay for supper? The boys are all stretched out inside. We were up early and worked hard all day. Their empty bellies'll be wakin' 'em up pretty soon." He grinned and chuckled a little.

"Aw, thanks, but now that George is gone I gotta lock up the saloon every night. Best get back to town. Borrow a fresh horse from you, though."

"Suit yerself. You gonna leave that paint here?"

"Uh. I don't think so. Might never see him again." Jake chortled and grinned big.

"Aw, c'mon now. I ain't that bad. Anyways, thanks for comin' out with the warnin'. Let's git that hoss for yer."

Jake rode out and frequently checked his backtrail all the way back to Springerville. He had Jasper on a tether, but the big paint insisted on pacing head-to-head with the bay mare Jake rode.

Long before daybreak the next day, he rode out to La Cienega. He arrived at dawn just as the crew was saddling up for the day's work. Clark was with them. Jake stopped short, dismounted, and called for Clark to come on over to him. Jake made a big display of showing a folded legal-looking document, and when Clark walked up, Jake handed him the document and said loud enough to be heard by the crew, "Alfred Clark, you've been served." Clark unfolded the paper and read what Jake had written inside: *Play along. Meet me down at the cottonwoods at the river.* Then Jake tipped his hat, remounted, and rode away.

Jake took off Jasper's bridle and slipped a loop over his ears and down his neck and let out the rope so the big black-and-white paint could enjoy himself cropping new spring grass growing under the cottonwood trees. He lit a cigar and sat on a rock, smoking, while he waited for Clark to show. It was twenty minutes later when he saw him trotting his horse toward him. He waved his hat over his head and Clark came right at him.

"What's all the cloak-and-dagger secrecy about?" Clark said as he dismounted and grounded his horse's reins.

"I don't want any of your crew getting any ideas. They all know I am district constable, so they'll just think I came out to serve papers on you. When really I got a lot to tell you."

"All right. Let's hear it."

"You or your crew never made contact yesterday with the Clantons, ain't that right?"

"That's right. We never saw anyone."

"Well, they made a raid on you, all right." Jake proceeded to inform Clark about all he saw at Cienega Amarilla and what he heard from Ike. The more he talked the darker Clark's expression became until by the time Jake finished he was downright infuriated.

"I want my steers back."

"That's why I came out here this mornin'. I figure Ike's about ready to pull out with that bunch a critters heading south. If you leave now you can catch him."

"Yes. He'll be movin' a lot slower. You've got to get right on down to Judge Hogue and file a complaint so he can issue warrants and we arrest those criminals when we catch up with them."

"I don't think that is the way to do it. For one thing it will show me up, and for the other it won't carry as much weight as an indictment. But if I testify before a secret grand jury, then my cover is protected and they can indict based on my testimony and anybody else's, for that matter. But, if you do catch them this mornin' with the stolen cattle, well then that's that." Jake let that sink in for a few seconds. "Or, if you don't catch 'em, once there are arrest warrants, then a posse can go get 'em."

"Or you."

Jake studied him for a long minute and said, "I don't know about that. Would have to be well worth my while."

"We wired William Ellinger and he is willing to throw some money to us, but he is most interested in getting Lee Renfro. He's authorized us to offer you a thousand dollars for Lee Renfro, who is already wanted, and he'll help out the association to make up a reward of five hundred each for Ike and Phin if warrants are issued for them. The Renfro reward is all secret and it's only for you and nobody else."

"Why's that?"

"I told him about your expertise and Texas reputation and he agreed it is more efficient to use a professional."

Jake liked the sound of that, but he knew Mary Jane would not. Besides, he was getting used to the comfy life in town. Life out on the range was losing its allurement.

"I'll think about it. Renfro already has a warrant out on him. Meantime, you better get on after Clanton and the grand jury to subpoena me if you need to."

"Yes. All right, then. Be seeing you," Clark said as he mounted and rode off. Jake watched him go until he was out of sight. He stayed where he was and mulled over in his mind all that Clark said. When his cigar was done, he stubbed it out with his boot, coiled the rope and tied it and the loop to his saddle, re-bridled Jasper, let him suck up some water from the river, slipped him a piece of hard candy, vaulted into the saddle and rode off back to town.

The next evening, just before sundown, Al Clark rode into town and tied off his horse at the rail in front of Brighton's saloon. He stretched the kinks from his big frame then went on into the saloon. He went up to the bar and said, "Overholt, please. J.V. around?"

"Willie said, "He's in the back. I'll get him for you."

Jake came out of the back room with Willie. As he grasped a bottle of Overholt from the backbar, he said, "Howdy, Al. What brings you to town?"

"Hello J.V. I was out on the range down this way and thought I would stop in for some refreshment."

"Well come on over and have a seat at the table. You hungry? We can fix you a sandwich."

"No, I'm fine. Thank you. This will do." He poured himself another whiskey and with a slow shake of his head in a low voice said, "He is a wily one. He got away," and stared into Jake's eyes.

"What happened?"

"We caught up with them all right, but they were coming toward us heading north. Ike said they were going down to gather in some of their herd on Eagle Creek when they came across a bunch of strays with my brand and were pushing them back up to my range for me." He raised his eyebrows in an astonished look and said, "Can you believe that?"

"Yes, I can. Ike thinks fast on his feet. He must a seen you comin' before you saw him. Thought up that scheme and had the bunch turned around by the time you came into view of them. Yeah, he's smart, all right."

"I sent the crew on up to the ranch with that bunch of steers and came right over here."

"Why didn't you arrest him? You know what I told you and you found him with your critters." Jake shrugged his shoulders just a little and raised his eyebrows.

"Because I did not want to take any chances that he would get off like he has all these past years. He has had many charges dismissed. This time, though, we got him if we get a grand jury indictment with our strong testimony and a warrant for his arrest. At least I got my steers back."

"Well, now, then we need to get up some warrants." Clark held his glass up and Jake clinked his against it. "I don't believe you've met my wife, Mary Jane. She's probably just about ready to ring the dinner bell. I'd like for you to meet her. Why don't you stay for supper?"

"Oh, thank you. Maybe some other time. I need to get back to the outfit. I'll go up to St. Johns tomorrow to meet with the district attorney. What do I owe you?"

"On the house."

"All right. Thank you. Next contact you should have is a subpoena to appear before the grand jury."

"Secret grand jury."

"Yes, of course." He smiled, stood, put his hat on, and said just above a whisper, "Good evening, Jake." Jake smiled back at him and cringed inwardly at the mention of his nickname.

JAKE LEANED AGAINST the stone of the courthouse wall by the steps to the entrance and deliberately breathed in the air. He struck a match against the stone, lit up a cheroot, got it going and smiled as the breeze carried the smoke away. He wanted some fresh air after spending almost all day in the stuffy, smoke-filled, grand jury room. His testimony was finished, but he was waiting to see if there would be any indictments. He was thinking about the reward money for Renfro and the lesser amounts for the Clantons. They were all rustlers and Renfro was a murderer. The evidence was solid. They all needed to be behind bars. Not that he was any angel. But he never murdered anyone, and he'd paid his dues for the mules he stole over ten years past. There was plenty of opportunity to rustle when he was a stock detective in Texas or commit other thievery or take bribes when he was a detective before that, but he did not. And now for two years he and Mary Jane were, if not of the best, then, among the respectable law-abiding citizens of the county. So, he was torn between going back out on the range for the reward money or sitting back and just being a good citizen. His reverie was disturbed by Al Clark swiftly clumping down the steps and calling out to Jake, "Fifteen! We have fifteen indictments!" He had a big wide grin across his face.

Jake nodded and asked, "When will there be arrest warrants?"

Clark came up next to him and said, "Anxious, are you?"

"Maybe."

"Well, there is one little problem. We still don't have an indictment against Lee Renfro."

"Why are they draggin' their feet?"

"Don't know. But I expect it will be shortly."

"I'll wait for that. No sense in me goin' back out on the range unless it's worth my while. Reward is still offered, ain't it?"

"Far as I know."

On the last Saturday night of April Jake was tending the bar along with Willie, and Mary Jane was waiting tables. A whiskey drummer came in the door and hurried over to the bar. He apparently espied Jake and scooted down his way. "You heard the news?" he said a little too loud and several heads turned in his direction. The murmur of the crowd hushed as everyone waited to hear. "Phin Clanton and some of his gang were arrested today by deputies Powell and Miller and their posse!" There was but a brief silent pause, then a general shuffling of boots and the talk started back up.

"Guess it ain't all that newsworthy," Jake said to the drummer who looked somewhat disappointed. "You know if they got Ike Clanton or Lee Renfro?"

"They weren't named in what I heard."

"All right. Let's see your merchandise list, anyway. Got anything new on it?"

After they locked up the saloon and were walking home Jake wrapped his arm around Mary Jane and said, "Warm enough?"

"Yes. It's not that cold." She hooked her arm around his, looked across at Jake and smiled. "Sounds like the sheriff is genuinely pursuing the Clantons. The rewards are all being eaten up."

"Well, there's that and there's this. I been holding onto this because there ain't been nothin' done 'bout it. This is top secret. Just between you and me, okay?"

"Of course."

"Been offered a special reward of a thousand dollars for Lee Renfro."

Mary Jane stopped in her tracks and squeezed his arm. "Who from? And why you? A bounty hunter?"

"Well, cuz a my previous experience and expertise." He smiled a little sheepishly and it could be seen in the moonlight. "The money's comin' from William Ellinger. It's a onetime thing, so it ain't like a all-the-time bounty hunter."

Mary Jane's voice took on a suspicious tone. "Does that mean you are going after him?"

"There ain't no warrant. And I ain't doin' anything without a warrant. But that's what I am sayin'. Maybe Phin's arrest might help that along."

"What you're saying then, is that if there is a warrant issued, you're gonna go after him?"

Jake stopped, turned to Mary Jane, held her gently by both arms and said, "Only—and I am being as honest as the day is long, I mean it—only if you agree. If you still don't want me out there, I won't go."

She stepped free of his grip, took his arm again and led off toward their house. "A thousand dollars, eh? How much of our savings did it cost us for the house, shop, and saloon?"

"Just about a thousand."

"So, we could replace our savings and keep adding to it as the months roll by." She paused as if she was mulling that over but kept walking. "That's not all there is, though, is there?"

"What a you mean?"

"Jonas Brighton. You know exactly what I mean. You miss the chase. You like being a detective. You want to hunt down bad men and bring them to justice. Don't you?"

"Well—"

"Don't you well me. You want to be out there searching out the clues, following the trail and making the arrest. Don't you?"

"Well—"

"You like the limelight. You want to be the hero."

"Well—"

She stopped abruptly and stepped in front of him, forcing him to stop. She had her jaw thrust out and glared at him with such intensity that he could feel it more than see it. "Well... you are."

"Huh?"

"You *are* my hero." Her whole demeanor softened, and she smiled at him with love and admiration as much as he could see as they came into the ring of light from a lamp in front of Kinnear's Saloon. "I love you mostly because you are who you are. You stayed off the range now for almost three years without any complaint or attempt to hornswoggle me into changing my mind. That's a man in my book and I don't want to hold you down. So, you go on out there." She took his arm again and started walking. "Just don't get killed. That would rile me good."

Jake laughed and took her in his arms, lifted her off the dirt, and hugged her tight. Then he set her down and kissed her sweetly on the lips. They started walking again and he said, "You are right. I do miss it. Guess it is kind of in my blood. Even all the time I'm in the saloon I'm listening for information that can be useful for... for anything." He grinned. "Just catching the bad men, outfoxin' 'em, trackin' 'em down. I like it. Gunplay ain't much fun, but you got a be good at it if you're to survive. That's why me and Wes were always practicin' with pistols and rifles." He looked at her with a little nostalgia in his voice and expression. "Sure would be nice if he were here."

"You talking about Wild West Texas Wes? Yeah. I miss him, too."

"Somethin' I never told you 'bout. It was before your Josh died. Me and Wes tracked down some rustlers. We came up on 'em and they skedaddled. We gave chase. Wes after one and me after 'nuther. Rope 'em, tie 'em up and bring 'em to jail. I had my feller on the ground and was tyin' him up when a renegade Comanch who was part a their gang got the best a me and was about to slit my throat when Wes shot him and saved my life. Over the campfire I told Wes I would never chase a varmint again. If they run, they're guilty, and I ain't takin' the chance a gettin' shot or stabbed so I ain't chasin' 'em. They run from me, they're gonna get shot."

"Now, you told me that to make me feel better about you going out on the range?"

"Well, just so's you would know I generally don't take no chances."

"Generally?"

"Sometimes you got a take little ones." He grinned.

They got to the door of their house and as he walked in Jake recalled Jim Loving's policy of not hiring married men for range detectives. One small hesitation because of thoughts of his wife could cost a detective his life. Got to remember that. Best not hesitate.

SIX

THE END OF IKE CLANTON • 1887

ON MAY THIRTEENTH, Deputy Sheriff Albert Miller rode into town and tied off his horse at the rail in front of Brighton's blacksmith shop. As he walked in the shop door he called out, "Yo, J.V. You around?"

"Right here," Jake called back as he came from the back of the shop with a rag in his hands. "Howdy, Al."

Miller smiled slyly and held up a folded official-looking document. "You know what this is?"

"Wal, seein' how I seen 'em before, and since it is in the hand of a deputy, I'd say pretty confidently that it's a arrest warrant."

"And you'd be pretty confidently right, 'cept it is not just one warrant but two." He slid the warrants apart with his free hand to reveal the other warrant. "One for Ike Clanton and the other for Lee Renfro. Ike for grand larceny and Renfro for murder and larceny. How 'bout that?"

"'Bout time, I say."

"Yep. Sheriff Owens wants me to deputize you special for this job and the two of us to go after these varmints. Are you up for it?"

"Reckon so."

"Okay. Raise your right hand. I, Deputy Sheriff Albert Miller, hereby deputize you, J.V. Brighton, to perform all the duties of a deputy sheriff in and for the county of Apache, Arizona Territory. Do you accept and solemnly swear to perform said duties?"

"I do."

"All right, then. Ain't got no badge. But it don't matter. You're a deputy just like me."

"In the mornin', then?"

"Yep."

"Okay. You can stable yer horse at my place tonight, and we can head out from there in the mornin'."

At dawn Jake and Miller were in Jake's corral saddling up. Jasper and Miller's horse were munching on hay the men had forked out for them. "That's a fine-lookin' horse you got there," Miller said.

"Yep. He's a real good boy," Jake said as he stroked Jasper's neck. He tied on his saddlebags, bedroll, and black slicker. He tied on his brown leather chaps too. He didn't know for sure if he would need his chaps because he had his beige canvas pants tucked into the tops of his spurred boots and that would probably be enough protection unless they got into some high and stickery brush. He wore his usual range garb of blue denim shirt, brown leather vest with his thirty-two caliber pocket pistol nestled into the right pocket, light blue bandanna, and his nutria Stetson Big Four hat. It was still cold in the morning so he wore his felt-lined beige canvas coat.

"I left my slicker at Baca's. Think we'll need 'em?" Miller questioned.

"Can't tell. We're gonna be in the mountains, so yer never know."

"Maybe I better go by and pick it up."

Jake strapped on his spare cartridge belt. Every loop had a forty-four cartridge in it and so did the pistol belt he buckled on over the top of it. He wore a cross-draw holster filled with an Army double-action, five-and-half-inch barrel, forty-four caliber pistol with a good-sized sheath knife on the opposite side. He picked up his Winchester model 1873, with octagon barrel in forty-four caliber repeating rifle, and stuffed it into the scabbard on his saddle so the butt faced forward.

"Wal, you're loaded for bear."

"Don't like to take chances. You don't look any lighter. Bet yer got a spare pistol in that saddlebag. Don't yer?" Miller didn't answer.

As they rode away from the corral Jake looked to the house where Mary Jane was standing in the threshold of the back door. She threw him a kiss. He pretended to catch it, press it to his lips and throw her a kiss. She pretended to catch it and press it to her lips. Then the riders were past the corner of the house and into the road leading out of town to the south through Eagar's. As they walked their horses along the road Jake said, "That Ike Clanton is a clever feller. He'd figger one a the first places a posse'd look for him would be Cienega Amarillo.

I'm thinkin' that place is probably deserted now that the word is out on the indictments. "What a yer think?" Jake twisted his neck to study Miller for a few seconds.

"Wal, I think yer probably keerect. What yer figger we ought ta do?"

"Ike. He never lets a penny slip through his fingers if he can help it. So he ain't gonna want a be losin' any livestock, even though there's Apache County warrants out on him. And he sure as fire heard about 'em. He's gonna want a be headin' south into Graham County, where there's less law after him and where he can sell his stolen beeves to a certain meat-packer." Jake emphasized the words meat-packer and glanced long at Miller to see if he grasped the import of Jake's statement.

"Once I heard Ike talkin' 'bout him and Phin and Ebin Stanley runnin' critters out onto a big grass southwest a Nutrioso for summer graze. He said there was plenty a water on the plain and the Black River was on the south of it. You know where that is?"

"Yep. The Horton brothers have a camp on the Black, and old man Wahl is down that way too."

"Yeah. So that's where we probably oughta start. See if we can cut any tracks leadin' south out a that meadow."

"Wal, the Hortons'll know if anything was goin' on around there. We should stop there and have a talk."

"Okay. What's it like if we just keep headin' south outta town?"

"You mean the trail?"

"Yeah."

"Ain't no trail. And I ain't in favor a climbin' the White Mountains. We can stick to the ravines in between the ridges. We'll be gradually goin' up. But not any steep stuff."

"Okay. So that's what we ought a do. Head down to that Horton camp. Don't yer think?"

"Yep."

It was slow going up through the mountains with pine trees and snow-covered peaks all around them but fortunately no snow where they rode except for a few patches in the shaded places. After a few hours they broke out of the timber and came upon a huge grassy tableland of about five by ten miles in measurement. As they rode across its low rolling hills at a trot, in view were grazing red Hereford cattle spread out over the plain that at a distance looked like red dots here and there. They struck the Horton camp just about noon as they first came to what Jake guessed was a full section of hayfields north of the river. There was a weir on the river that could divert a flow of water into the hayfields through a well-constructed ditch system. The camp proper was located on the south side of the North Fork Black River, just west of the confluence with the East Fork Black River. They splashed across the river and rode up to rustic structures of two small cabins, a privy, a shed, corrals, and a few small outbuildings that made up the camp situated on the edge of a patch of pine and juniper with a meadow in front that ran down a hundred feet to the river. The whole outfit was in the shadow of the north face of a low mesa wall that had been carved out long ago by the river.

Two shepherd-looking dogs came charging out, chaotically barking and running circles around the horses until Jasper caught one of them with his hind hoof. The dog yelped and the two of them retreated to a safe distance away. "Hello, the house," Deputy Miller hollered out.

Women appeared at each of the doors to the two cabins. One was drying her hands in a dish towel and hollered, "Brownie. Scruffy. Hush yer yappin'!!."

Miller and Jake walked their horses up closer to the cabins. Miller removed his hat and said, "Deputy Sheriff Albert Miller, ma'am. And this is Deputy Brighton. Any of your menfolk around?"

One of the women spoke up. "Depends. Why you lookin' for 'em?"

"We're in search of two wanted men. Ike Clanton and Lee Renfro. You seen 'em?"

"Don't surprise me. They's livestock thieves, as sure as can be. We're missin' a mule our men are out lookin' for right now."

The other woman chimed in, "Yeah, and old man Wohl is missin' a whole string a horses. Clantons, sure enough. Our husbands went over to Wohl's this mornin'."

Jake noticed a teenaged girl watching from back in the shadows of the interior of the cabin of the woman who spoke first. And, as they were talking to Miller, little heads appeared from behind the skirts of both women. There were probably more children around somewhere out of sight, someday to be ranch hands out in this lonely place.

"All right, then. We'll be headin' over there. Thank you, ma'ams." Miller re-sat his hat and tipped the brim. Then he and Jake turned their horses and rode out.

"Reckon they's scratchin' it out up here," Jake said.

"Truth be told, they're doing pretty well. They put up a good crop a hay, feed right here in the winter, graze in the summer, don't have to move the cattle around much. Fattens 'em good, and they drive to market in the fall—usually Fort Apache or the San Carlos Reservation. Good Herefords."

"They Morman?"

"Don't know. Why?"

"Just thinkin' if they were, they could get a lot a help up here."

"Uh-huh."

They arrived at Wohl's camp an hour later and in no time cut the trail of a band of horses leading off to the south. "We follow that track out and I bet we run into the Horton brothers," Jake said.

"We better say howdy to old man Wohl first."

"Yeah, before he blows us apart with that scatter gun he's a holdin'," Jake said as he looked to the cabin door where an old feller was standing with a shotgun aimed right at them.

Miller and Jake held their hands up and walked their horses to the cabin. He had the drop on them, and Jake knew it as he squinted his eyes against the sun. "Howdy, Mister Wohl. I'm Deputy Miller and this is Deputy Brighton. We have arrest warrants for Ike Clanton and Lee Renfro. You seen 'em around?"

"Wal, it's 'bout time. Yer finally gonna arrest those scoundrels. No, I ain't seen 'em. But I know that Ike Clanton's been around. Renfro, I don't know 'bout that murderer."

"How do yer know Ike's been around?" Jake said.

"Cuz all my horses is gone. They was here two days ago. Now

they ain't."

"We cut a trail a horses over that a way." Jake pointed to the area where they found the tracks. "Is that the way the Hortons went?"

"Yep."

"Okay. Thanks. We better catch up with 'em," Miller said and reined his horse around. "Be seein' yer."

"Good luck. Bring my horses back," old man Wohl called out as the riders loped on out of the camp.

Another two hours and they caught up with the Horton brothers. Miller hailed them down and they struck out after them. They were heading north so probably they gave up on the trail and were going home. First thing Jake took note of was they were well armed with pistols, rifles, and knives. And everything was pointing at the two deputies.

"Whoa, now, boys," Miller called out as he raised his hands. "We're deputy sheriffs out after the Clantons."

As the distance closed between them, Miller showed his deputy's badge and Jake showed a detective badge he had from his days in Missouri. Everyone sat their horses and remained cautious.

"Wal, ain't that grand? The law finally come to do their job," the younger of the two brothers said with a sneer.

"You been on the trail of old man Wohl's horses?" Jake said to the older brother.

"Yep, and our mule too."

"Wal, we got warrants for Ike Clanton and Lee Renfro. Yer can rest assured we're gonna get 'em. There won't be no slippin' away this time. Legally or any other way." Jake's voice was authoritative and he looked straight into Horton's eyes with that death challenge that let the recipient know he had killed men.

"Wal, that's mighty fine, neighbor. How kin we help yer?"

"We need someone to help us git around these mountains. Someone who knows their way. We can follow these tracks out well enough, but we don't know where they might take us and what might be on the other side, if yer git my drift."

"Yer think we need that?" Miller said.

"Wal, I'm sure yer could git us down to Clifton, but there is a lot a mountain between here and there, and we need someone who knows all the good outlaw hidin' places and can keep us from gittin' lost," Jake said with a grin and the Horton brothers chuckled.

"Yeah. Reckon yer right. Can one a yer help us out?"

"I will," the older brother said. "My little brother here can watch over the camp and take care a the women."

"All right, then. Let's git back on this trail," Miller said.

"There's a camp spot about three hours south. The thieves stopped there and camped. That's where we turned around. We was plannin' to ride out directly in the morning with better supplies. We can camp there for the night."

As they followed out the tracks, they rode along the base of a long ravine between the mountain peaks. It was rough country and the slopes on either side of them were steep and densely treed. Jake kept his head on a slow swivel, staying alert for any sign of movement or some out-of-place shape or color that would be more than likely human rather than natural. Because of the strong breeze through the treetops, it sounded like a rushing river all around them, and he could hear very little if anything at all less than a yell.

The sun was below the tops of the mountains and the light was failing fast when they arrived at the campsite the Horton brother talked about. They took care of the horses, got a fire going, ate their supper, smoked, and talked it up for a while, then bedded down.

Horton of habit was up an hour before first light. He got the fire built up and put on a pot of coffee. When the fire was going good, he went down to the river and filled a canteen with water. While he was kneeling down to fill the canteen, he saw a movement on the other side of the river. It was only about sixty feet across at that point and running three or four feet deep. He slowly stood up and raised his hands above his head. When he did, there was the sound of a short, low growl and movement through the brush. Then nothing.

Back at camp he got a pot of water boiling, then mashed in a hunk of hardtack to soak and laid a slab of bacon in a skillet. In a few minutes the aroma of the frying bacon aroused Jake and Miller and they finally stirred into full consciousness. "Smells like we got some chuck goin'," Jake said sleepily.

"Yep. And lucky for yer, I am still here to cook it for yer instead a bein' someone else's breakfast."

"What a yer mean?" Miller said.

"Lion. That's what I mean. Down by the river."

"Cougar?"

"Yep. He was acrost the river from me. At first, I thought it might be one a these thieves we been chasin'. Then I figgered what it was and I stood up and made myself look big. Wal, he made a snort and moved off. Coulda got us in our sleep."

"Yeah. Ain't that the truth?" Miller said as if he was mulling it over to himself.

"Wal, that'd been a real shame cuz then we couldn't et this fine-smellin' chuck yer got here," Jake said as he tugged on his boots.

Within an hour they were on the move again and after they crossed the river Horton said, "Wal, now that we crossed the Black River, we are in Graham County. You boys got what-a-they-call-it?"

"Jurisdiction."

"Yeah. Jury diction down here."

Miller said, "A lawman sworn in anywhere in the territory of Arizona has jurisdiction anywhere in the territory. It don't matter."

"Wal, good then."

Jake was leading the little posse and as the best tracker he was interpreting the sign and following the trail. After several hours he pulled back on the reins and stopped Jasper in his tracks. "Lookee here," he said. "They's tried to wash out their trail by draggin' it with brush. Wal, we'll just follow the drag then."

Another mile and they came to a deserted camp that had obviously been used several times. Off a way from the camp was an entrenchment with a revetment of logs and stones. Jake looked around the camp and said, "Looks like they's camped out here for a while, and from the look of that trench over there, they's willin' to fight to the death." Then he dismounted and with his finger nudged the edge of the ridges of the hoofprints of all the horses. The dirt was still fairly compact and not crumbly. "Reckon we're 'bout two days behind 'em. Trail's leadin' south." He looked to the gray sky. "We better git goin'. This sky looks like it could open up any minute and wash out the trail." He remounted and they all headed out down the trail of tracks to the south.

When he felt the first drop of rain, Jake stopped and put on his slicker. With the first boom of thunder, he started keeping an eye out for shelter. With the flashes of lightning and crashes of thunder coming closer and closer to them they took shelter in a thick copse of pine trees. Then the wind came up and tore through the tops of the trees and buckets of rain poured from the sky. The tree canopy protected them from about half the volume of falling rain, then it got vicious and started coming at them horizontally. They were being soaked and thrashed by the wind as they struggled to keep their horses under control and remain in the trees. Fortunately, the lightning strikes were not close enough to completely spook the horses so they were able to get through it without a runaway. The storm blasted its havoc for about twenty minutes. Then it dissipated as it moved on, followed by cloudy blue sky. Jake urged Jasper out from under the dripping trees and looked to the south. Nothing. The tracks were all washed out. He pulled his hat off and shook off the rain beads.

"Looks like that's the end a that trail," Jake said as he stepped out of the saddle and shrugged out of his slicker. Turning to Horton he said, "We might as well camp here, and in the mornin' you might as well head back to your outfit. How do we git to Clifton from here?"

"Here. I'll show yer the easiest way for yer to foller. It ain't the shortest. But I heard yer say the Clantons have a cow camp at the Blue and the San Francisco. I kin point yer in that direction so you kin look around. Yer kin ride the San Francisco right on into Clifton. If'n we git on top a this here ridge, I'll show yer."

On top he pointed east. "See that medder out there, greener the rest a 'em. Runnin' northeast to southwest. Shaped kind a like a spearhead?"

Jake and Miller peered into the distance and Jake said, "Oh, yeah. I see it. Yer see it, Al? Right there 'bout five mile out?" He pointed in the same direction as Horton.

"Oh, yeah. Got it."

"Okay. Wal, yer ride straight east to the medder over thar. There's a creek due east a the medder. It turns southeast. Yer kin foller it all the way downstream to the Blue and turn south on the San Francisco where the Blue runs into it. River runs right through the middle of town at Clifton."

Jake took out his pocket compass, flipped open the lid, turned the compass until the needle was pointing to north, sighted over the meadow to a prominent peak beyond and noted the bearing to the peak. Due east.

"Whatcha doin' there?" Horton asked.

"Wal, this here is a compass. Yer can find directions on it. See that highest peak out there? Wal, it's due east a here and the meadow is due west of it. So, as we come down off this mountain, I can stay on a course of due east using this compass to take bearings on that peak and run smack into that meadow, even though I can't see it. Yer foller?"

"Uh-huh. 'Course I kin do the same thing without no compass."

"Yeah, wal, I ain't so gifted. And up here in these mountains I like to be sure 'bout what I'm doin'."

In the morning, Horton was saddled and ready to go. "All righty, then. I'll head back to the barn. If yer see a dun jenny with red muzzle, that's probably my Judy. And she'll answer to that name. Ain't got no brand on her, but she's got a big scar down her right flank where she run into a fence spur a few years back."

"Be more sure if she was branded," Jake said with a hint of an accusatory tone in his voice.

"Yeah. I know. Wal, maybe I'll git lucky. If'n yer want a git back faster on yer way back, yer can come up Eagle Creek 'til yer hit the high mountains. Then turn east and yer'll run back into the Blue. Yer probably kin find yer way from there. Good luck. See ya." He turned his horse and rode away.

JAKE AND MILLER found their way to the confluence of the Blue and San Francisco Rivers. There were a few cows scattered around, so Jake said, "Let's take a look around and see if we can find their camp."

They found a well-used campsite but it was deserted. "Could stay here for the night. But they might come back and catch us sleepin'," Miller said.

"Yeah. Let's move downriver a ways and see if we can find a place to set up a camp without putting a lot a campfire light out. Take a couple a days to search out this place for rustled cattle."

They were undisturbed through the night and spent the day searching the area of what Jake thought was probably the Clanton camp. But they didn't find anything more than the one campsite and a dozen or so steers. All the beeves were carrying a big JU brand on their left sides, which Jake knew was Phin Clanton's brand. They roped a couple of the steers and Jake inspected the brands. As far as he could tell they looked legitimate, and the ears were cropped and slit like both Ike and Phin talked a lot about. Because of that their beeves couldn't be rustled.

"Wal, Phin's in jail and Ike's probably hidin' out somewhere. The gang's all split up. But, someone's gonna come back for these critters and trail 'em to market. We could stay here a few days and see if that happens," Jake said.

They waited two days and gave it up. On the morning of the third day, they made their way down the San Francisco to Clifton. They rode down the main street until they came to the end of the street where about a couple hundred feet past it there was a large building with corral lots next to it. In the corrals were cattle, pigs, and sheep.

"That's what we're lookin' for," Jake said.

"What's that?"

"See the sign? ABC Meatpacker?"

"Oh, yeah. That's where Ike told yer he was sellin' his beef."

"Yep. Let's go in and have a little talk with the owner."

"Howdy," Jake said to a feller sitting at a desk in a little office. A bank of file cabinets piled high with all kinds of ledgers and documents was behind the desk, and the desktop itself was strewn with what looked like orders and invoices.

"What can I do for you?" the man answered as he eyeballed their badges. "Ain't seen you around these parts before."

"We're out a Apache County lookin' for Ike Clanton or Lee Renfro. You know them?"

"Ike, I know. Buy beef from him. Never heard of the other feller."

"Seen Ike lately?"

"He hasn't been here in over a couple a weeks."

"Know where he's stayin'?" Jake asked.

"Nope."

"Wal, all right. Thanks."

"What's he wanted for?"

"Grand larceny. Cattle theft. Those beeves he's been sellin' yer were stolen. You know about that?" Jake looked hard at the man who gulped audibly.

"No, sir. No, sir. I don't know nuthin' 'bout that."

"Wal, that's good because if yer did, it'd be accessory. You don't want that, do you?"

"No, sir. No, sir."

"All right, then. Yer can maybe help us. Ike got a watering hole here in town he likes?"

"You mean a saloon? Oh, yes. He's always over at the Cactus back up Main Street."

"Thanks. We'll check back in a few days. See if he was back here."

They got no help at the saloon, so Jake said, "Let's go down and talk to the sheriff at Solomonville. What's his name?"

"Crawford."

"Yeah. We might get lucky and he have them in jail." Jake grinned at Miller who shook his head.

They rode on down to Solomonville and visited with Sheriff Crawford of Graham County. As they came out of his office and were mounting up Jake said, "Wal, he was cordial enough but didn't have no information for us 'cept for that Little Steves Ranch he said Ike and Phin been seen at. His askin' for wanted posters made sense. We probably ought to get 'em out when we get back." Jake looked around and spied a hotel. "I don't know 'bout yer, but after four days in the saddle I could use some rest."

"That sounds just right, compliments a Apache County, a course."

"A course."

They holed up for two days and on the morning of the third day as they walked to the livery Jake said, "I don't know this country. Ain't ever been here afore. I guess we want to make sure Clanton and Renfro didn't get off to the south to Mexico. Any ideers on how to check that out?"

"Well, one of us should go west to Fort Thomas and the other south down to Fort Bowie to the railroad. Do a lot a askin' around."

"Sounds good. Which one do you want?'

"I'll head over to Fort Thomas. Friend a mine is over that way." He smiled.

"Uh-huh. Okay. What a I do? Just head south outta here?"

"Yep. Hope yer don't run into any 'pache." This time he grinned. "It's a good hard day's ride. Mine's not as bad, but there's a couple a settlements to stop in along the way."

"All right. Meet back here day after tomorrow?"

"Yep."

JAKE RODE BACK into Solomonville late in the afternoon after three days of baking in the desert sun. He went right to the livery, reined Jasper in at the door to the barn, dismounted, pulled his hat and bandanna off and mopped his forehead then down the sides of his face and around the back of his neck. Jasper was lathered up around the saddle harness and his mouth was sticky. Jake led him right over to the stock trough and let him drink his fill. Then he found a hitch ring in the stables and tied Jasper off. He picked up an empty galva-

nized bucket, filled it with water at the stock trough and carried it
back in to the stables.

"Yo! Howdy. Oh, it's you again. Back from your ride south?" The
voice came from the opposite end of the barn where the livery man
came in from the back lots.

"Yeah. Me, again. Got any burlap? Wanna wash down my horse."

"Here you go." The feller handed Jake two burlap potato sacks
folded flat.

"Thanks. Where's a fellow git a bath around here?"

"Down at the Chinaman's on the other end of town."

"Okay. Thanks. See anything of Ike Clanton while I was gone?"
Jake asked as he tethered Jasper to the hitch ring with a short length of
rope and loop around his neck. Then he pulled the saddle off his back.

"Nope. Like I said before. Ain't seen nuthin' a him for a good couple
a weeks."

Jake pulled the bit out of Jasper's mouth and hung the bridle on a
nail on a post. Then he poured the bucket of water over Jasper's back.

"Okay. Thanks."

"See any ' 'pache? Since that big shaker we had three weeks past
they's been dancin' nonstop. They's think it was some kind a sign."

"Yeah? Didn't see any Apaches. Just sagebrush and juniper."

Jake finished washing Jasper, gave him a piece of hard candy,
forked in some hay to his manger, and poured oats in next to the hay.
Then he walked down the dusty main street to the hotel and dropped
his rifle and saddlebags from which he pulled a clean union suit and a
clean shirt. Then he headed for the Chinaman's. He felt in bad need
of a bath. It'd been long over a week and he had been detecting his
own environment for the last few days. His shirt was crusted with
salt sweat and his union suit was rubbing him the wrong way.

After his bath Jake felt better. He was leaning back in a chair on
the porch of the hotel with his boots crossed up on the rail, sipping a
whiskey and smoking a cigar. The porch was shaded by the overhead
and it was cooler there than inside the hotel bar. He was waiting for
Miller who came riding down the street after Jake had been sitting

there for about half an hour. When Miller was abreast of him, Jake called out, "I don't see no prisoner."

"Don't look like yer got one neither."

"Yeah," Jake chuckled. "Go on put your horse up and come on back. I'll buy yer a drink."

Once Miller had his drink and his cigar lit, Jake said, "Yer know that Little Steves outfit Sheriff Crawford was talkin' 'bout? He said that the Clantons stop by there from time to time with small bunches a cattle. I'm for headin' over there and see if ol' Ike's been around there lately. Might even be there now."

"That's probably a good ideer. Probably ought a stop by their camp at the Blue and San Francisco again. See if anyone's there or been there since we left it."

"Yeah. In the mornin' we'll have to git directions from there to Little Steves."

"Yep."

The next morning they were at the sheriff's office waiting for him when he showed.

"Howdy, Sheriff," Jake said. "Wonder if we could have some directions from yer?"

"Why, sure. Come on in." He unlocked the door and they all went through. "Ain't got no prisoners, so I don't have a night man here. What can I do for you? Be just a few minutes and I'll have coffee ready."

"Wal, thanks, Sheriff, but we had coffee over the hotel. We're gonna take today to rest up the horses. But tomorrow we want to go back up to the Clanton camp on the Blue and over to the Little Steves you told us 'bout. Can you give us directions?" Jake said.

"Sure. It's easy. Head back up to Clifton and follow the San Francisco to the Blue. When you're done there, you want a head about five mile up the Blue and then turn due west for probably 'nuther fifteen miles as the crow flies until you come to the only north-south creek flowin' this time a year. That's Eagle Creek. Foller the creek north for about five miles and you come to where Willow Creek comes in from the northwest. The Little Steves is right in the fork of the creeks. You can see the lots and buildings from the fork. They call it the Eagle Ranch, too. Sheep and cattle. They ought a be done with the shearin' by now so yer won't have to hep out." He grinned and chuckled.

"All right. Thanks, Sheriff."

"You betcha. Good luck to ya."

As they rode out of town Jake said, "Wal, they weren't 'xactly detailed directions, were they?"

"Nope. But I think they'll git us in the general area."

"Hope so. My butt's gettin' numb. It ain't used to all this ridin'. Oh, I rode a lot a days in a row in Texas but not here lately." He grinned at Miller, who smiled back.

"Yep. Saddle's a little tougher than a saloon chair." He grinned at Jake, who smiled back.

They stopped for the night at the Clanton cow camp. The same steers were there. No less, no more, and there was no sign of any human presence while they were gone. After supper at the campfire Jake said, "Hard to believe ol' Ike'd leave these beeves here instead a runnin' 'em into his meat-packer in Clifton."

"He must be really sceert and hidin' out somewhere. Not takin' any chances."

"Yep. And that means we ain't probably gonna ever find him. Even though we don't think he hightailed to Mexico, he could have. Or he could have scooted over to New Mexico. Or he could be hidin' out in the mountains. So I guess we just do what we can. Ain't gonna git tangled up in those mountains, though. I say we check that there Eagle Ranch and if we have no luck there then head on back to Springerville."

"Yep."

———————

THE HORSES SMELLED the water of the creek and on their own stepped in to a lope. When they arrived at Eagle Creek, they let their mounts drink while they filled up their canteens. They remounted, and while still sitting in the saddle, Jake pulled his spyglass out of his saddlebag to search south, west, north, and east over the rolling terrain of short tawny grass heavily spotted with juniper. It was an overcast day, so he had no problem with glare from the glass. "Looks pretty deserty down there to the south. North looks more hospitable. Sheriff said the ranch is north a this fork in the creek. If it's the right fork. I think I see a windmill 'bout five mile out and—whoa now—what's this?" Jake held the glass steady then pulled it down to see with the naked eye. "Riders. Three a them. See 'em comin' from the west over there?"

"Yep," Miller said slowly as he strained to see. "Anyone we know?"

Jake pulled the glass back up and said, "No. Look like Indians. Here, you take a look."

Miller looked through the spyglass and said, "Apache. Look like scouts or Indian Police. They's turned and coming our way."

"Should we make a run for it?"

"Nah. Runnin' from 'pache is like a rabbit runnin' from a coyote. If the rabbit don't git to his hole, the coyote always wins. And we ain't got any holes out here. I think we should ride toward them so's we don't look afeared."

Jake reined Jasper to his right and led off up the creek.

Miller pulled up beside him and said, "Make sure to keep yer gun hand close by yer pistol and yer rifle acrost yer lap. Keep a close eye on 'em. If they try to surround us, we got a git back-to-back to fight 'em off. Yer ever done any Indian fightin'?"

"Onced. In Kansas. Back in sixty-seven. Cheyenne. We jumped a small war party. They put out a hellacious amount a lead but, one a our fellers wounded one of 'em and they took off runnin'."

"Wal, we'll see what this bunch does."

Both parties kept coming with Jake and Miller riding the east side of the creek and the Apaches on the west side. When they were directly across from each other they all stopped.

"One a them is a Indian Police. See the badge he's wearin'? He's a breed. Long red hair. Army scout too. Wearin' sergeant's stripes," Miller said. "Got a bad eye, too."

The policeman raised his right hand, and both Jake and Miller raised theirs.

"Howdy. Peace," Miller called out.

"Howdy. Peace," the policeman repeated with a curious little smile.

Miller pointed to his badge and said, "We're deputy sheriffs searching for rustlers and murderers."

The policeman pointed to his badge and said, "Me, too," and smiled. "Reservation cattle missing."

"You from San Carlos?" Miller asked.

"Yup."

"What's your name?"

"Mickey Free. Lieutenant Mickey Free, San Carlos Tribal Police and army scout."

"You say you're losing cattle to rustlers?" Jake said.

"Yup."

"You ever heard of Ike Clanton?"

"Nope."

"He's a rustler we have a warrant to arrest. Who do we see at the reservation to talk about rustlers?"

"Al Sieber your best bet. He chief of scouts. Captain Pierce is agent."

"You speak good English."

"Mexican and Apache, too. Irish Mexican. Adopted by Apache when I a kid." He grinned.

"Looks like you got company coming," Miller said as he looked past them. They twisted in their saddles to see a rider coming at a full gallop with a dust trail a hundred yards long streaming out behind him.

They waited for him to come up to them and when he did, they conversed in Apache while Jake and Miller looked on. Presently, Mickey Free said to them, "We got to go. Good luck to yer." They wheeled their horses and in a cloud of dust rode away. The messenger loped along behind them.

"Wal, that must a been burnin' news. I heared from the stableman in Solomonvlle that the Apache are all stirred up over that earthquake. Maybe there's trouble on the reservation," Jake said somewhat contemplatively. "Wal, whatever it was, guess we might as well git on up to the Eagle Ranch. Dern. Didn't even git a chance to verify that the ranch is north a here."

After about a mile they came upon country populated with sheep and Longhorns. It wasn't long and a pair of herding dogs were barking at them and ran circles around them all the way to the gateposts of the Eagle Ranch. There was a man standing there with a rifle, clearly waiting for them.

"Howdy. We're deputy sheriffs from Apache County lookin' for Ike Clanton and Lee Renfro. Yer know them?" Miller said down to the man.

"Yup."

"They been here lately?"

"What they wanted for?"

"Clanton for larceny and Renfro for murder and larceny."

"Any reward?"

"Two-fifty each. But you got a give information that gets them found and arrested and convicted. You got that kind a information?"

The man leaned his rifle against the gatepost, retrieved the fixings from his pocket and rolled himself a smoke while Jake and Miller looked on. Finally, after he had fired a match, lit up, sucked in a drag and blew it out he said, "Nah. Guess I don't. Clanton was by here 'bout a week ago, though."

"What's your name, sir?" Jake said.

"What's yours?"

"J.V. Brighton and this is Al Miller."

He pulled a drag on is cigarette and said, "George H. Stevens. Sergeant, Fifth Calvary, retired."

"Sheriff Crawford told us about you. Said yer were a good man," Jake lied.

"Don't know 'bout that. Just tryin' to get by."

"Yer have a crew here? One of 'em might know somethin' about Clanton and Renfro?" Jake stared down at Stevens. He looked away.

"Got three hired help right now. They're up in the barn if you want a talk to 'em."

"We'll do that. Any other place around here Clanton or Renfro might be holdin' up?"

"Which way'd yer come from?"

"We come over from the Blue. Gonna head north out a here and back to Springerville."

"Uh-huh. Wal, the onliest other place around here is old Peg Leg Jim's 'bout five, six mile up the creek. He's got a purty good cabin up there. His last name is Wilson. Yer welcome to stay for supper. Got a purty good beef stew. Missus is off down to Solomonville visitin' her sister, so it ain't fancy but it's good. 'Course it's a little early. You'd have to wait a bit."

"Obliged," Jake said with a smile. "But we are anxious to git back. Been out over two weeks. We'll just talk to yer crew and head on up to that Peg Leg's place."

AFTER A FRUITLESS half hour talking with Stevens' crew the two lawmen rode north and struck James Peg Leg Wilson's cabin about an hour before sundown. It was a new looking log cabin that looked pretty weathertight with a solid-looking wood shake roof and a covered front porch. A stone chimney at one end topped out a stone fireplace. As they rode up to the cabin they saw a man sitting in a chair on the porch with a rifle across his lap. Miller said quietly, "Yer know, that name James Wilson sounds familiar. I think I saw a wanted poster out a New Mexico. Cain't be sure though."

"Wal, that'd make sense. Clanton'd hole up with another outlaw. Best watch real careful like." They rode on up and said howdy.

Up the creek about three hundred yards there was a small meadow where they staked the horses on long tethers. They would have hobbled them but Peg Leg said that every once in a while a bear'll come down the creek and there were cougar around too. Naturally, Jake slipped Jasper a piece of hard candy before he left him.

Wilson was a hospitable feller of about forty with a brown beard and hair, rosy cheeks, sun-wrinkled face, and gnarled hands. He was kinda skinny and bent over. His union suit was dirty and stained and, besides his britches with suspenders and his boots, that's all he had on. But there was a delicious-smelling rabbit stew in the kettle over the stone hearth and he was pulling two extra bowls down from the shelf so the stained armpits of his faded union suit could be ignored.

The lawmen dropped their saddles in the corner of the cabin where the end of a bunkbed sat. There was an old wood table with four chairs in one corner and a regular bed butted up against the wall of another corner. The wall on the fireplace side adjacent to the last corner was filled with a wooden fixing counter with cabinets underneath. The place had a funny smell to it, but Jake ignored it.

"Wal, glad to have yer boys in for supper," Wilson said in a grizzly old voice. "Don't git much company out here. Oh, one a the Little Steves crew come around lookin' for strays ever onced in a while. They's have no time to set an talk, though. Speakin' a which, let's go out on the porch and set a spell." He grinned friendly-like, revealing a mouthful of decayed teeth. "Who'd yer boys say yer was lookin' for?"

Jake shook and bounced a crooked wooden chair around to test its strength and, satisfied, sat in it and leaned it back against the cabin wall. He pulled a cigar out from his shirt pocket underneath his vest, snapped a match with his thumbnail, and lit the cigar. He got it going good and looked from under his brow at Wilson who was nearly drooling. "Want a cigar?" Jake said to him.

"Sure would."

Jake slowly reached to his shirt pocket, stopped and said, "We're lookin' for Ike Clanton and Lee Renfro. You know 'em?"

He looked away and said, "Wal I heared a 'em. Don't know 'em." Then he fastened his eyes on the lump under Jake's vest formed by his hand at his shirt pocket which he still had not moved.

"That right? We hear tell Clanton stops by here purty regular."

"Wal, I don't know where yer heared that from. Ain't true."

"We have our sources." Jake pulled his hand out from under his vest and palmed a short cheroot. Then he twirled it in his fingers.

"I guess it's what a feller means by regular. He's been by a time or two, but I don't know him." Wilson feigned a look of truthfulness.

"When was the last time he was by?"

"Wal, just so happens it twas 'bout a week ago."

"Say what he was doin' or where he was goin'?"

"Nah. He ain't much a talker."

"Wal, I know him and so does Al here. Would yer say Ike is a talker or not, Al?"

Al lifted a boot up onto a chair seat and leaned on his thigh. "Ev-er'body knows Ike Clanton is a talker." And he stared accusingly at Wilson. Jake continued to twirl the cheroot and stared hard at Wilson.

Jake said slow and low while he speared Wilson with eyes that threatened sure death, "I think he comes by here purty regular, and I think yer know him purty good. Now we got a warrant for his arrest, and if yer don't tell us what yer know, we can arrest yer and take yer to jail as a accessory."

"Oh, all right! Gimme that cigar." He snatched it out of Jake's hand, scratched a match on the cabin wall, lit the cigar and puffed it until the tip glowed red. "I know him. Kind of a friend. So, naturally, I ain't real interested in helpin' yer fellers. But, he ain't a good enough friend to git thrown in jail over." He puffed the cigar and blew out big puffs of smoke. "Ahh. Tha's real good."

"What about Clanton?" Miller said.

"Oh, yeah. Like I said, he was by 'bout a week ago. Said the law was after him and he was hidin' out in the mountains. Comes down to et some a my stew or set down for breakfast."

"How often?" Jake said.

"Huh?"

"How long between his visits?" Miller sounded a little perturbed.

"Oh. Usually 'bout onced a week."

"Uh-huh. So, he's due any time now."

"Yer could say so, I guess."

"Wal, reckon we'll be spendin' a few days with yer, Peg Leg." Jake smiled big.

"Tha's fine by me, Long as yer got more a them cigars."

"Oh, I got plenty."

In the morning Jake and Miller were set down at the table drinking their coffee and Peg Leg was at the hearth frying up a slab of bacon. He had beans bubbling in a pot set next to the small fire and a Dutch oven full of bread dough buried in the coals.

"Wal, we're 'bout ready here, boys. Soon as this sow belly is done, I'll pull out them biscuits. Mmmm. Makes my mouth to water just a think 'bout it. Eh? Who's that a comin' up?"

Jake and Miller both heard the rider come up to the cabin before Wilson and were at the door. Jake snatched up his rifle from where it was leaning against the wall next to the door. Miller was to his right and behind Jake. Slowly, Jake cracked the door and saw who it was.

"Howdy, Jim. I smelled that bacon a mile up the trail. Reckon yer got some to share with a ol' desperado?" Ike Clanton sat his horse in front of the cabin and obviously thought he was talking to Peg Leg through the cracked door. He held his horse's reins in his hands crossed on the horn of his saddle, had his hat pushed back and was full of grins. When Jake opened the door wide and stood with his rifle held in both hands low across his body, Ike saw him and his grin faded considerably. "Why... howdy J.V. What yer doin' down here? I ain't got no more cattle fer yer to count."

Miller peered around Jake's side and his face came into full view. Ike saw him and his grin disappeared to be replaced by a frightful look. He pulled back on the reins to back up his horse.

"Throw up yer hands, Ike. Yer under arrest!" Miller yelled.

Clanton wheeled his horse to make a run for a trail through the timber beside the cabin. His horse gave a deep throaty groan in protest of the jerk on his bridle. But he obeyed the rein and in a spray of dirt and dust kicked up by his hooves, he spun to his left. Clanton wildly slashed his spurs across the horse's sides from girth to flank and the horse jumped into a full run.

"Halt! *Halt!*" Miller shouted.

Jake hollered, "Stop! *Stop!* Ike, don't run."

Jake raised his rifle up to his shoulder, took aim and held it for a few seconds. Miller aimed his pistol. About twenty yards out, Clanton reined the horse to the left where the trail turned, unsheathed his rifle and laid it across the crook of his left elbow pointed at Jake and Miller. Jake squeezed off a round. The forty-four slug hit Clanton under his left arm and passed through his body. Jake levered in another round and fired again. The second shot hit the saddle pommel and grazed Clanton's leg. He hung on for a couple of seconds and then fell from the saddle. His horse went on a few feet and stopped.

"Yer got him!" Miller exclaimed.

"What'd yer do that fer?" Wilson said loudly from the cabin porch.

Jake lowered the rifle and held it at the ready across his chest. He walked cautiously along with Miller to where Clanton was stretched out motionless, facedown on the ground. Miller nudged the body with the toe of his boot. He did not twitch, move, or groan so they dropped to their knees and rolled him over. There was no life in his eyes. He was dead.

Wilson came limping up and when he saw the dead Clanton he screeched, "Yer kilt him! Yer kilt him!"

Jake stood up slowly and looked at Wilson with sadness in his eyes and a downturned mouth. "Sorry. He was kinda my friend, too."

"Wal, then what'd yer kilt him fer?" Wilson said huskily.

"Nothin' else I could do. He was goin' to shoot us. It was self-defense. I ain't no killer. I ain't likin' this a'tall."

Wilson shoved his hands in his pants pockets and scowled at a dirt clod that he kicked with his good leg and almost fell down doing it.

"Wal, guess we better figger out what to do from here," Miller said as he holstered his pistol. "Cain't haul him back to St. Johns. Be too stinky by the time we got there. Buzzards be followin' us all the way. Just about as far down to Solomonville."

"Aw, ya'll wait here. I'll take Ike's horse. Get some hep down at the Little Steves and bury him proper off to the side a the cabin there. There's some other graves over that a way."

They watched him ride off and Miller said, "Smell that?"

"Burnin' bacon." Jake looked at Miller, Miller looked at Jake. They hurried back into the cabin.

There was just a little smoke in the cabin and Jake said, "Quick! Git that skillet off the fire. I'll pull that Dutch oven outta the coals."

Five minutes later they were chowing down on the breakfast they expected earlier. Bacon, beans, fresh biscuits, washed down with fresh coffee. After breakfast they sat on the porch, smoking cigars and sipping coffee.

"Wal, what a yer think?" Miller said. "Should we ride on down to Solomonville and report the killin'?"

"Are yer sure we're in Graham County? We could be on the reservation for all we know."

"Cain't be sure, but I think we're just over the line into Graham."

"Wal, it'd be two days back to Solomonville with a pack horse. Five days from there back to Springerville and the better part of a day on up to St. Johns. I say we git this culprit planted and head right out for the barn. We can send a wire to Sheriff Crawford," Jake said then swished some coffee and swallowed it.

"Yeah. Sounds good to me."

"S'pose we ought a git the body covered up proper," Jake said.

They brought a canvas tarp out of the cabin, dragged Clanton's body up to the porch, laid him on his back, crossed his hands on his chest, and draped the canvas over him.

"Wal, all right. Let's go check the horses." Jake said. As they hiked up the creek he said with a slight smile and his head hung down a little, "Yer know… if ol' Ike didn't point that rifle at us, I don't know if I woulda shot him."

"Yeah. Don't fret none. I was just about to pull the trigger when he fell off his horse. Yer got those two rounds off fast. Like yer done it before."

"Yeah. I killed a few men in my time. But they were killers and deserved it. All bad men tryin' to kill me. I ain't so sure ol' Ike deserved it. I think he might a been goin' to lay down some lead to get us to duck away so's he could make a run for it. Nah. I think I shot too fast. He probably couldn't a hit us anyway, snap shootin' like he was gonna off a runnin' horse."

"Wal, like I said, I wouldn't fret none 'bout it. What's done is done. But, just wonderin'. Yer got lawman 'sperience?"

"It ain't no never mind." Jake quickened his pace so as to outdistance Miller.

An hour later Peg Leg, George Stevens, and two of his men showed up. Miller pulled back the tarp and said, "Ya'll recognize this feller?"

They all pulled off their hats and George said, "No doubt 'bout it. That's Ike Clanton. Right, boys?" The two hands nodded their heads and mumbled their agreement.

"All right. We can dig the grave right over here," Peg Leg said as he limped over to a spot under a tree. "Dig it out here a ways so we's don't got a fight no roots."

The two hands pulled off picks and shovels they had tied to their saddles and attacked the earth where Peg Leg stood. As the digging continued there was room for only one man at a time in the hole. So, Jake, Miller, and George pitched in and a rotation of diggers went on with each man shoveling and throwing dirt or swinging the pickax as fast and hard as he could. When one man was out of breath, another jumped in. It went faster too because the dirt was not hard or too sandy. At the end of an hour they were waist deep. Another half hour and they were shoulder deep.

"That should do it. Don't yer think?" Miller said. Everyone, breathing hard as they were, agreed. They carried the body over, wrapped and tied it up good in the tarp and rolled it into the grave. It hit the bottom with a thud, and they all went quiet.

After a minute, Peg Leg said, "Lord," and in one swish they all pulled off their hats, held them low in their hands and bowed their heads. "Ike was a friend a ours. Oh, he was a desperado, fer sure. But we all done bad things one time or anuther. So, we hope you'll fergive his sins and let him ride through them purly gates. Amen." And they all said amen.

Jake threw in a couple of shovelfuls of dirt and handed the shovel to Miller who did the same and handed it to Peg Leg and he passed it on to the others. When the body was covered over with dirt he said, "Wal, we got a git on the trail. Ya'll can finish up here. I wouldn't put no grave marker up. He was kind a famous and grave robbers might come along and dig him up. Maybe just take that rock over there with the natural craggy X mark on it and set it in the dirt at the head. Let the weeds and stuff grow over the fresh grave. That'll mark the grave for anybody who needs to know. What do yer think?"

"Probably a good ideer," Peg Leg said. "Yer know he's got a sister up at Nutrioso. Mary Stanley."

"Yeah. That's right." Jake turned to Miller and said, "We should ride back up that way and let her know. And we can take Ike's horse and saddle to her."

"Sounds right," Miller said, and Peg Leg nodded his head yes.

"Just head northeast out a here and pick up the Blue?" Miller said. "Then north to Cienega Amarilla? That right? We know the way from there."

"Yup."

———————

LATE SATURDAY, AFTER suppertime, the deputies rode into Springerville. Jake put Miller and his horse up at his place, and Mary Jane fixed them a little something to eat. Next morning Miller went on his way to St. Johns. He and Jake agreed to meet in St. Johns on Monday and make their report. After he was gone, Jake sat at the table drinking coffee. Mary Jane was at the sink cleaning up.

"I feel awful 'bout shootin' ol' Ike," Jake said.

Mary Jane dried her hands on a towel, picked up her coffee and sat down across from Jake. "Wasn't he a killer?" she said with a curious look on her face.

"That's the funny thing. I ain't never heard a Ike killin' anyone. Oh, he puffed himself up and all, but I never even heard rumors. And that's the burr under my saddle. I wish he'd never pointed that rifle at us."

"Well, sweetheart, he did." She stood and draped her arm over his shoulders. "There's nothing else you could have done. You had to defend yourself."

"That's what I said. But a feller always has a choice."

She scooted a chair over next to Jake, sat down, and took his free hand in between her hands and gently caressed it. Softly she spoke. "Yes. A fellow does always have a choice and hopefully he chooses right. Your instinct was to defend yourself and Deputy Miller. That instinct comes from more than just fear and self-protection. You got other people to think of. Me and maybe somebody else. If you went and got killed, what would happen to us? Besides, I didn't really care for that old blowhard anyhow. Not that it makes it right. Let's just say I don't miss him. And I sure would miss you if you were killed. You know that's why I hate this range business."

"Well, I'm takin' a couple a weeks to rest up, but...." Jake gave her a suspicious look and said, "What do you mean 'maybe somebody else?'"

Mary Jane smiled coyly. "I mean, maybe we have one in the oven."

Jake jumped up and took Mary Jane in his arms and beamed a wide grin at her. "Here we go again," he said. "Let's hope we make it this time."

"Hold on now," she said. "It's still early. I'll know for sure in another couple a weeks."

"That's gonna be a long time to wait. Think I'll go to church today. Need to repent and give thanks too. You want to go?"

"Sure."

Jake sat in the pew and stared the whole time at the Crucifix on the wall at the head of the church. Neither he nor Mary Jane went forward for Communion.

―――――――――――――

THE DRY, WINDY, and dusty day was getting on, well into late afternoon, when Jake tied off Jasper at the rail in front of the courthouse and walked in to the sheriff's office. Miller and AG Powell were there playing rummy.

"Howdy, boys," Jake said as he loosened his stampede string and pushed his hat back on his head. "Didn't know yer were comin' in, George," he said with a smile at Powell.

"Ran into Al on the trail, so thought I'd just come on in with him."

"Wal, Sheriff Owens ain't here, and the DA is in Prescott. We got no one to give a report to," Miller said as he threw a card into the pile of discards.

"Wal, how 'bout Judge Martin. He around?"

"Don't know. Let's go see."

The Justice of the Peace was in, and sitting with him in his modest chambers chewing the fat was J.F. Wallace, editor and manager of the *St. Johns Herald*.

"Hello, Judge. Mind if we interrupt? We got a report to make on Ike Clanton, and the sheriff and the DA ain't here," Miller said sort of apologetically. Wallace sat up straight in his chair and fumbled for his notebook in his outside coat pocket.

The judge leaned back in his chair. "Make your report," he said.

Miller spelled it out in detail with Jake commenting here and there. And the editor was making furious notes. When they were done, the judge said, "Okay. Your report is duly noted. You can go ahead and send your wire to Sheriff Crawford."

"Okay to print this, Judge?" Wallace queried.

"Sure."

"Can you boys give me about an hour to write this out and you can check it over?"

"Maybe. If yer buys us a drink or two over to the Monarch while we wait," Miller said.

"Deal."

The story came out in the June ninth edition of the *St. Johns Herald* just as Miller and Jake had reported it. For days after, a lot of folks came in to the shop and the saloon and congratulated Jake. Others, cowboys and outlaws, gave him the stink eye. Every time he was either congratulated or criticized there was a little queasy feeling that came up in his gut.

Two weeks later on a Saturday night, Jake and Mary Jane were walking home from the saloon. She had her arm hooked in his like always and she looked over at him for a long minute.

"What?" he said.

"Well... we didn't make it."

He stopped up short and stood in front of her. "How many times we gonna have to go through this?" His face showed a painful exasperation.

"I know, sweetheart. I don't know if I'm used up or what."

"Probably me, not you. 'Course, neither one a us is a spring chicken." He laughed. "Aw, what the heck. We'll just keep on havin' fun tryin'."

She gripped his arm tightly and pressed in close as they finished the walk home.

BUT LEE RENFRO, with the thousand-dollar reward offer to Jake from William Ellinger, was still out there somewhere, and word came in that he might have been in on a horse-stealing that ended up with the thieves being killed by a posse and one escaping. One of the killed was the Ace of Diamonds. So, Jake decided to mosey on up to St. Johns and see what he might find out. He walked into the courthouse and shoved the door against the wind to latch it closed. In the sheriff's office, he found new Undersheriff Art McDonald there cleaning his pistol.

"Howdy, Art," he said cheerily.

"J.V. How yer doin'?"

"Fine. Got any coffee?"

"Yeah. Just made a fresh pot. Still hot. Right over there."

Jake poured himself a cup and stepped back over to the table where Miller was sitting. He pulled a chair out from under the table and sat in it. "How's that Colt holdin' up?"

"Right good. Yes, sir. Put a lot a rounds through this big boy. Practice and all. But yer didn't come all the way up here just to jaw 'bout my pistol, did yer?" He looked askance at Jake with a little smile on his face.

"No, I did not. I heard about the Ace a Diamonds gettin' kilt by some ranchers for stealin' horses. That right?"

"Yup. Accordin' to the buckboard driver from Springerville. Probably where yer heared it. They were up on the headwaters a Eagle Creek at Charlie Thomas's ranch. Partook of ol' Charlie's hospitality. He give 'em somethin' to eat and told 'em to move on. Jack Cooper and Bill Eaddy were stoppin' at Charlie's too. Next mornin' Cooper went out to catch the horses and five were missin'. They followed the trail and caught up with 'em. Had a shootout. Long Hair and Diamond were kilt, and Renfro skedaddled."

"Sure Renfro was one of 'em? I heared they weren't sure."

"Wal, that's right. But, birds of a feather—"

"Yeah, probably so. Heared anything else 'bout where he might a run off to?"

"Nah. But, he probably thinks he's safe up in them mountains. Could be anywhere up there. Thousand different places to hide out."

"Wal, thanks for the coffee. Think I'll mosey on over to the *Herald* office and round up ol' Wallace. See if he's heared anything more. When yer gonna visit down our way?"

"Oh, one a these days soon."

"All right. We'll be lookin' fer yer. See yer then."

There was no more information to be had, so Jake thought about it for a couple of days and made his decision. This was the first news in a long while about the possible whereabouts of Renfro, so he filled his saddlebags with provisions and rode on out leaving a trying-to-be-brave and encouraging-but-sad-looking Mary Jane at the door to their house. His first stop was the Thomas Ranch. He had a plan.

———————

IT WAS A bright and calm day in the White Mountains when Jake rode into the canyon of the Thomas Ranch. He spotted a cowboy in a big meadow pushing a bunch of cows to the other end, where there were about five bulls that he could see grazing away. He loped ol' Jasper on over there, slowed to a trot and finally a walk when he got close to the man. He hadn't ever met Charlie Thomas, so he had to assume it was him.

The feller reined in his horse, and Jake saw his hand move to the butt of his holstered pistol. Jake raised his hands and called out, "Hold on now. Name's J.V. Brighton. Detective for the Apache County Stock Growers Association." He got to about ten feet away and stopped Jasper.

"What a yer want with me?"

Jake nudged Jasper, and they edged in a little closer. "Hey, you Charlie Thomas?"

"Maybe."

Jake pulled aside his vest and revealed his detective badge and said, "I am lookin' for Lee Renfro. Yer know him?"

"Cain't say I know him. Know who he is."

"Wal, I hear tell yer had a run-in with him ta other day. I ain't carin' 'bout the other two fellers. They were killers and got what they deserved, but I want this Renfro feller. Yer know where he might be?"

"Ain't sure it was him, but whoever it was he ran off to the west. Probably onto the reservation over to Rio Bonito way."

"Much obliged." Jake tipped his hat, turned Jasper and rode south.

Two days later he rode onto the San Carlos Apache Indian Reservation late in the afternoon. He saw some soldiers and walked Jasper over to them while he pulled off his bandanna, raised his hat, mopped his brow and his neck, and was about to retie it when he noticed the backs of his hands were sweating so he wiped them dry too.

"Howdy," he said to them as he revealed his badge. "Can yer point me to Al Sieber?"

One of them said, "Pinkerton?"

"Apache County Stock Growers."

"Say!" Another said with a small degree of wonderment. "You the one who kilt Ike Clanton? We heared 'bout that just ta other day."

Jake stared at the soldier for a few seconds just to freeze his guts and said sternly, "Sieber?"

The kid pointed to a tent standing off by itself from the other tents down a ways from where they were. "Obliged," Jake said and trotted Jasper off to the tent.

The tent flap was open, so Jake walked in and saw a man about his age sitting at a table in his union suit with his left leg up on a pillow on a cot next to the table. He had black hair and mustache, was of average build, and had keen, intelligent dark eyes.

Jake said, "Howdy. You Al Sieber?"

"Twas. Now I am just a shot-up old Army scout fightin' to keep my leg the doc wants to saw off. How's that for cryin' in the milk?"

"Not bad. I'm Detective J.V. Brighton outta Apache County." Jake pulled his vest lapel aside to reveal his badge. "What happened to you?"

"Aw. We had some trouble here 'bout a month ago. Apache Kid settled an old score, Apache on Apache. Captain Pierce, the agent, said he had to go jail anyway. The Kid's friends didn't like it and started a scuffle. I took a bullet that shattered my ankle all to pieces. Apache Kid and his friends broke outta the reservation, and my scouts and the tribal police are out lookin' for 'em. That's it."

"Would one a yer scouts be a feller name Mickey Free?"

"Sure is. How'd you know that?"

"Ran into him out on Eagle Creek last month. He had to leave sudden like. Thought it might be cuz a some trouble here. Guess it was, huh?"

"Reckon so. Anyways, what can I do for you, Detective Brighton?"

"Wal, I'm a stock detective chasin' down rustlers. That's what I was doin' when I ran into Mickey Free—"

"Al?" a man called out as he walked into the tent. "Oh. Sorry. Didn't know you had company."

"Captain Pierce. This is J.V. Brighton. Stock Detective outta Apache County. I believe he's the feller who killed Ike Clanton."

"Oh, yes. The one Sheriff Crawford was telling us about. Pleased to make your acquaintance, Mister Brighton." He held out his hand, and Jake shook it saying, "Likewise."

"I believe he was about to tell me something about Mickey Free," Sieber said.

"Yes. I was telling Mister Sieber that I met Mickey Free on Eagle Creek when I was on the hunt for Ike Clanton. He said he was lookin' for reservation cattle and the rustlers who took them. So, I thought maybe we could work together. I have a lead on a gang working out of Rio Bonito. I don't know that country, and I thought we could team up together to search out there for reservation cattle and rustlers."

"That sounds like a good idea. What do you think, Al?"

"Well, you know Mickey's out chasing the Kid, and I can't spare any scouts. But maybe you can set him up with some tribal police who know that Rio Bonito country."

"Yes, I think so. Think we need to run it by Marshal Meade?"

"Nah. You got the authority here. They're policemen of the Apache not deputy U.S. Marshals."

"Yes, I think you're right. I'll send him a courtesy note, anyway—just to let him know what we're doing. Meantime, let's go on over to the guardhouse and see if we can recruit some knowledgeable policemen."

"Shouldn't have any trouble with that," Sieber said. "They all know their way around pretty good in those mountains. When you're done, come on back and have a drink. My ankle is killing me and needs some dulling out."

"Okay. Thanks."

"Captain Pierce?"

"Ah. No, thanks. I have paperwork I need to finish. Which reminds me. Mister Brighton, could you give us a minute? Thank you."

Jake stepped outside and found some shade to stand in while he waited for them to finish their business. Presently, Captain Pierce emerged and said, "Over this way."

Captain Pierce made arrangements for three tribal police to accompany Jake, and when all was set in place, Jake went back over to Sieber's tent. He already had a bottle of Kessler out and a glass full that he was sipping. "Come on in," he said when Jake appeared at the open tent flaps. "Can I pour you a drink?"

"You betcha. Care for a cigar?"

"Don't mind if I do."

"Where does a feller get some chuck and a place to bunk around here and care for his horse?"

"Well, right here. They'll be bringing in my supper, and I'll share it with you. You can bunk in that cot right over there. Breakfast in the morning. What time you pulling out?"

"Sunrise."

"Okay. I'll have them bring in the breakfast at dawn. You can turn your horse out in that corral over yonder. There's feed and water there and a guard so's your horse don't go missing. How's that?"

"Mighty fine of you." Jake smiled and puffed his cigar. "I'll be back in a few minutes."

Jake reappeared at the tent again, and Sieber said, "All right, then. Let's get to drinking and telling each other lies." He grinned. "Where do you hail from?"

"Originally?"

"Well, say, right before the war."

"Oh. Well, Indiana but, I joined up in Illinois. Twenty-first Regiment Illinois Volunteer Infantry."

"Oh, yeah? I was First Minnesota Volunteers. Made it through Fair Oaks, Antietam, Fredericksburg, Chancellorsville. Gettysburg got me though. Almost took my leg." He raised his right leg a little with a bit of a sour look on his face. "And now I got this one they want to take off. No sir. Not now. Not ever." He gulped down a pretty good slug of whiskey.

Jake sipped his whiskey, puffed his cigar, and blew a big cloud of blue smoke up over his head. "Yeah. I made it through alive too. But it was not pretty. Enlisted December sixty-three. Got captured in July at Tunnel Hill, Georgia. Did time at Andersonville—" Sieber made a loud whistle. "—finally moved me to Charleston where I got released in December. Sick for a long time. Finally mustered out as a corporal in San Antonio in December sixty-five."

"Yeah, I mustered out as a corporal in Elmira, New York. Came west in sixty-six."

They went on with the stories of their adventures late into the night until Jake said he needed to hit the hay. Sieber laughed and called him a sissy, but Jake hit the rack anyway and was soon snoring away.

In the morning Jake's head throbbed a little and he felt wrung out, but he made it through breakfast while Sieber slept, and Jake was gone before he woke up.

On the second day out with his tribal police force they were in the mountains on the Rio Bonito plateau when about a hundred-fifty yards out a fellow on foot and in his shirtsleeves came out of a canyon mouth. Jake and his posse closed to within twenty yards when Jake halted and dismounted. They all dropped from their horses. He couldn't be sure, but this feller looked like he could be Lee Renfro. He called the English-speaking policeman over to him.

"Yer two go on over and tell him we're from the southern country and ask him to come over and talk to me about the trails up here."

They went over to the feller, talked and gestured for a minute, and sure enough, the feller started to come with them over to Jake. Meanwhile, he and the other policeman pretended to be fixing their saddles. Jasper stood between Jake and the feller who Jake watched from underneath the rim of his hat over the seat of his saddle. When he was ten to fifteen paces away Jake clearly recognized Renfro. Jake drew his pistol and stepped to the side way away from Jasper.

"Lee Renfro! Throw up yer hands!" Jake called out loudly. Renfro stopped walking and stood still looking like he was confused. He was about ten paces away.

"Throw up yer hands, Renfro!" Jake called out again. He still didn't move, even though Jake clearly had the drop on him as he pointed his pistol directly at Renfro's chest.

"You're under arrest. Now throw up yer hands!"

With that, Renfro's face turned sour and he jerked his pistol out of the holster. He cocked the hammer and raised the six-shooter to point at Jake and that's as far as he got. His expression changed to shock and horror as two forty-four slugs tore through his chest and came out his back. The impact threw him to the ground. Jake came running up to him, and as Renfro's face began to turn white, in gasps over a sucking air sound from his chest, he gurgled, "Did you shoot me fer the money?"

Jake said calmly, "No. I shot yer cuz yer resisted arrest."

In between gasps, Renfro said, "I suppose it's all up with me. Will yer send my watch and other stuff to my brother in Cowboy, Texas?" There was just a slight pleading look in his eyes for a few seconds. Then they looked off into the distance and the sucking air sound ceased. He was dead.

Jake shook his head side to side and hollered. "Let's get after the rest of 'em." He vaulted into the saddle and ran Jasper up the canyon. They got to the camp and only one horse and saddle were there. Jake supposed it was Renfro's. There was a bed of hot coals in the fire ring and camp pots and stuff scattered about that indicated to Jake a rapid departure by persons unknown. He had a choice—go after them or take Renfro's body back to federal authorities. He chose the latter because it was Renfro he was after and he got him, so the job was over as far as he was concerned. But he told the policemen they could pursue the fugitives if they wanted. They did and took off after them in a cloud of dust.

He led Renfro's horse to where the body was spread out on the ground and got the corpse up and tied to the saddle. Then he started for Fort Thomas about twenty-five miles to the west, which was much closer than San Carlos. It was just past noon, so he figured he could make it before dark. The problem was water, and that meant he had to stay by the creek heading south. Then take one last big refill and turn west across the desert until he struck the Gila River somewhere close to Fort Thomas. After an hour of riding, he saw a shadow move across the ground in front of him. Then another went across. He looked to the sky and saw six buzzards circling low overhead.

"Don't git too excited," he said out loud to no one. "I ain't about to be buzzard bait. Yer might as well just fly away. No? Okay. See yer at Fort Thomas."

It was dusk when Jake rode into Fort Thomas. The wind was blowing hard and dust was swirling everywhere. Things were banging around as if they were about to break loose from their moorings and go flying off in the brownish-orange sky. He found the provost office and tied Jasper off out of the wind, moved his badge from his shirt to the lapel of his vest and went in the office, forcing the door shut behind him. There were two soldiers in not-so-clean white shirts sitting at desks—one on the left wall and one on the right. They were each working on some kind of paperwork, and Jake wondered where their blue coats were until he saw them together with their hats hanging on pegs on another wall where there was a rack of rifles.

"Howdy," Jake said. "Got a outlaw body outside. Shot him on reservation land."

"Aww," both soldiers groaned. "Why don't yer take him on in to the agent at San Carlos?"

"Horse is done in. Got a rest him."

"Now we gotta do a bunch more paperwork and get up a detail to bury him."

Jake glanced back over at the coats on the wall and saw that one of them had corporal stripes on it. "Yer the corporal?" he asked.

"That's right. Gimme what yer got."

Jake handed him the warrant. He unfolded it, read it, and said, "Wanted for murder out of Apache County. Reservation's Indian land."

"Yeah. I know. It was up on the Rio Bonito. I tried to arrest him, but he pulled on me and I had to shoot him. Captain Pierce gave me three tribal policemen to posse up with me. They can verify my story. I sent them after the rest of the gang and came down here with Renfro's body."

Then another older soldier and a deputy U.S. marshal walked out of the office behind the corporal. "It's okay, Ross. We can handle it. I'll clear it with Captain Pierce." Then he turned to Jake. "I'm Sergeant Whitehead," he said firmly and seriously as he looked at Jake's badge. And before Jake could answer he said, "Yer a detective?"

"Yes, sir. For the Apache County Stock Growers Association."

"Wal, we heard yer story. What're yer doin' chasin' murderers on Apache land?"

"It's for murder and grand larceny. He was part of the Clanton crew. He was a rustler and a murderer. Had a tip from Charlie Thomas out on the head of Eagle Creek that he mighta been over to the Rio Bonito. Thought he might be rustlin' reservation cattle. So, we went over there to find out. He murdered a fine man. Ike Ellinger. A rancher from over toward Socorro."

"Uh-huh."

The deputy marshal stepped forward and offered his hand. He was tall and lean with an oversized handlebar mustache that made his face look smaller than it was. "Joe Turner," he said.

"J.V. Brighton." They shook hands and the deputy's eyes widened a hair.

"Heard 'bout yer. Twas 'bout a month ago yer kilt Ike Clanton. Didn't yer?"

Jake was starting to feel a little uneasy so he just nodded his head yes.

"Wal, Marshal Meade might like to meet yer. Think yer might be up for that?"

"Depends. Why would he want to meet me?"

"For a job," Turner chuckled.

Jake stared at him for a long minute but, kept his expression stoic. It was a curious thing. Him a deputy U.S. marshal? "Maybe. I'm in Springerville. Got a saloon and blacksmith shop there."

"So. Detective work yer hobby?"

"No. I got past 'spereience. Twas asked to do it."

The deputy looked at Jake with a curious expression and said, "Where you hail from?"

Jake stared hard at him for a few seconds and said, "Texas." Nobody said anything else, so Jake said to the corporal, "Yer got that paperwork ready for me to sign?"

"Right here. Just make yer mark on that line there." He pointed at a line on the document. Jake picked up the paper, read it over, and signed his name on the line and printed it underneath.

"Much obliged," he said. "Any place to get a room here for a couple a nights?"

He got directions, then went into town to get Jasper settled in the livery and himself in a house that had rooms to let. On the second morning he restocked at the general store and started out on the long ride back to Springerville.

SEVEN
POLITICS • 1887

FIVE DAYS LATER, he rode into Springerville and stopped at his shop. He walked in and saw his hired man sweating over the forge with a heavy piece of metal. The fellow didn't see Jake because he was totally involved in the piece he was working on, so Jake stayed back and watched him work. The man pulled the piece out of the forge, and it sizzled red-hot in the tongs as he transferred it to the anvil. As he began to shape it with his hammer red sparks flew off with every blow of the steel mallet in his hand. Mentally, Jake fell in with the rhythm of the swing of the hammer and could almost feel the hot soft metal give way to the blows and take on the shape it was destined to become. He felt as if he were back in the shop again plying his simple but skill-demanding trade, and there was a mild yearning in his being to return to the forge and the anvil. He was sort of dreaming along like that when the hiss of steam brought him back to the present moment and, when he saw the piece come out of the water, he said, "Howdy, Abner. How's it goin'?"

Abner jumped a little but held on tight to the tongs. "Oh. Howdy, boss. Yer startled me a bit there. Didn't see yer come in."

"Don't let me interrupt yer work. I just got back into town and thought I'd stop in and see how things are goin'."

"Oh. We're holdin' on. Got two jobs behind this one."

"Okay. Well keep up the good work. I got a git up to the house."

"Yes, sir. Well, welcome home."

He stopped in at the saloon to talk to Willie to see how things went in his absence. All was doing fine, so he went on home and put Jasper up for a good long rest. Mary Jane came out to the stable, sneaked up behind him and said, "Well look what the cat drug in."

Jake, startled, said, "Yow! Yer 'bout scared the pants off a me."

"That wouldn't bother me none," she said huskily as she wrapped her arms around him and hugged him tight. "Missed you."

"Yeah. I missed yer too. Glad to be home." He hugged her tight and planted a big one on her eager lips. Then he finished with Jasper, gave him a piece of hard candy, stripped, pulled down his union suit, and while still with his boots on, washed up, and toweled off with the towel she handed him. He took Mary Jane by the hand and they skipped off to the house.

After their romp in the bedroom, they sat at the table sipping whiskey. "Well, tell me what happened," Mary Jane said solemnly. "I can tell yer broodin' 'bout something. Yer weren't exactly a ruttin' bull in bed."

"Jeez, Mary Jane. Yer don't have to be so, so, so…."

"I'm sorry. Don't mean to hurt your feelings. It's not that important to me anyhow. You are all I care about." She grasped his hand and squeezed tight while she smiled all her love at him. "Love you way too much to do you any kind of wrong."

"Me too. And you're right," he said admittedly as he dropped his head and gazed at the tabletop. "I got a lot on my mind." He paused and took a deep breath. "Had to kill another man. That makes eleven," He looked up at her with eyes full of remorse mixed with a pleading for he didn't know what.

"Renfro?" Jake nodded his head yes. "Was he gonna shoot you?"

"Yeah, I had the drop on him and he still went for his gun. Had to shoot him."

"I understand how you feel, honey. Don't matter that he was a murderer who killed who knows how many more men than Ellinger and sure woulda killed you too. He was still a human being whose life you had to take, even though it was at the call of the Almighty. His time was up."

Jake brightened a little and said, "Yeah. That's right. I got a keep things in what-a-they-call-it?"

"Perspective."

"Yeah. Perspective. That way I won't get so melancholy." He smiled at her. "And you might be lookin' at a future deputy U.S. marshal."

Mary Jane's eyes widened and her smile broadened with a hint of reserve. "What's this about?" she said over the rim of her glass as she sipped some whiskey.

"Wal, I ran into a deputy out a Tucson who heard my story of the Renfro shootin', and he thought the marshal might want to talk to me about a job. How's that?"

"Wow. That's quite an honor but," her countenance darkened, "you know I don't like all this dangerous lawman work, so I can't be overjoyed. But if you are happy, I am happy." She raised her glass and said, "Here's how."

"Here's how." And they clinked glasses. "I'm goin' up to La Cienega Ranch day after tomorrow to see Clark 'bout that thousand-dollar reward. Give Jasper and me a day to rest up."

———————————

"SINCE THE SHOOTIN' happened on the reservation, I had to leave Renfro's body at Fort Thomas. Made my report and signed the federal paperwork. It's all in the record down there. I don't have no corpus delicti, but I got a record of it on file." Jake grinned and sipped his sweet tea. He and Al Clark sat on the porch of the La Cienega Ranch house. Both their glasses were about half empty when Jake finished his story. Clark gave him a slight cordial smile, and Jake's grin faded to a frown. He said with a certain anticipatory curiosity. "Now, I'm here to collect my thousand."

"Yes. Well, I don't have the cash on hand. I will have to wire Ellinger for it. Take a few days. But... maybe we better keep quiet about this for a while. What with that killing up on Eagle Creek, the horse thieves Charlie Thomas shot, and Clanton and now Renfro. There's been a lot of killing, and I feel like people are getting nervous about it."

"Why would they be nervous? We're cleanin' out the murderers and thieves for them. Think they'd be happy."

"I'm getting ready to ship a herd to Springer, New Mexico. Why don't we wait until I return before we make any announcement?"

"You gonna have my money before you leave?"

"Oh, yes."

"Cuz I did recover your twenty steers and rid the Territory of the Clantons and the murdering Renfro. Exacting revenge for Ellinger."

"Yes. Yes. Don't worry. I'll deliver it to you personally when Ellinger wires it in."

"All right, then. Wal. Reckon I better mosey."

Jake rode out in the direction of Springerville and doubled back in a wide loop toward St. Johns. He came into town and stopped at the M'Cormick House where he stabled Jasper and got a room for the night. Then he went over to the Monarch for a drink. George Powell was there and a few other fellows Jake knew. He bellied up and shot the bull with them for a while. In the course of their jawing, he learned that the correspondent for the *Apache County Critic* out of Holbrook was in town. He stayed for a couple more drinks, then he headed to the café for supper.

After supper he stepped out onto the boardwalk, wiped off the sweatband of his hat with his bandanna, put on his hat, stuffed his bandanna into his pants pocket, lit a cigar and walked the short distance down to the stables at the M'Cormick House. There, he sat down with his back against the wall of Jasper's stall and cleared away the straw to bare dirt where he could ash his cigar. Last thing he wanted was to start a fire and burn down the town. As soon as he sat Jasper nickered and pushed his nose against Jake's shoulder. Without even thinking about it Jake pulled a piece of hard candy from his coat pocket and held it up for Jasper who nibbled it off his hand.

"Well, Jasper, ol' buddy. I got a suspicion I ain't gonna git paid for Renfro," he said out loud. "I think I need some insurance and that *Critic* correspondent is probably the feller to gimme it." After the second piece of hard candy he gave Jasper he had to move away so Jasper couldn't pester him anymore. He sat brooding a while longer, then stood up, gave Jasper another piece of candy and stroked his neck while he munched it. After that he walked out of the stable, ground his cigar butt into the dirt with the toe of his boot and went upstairs to his room. He kicked off his boots, stripped down to his union suit, opened the window for some air, warm though it was, propped up the pillows on the bed, picked up his dime novel of one of the Old Sleuth adventures, flopped onto the bed and by the light from the window absorbed himself in the detective story.

In the morning at breakfast he spied the *Critic* correspondent sitting at a table with J.F. Wallace, the *Herald* manager. Jake paced himself so he could stay up with them and pay his tab the same time they did. They all caught the others' attention and smiled and nodded greetings. The two newspaper men walked out of the café, and ten seconds later Jake did, too. He walked casually at a distance behind them and observed them both go into the *Herald* office. Across the street was the general store, so he walked over, bought a newspaper while keeping an eye out across the street, and came out and sat in one of the chairs on the boardwalk shaded by the overhead cover. Two hours went by and finally the correspondent came out of the office and immediately headed for the doors of the general store. Jake stood up and said, "Howdy, William."

"Hello, J.V.," came the reply with a mild curious expression.

Jake faced him squarely and in serious tone of voice and countenance said, "I don't wanna beat around the bush so I'm givin' you the exclusive on this. I killed Lee Renfro. I'm stayin' at M'Cormick's. Come to my room in five minutes and I'll give you the whole story."

"Er... All right. I'll be there."

Jake tipped his hat and walked away smartly. Five minutes later he answered the light knock at his door. Jake ushered in the correspondent and looked down the empty hall to his right and to his left and shut the door. He pulled a chair over for William to sit in next to the bureau and sat down on the bed across from him.

"I give you first shot at the story on the condition that you do not print it until I say it is okay. Do I have your word?"

"Yes, but why all the secrecy?"

"I don't know. Certain people want it that way."

William opened a large notebook, propped it on his knee, opened his fountain pen, poised it to write and said, "Okay. Shoot. So to speak." He made a small grin with a little chuckle.

"Well, I was workin' as a special agent for the stock raisers' association to catch rustlers. As you know, I got Ike Clanton, and Phin Clanton was arrested. All the rest of the gang hightailed it outta the county except for Lee Renfro. I got word that he was out on the Rio Bonito so I went lookin' for him." Jake laid out the whole story for him in detail.

J.V. BRIGHTON WAITED a week and there still was no word from Clark, so he decided to ride on over to the La Cienega Ranch and find out what was going on. He found one of the hands in the barn.

"Howdy," he said. "Al around?"

The hand looked up from his saddle work and said, "Howdy. Nah. He's over to Springer, New Mexico."

Jake held his emotion in check and said, "When's he comin' back?"

"Should be 'bout a week, I reckon."

"When he gits back, could you tell him J.V. Brighton was lookin' for him?"

"Will do."

"Obliged." Jake vaulted into the saddle, made an angry ride straight to St. Johns and lunged through the doors of the *Herald* office. William, the *Critic* correspondent was there.

"You can release the whole damn story," he said loudly.

"What happened?" William asked.

"Never you mind. Just print it."

When Jake returned to Springerville, there was a telegram waiting for him. Next morning he was tying his saddlebags and bedroll to his saddle. Mary Jane handed him a slab of bacon wrapped up in butcher paper and he stuffed it into one of the bags. Then he turned to her and said solemnly, "Don't know exactly what Marshal Meade has in mind, so I don't know how long I'll be gone. You'll wait for me, won't you?" He grinned.

Mary Jane threw her head back and laughed heartily. "Well, I might ride out for the big city of Albuquerque if you take too long gettin' back." He snatched her up and kissed her passionately then held her back, gazed into her eyes and just loved her with his unabashed expression of affection. Without another word he stepped into the saddle, clicked up Jasper, and headed south out of town.

IT WAS EARLY morning and already hot. Jake walked into Sheriff Crawford's office in Solomonville and found him playing solitaire and drinking a cup of coffee. Jake arrived in town the day before for a pre-arranged meeting with U.S. Marshal Meade. "Howdy, Sheriff."

"Howdy, yerself. How's the ride down?"

"Not bad. Gittin' used to it," he said with a smile. "He here yet?"

"Not yet. Probably he'll git off the train at Bowie and ride up here. Should be around noon. Wanna play some rummy to kill the time?"

"All right. Penny a point?"

"A real gambler, huh? Okay. Penny a point. Got a pencil and pad right here."

Jake was down twenty cents when U.S. Marshal William K. Meade rode up. They heard his horse snorting, pawing the dirt and grinding his bit, so Jake got up and looked out the window. He saw the badge and that is all he needed to see. "Wal. This is lookin' purty good right outta the chute. Marshal saved my bacon or yer could a been into me for a bunch," Jake said with a laugh and Sheriff Crawford joined in.

"Wal, I didn't tell yer, but I got a purty good repatation when it comes to rummy."

"Cain't catch any rustlers, though," Marshal Meade said as he walked in the door.

"Can. When they ain't on federal land," the sheriff growled with a sour look as he re-shuffled the cards.

"Wal, you go on and play your cards. We got business to transact; real lawman business." Then he turned to Jake, "Marshal Bill Meade," he said and held out his hand to Jake for a shake. He was an average-look-ing feller with a black mustache and hair, deadpan eyes, and solemn facial expression with a down-turned mouth. "Let's git some dinner. It's been a long time since breakfast." He held the door open for Jake who looked back at the sheriff as he went out.

"Yer don't know what real lawman work is cuz yer spendin' all yer time politikin'," Crawford said.

Meade and Jake walked about five paces and Meade said a little too loud, "We need more like John Slaughter down in Cochise County. Now, there's a lawman for you. When we sit down for dinner, I'll tell you what I have in mind for you." Before that, though, he interrogated Jake on his politics to which Jake admitted he didn't have any which seemed to throw Meade into a tizzy. So, Jake made attempts to avoid the topic, difficult though it was.

Finally, Jake said, "Sheriff Crawford seemed like a purty capable feller and he was a big help to me in the Clanton pursuit."

"Oh, he's alright and he is a Democrat. I just like to needle him."

"What'd yer have in mind fer me?" Jake said to get off the subject. He slurped up a big spoonful of chili and bit off a hunk of tortilla.

Meade wiped his mustache on a napkin and said, "I heard about how you took care of Ike Clanton and Lee Renfro. I got a feller I need catching. Name is Mark Cunningham. He's been rustling cattle off the San Carlos and the Fort Apache reservations. He's got a ranch right on the border of the San Carlos, and he goes across all the time to steal cattle." He stopped and scooped up some chili, twice, plus a chomp of tortilla and when he swallowed it, he washed it down with a big gulp of coffee. The coffee dripped from his mustache in tiny beads. "He's here in Solomonville all the time, and I need someone to catch him and arrest him, and I ain't got a deputy to spare so I thought I could employ a man of your apparent talent.

"You got a warrant?"

"Nah."

"How am I gonna arrest him without a warrant?"

"You got a get the evidence then arrest him and file the complaint.

I'll make you a special deputy U.S. marshal. You ain't sworn in. You're appointed by me and it is a temporary position depending on how good you do. You interested?"

"What's the pay? My wife will want to know." Jake grinned.

Meade did not. "Pays sixty a month plus expenses. You provide your own saddle, firearms, gear, and horses. So, are you interested?"

"Reckon I'll give it a whirl." Jake smiled friendly-like.

Meade did, too. "Good. You'll have to come with me back to Tucson to do the paperwork. Then you can come back here and catch that varmint Cunningham."

WHEN THE TUCSON to El Paso train stopped at Bowie Station, Jake jumped down from the coach and hurried to the stables where he had put up Jasper while he was in Tucson. There were black clouds building up over the mountains to the north and he wanted to beat the rain to Solomonville. It was hot and sticky and a new swarm of flies was everywhere. Jake and Jasper were loping away on the trail by midday and just barely staying ahead of the flies. Every time Jake reined Jasper back to a trot they caught up, swarmed around them and started biting. Jasper swished his tail wildly, crow-hopped and kicked to get them off of him. Jake swatted with his hat and that raised a sweat only to send the flies into more of a frenzy. They stepped back up to a lope and stayed at that pace until a stiff breeze kicked up. That kept the flies away so they could slow back to a trot and a few restful walks.

They traveled through the barren dirt, sagebrush, and the sparse juniper while the thunder clouds approached closer and closer. The breeze became a light wind and in another half hour it was a gale as the thunderstorm bore down on them. Dirt and tumbleweeds were flying everywhere and day was turning to night. Jake navigated by sense of direction alone, generally bearing north, because he could not see more than fifty feet in front of him. He was worried about going off the edge of some unseen gully or low mesa so he reined

Jasper to a walk and they picked their way slowly. Lightning flashes and the rumble of thunder were around them, and now he was worried about being struck by lightning. Luckily, they came upon an overhang of boulders and huddled under the rocks. The great shafts of brilliant electric white with streaking lacy strands shot from the black cloud and blasted the ground all around where they were holed up. It hissed, snapped, and exploded in a brilliant white flare. The hair of Jasper's mane and forelock stood straight up and he desperately wanted to bolt and run for his life, but Jake stayed in the saddle and held him back with a strong grip on the reins. When the rain came, Jasper surrendered because it was not just rain. It was a burst from the clouds of a sheer wall of water, and there was no seeing through it. It was like looking at a roaring waterfall. Little streams of water began pouring down the rocks on either side of them. In front of them and a little below a spontaneous fast-moving stream of muddy water suddenly welled up and surged past. Jake crossed himself and thanked his guardian angel for helping him find the small place of refuge they had ducked into.

The downpour lasted twenty minutes. As the storm moved away to the southwest, the sun, sitting low on the horizon, shone through the sheets of rain so that it looked like a colorful drapery of orange-red hanging in the sky underneath the black cloud. In but a little while it all faded in the distance and the sunshine returned to the desert. "Whew, Jasper," Jake said. "Thank our guardian angel for savin' us from that devil storm. Let's git on up to Solomonville. Looks like another is on the way."

Jasper jumped the flooding stream almost all the way across, but came up short and almost lost his footing. He got it back and scrambled out of the gully. They headed north at a lope but were slowed up every now and then by fresh-cut streams of muddy flash flood water, several of which were tumbling pretty good-sized rocks along in their current. Jake had to carefully pick where and how to cross and avoid quicksand as well.

They were about two miles from Solomonville and Jake started to think they were gonna make it without getting wet, even though there was black cloud and lightning all around them. Then he cursed himself as he felt the first drop of rain on his face, stopped and shrugged into his slicker. In two minutes they were caught in the open in the middle of a heavy shower of rain. They trudged through it and came to the livery barn, went in and were thankfully out of the rain.

"Well, lookee who's here!" exclaimed the stableman.

"Howdy, agin," Jake said. "A course I need some burlap to rub down my horse." He shook out of his slicker, shrugged off his suspenders, took off his shirt, unbuttoned his union suit and pulled the top down to his waist.

"Got wet, huh?" He turned his head and spat out a stream of tobacco juice.

"Sweat."

"Uh-huh. Them slickers ain't the coolest thing in the summer. Here's yer burlap. Same rates as last time."

"Okay. Obliged. Need to git my saddle on a tree to dry out. Yer got any open in the saddle room?" he asked as he uncinched the saddle.

"Right over there. Got three empty trees. Yer can have yer pick."

"And my saddle blanket and bedroll?"

"Wal, probably best to lay them out in the shop. I keep the forge goin' all the time so it's purty warm in there."

"Obliged agin. I'll pay extra for the special handlin'."

"Aw, shucks. No extra charge fer doin' nuthin'."

Jake smiled and pulled the saddle off Jasper.

IN THE MORNING, after he fed and watered Jasper and had his own breakfast he saddled up and rode out to the Cunningham ranch. The saddle was not entirely dry and soon his britches and union suit were damp. But he figured as the day wore on they would dry out before he got a rash.

He purposely circled around the ranch headquarters and out onto the range of the ranch. It wasn't long and he came across a bunch of yearling and two-year-old Longhorn steers. They all had fresh Cunningham Circle MC brands on them. No doubt they were reservation cattle, but how to prove it? They could always claim them as mavericks. Gonna have to git some testimony, he decided. He took note of his position with his compass by triangulating bearings to prominent features of the terrain. He wrote them in his notebook and rode out.

Back in Solomonville he tied off Jasper at the sheriff's office and walked in the door to be met by Sheriff Crawford and one of his deputies. The sheriff looked grave, but Jake said howdy just the same. "Sorry, J.V., but I got a warrant for yer arrest."

"What're yer talkin' 'bout? Who's the affiant?"

"The what?"

"Who filed the complaint?"

"Oh. That would be Mark Cunningham himself. Claims you murdered Ike Clanton."

"Lemme see that." Jake snatched the warrant out of Crawford's hand and read it over quickly. "It's dated day before yesterday. He must of known I was comin' after him. He don't know me, and I don't know him. So, how'd he know I was after him?" Jake glared at Crawford suspiciously.

With the innocence of a cherub written all over his face he said, "I ain't got any ideer. I never said nuthin'. Yer ain't gonna make trouble, are yer?"

"I'll go quietly long as yer promise me yer'll wire Marshal Meade 'bout this."

"Oh, yes sir. I surely will. Yer'll pay for the telegram, a course."

Jake ignored him and said, "You can come with me or send your deputy so as I can put up my horse at the stables. And, the county'll pay for it, a course," he said with some sarcasm.

———————————

THINGS WERE SLOW in Graham County so Jake's hearing was set

for August 8. It lasted all of five minutes and the charges were dismissed against Jake because Cunningham failed to show and give testimony. Jake and Deputy U.S. Marshal Will Smith from Yuma, who was sent by Meade to see what was going on, joined up and left immediately to recover the cattle Jake had discovered at the Cunningham Ranch, but they could not find Cunningham.

"Wal, let's bunch up these critters and git 'em back to the reservation," Jake said as he and Smith looked out over the range where the cattle were grazing. "Yeah. I suspect that Cunningham is being protected by someone of influence around here," Jake said as he pulled his hat down to block the sun. "I heard rumors that they's tryin' to get a grand jury up against me. Can't let it stop me. They's a lot a rustlers down this way and I aim to catch 'em."

"Yep." Will said and spurred his horse off to start rounding up the cattle Jake had pointed out.

SINCE HE WAS a federal officer now, Jake managed to talk Sergeant Whitehead into letting him bunk in a vacant room of the NCO quarters of Fort Thomas. That gave him an address and a central location for working the reservation and Graham County, which is the section of the Tucson District that Marshal Meade wanted him to work. As time went by Mary Jane sent him clippings from the *Herald* and Critic. Both newspapers had turned against him and were spewing vituperative epitaphs about him throughout the month of August. The *Critic* correspondent called him a hired assassin, a hired thug constituting himself judge, jury, and executioner and advocated for a grand jury investigation. But the one that stuck the most in Jake's craw was the published denial of the Apache County Stock Raisers Association of any involvement with J.V. Brighton of any sort. "Yella belly traitors," he muttered to himself. That meant of course he would not see any reward money either from the Association or Ellinger. "They got what they wanted and left me out in the cold." He was talking to himself in his room. "Lucky I got this deputy marshal job. Stay down here for awhile. Won't run into those Apache County cowards." And he took another drink of whiskey.

He devoted his time to investigating and catching rustlers, recovering stolen livestock, and teaching the Apaches how to brand cattle. After a little over two months away from Mary Jane he decided to go on up to Springerville for a visit. Marshal Meade gave him some official documents to deliver to the Navajo Reservation Indian agent who agreed to meet Jake in St. Johns.

"WELL, DEPUTY U.S. Marshal Brighton," Mary Jane said with a little smile as she eyed Jake over the rim of her coffee cup. "Sounds like you've been busy."

"Yeah. But it's good to be here at home with you, my love. And no thanks to these yahoos around here. Them and that so-called Equal Rights party. They's hornswoggled me good. That Clark is the worst of 'em all. He played me like a fiddle." Jake screwed up his face as if he were being tortured.

"Maybe he didn't have any choice. Maybe he got played."

"I don't think so. Where the almighty dollar is king, there is treachery. Oh, well, what is done is done. But yer can be sure I won't be dealin' with 'em anymore." He took a drink of coffee from his cup and looked to Mary Jane for confirmation.

"Yeah. I think you are right. Besides, we got other problems."

Mary Jane got up and went to her big sideboard and picked up two ledger books. She plopped them down on the table in front of Jake and indicated that he should open them and look at the books of their businesses, which he did. Mary Jane watched while he studied the entries, and after about fifteen minutes, he looked up and said, "This ain't lookin' too good. We barely got our heads above water. Lucky I got my marshal salary."

She went around and sat in a chair across from him and leaned in on her crossed arms. "It is," she said tersely. "But you know I don't like you being a lawman. Regular old detective, not a stock detective, is all right. Lawman ain't. Even though I am proud a you and glad you are happy, you know I don't like it."

"Yeah. I gotta say I am gittin' kind a tired a killin' folks, bad as they are and deservin' it." He paused and pulled a cigar from his shirt pocket and a match from his vest. He was about to strike the match on the tabletop when he got a don't-you-dare look from Mary Jane, so he quickly averted and scratched it on the underside of the table. The cigar well lit, he said, "I met Virgil Earp in Tucson. You know who he is?"

"Think I heard of him."

"Well, he's Wyatt Earp's brother and was in that gunfight in Tombstone a few years back. He's the marshal in Colton, California, now and he was tellin' me all 'bout the opportunity in California."

"That lawman opportunity?"

"Not altogether. I was thinkin' maybe we ought a pull up stakes here, sell out lock, stock, and barrel and see what we can find in California. Sound interestin'?"

"Anything that gets that badge off your chest sounds good to me." She had a grin, but he knew she was dead serious. "You thinking about selling even our furniture and all? What about Jasper?"

"Yeah. We'll need the grubstake. Don't know how much we could get for it, but every little bit helps. We can always rent if we need to. Jasper? Wal, I hate to, but I'll probably give him to Ben Irby over the Hashknife. At least that way he'll be with Texans working stock." She looked skeptical but still smiled. Jake knew she would accept almost anything to get him off the range.

"I got to ride up to St. Johns tomorrow and deliver some documents. You want to ride along?"

"Sure."

The next afternoon, late, they walked together into the Monarch Saloon and Billiards establishment in St. Johns. Jake had his shiny marshal's badge pinned prominently on his coat lapel and was resoundingly greeted by all sorts of those at the bar and billiard tables. Even the poker players got up to slap his back. It was the first opportunity they had to show their appreciation for his work in helping to clear the outlaw pox from the Round Valley and surrounding ranches. Mary Jane deliberately faded into the background and let Jake have his day. At least the common folk appreciated what he had done, even if he wasn't all that altruistic about it.

In the morning after they finished their breakfast, they walked down to the livery to retrieve their horses and while they were saddling up Jake said, "Let's just walk down Main Street leadin' the horses and say howdy to the folks." And they did, waving and saying hello to folks as, with Jasper and the other horse clopping along behind, they passed the blacksmith shop, café, saloons, barber shop, general store, meat market, marshal's office, dentist and doctor offices, back past the hotel, the Catholic Church and LDS Church, where a little gathering of Mormons waved and called out their hello and thank-you. "Maybe I should run for sheriff in eighty-eight," Jake said with a grin.

But when they came to the courthouse Jake stopped and gazed at it for a minute, dropped his head and slowly turned it side to side. Mary Jane curled her arm inside his and pressed in close while Jasper nudged his back with his nose and nickered softly. Jake pulled a piece of hard candy from his coat pocket, smiled at Mary Jane and Jasper as he gave the candy to him. Then he said, "Let's git on outta this place." They mounted and rode out of town.

But as it was, the Thanksgiving, November 24, edition of the *St Johns Herald* reported:

J.V. Brighton, Deputy United States Marshal, came in last Tuesday, afternoon, and was around town shaking hands with his numerous friends.

PART II

ONE

ADIÓS, ARIZONA, HELLO, CALIFORNIA • 1888-1892

"SO YER FIXIN' to head out for California, eh?" queried Ben Irby, superintendent of the Aztec Land and Cattle Company's Hashknife Ranch, as he and Brighton walked toward the barn at the ranch headquarters. Jake led Jasper behind him by the reins.

"Yeah. It's time to cash outta Apache County. Startin' to git in the same ol' rut I was in Texas. Yer know, killin' bad men." He glanced at Irby with a weak smile. "S'pose I got yer to thank fer that."

"Me? What'd I do? I hardly know yer." Irby said incredulously with a slight arch of his eyebrows.

"Yer told Alfred Clark all about my stock detective history in Texas, and he hung the carrot in front a my nose and snatched it away."

"Yeah, well then, I didn't know yer wanted to keep it quiet until I got yer letter. I didn't say nuthin' after that."

"I know. Don't hold it agin yer." He gave Irby a slight pat on the back. "And I am much obliged for yer takin' in Jasper. It's good he'll be with Texans. He was born in Texas."

"Aw, my pleasure. If he's half as good a stock horse as yer say he is, we'll be the ones who are obliged."

"He's picky 'bout who rides him, though. Been known to throw more than a few cowboys. The way to git on his good side is through his sweet tooth. He loves that orange-flavored hard candy. I have some left. Here, take it," he said as he pulled a bag out of his coat and handed it to Irby.

"Spoilt him, huh?"

"Sorta."

"Wal, he'll be fine. We take good care a our horses here on the Hashknife. If he don't cozy up to anybody for a while, that's fine. We're patient."

"Thank yer kindly."

"Yer know, I know a feller out in California who's bossin' a ranch for that giant Miller and Lux Company. Yer ever heared a 'em?"

"Yeah. Virgil Earp told me 'bout 'em."

"Oh, that's right. Yer was a deputy U.S. Marshal. Ain't that right?"

"Yeah. It was only temporary. Cleaned out a lot a the rustlin' down in Graham County and the San Carlos Reservation. Afterwards, the marshal said he didn't have the budget anymore to keep me on."

"Yeah. Well, let me scratch out a note a recommendation for you to take to my friend in California."

"Okay. But don't say nuthin' 'bout my stock detective 'spierence."

"Ain't that the point a yer goin' out there?"

"Nah. I'm outta that business. Just say I'm honest, reliable, and a hard worker. That's good 'nuff."

"All right. I'll go over to the office and be right back."

Jake pulled the saddle and blanket off of Jasper's back and carried them over to an empty tree in the tack room. He slipped the bridle off Jasper's nose and hung a feedbag of oats on him, which he immediately dove into and started munching joyfully. Jake found a couple of curry brushes and set to work brushing the big black-and-white paint all over, not just his back. Then he picked up a comb and pulled it through his golden tail and mane. By the time he was done, Jasper looked as handsome as could be. He pulled off the oat bag and brought a bucket of water to him and let him suck down as much as he wanted. When the bucket was empty, he set it aside, wrapped his arms around Jasper's neck, and hugged him tight. "Wal, ol' pard," he said low and quiet like. "This is the end of the trail for us. Gonna miss yer, big feller. You been the best...." He couldn't go on because the lump in his throat took his voice away. And Jasper nickered and reached around to nuzzle his leg. He didn't even sniff for candy while he rubbed his cheek against Jake's leg, who at that moment had a tear streaking down his cheek. A tear he quickly wiped away when Ben Irby came in the barn.

"Yer 'bout ready?" Irby called out. "I got a mare saddled for you at the rail."

"Obliged, Ben. I'll leave her for you at the Holbrook livery, like we said. Mind if I put ol' Jasper out in the lot?"

"Nah. Go ahead. He might as well git to know everyone right from the git-go. Here's the note. Feller's name is Gus Reynolds on the Santa Rita Ranch in Merced County. He's a Texan. Been out there three or four years. Teachin' 'em how to punch cows," he said with a grin.

"No offense, but I hate cowboyin'."

"None taken. They farm on that ranch, too, yer know. Yer got any farmin' 'speerience?"

"Yeah. I do, plus the blacksmithin'."

"There yer go. Ought ta be somethin' for yer ta do there." He walked off to where the mare was hitched and waited for Jake. A cowboy and his horse needed to be left alone at a time like this.

Jake led Jasper out to the corral where there were about seven other horses, opened the gate, and closed it behind Jasper. He unbuckled and slipped the halter off of Jasper's head and noticed his ears were pricked up, but he wasn't paying any attention at all to the other horses. Jake opened the gate, and Jasper tried to go through with him, but Jake pushed him back and closed the gate. The big black-and-white paint hung his head over the top rail and nickered loud with deep-toned gurgles in his throat. Jake pulled out two pieces of hard candy from his pocket and held them in his palm in offering to Jasper. But Jasper did not even sniff the candy and threw his head back in protest. "Wal, that's the first time yer ever did that," Jake said to him. "Yer might be takin' this harder than me." And he hugged him again. "Best to git on outta here," Jake said just above a whisper.

He turned and hurried over to where Irby stood. As he went, he covered his ears with his hands. Jasper was whinnying for him. He took the mare's reins from Irby and jumped into the saddle. Jasper whinnied louder. Jake looked back at him, teared up, and looked at Irby who said, "Good luck to ya." Jake reined the mare around and spurred her away, not looking back. Jasper flattened his ears, flared his nostrils, reared and crashed the gate and kicked at the top rail of the fence but, it was too stout and would not budge. He was trapped, and his pardner of five years was leaving him. After no short while, he gave up the thrashing and went off by himself in the lot and stood staring in the direction Jake had gone. Then he hung his head and moaned pitifully.

Jake kept the mare at a trot all the way to Holbrook. On the way he thought a lot about Jasper and the scrapes they had been in together and gotten out of together. If it wasn't for Jasper, Wes Wilson probably would have been killed twice. Once by that Jonesboro feller and for certain by that weasel Vern Conroy. It was Jasper's speed that got Jake where he needed to be to save Wes's life. And again the tears came. This time he couldn't stop them as he sobbed for several minutes. Finally, he got to Holbrook and stabled the mare where he paid the stable boy two bits to feed, water, and curry her. Then he walked across the dirt road to the boardwalk and on to The Cottage Saloon, where he stopped and took down two whiskies in two swallows, wiped his mustache on his coat sleeve, and left for the Holbrook House where Mary Jane waited for him to arrive.

Jake opened the door to their room where he found Mary Jane sitting in a chair thumbing through the Montgomery Ward catalog. She stood up when he entered, tossed the catalog on the bed, and stared at Jake with compassion written all over her face. He went to her; she went to him. They embraced, and Jake held her tight. "How'd it go?" she whispered in his ear.

"Hard," he said. "As hard as losin' you or Wes."

"I am so sorry for you. And for Jasper."

"Maybe we ought to bring him with us. I don't know."

She leaned back away from him and looked intently into his eyes. In a soft but firm voice she said, "I know it is very hard to lose a loved one. I've had to do it three times with the children I lost. But, in time we get over it and get on down the trail. As I said when we went over this ground before, I would have liked to bring Jasper along too. But we are looking for things for you to do that don't require a horse. Ain't that right?"

"Yeah," Jake said remorsefully as he stared at the floor.

"Besides, look at this in the paper. Some German's invented a horseless carriage. Not too far off and we won't even be using horses anymore," she said in an attempt to be cheery.

"Yeah. Okay, let's have some supper." He tried to look reassuring with a meek smile but apparently was not very convincing.

"You better?" Mary Jane asked.

"Yeah, I'll get over it. Let's go."

———————

IN THE PITCH-dark of morning an hour before dawn Jake caught two mules in the lot and slipped halters over their ears. Two other hands already had their mules at the feed trough.

"Mornin', Steve. Alvin," Jake said as he led the mules up to the trough where he had already forked in their first ration of hay.

"Mornin', J.V.," Alvin said. Steve said nothing.

He tied off the mules so they could chomp the hay but not move away. In the light of the lantern on the ground, he harnessed them up for the day's work. They would be pulling a hay mower all day. When he finished harnessing, he poured in a couple of coffee cans of oats for each of them. "Feels like it's dry enough to start mowin' at first light," Jake said.

"Yep," came the answer from Alvin. Again Steve said nothing. Then Jake went to the house.

Amid the soft glow of the oil lanterns on the shelves Mary Jane set Jake's breakfast down on the table in front of him. He set down his coffee mug and dug into the fried eggs, bacon, potatoes, and toast with a modest gusto. "Boy. I know I keep sayin' it, but they's have the best eggs ever here at the Santa Anita."

"Must be the feed," Mary Jane smiled. "Whatcha doin' today?"

"Still mowin' hay. Second cut."

"Well. Be careful. Don't fall off the mower. Might get cut up into little pieces." She grinned.

Jake screwed up his face and looked up at her. He swallowed his mouthful and said, "You don't have to be so colorful."

"Just want to make an impression so you stay safe because you might have another mouth to feed," she smiled mischievously as she leaned back against the sink counter and folded her arms across her chest.

He stopped chewing, swallowed, wiped his mustache with a napkin, scraped his chair back, stood and slowly stepped toward her. He gave her a big question mark look.

"Yup," she said. "'Bout three months along, near as I can figure."

"Yahoo!" Jake called out loudly. "Maybe this time we'll make it." And he pulled her up and swung her a couple of turns around the kitchen. Then he suddenly stopped. "Better go easy," he said. "Don't want to upset the apple cart." He gently patted her tummy. They laughed and enjoyed the moment for a few more minutes until Jake said, "Got my dinner packed?"

"'Course I do. Don't I always?" she said as she put a covered tin lunch pail on the table along with a canteen of water.

Jake smiled, gave her a kiss, and said, "See you at supper." Then he went out into the dark and headed for the side of the barn where the team he had harnessed was licking the last of their oats from their feed troughs. The first faded gray light was beginning to show over the tops of the distant Sierra Mountains. Jake glanced up at them, then tied his lunch pail to the harness of one of the mules, unhitched them, vaulted up onto the back of one of them and started him off down a narrow farm road with the other in tow. The river was behind him and in the early morning air he could smell its particular odor carried on the breeze that tickled the back of his neck. Soon, though, as they came upon a field, the scent of the river was displaced by the aroma of freshly mown hay. Jake looked out over a broad expanse of low rolling hills that appeared to have been painted in gold. Immediately before him was a field of tawny green hay that gently swayed in the breeze. The field was fenced in by barbed wire and hand-split wooden posts with a gate where Jake stopped the mules.

It looked like Steve and Alvin had just started mowing. Jake needed to hurry over and hitch the mules to his mower where he left it at the end of the day before. The other two mowers were staggered and Jake needed to get his in the right position so that three swaths were cut at the same time by the three staggered mowers. He got the mules hitched, tied his lunch pail to a rack on the mower, stepped up onto the rusted steel frame, sat in the polished steel seat of the mower, pulled a lever that dropped the scissor blade parallel to, and four inches above, the ground, released the brake and slapped the mules' backs with the reins. With the blade engaged and scissoring, off they went, mowing hay.

It was a typical summer day that wore on in the San Joaquin Valley. Jake and the other two mowers had opened their umbrellas that were attached to the backs of their seats to shade themselves from the sun, which when it reached its zenith was making the steel of the rigs too hot to touch with bare hands. It was also the time for the dinner break. The mules were unhitched and trotted over to a creek lined in willows, watered and hobbled so they could crop the grass patches beside the willows but not get too far away. The men sat at an opening in the willows on the grassy bank in the shade of great big sycamore trees where Alvin and Jake talked while they ate their dinners. Steve sat off by himself like he always did.

When the sun touched the western hills and the air was cooling the men ended the day's work. They unhitched the mules from the mowers and trotted them back to the lots for the night. When Jake arrived, he saw Alvin rinsing his face in the stock trough and Steve struggling with one of his mules. He got his mules inside the corral and shut the gate behind him. When he turned back around, he saw that Alvin was staring at Steve, who was jerking the mule's halter and slugging it in the neck. Jake charged Steve at a full run, slammed into him, and knocked him off his feet to the ground. The mule backed away and trotted off to a safe corner of the corral. Jake shouted, "What're yer doin'?" He glared at Steve with eyes aflame in anger and body poised for combat.

"Son a bitch tried to kick me," Steve yelled back.

"Ain't no call to beat the animal."

Steve jumped to his feet. "How 'bout I beat you, then?"

He charged Jake with his head low so he could butt him like a bull, but Jake sidestepped him and he flew to the ground again. He sprang up and pulled a big jackknife from his pocket, opened the blade, and brandished the knife at Jake. With his face twisted in a hateful look, he leaped at Jake like a cougar and slashed at his head. Jake backpedaled and tried to duck away, but the sharp blade caught him on the left cheek. A four-inch slice opened up and blood gushed forth from the cut. He pressed his hand against the wound and staggered backwards. Steve moved in, and was about to thrust the blade into Jake's gut, when Jake heard a whang sound and saw Alvin knock Steve silly with a whack to the back of his head with a shovel. Steve dropped the knife and fell face-first to the ground.

Alvin stood over Steve with the shovel across his body at the ready and said, "I don't mind a good knife fight, long as both fighters got knives."

"Much obliged, Alvin. He'd a stabbed me, sure. Might a even kilt me. That woulda upset my wife," Jake said with half a grin.

"You're welcome. Glad you didn't get killed. Wouldn't want Mary Jane to be upset. But you got a get that cut sewed up."

"Yeah. Mary Jane'll do it. She's good at that. Uh-oh. Here comes Gus."

The ranch foreman rode up, sat his horse, pushed his hat back and said, "What's goin' on here?"

Alvin looked at Jake, and Jake looked back at Alvin as if to say he should tell him. "Well, a little skirmish, boss."

Reynolds looked at the unconscious Steve on the ground and at Jake with his hand over his cheek and blood all over it. Then he said, "Looks to be mor'n a little skirmish. He dead?" He nodded toward Steve.

"Don't rightly know, boss. Haven't checked him yet," Alvin said and squatted down and rolled Steve over to see that he was breathing. "Looks like he's still breathin'."

"What happened?"

"Well, you know how Steve is. Said ol' Jinks there tried to kick him, so he was punchin' him in the neck. That ain't right and J.V. knocked him down. He got up with a knife and slashed at J.V. Got him in the cheek and was gonna stab him when I whacked him with that shovel. Ain't a fair fight unless both fellers got knives."

"Uh-huh. Wal, ol' Jinks don't kick for no reason. Brighton, yer better git that cut sewed up. Alvin, throw a pail a water on Steve. See if he comes to."

Steve did not revive. "All right. Let's git him over to the bunkhouse. Got a wire the headquarters. See what they want to do," Gus said as he dismounted. "Can yer make it home all right?" he said to Jake.

"Yeah. I'll be fine. Don't worry 'bout me."

When Jake walked in the door. Mary Jane turned from her sink to greet him, she screamed. "Great balls a fire! What happened to *you?*"

"Got cut in a fight."

"With who?"

"Steve."

"Oh. Yeah. He's a strange one. Let me look at that. Mmm. Still bleedin'." She pulled a clean towel from a shelf under the counter, folded it, and pressed it onto the wound. "Hold that there tight. I'll get some water boilin'."

She had a kettle of water already on the stove keeping it hot so it didn't take long for it to boil. She wiped the cut as clean as she could with the towel and pressed it again with instructions for Jake to hold it. Once the water was boiling, she poured some into a clean pot, opened the ice chest of their icebox, and with an icepick chinked off a fairly good-sized chunk of ice and put it in the pot to cool the water. "Turn your head to the side," she said and began to wash the cut with the towel and cool water. "That's pretty deep. Gonna leave a nice scar." Jake gritted his teeth as she cleaned the wound. She then got a needle and thread from her sewing basket and poured a little boiling water over them. Lastly, she scrubbed her hands good and poured some diluted carbolic acid over the needle and thread and into the cut to anesthetize the wound a little bit.

"That Steve was sluggin' poor old Jinks. Yer know I can't abide cruelty to animals so—"

"Don't talk. Your cheek moves when you talk. It'll throw my seam off line, and I want to keep this as neat as possible so your pretty face isn't too badly marred." She smiled jokingly at him, and Jake rolled his eyes. Then she started stitching, making sure she had plenty of skin and went deep enough to hold the cut closed. Jake groaned and groaned, but never did he yell or scream or anything. He didn't grin, but he did bare it through twenty close-knitted stitches.

When she was finished, Mary Jane stepped back and admired her work. "I always was an expert seamstress," she said with a wry smile. Then she made one last pass with a clean towel and added a little more diluted carbolic acid. The bleeding had been staunched, and she seemed to be satisfied. "There now. We'll bandage that up and you'll be almost as good as new except you'll be sore for a few days. But I'll take care of you."

"Uh-huh. Doubt if Gus'd go along with that. We got hay to mow and now we're short a hand."

"Well, you gotta keep those stitches clean. No dust and the like. And no more fightin'. You're too old for that. Gotta control your temper."

"Aye, aye. Captain," Jake said and saluted her in military fashion.

Steve ended up in a sanitarium down Stockton way, never to be the same again.

JAKE SAT IN the kitchen at the table nursing a cup of coffee while he tried to concentrate on reading the newspaper. He'd been up all night and was pretty rummy. Mary Jane's screams were becoming more intense, and in his concern for her, it was impossible to ignore while nerve-wracking at the same time. It'd been several years since he went through this with his little Martha born in seventy-three to him and his former wife, Matilda. They were both killed in a tornado in Kansas while he was in prison. So, even though it was cold outside, he went out onto the porch, lit up a cigar, and continued to read about the now-famous Nellie Bly and her around the world trip. The news was all about her adventure and the reception upon her return to New Jersey four days ago on January twenty-fifth. It annoyed Jake that they were always behind in hearing the news because it usually took three to four days before the

San Francisco Examiner arrived at the ranch in the mail. Nothing he could do about it, though. He and Mary Jane had been following Nellie Bly's progress on her circumnavigation of the globe. She became a sort of hero for them after they obtained and read her book on her undercover work at the Women's Lunatic Asylum in New York.

Twenty minutes passed and the screaming stopped. Jake listened intently through the walls not knowing if she would start up again or a little baby cry might come out. After a couple of minutes more and no sounds at all, he tossed his cigar and hurried in to the bedroom door where he stopped to listen. He heard the midwife say, "She is a quiet little girl with beautiful skin. Here. You take her." Jake cracked the door and slowly eased it open. "Come on in, Jake. We're all done here. You're the daddy of a new baby girl."

Mary Jane was holding a little bundled up newborn girl and smiling and cooing. "Come over and see her, honey," she said.

"Is she all right? Everything okay?" He smiled down at the baby.

"Yes, she's fine. All perfect. Fingers, toes. Look at these dimples. Want to hold her?"

"Not yet. Too small. Let her git some beef on her so I don't feel like I might break her."

Mary Jane giggled and said, "You're silly."

"We gonna name her what we said if it's a girl?"

"I think so. Don't you?"

"Might as well. Nellie Bly it is. Our little hero, Nellie Bly Brighton."

Three months later Jake stood proudly in his black suit with Nellie Bly, wrapped and dressed in white in his arms and Mary Jane at his side. Gathered around them dressed in their Sunday-go-to-meeting duds were Alvin Best and his wife and Gus Reynolds and his wife. They were centered on the baptismal font of the chapel of the Santa Anita Ranch. A warm and gentle breeze curled its way through the open doors and tickled the back of Jake's neck. The priest reached for Nellie Bly, and Jake handed her over. He proceeded with the rite, sprinkled her with water, and said the words that made Nellie Bly a Christian like her ma and pa.

Afterwards, over at the Brighton house, Mary Jane put on a little reception for everyone. Little, she said, but little it was not. The table was almost spilling over with food.

"Where'd yer git them ribs, J.V.?" Alvin said in between chomps on rib bone.

"Little trick I learned back in Kansas City, which of course yer know is famous for its spareribs. A butcher from Canada was cuttin' ribs from the top of the rib cage between the spine and the spareribs, and they were so tasty and leaner. So I asked Acilino to cut us some racks out a that hog he was butchering. I grilled 'em up this mornin'. And, wah-la. Here yer are."

"Well, they are mighty fine. And so are that wife and daughter a yers, I might say."

Jake looked to Alvin with true appreciation in his expression and said, "Thank you, Alvin, and thanks again for saving me for them."

"Aw, sure. That cut looks like it's gonna leave a pretty manly scar." He grinned and Jake grinned as he rubbed the scar on his face.

"Where'd yer git the name Nellie Bly?"

"Nellie Bly is that famous newspaper woman who just got back from circling the globe. You heard a her, ain't yer?"

"Nope."

"We figgered we would honor her by naming our baby after her."

"Well, I reckon that's fair enough. 'Scuse me, I'm gonna git some more a them beans."

After everyone left, and Jake and Mary Jane were at the sink washing and drying the dishes, Jake said, "Did you read that letter from Ben Irby?"

"No, I haven't."

"Well, he says all is pretty much the same around there. They got a half a foot a snow on the ground right now. Jasper is out of his melancholy, and Irby has taken him as his own. Says they're getting along just fine."

"That's good. Makes you feel better, I bet."

"Sure does."

TWO YEARS LATER, on a clear spring day at dawn, Jake was leading two teams of Belgian draft horses out to the fields to harness up to the harrows for the day's disking. He was riding one of the ranch horses so he could return to the lots once the teams were hitched up and return with a wagonload of seed and equipment for planting. About a half mile from the house his horse stepped in a hole, lurched violently, threw Jake to the ground and fell on top of him. He heard the crack before he felt anything of his right femur snapping in half. Then the horse rolled off him, got up, and ran for the barn. The numbing electric-like tingling running up and down his leg and the jagged bone sticking out through a rip in his pants let him know for sure that his leg was broke. His back hurt bad and he feared it might be broken too. Luckily, the leg wound wasn't bleeding a whole lot so he figured the artery didn't get punctured. He started to toss around trying to figure out what he was going to do when, in just a few minutes, Alvin came running up from the field. "Jake? *Jake!,*" he hollered as he got close. "I seen yer go down. Yer okay? Are yer hurt?"

"My leg's broke. See?" Jake said with a grimace.

"Yer startin' ta blanch. Here," Alvin said as he took off his coat and laid it on Jake. "I better stay with yer a bit. Then I'll git a wagon, cuz yer ain't gonna walk on that leg even with a crutch." Five minutes later Alvin was looking back toward the lots and saw someone coming. "I think it's Ditzen. He was gonna hunt out here today. Yeah, it's him. I'll fetch that wagon and we'll git yer to Doc Wade in Los Banos."

Fourteen miles it was. Three hours of pain from hell as he was jarred constantly and rolled around in the back of the wagon. He passed out twice, and they revived him with splashes of water. Finally, mercifully, they arrived at the doctor's office where they helped him onto an exam table.

"Well, this looks serious, J.V. Lucky for you, I happen to have some ether on hand. It will greatly reduce the pain when I set that compound fracture of your femur. Then I have to sew up that gash. Don't know how well the muscle will heal up. You're gonna be in a splint and on crutches for a good three months."

"Ohhh. Glad to hear it, Doc. Think I could have some ether now?" Jake groaned. "This is worse pain than the gunshot I got in the other leg. And my back is killin' me. Seems like the whole thing is on fire."

"Let me check your backbone and ribs. That hurt? No? You probably got some internal injuries to your kidneys. We'll check your urine when I am done with your leg. Just breathe in these vapors," Doc Wade said as he unscrewed the cap of a brown bottle and held it to Jake's nose. "That's right. Breathe deep." In no time, Jake was smiling, calmly breathing and giggling. "Think I could have some for the ride back to the ranch?" He said with a dumb smile on his face.

After Jake was all patched up, Doc said, "You're gonna have to change this bandage every day for a week and every other day for another week. I put a three-board splint on to immobilize the leg and to allow you to be able to change the bandage without loosening the splint. Those stitches need to come out in two weeks. You should come back for me to do that and have a look at everything to see how you are healing. There is blood in your urine, so your kidneys are definitely injured. Just keep an eye on your urine. If the blood becomes heavier, you get on right back over here. Any questions? No. Okay." Doc gave him crutches and sent him home with Alvin and Ditzen. They helped him outside because he was still woozy.

"Here, let's lift him up on the wagon, Ditz. Don't move yer leg none. I'll pull him up. You hold his leg. There. That's good. Okay. Sit on this pad here we made yer. Now, put your leg on this pile of burlap. There. How's that feel?"

"I feel just fine." Jake smiled and looked a tad bit looney. "Don't fergit to stop by the drugstore and git me some Laudanum. They say I'm a tough one. But that's only if I have to be." Again, he smiled like he was drunk.

Jake grimaced as he stumped up the steps to the porch with Alvin and Ditzen on either side of him. He was more sore from the wagon ride than the fractured leg. Apparently, Mary Jane heard them because she swung open the door, gasped and exclaimed loudly as she wiped her hands on her apron, "Jumping Jehoshaphat. What now?"

"Horse fell on me. Broke my leg."

"Well. My word. Here. Let's get him on the bed."

"I can make it on my own," he said firmly as he hobbled with the crutches to the bedroom and sat down on the bed. "Can you just lift my leg as I lay back? Thanks."

"There. Okay. Thank you, Alvin and Mister...?"

"H.G. Ditzen. I was just over hunting on the ranch when I ran across these two."

"Well, thank you, Mister Ditzen. I guess we can take it from here."

"All righty, then. If you need anything, just holler," Alvin said. "Oh, here. Jake wanted us to get this for him," he said as he handed her the Laudanum.

"How much do we owe you?"

"It were two bucks, but...."

"Nonsense. Don't even say it. If you could wait on the porch, I'll be right out with the money."

She went to the bureau in the bedroom, pulled open a drawer, took out the clothes, lifted the false bottom and retrieved two one-dollar notes. She glanced at Jake on the bed and he nodded his head with a proud smile. "Protect the assets. Good girl," he said.

Mary Jane came back in and Jake said, "Can you spoon me some of that Laudanum? My leg is on fire and my back is killin' me." She did, then went to tend to Nellie Bly.

Two weeks later, Mary Jane was finishing her wash-up and said to Jake, "Today's the day we take you back to Doc Wade to get those stitches out and check you over."

"Nah," he said gruffly. "Ain't gonna do that. You can take 'em out just fine. Ain't no more blood in my urine. He just wants to charge me another office visit. Cost the ranch enough as it is. We're much obliged to Gus and Mister Miller for that. Here." He threw the cover back. "Just give me some more Laudanum and pull 'em out."

"All right. Here you go," she said as she held the spoonful of the opiate to his lips. "Now, that's the last of it, and it's the last you're gonna get. You're startin' to get addicted to this stuff."

"Aw. No, I ain't."

"Yes, you are. And I don't want to hear any more about it." She gave him a very cross look and left the room to retrieve her straight razor and tweezers. She washed them in soap and hot water along with her hands and returned to Jake where she removed the bandage. Gently, she cut the stitches with the razor and pulled them out with the tweezers. They came out nice and easy with no bleeding. "Good," she said. "Now a clean bandage and we are all done."

"Thank you, nurse Mary Jane," Jake said lewdly with a devilish grin. Mary Jane stared at him in disgust and left the room making a show of disposing of the Laudanum bottle.

THREE MONTHS LATER, Jake sat at the kitchen table playing solitaire and with his good leg and foot he gently rocked Nellie Bly who was sitting in her swinging shoe fly rocker. Mary Jane came in with her empty laundry basket and said, "Getting warm out there."

"Yeah. Want to play some rummy? Ain't it 'bout time for me to git this splint off?"

Mary Jane stepped around the table and checked on Nellie Bly, who she gave a little love poke and cooed a smile out of her. "You're such a good little baby," she said lovingly.

"I talked to Gus, and he wants you to go back to see Doc Wade to take off the splint—at ranch expense, of course."

"Wal, I guess we can do that one last time."

The next day, Alvin hitched up ol' Jinks to a buggy for them and off they went to Los Banos. In Doc Wade's exam room after the splint was off and Jake had his britches off, the doc massaged his leg at the fracture point and said, "Any pain? No. Okay." Then he began to manipulate the leg through the normal motions. "Pretty stiff, eh? I'll give you some exercises to loosen that up. Okay. Let's test its weight bearing."

Jake hopped off the table landing on the foot of his good leg and gingerly began to shift his weight to the bad leg. "Got some pain there, Doc."

"Uh-huh. I was afraid of that." Doc Wade stroked his gray goatee and said, "Try to take a step."

Jake did but could only put just a little weight on the bad leg.

"Well, you're gonna have to work through that as best you can. Gradually, it should get better. Use a crutch or cane as much as you need. But you probably won't ever walk without a limp and shouldn't ever ride a horse again."

"That mean I'm a invalid?" Jake said as he looked at Mary Jane with some amount of appeal in his eyes.

"Well, I don't know if I could certify that. But, certainly disabled to some extent."

"I applied for a invalid pension in Kansas back in eighty for my back and kidney and bladder problems from scurvy and dysentery, when I was a prisoner at Andersonville during the Civil War. But I didn't get it. Probably cuz they weren't permanent like this one. This ain't military, though. Oh, well. Let me borrow one a those crutches from yer, Doc."

A month later Jake was getting around on a cane, and a month after that he wasn't using anything, but he had a definite hitch in his giddy-up, and his kidneys were pretty much sore all the time with an occasional red tinge in his urine. After Mary Jane had Nellie Bly down for the night, she came into the kitchen where Jake sat at the table sipping a glass of whiskey. She took a glass down from the cupboard and sat down across from him. "I'll take some of that," she said. "I'm plum tuckered out tonight." Jake silently poured some whiskey in her glass. "Here's how," she said as she raised her glass. Jake clinked her glass with hers but still said nothing. She studied him for a minute or two and said, "Cat got your tongue?"

"Aw. I's just thinkin'." He took a swallow of whiskey and said, "I ain't much use around here no more. I think we need to move on and make room for a workin' hand. Gus ain't said nuthin', but I know he's been thinkin' it. Would, if it were me. What a yer think?"

"Well, sure enough, what with that gimp leg you can't do the work you hired on to do. But, I kind of like it here. Been here four years. Settled in. Maybe there's some kinda other work you could do. They are inventin' all kinds of new machines now."

"Yeah. I know. But I ain't gettin' any younger, and I always got these aches and pains from the war and now more from the horse fall. Not like it was when me and Wes was ridin' the range. Didn't seem to ever think 'bout my aches and pains back then, even when that devil Conroy shot me in the leg."

"I ain't gettin' any younger either, and I got a daughter to raise up. Where you thinkin' about goin'?"

"Wal, how does applying my detective skills in the big city sound?"

"San Francisco?"

"Might as well. We got money saved up to carry us through until I get some cases. So…." he shrugged his shoulders. "What a you think?"

Mary Jane looked like she was tossing the idea around in her head, then raised her glass and grinned. "Might as well. Here's how."

"Here's how." Jake said with a matching grin and clinked her glass.

TWO
ANOTHER BAD MAN • 1892-1893

THE PALMER SALOON, a local watering hole on Clayton Street in what became known as the Haight-Ashbury District of San Francisco, was a regular stop for Jake on his rounds around the town. Usually, he had a drink or two there on the way home, just to see if he could catch any buzz that could prove profitable. If he struck out, then he just went on home and had a drink with Mary Jane before supper. Plus, it was a good spot to warm up after a day out and about in fog city. He was about two months into this routine when he finally struck paydirt.

Jake leaned on the bar with his right foot on the brass rail to rest his bad leg. He wore his black three-piece suit with a collar and gold paisley cravat. He was about halfway through his first Kessler whiskey when Edward Palmer came from the back room and motioned Jake down to the end of the bar. Palmer pushed his large frame past the bartender on duty and slipped down to the end of the bar. He brushed back the forelock of his balding head and in a hushed tone with his back to the other patrons at the bar, Palmer said, "So you are a detective, Mister Brighton. Ain't that right?" He shot a quick look over his left shoulder, turned back and bored in on Jake.

Although he tightened up inside like a strand of pulled barbed wire, he never revealed anything of the sort in his expression or physical countenance. "Yes. That's correct," Jake answered in an equally subdued tone.

"Well, I got a situation that needs lookin' into. How much do you charge?" Jake was long prepared for that question and answered with firm conviction, "Seventy dollars a day plus expenses," although he would have easily negotiated.

"All right. And you are sworn to secrecy, right?"

"Yes, sir. Utmost discretion."

"Uh-huh. Whatever that means. Well, I suspect my Amelia is stepping out on me. I need someone to follow her and get the goods on her. Think you can do that?"

"Most assuredly. I'll have a contract tomorrow for you to sign. Is that soon enough or do we need to start right away?"

"No, that's fine. Just tears my guts up to think this is happening. I took her off the streets when she was just eighteen years old and gave her a fine life. But I got to protect my assets, you know, and there ain't no double-dealing little bitch gonna play me for no fool. You get my drift?"

"I sure do. Why don't you meet me at my office about noon tomorrow, and we can sign the contract and get started? Bring a photograph of Amelia."

"All right," he grumbled.

At the appointed time, Palmer filled the doorway of Jake's small office and groused, "Here I am. Let's get this done."

"Good day to you, Ed. Here, have a seat. You can read over the contract right here."

"Just give it to me. I'll sign it. You cheat me at all, you might make your wife a widow."

Jake ignored his words and set the contract in front of him, dipped a pen and handed it to him. Ed scribbled his name on the line and handed it back to Jake. He blotted the wet ink, looked it over, put it in the drawer of his small desk, and sat in the desk chair. "Now," he said, "if you have a few minutes, I have a few questions."

"Go ahead."

"Okay. I notice that you are the bartender at the saloon on Sunday and Monday nights. Is that correct?"

"Yeah."

"And is that when you suspect Amelia is—as you say—stepping out on you?"

"Yeah."

"Okay. What is the address of your house?"

"It's farther on up Clayton at number thirty-eight."

"Is that her photograph? May I have it? Mmm. Lovely lady."

"Yeah. Maybe *too* lovely. I'm beginning to think she married me for my money. It ain't a whole lot, but it ain't a little either."

"Well, tomorrow is Sunday. I'll start tailing her then."

Jake continued to ask more questions until Palmer left.

On Sunday evening, he positioned himself where he could see the Palmer house's front door but was well out of sight. He remained there for five hours and gave it up because there was no movement either in or out by Amelia. Palmer would be home in an hour, so if she had been out, she surely would have returned by now.

On Monday, however, he got in position earlier and at about five thirty p.m., the front door opened, and she appeared dressed to the nines. She wrapped herself in a long black coat, pulled the netting down over her face and locked the door behind her. Then she immediately made for the cable car on Seventeenth Street. Jake followed well behind her and when the car stopped, he watched her board and go immediately to the covered cabin where a gentleman gave her his seat. He stumped along as fast as he could, caught the car, hopped on and hung outside where he could observe her. At Market Street she disembarked and caught the Market Street trolley and rode it to the Ambrose Hotel. There she left the cable car and entered the hotel at a side door on Annie Street. It appeared as though someone was there waiting for her. Jake had a hunch and went through the hotel lobby to the lounge, and there she was already perched on a stool off to the side talking to the bartender and smoking a cigarette.

Jake stepped across the lobby to the front desk and bought a copy of the Examiner. Then he selected a chair against one wall from which he had a clear view of Amelia and the expanse of the entire lobby. It wasn't long thereafter that a dapper young man, who looked to be about thirty years old, pranced in through the front doors and across the lobby directly to the lounge where he went right to Amelia, caressed her and kissed her. The bartender brought him a drink without him even ordering. They obviously had done this before, probably several times. The two lovers swooned over each other for about a half hour. Then he escorted her up the grand staircase.

Jake, acting casually as if he were a guest at the hotel, strolled up after them but stayed far enough behind so as not to be detected. But it didn't seem to matter because they seemed indifferent to any sort of discovery. They were not in the least acting surreptitiously. They ascended to the third floor, walked arm-in-arm down the corridor while Jake waited at the top of the stairs and peeked around the corner just in time to see them disappear through a room door. He tiptoed down the corridor and memorized the room number. It occurred to him then that the young man did not stop at the desk for a key. He already had the key on his person. This was shaping up like a regular Monday night tryst with these two. There were a couple of upholstered chairs at the end of the corridor, so Jake went down and took one of the seats to wait out the lovebirds.

After a couple of hours and having read every word in the newspaper he laid his head back and the paper over his face. He dozed for another hour and a half when, for some unknown reason, he snapped awake. He pulled his watch from his vest and noted that it was nine thirty. He stretched and walked around a little, then sat down again. At ten the room door opened, and he quickly picked up the paper to hide his face. The young man took Amelia on his arm and escorted her back downstairs to the lounge. Then he left through the main lobby. Jake looked back to Amelia just in time to see her hand the bartender some money and leave through the side door. So, she was working. Is that it? Not an affair?

Jake followed her home. She was in the house by eleven, and that was that. But he was curious about the young man. He would take it up on the morrow.

About two in the afternoon, Jake strolled up to the front desk of the Ambrose Hotel with a porter following him, carrying Jake's valise. "Hello," Jake said to the desk clerk. "I'm just in from Kansas City and would like room three-o-eight for the night. It's a rule of mine. Whenever I am in a hotel of three or more floors, I always take room three-o-eight. My wife died in a room three-o-eight, and it comforts me to know I am closer to her." He smiled big and pleasantly at the clerk who stared at Jake like he was some kind of nut escaped from the freak show.

"I am sorry, sir. That room is booked. May I offer—"

"No, no. I *must* have that room. Can't you put them in another room?" Jake's smile was gone and his voice a little gruff.

"I'm sorry, sir. The suite is on long-term booking for weeks ahead."

"Every night?"

"Yes."

He puffed up and said, "Well, that's just preposterous. I must say good day to you, then."

"Good afternoon, sir."

Jake strode out the revolving doors with the porter following him, handed him a fifty-cent piece and asked him to hold the bag in storage for him. Then he walked the few blocks over to and down Second Street to the docks and passed the afternoon away watching all the maritime activity. When he thought the time was about right, he headed back to the hotel and took up his usual spot. Luckily, the day clerks were gone from the front desk and replaced by the night clerks or Jake might have been recognized as a nuisance. He waited for three hours and gave it up. But he was sure his hunch was right, so he came back the next day at the same time, and sure enough, in an hour's time he saw a lovely and well-dressed young lady come into the lounge from the side door. And a half hour later, this time a well-dressed man of about his own age, came in and went right to the lady at the bar. Jake waited and when they left he followed them to... suite three-o-eight. So that was the game. Somebody was running a high-class prostitute ring through the Ambrose Hotel, and his client's wife was back in the game. He had to be sure, though. He went back downstairs and booked a suite for the night. Then he went over to the lounge.

"Howdy," he said to the bartender. "Do you happen to have any Overholt whiskey?"

"Yes, sir. Right here," the bartender said with a smile as he turned and took down a bottle from the backbar. "Can I mix something for you or do you want it neat?"

"Yes. I believe I will have a Manhattan."

"Up or on the rocks?"

"Up will be just fine. Dining room is open 'til eight, isn't it?"

"Yes, sir."

"My name's Jonas V. Brighton. And yours, sir?" Jake smiled pleasantly and made himself to appear as a friendly fellow.

"Jack Sprat," he said with a deadpan look as he held out his hand for a shake.

"Ha, ha. That's funny."

"No. That is my real name. Jackson Wayne Sprat at your service."

"Well, I'll be. Your ma and pa must have had a particular sense of humor." Jake took a sip of his cocktail. "That's a pretty good drink you mixed up there, Jack."

"Thanks. What'd you say your business is?"

"I didn't. But since you ask, I'm in the security business."

"What kind a security? Banks and stuff. Hotels?"

"Personal protection. My last engagement was with Annie Chambers. You ever hear of her?"

"Nope. Can't say I have," Jack Sprat said as he polished a glass and set it with others underneath the bar.

"She's the most notorious madam in Kansas City and runs the most elegant house. I was her bodyguard for five years."

"What happened?"

"Why I'm here and not there?"

"Yes." Sprat looked a little suspicious like he was waiting to hear the same story he had heard over twenty years behind the bar.

"Well, I don't know if I should say. After all, we just met." Jake turned his smile into a frown and glared at Sprat with his dark challenging eyes, hoping to send a little chill up his back. It didn't work.

"Suit yourself. Doesn't make any difference to me."

"Well. I think I'll have some supper," Jake said as he tossed down the rest of his drink. "I'll be around again. By the way, you know of anybody who might need some personal security?"

"Well, I don't know if I should say. After all, we just met." He cracked a little smile.

"*Touché.* I'll be seeing you, and we can get to know each other better." Jake gave him his friendly smile, left and went to the dining room.

After supper he returned to the lounge, sat again at the bar, lit a cigar, and ordered an Overholt neat. He nursed it for a half hour and ordered another. Sprat was still pouring and splitting his time between Jake and two gentlemen at the other end of the bar. Jake was just making small talk and after a half hour passed, the two men left. Just a few minutes later the lady of the night came down the stairs in a hurry and looking a fright. Her client for the night was coming after her, and he did not look happy. She hustled over to the open end of the bar where she could get behind Sprat and Jake saw his opportunity. The man's face was red and he was sputtering all kinds of expletives. Jake moved to head him off and got between him and the lady.

"Whoa now. What's the problem here?" Jake said as he held the man back by the lapels of his coat.

"She stole a hundred dollars from me. That's the problem. Get your hands off me. Who do you think you are?"

"Hotel security, Mister...?"

"Johnathan Q. Robinson. That's who. And I'll not be victimized by this little tart."

"Okay. Oaky. Let's calm down. Here, sit down before you go into a apoplectic fit." Jake muscled him into a chair in a corner away from the passage to the lobby. "Here, sit here. Might be some newspaper reporter in the lobby."

"There better not be. That's part of the guarantee."

"Yeah. We do the best we can, but you never know, there could be some new guy we don't know about. So, let's just sit and relax quietly while we figure this out."

"There's nothing to—" he started to say loudly.

"Tut, tut. Let's stay calm, Mister Robinson. Now, Vicky, did you take a hundred dollars from Mister Robinson?" Jake kept his eyes on the client while he spoke.

"Well...."

"Tell the truth now."

"He was gonna cheat me out of five dollars, so I grabbed his wad and hurried down here so Jack Sprat could take care of it. He owes me ten dollars. Here. Here's his cash." She handed it to Jack Sprat, who took it and pulled a ten from the roll.

"Hey! What're you doin'? That's mine," Robinson said and started to rise, but Jake held him down.

"Is that right, Mister Robinson?"

"She wasn't worth ten dollars."

"That's cuz I wouldn't do the sick things he wanted me to do," Vicky said with indignation.

"Well, now. That's a whole different story. Now you know the house does not like a welcher and perversion is only tolerated if the girl is game. She clearly is not. Therefore, you owe her ten dollars, and you are going to pay it because you don't want this to somehow get out onto the street. Do you?" Jake held his hand out for the cash roll, and Sprat put it in his hand. He tucked it in Robinson's coat pocket, put his hat on his head, and manhandled him through the side door. "Now. Good evening, Mister Robinson." The gentleman huffed and puffed but did not resist.

"I didn't know the hotel put on a security man." Jack Sprat said as he handed a whiskey to Vicky.

"Thanks," she said. "I can use it."

"Oh. I only said that to sound official."

"You handled it well. I'm afraid I would've roughed him up a bit."

"I can do that, too. But why risk getting a bad name for the business, eh?"

"Maybe Sharkey should meet this fellow. By the way, how'd you know my name was Vicky?"

"I heard Mister Robinson call you Victoria. I figured you would go by Vicky. Made it sound like we knew each other."

"You're pretty sharp, ain't yah?" She smiled and moved closer to Jake with a clear message of seduction in her countenance.

"Well, thank you, darlin', but I am married, and unlike these male sluts you service, I stay true to my own. Not that I wouldn't enjoy your company if I weren't married. I think I would." He smiled and gave her his bedroom eyes look.

"Oh, my. Now I am all aflutter."

"Here's how," Jake said as he held his glass up for a toast.

"Huh?" they both said.

"Cheers."

"Oh, yeah. Cheers."

"Who's that Sharkey fellow you mentioned?" Jake asked.

"Well, I tell you what. You tell me why you left Kansas City, and I'll tell you about Alan Sharkey."

"Deal. It's simple. I got in some trouble with the law and decided to get outta town. There's no way I was going to jail. Spent four years in prison already. Don't want any more."

"What was the trouble with the law?"

"I hurt a fellow pretty bad." Jake drilled through Sprat's eyes with his deathly stare and this time was sure he sent a chill up Sprat's spine. "They got a warrant out on me. No reward, though. So don't ya'll get your hopes up." He grinned to ease the tension.

"Spend time in Texas?"

"A little. You could tell, huh?" Jake took a sip of his whiskey and checked over the rim of the glass to see if he had blown his story.

"I used to live in Texas," Jack Sprat said. Jake tensed. "Down San Antone way. Many moons ago." Jake relaxed. "Came west for the gold and ended up working the saloons around Angels Camp. Got tired a all that and came down to the big city 'bout ten years ago. Been here ever since."

"Well, you know what they say. You can take the man outta Texas, but you cain't take the Texas outta the man. Here's how." And he raised his glass. This time they both responded, "Here's how." And Sprat said, "Yep. It brings back memories. Oh well, those days are long gone. So, you want a hear about Alan Sharkey. Mean son a bitch. Killer. He's the boss of this outfit. Hah, hah. You got me talkin' like my ol' Texas self."

"It sounds real nice," Vicky said.

"Well, anyway. He come up outta the docks and has a gang runnin' prostitution, extortion, bribery, and opium he deals with the Chinese. Strong-arms his way in everything he does, but he's smart. He set up this operation, got a lot of the law looking the other way. Me and all the girls work for him. I set up the appointments, and they do the work."

"How long you been here in the Ambrose, and what does the hotel have to say about all this?"

"We been working this for six months now," Vicky said. "And doing pretty good except for creeps like that Johnson. First time we seen him here, huh Jack?"

"Yep. Girls get half the fee. I get fifty cents, and Sharkey takes the rest. Hotel gets nothing unless they'd like to have the building burn down."

"Pretty slick. Well, tell you what. I'd like to stay and jaw with ya'll, but I got to get to bed. Headin' down to San Jose early in the mornin'."

Vicky made a pouty look, then grinned. "Here's how," she said and they all tossed down their drinks.

The following Monday Jake showed up at the lounge ahead of Amelia and started talking with Sprat. There were two men at the other end of the bar and a man and a woman at one of the small cocktail tables.

"Who you got working tonight?" Jake said in a semi-low voice.

"Girl named Amelia. But I don't know if she's gonna work. I don't have any appointments set up. Here she comes now. Hear that tap at the side door?"

It was Amelia who came in and surveyed the room in one sweep. She smiled at the couple at the table and looked at the two men, but they were busy in their conversation. Then her beautiful eyes lit on Jake, and she smiled at him ever so sweetly. Just barely touching him, she quietly swished by on her way to her usual corner perch. Her perfume was intoxicating. Jake had to rein in and remind himself that he was spoken for. She sat up on the barstool and removed a cigarette from her little purse. She gave Jake a devilish look as she waited for him to light her cigarette, which he did with a match from a book of matches placed by ashtrays on the bar.

"And you say this beauty's name is Amelia, Jack?"

"Yes, sir."

"Well, if I were younger and not married, I sure would be sparkin' up to you, Amelia."

"Why, thank you Mister?"

"Brighton. Jonas V. Brighton."

"But you know, Mister Brighton," she cooed and fluttered her eyelashes at him, "you being married doesn't bother me." She glanced at Sprat and said, "You tell him the deal?"

"Sure did."

She smiled with a lot of pearly white showing and a big look of query in her eyes. "Well?"

Jake took her hand, caressed it, stared deep into her eyes with his own dark liquid eyes that could melt the hardest heart and said, "You are very beautiful, and I would love to spend some time with you—" She threw her arms around his neck and kissed him all over his face with hot, panting breath. Jake chuckled, pulled her arms down and gently urged her away from him. Again, he gazed into her eyes and said, "I can't. I took an oath."

She pulled away, took a drag off her cigarette and said, "Well. She's a lucky woman. I admire you for that. Ain't that right, Jack? But, if anything ever happens, you come look me up, you hear?"

"I hear. How long you been working for Sharkey?"

She shot a look at Jack, and he said, "He's okay. He already helped Vicky out of a jam."

"What was that?"

"Fella was tryin' to cheat her, and Jonas got her fee and sent the fella on his way."

"Well, that's good of you to help us working girls. Lord knows we need it. Me and Jack started out together here 'bout six months ago."

"Business been good?"

"Not too bad, I'd say. Wouldn't you, Jack?" He nodded his head and went to serve the couple at the table. They talked for another hour until Jake took his leave.

Two days later in the back office of the saloon, Jake handed his written report to Ed Palmer along with a bill in the amount of four hundred dollars. Ed read the report and growled. "Alan Sharkey. That son of a bitch snaked my Amelia back into the business, and now I got a divorce her to save face. Damn!" He sat in his desk chair and dropped his chin to his chest. As he spun to open the safe, the door to his office swung open and there was Amelia. "What're you doin' here?" he said sharply.

"What's he doin' here?" She scowled at Jake most unpleasantly.

"He's a detective I hired to follow you and get the goods on you."

"Well, you sure did that, didn't you? You lyin' dog," she sputtered loudly. "We'll see what Alan Sharkey has to say 'bout this." And she sprang out the door.

"Sorry 'bout that. Here's your four hundred. I'll need you to testify if it goes to court."

"Certainly." That was it. Jake left Palmer with his chin on his chest as before and went home.

The next day, midafternoon, Jake was on the sofa reading the Examiner when there was a knock at his front door. Mary Jane was in the back with Nellie Bly. He got up from the sofa and opened the door to see men standing there three abreast on the stoop. Right away he sensed the bad in them, and the one in the middle he knew right off was a killer. They wore dark suits and ties with bowler hats on their heads except the middle one wore a silver silk vest and a huge diamond stickpin in his red silk cravat.

"Yes? Good afternoon," Jake said. "What can I do for you?"

"More like what we can do for you, Mister Jonas V. Brighton," the deadly one in the middle said.

"Sorry. You have me at the disadvantage."

"Don't we now. Name's Alan Sharkey." He waited, probably for reaction but got none. Jake held his stare eye to eye. "Heard you had some doin's with one of my girls last night."

"Hey, I's just doin' my job. I was hired by her husband to investigate her activities."

"Uh-huh. That fat SOB Ed Palmer. Well, look here. I don't have the time to stand here and confab with you all day. I'm here to let you know I know where you live and I don't want to hear 'bout any testimony in court 'bout my business. Is that clear?" he said with a cold, deathly stare. "You have a wife and a daughter, don't you?"

"Well, yes." Jake pulled a cigar from his vest pocket and said, "I think I understand." He fumbled the other pocket as if he were searching for a match when, faster than the snap of a rat trap, he had his pocket thirty-two pressed into Sharkey's forehead. The man showed no fear, only surprise, and Jake held his attention with a deadly glare. "If one a you two others even twitch, Mister Sharkey here ends up with a hole in his head. Is that clear?" he said through clenched teeth. A slight smile came across Sharkey's face and he held it. "You two, real slow and careful take out your pistols, all of them, and put them on the ground." He waited as they complied and Jake said low and slow, "I said *all* of them."

They each pulled out another pistol.

"Now move way back, slowly." He quickly frisked Sharkey and took a pocket pistol from his vest and a sap he had in his belt on his backside.

"You're pretty efficient, Mister Brighton."

Jake pressed the pistol harder into Sharkey's forehead and a red welt started to come up. Sharkey's smile disappeared. "You made a big mistake threatening my family. That's what bad men do, and now I'm gonna have to kill you."

He just started to squeeze the trigger when a voice behind him called his name gently and calmly. It was Mary Jane.

"Jake. Not with Nellie here. I don't want her to see it."

The first sign of concern began to reveal itself in Sharkey's eyes. Jake hesitated as if he was thinking it over, then he lowered the pistol and pointed it at Sharkey's heart. "Now, yer best git along and hope I don't never see yer again, cuz I'll kill yer on the spot and there won't be no woman and child there to save yer."

Mary Jane glared at Sharkey and said, "You don't know how lucky you are, mister. This here is Rawhide Jake Brighton out of northwest Texas. If you never heard of him, then it's probably good for you."

"Now git," Jake growled.

The other two toughs turned and hurried away. Sharkey gave Jake one last deadly look, tipped his hat to Mary Jane, said "Good day," turned his back to them and walked away. Jake and Mary Jane watched them go until they turned a corner and were out of sight.

"We have to get out of town tonight," Jake said low and slow as he stared after the gangsters. "Pack only what we can carry with us, Mary Jane. Leave everything else behind."

"But…?"

"He's gonna come back and burn the house down. If I cain't kill him, then we got a run from him. Ain't cowardice. Just the way it is with bad men like him. Let's pick up these shootin' irons."

THREE

THE CHRIS EVANS CASE • 1893-1894

"WHERE WE GOIN'?" Mary Jane said as she lugged Nellie Bly on one hip and carried a big suitcase in her opposite hand.

Jake carried four suitcases, one in each hand and one under each arm. "Well, we could go north, south, east, or board a ship for the Orient. We liked it in the San Joaquin Valley, didn't we?"

Mary Jane nodded her head yes. "Let's just get on the train and head east then. I been readin' in the paper 'bout the train robbers Sontag and Evans. Maybe we just mosey on over to Visalia and see if we can be of service—for a fee, a course." He grinned.

They drug their suitcases on board the Seventeenth Street Trolley where the driver patiently waited for them before he engaged the cable and got the car moving. Thankfully, they only had to make one car change and that was at Market. They rode the Market Street car all the way to the ferry terminal and in three hours were on their way across the bay to Oakland from where they made their way by stagecoach and train all the way south to Visalia. It was a long, hot, and bumpy journey, but they arrived just a little worse for wear.

"You say the home is owned by a Missus Evans?" Jake said to the real estate agent.

"Yes. That is correct. Well, should say, it is foreclosed. The mortgagee technically owns it. Her mother lives next door and is caring for the children while she and her oldest daughter, Eva, are out on tour with her theater company."

"How long has it been vacant?"

"Just about six months."

"Is their theatrical play about the train robberies?"

"Yes."

"I think I have heard of it. We'll have to go see it, Mary Jane."

"Yes. Is it playing locally?"

"No. I believe they're up in Modesto."

"Well. All right. We'll take the house. The furniture comes with it, right?" Jake said as he sought Mary Jane's unspoken approval and got it.

"Yes."

"When can we move in?"

"Well, as soon as you sign the lease."

————————————

JAKE TOOK ON odd jobs, and Mary Jane provided childcare for the Evans children as well as her own Nellie Bly. Jake got more steady work at a lumber planer mill in Visalia, and he and Mary Jane were becoming fast friends with Molly Evans when she was in town. She was very appreciative of Mary Jane caring for her children, and her mother had all good things to say about the Brightons. Meanwhile, Chris Evans was still on the loose hiding out in the Sierra Nevada foothills.

One day Jake thought he would go down to the sheriff's office and say howdy. It was only a quarter-mile walk he thought he could make easily. Unbeknownst to him U.S. Marshal George Gard was there from Los Angeles. Jake introduced himself and started talking with Gard.

"Yeah, me and the missus, came out here from Arizona in eighty-eight," Jake said as he lit a cigar. He could tell nobody was listening, not Gard, not the sheriff nor his deputies. So just to grab their interest he said, "I was constable in Springerville and worked for Bill Meade down in Graham County chasing rustlers for about six months."

"You were a deputy U.S. Marshal?" Gard said.

"Special *temporary* deputy Marshal. After I killed Ike Clanton and Lee Renfro, he wanted me to go in and clean out the rustlers that were stealin' from the San Carlos Apache Reservation."

"Yeah. Think I heard 'bout that. So, you're that feller, eh? How come Marshal Meade didn't swear you in regular?"

"Well, I got the job done, and then he said he didn't have the budget no more."

"Uh-huh. No offense, but you don't look much like a rough and tough *hombre.*"

That annoyed Jake, and it showed in his eyes for just a flash. Then he took a drag off his cigar, turned his head and blew the smoke out, turned back, and with a hard stare at Gard, said, "Horse fell on me and broke my leg in ninety-two. Ain't been the same since." Then he cheered up and said, "But, mostly, I am a detective. Been working some cases in San Francisco and got on the wrong side of Alan Sharkey. You may have heard of him. Had to get out of town in a hurry. He threatened to harm my family. Don't know whether the house we were living in is still standing or not." Jake shrugged a little and smiled.

"I heard of Sharkey. Lucky you're still standing," the sheriff said.

"He is, too," Jake said with just a hint of bravado. "Listen, I've talked your ear off. I just came down to introduce myself. If you hear of any cases that need investigatin', let me know. We're rentin' the Evans house."

"Well, good to meet you. I'll let you know if anything comes up," the sheriff said. Jake glanced at Gard and saw that he was thinking.

"Yeah. Okay. So long."

On the same day, well past sundown, Mary Jane had the children all down for the night and was sitting with her knitting when she heard a light knock on the front door. Jake was down at the barn so she took the shotgun down from the shelf and with it pointed at the ground she opened the door a crack. "Yes?" she said.

"Hello, ma'am. Sorry to disturb you. I am United States Marshal George Gard. Is Mister Brighton available?" He showed his badge pinned to his vest under his coat.

Mary Jane studied him for a long minute, then said, "He's down at the barn. I believe he is alone."

"Good. I have a proposal for him. Might involve you too." He smiled ever so slightly. Mary Jane pointed to the barn.

Jake was painting a shelf for the kitchen and heard Gard coming up to the barn, but he could not see who it was as he was looking from the light into the dark. He shaded his eyes and heard Gard call out, "Yo. Brighton. It's Marshal Gard."

"Oh. Howdy. Come on in."

The marshal slid over to an inside corner, hidden from outside, lifted a boot onto a small stool and snatched up a piece of clean straw. "Well," he said. "I wired Meade to verify your story. Guess you were a hero around those parts."

"Don't know 'bout that. Just tryin' to do my job."

"You must a done it pretty good. Ever do any undercover work?"

"Oh, yeah. I had a big Missouri case back in eighty. Two boys murdered their pa. I moved in next door to them, got their confidence, and they confessed the whole caper to me. Made the news all the way to New York City. Then I worked undercover for the stock raisers association in northwest Texas. And sort a undercover in Apache County, Arizona."

"Texas, huh? Brighton, huh? You wouldn't be Rawhide Jake Brighton, would you?"

Jake got serious and said, "What's on your mind, Marshal?" Gard stared at Jake for a long minute, looked away, then looked back, but apparently decided not to pursue it any further.

"Well, you know that Chris Evans and John Sontag and their gang are wanted for murder and train robbery. In their last train heist, they broke into the U.S. mail and so now I got jurisdiction and a reason to go after them." Jake tensed. Gard went on, "I don't think the sheriff's been getting after it as much as he could. So, I got up a small posse, but I'd like to get an experienced man on the inside. Looks like you might already be all set up. Would you be willing to take on the case? Evans is the most wanted man in California. And he is a flat-out killer. Hates 'blood-hunting,' as he calls them, company officers and detectives. Just last month they stopped the Sequoia Mills stage looking for detective Will Smith to kill him. Luckily, he wasn't on board. This ain't no easy-as-pie job. It'd be dangerous, for sure."

"What's the pay?" Jake smiled as he wiped his hands on a rag.

"Do you have a fee schedule?"

"I do, but since I would be on this job every day, I doubt you could afford a month of my fee."

"Uh-huh. Well, how about I pay you a regular deputy's salary of a hundred a month?"

"What about my wife? She'll be in on it and riskin' her life, too."

"Yeah." He scratched the back of his head under his hat. "How about another fifty a month for her?"

"And the bounty? Here tell the Southern Pacific has a eleven thousand dollar bounty out for Evans, dead or alive."

"Well you'd have to work that out with the S.P."

Jake held out his hand. "All Right. Deal."

"Okay. Well, you get in cozy with those folks and see what you can find out so we can build a case of evidence. Want to recover all the loot they stole, too."

"Yes, sir. Will do."

JAKE AND MARY Jane became more and more a part of the Evans family as they gained their confidence. Jake did a lot of odd jobs around the houses, fixing fences and whatnot. Mary Jane was very busy with the children. Molly Evans was quite happy with how her children were being cared for. But on one occasion she got curious. "You Brightons seem to be traveling light," she said when just she and Mary Jane were alone in the sitting room one evening. "You have to stay on the move?"

Mary Jane sat for a long few minutes staring at her hands in her lap. With a serious concerned look on her face she said, "Promise you won't say anything to anybody?"

"My goodness. Of course. What is it, for heaven's sake?" Molly said with some alarm in her voice.

"Well, you know how your Mister Evans is hiding out from the law?" Molly nodded her head yes. "Jake has a warrant out on him from Arizona, so we ain't been stayin' in any one place very long. If you get my drift."

"Oh, my—yes. I get your drift and I sympathize completely. What's he wanted for?"

"Bank robbery and assault. Feller got shot when Jake was robbin' the bank. So, we skedaddled outta there in a hurry and been runnin' ever since. I hope this doesn't change anything between us."

"Of course not. Believe me. I think we are birds of a feather. Chris will be glad to hear that a colleague, so to speak, is watchin' after his place and family."

"Well, we're doin' what we can." Mary Jane made a weak smile at Molly. Later, when she told Jake he said she was getting almost as good as him. And all seemed just hunky-dory until one day Jake came back from downtown with news.

Jake came in hurriedly through the door and caught Mary Jane. "Chris is wounded and in jail up in Fresno. Sontag's in the hospital." Mary Jane's hand reflexively went to cover her open mouth and her eyes flew wide open. "I got to tell the family. Let's gather them up after the children are in bed."

Both Eva and her mother, Molly, happened to be home, and Molly's mother-in law, Isabella Byrd, with her two sons, George and Ed, came over from the house next door. Jake and Mary Jane had them all assembled in the front room of their house.

Jake stood up and motioned for the hubbub to cease. "Just gonna say it right out. All the talk today downtown is about, well, Chris and John were shot and captured. John's—"

Eva screamed, and all the other women gasped. "What happened?" Eva shrieked. "My father and my fiancé. Are they all right?"

"Word is John's in the hospital, and Chris is in jail. Chris can't be too bad off, but I don't know about John."

"Where are they?" Eva demanded.

"Fresno."

Molly Evans sat with her face in her hands and rocked back and forth ever so slightly. Isabelle and her sons looked as if they didn't know what to say or do.

"We got to go to them—*tonight!* J.V., you hitch the mules to the wagon. Mother, you and I will head out tonight. Take Joseph with us. When we get too tired to drive, we'll stop and sleep under the wagon."

"Joseph?" Molly said weakly.

"He's your oldest son. He needs to be with us. I can't do everything. Get the guns. J.V.? Git goin'."

"Eva. Do you think it might be better to wait for daylight? See where you're goin' better?" Mary Jane said.

"My father is lying in some cold jail, shot, who knows how bad. He needs me, and I need to be there as fast as I can." Her chest was heaving and she started to sob. She wiped her eyes on her sleeve and said more calmly and resolutely, "Now let's git goin'."

"Jonas, she sounds determined. Maybe you better go along, too," Mary Jane said.

JAKE STOOD BACK a ways from the cell block while Eva, Molly, and Joseph were in there visiting with Evans. He could hear Eva's heavy sighs but not what they might be saying. After about a half hour he heard Evans call for the jailer. The jailer came back and said to Jake, "He wants to see you."

"Me?"

"Yeah. Put all your pistols and knives out on this table."

"All right," Jake said and unloaded his hardware. He followed the jailer to Evans's cell.

"I'll leave you outside the cell. Miss Eva and the others can stay inside." Jake nodded his understanding.

Chris Evans stood in the middle of his cell with his Eva on his arm at his side, Molly hugging him on his wounded side, and Joseph behind him with his arm over his shoulder. He and his younger partner, John Sontag, were made the most notorious and famous outlaws probably since the James Bothers by all the hyperbole and constant coverage of the overexcited San Francisco press. And there, standing in front of Jake, was the great mythical train robber and killer with his doting daughter, devoted wife, eldest son, his left arm in a sling and left eye with a bandage on it. Jake stared at him for a few seconds until Eva began to weep. Evans was not a tall man—more like about Jake's height, but thinner. And he sported a full and thick dark brown beard like that of a Cossack. Jake waited for him to speak.

Evans stepped slowly to the cell bars with Eva at his side and held his hand through the bars. "Chris Evans," he said with a hard and steady gaze into Jake's eyes who returned the challenge with his own strong and unwavering stare. "Eva and Molly told me all 'bout what you're doin' for us, and I am much obliged."

Jake took note of Evans's sincerity and determined that despite all his capers, he appeared to be quite the family man. Jake softened his stare and while still looking at Evans shook his hand and said, "They seemed like they could use a hand. I ain't got a steady job so I got the time to help 'em out."

"Well, like I said, I am much obliged for everything and especially for bringing Eva and Molly and Joseph up here to see me."

WHILE CHRIS EVANS was in jail awaiting trial, John Sontag died of his wounds received at the Stone Corral shoot-out. Eva apparently did not take her fiancé's death hard as she continued to play in melodramas throughout the Valley to try and gain sympathy for her father. It didn't work. In December 1893, Chris Evans was convicted and sentenced to life imprisonment. All the newspapers took special note of how Eva wept bitterly upon hearing the bailiff announce the jury's decision.

But, Eva, being a young woman not used to things not going her way, approached Ed Morrell. He was an ex-con from San Quentin and happened to be a waiter at a Fresno restaurant. He was delivering Evans's daily meals to him. After one evening meal delivery Eva followed him out of the jail. She caught up with him and said, "Mister Morrell, may I speak with you for a moment?"

He turned around and smiled. "Yes, ma'am, what can I do for you?"

"You know who I am?"

"Why, yes. See you all the time with your father."

"And you like my father. Isn't that right?"

"Yeah. I think highly of him."

"Well, then would you be willing to help break him out of jail?"

"Yes. I think I would."

"Okay. All you have to do is smuggle a pistol in with his supper. Can you do that?"

"Yes, ma'am. Easy. That old turnkey doesn't ever check the tray. I was thinkin' 'bout doin' it pretty soon myself."

The very next evening Morrell arrived at the jail as scheduled with Evans's supper. Under a cloth napkin he'd hidden a pistol. The jailer opened the gate for food delivery on Evans's cell door, and Morrell handed the tray through. He caught Evans's eye and motioned with his eyes for Evans to pay attention to the lump under the napkin. Evans pulled the six-shooter, let the tray clatter to the floor, and pointed the gun at the jailer. "Now, open this door."

As soon as the jailer had the key turned, Evans kicked the door open and he and Morrell ran out into the street where they just happened to bump into the Fresno city marshal, who tried to stop them, but Evans shot him in the shoulder. Then the two escapees grabbed up a horse and saddle at the livery and ran for the mountains.

The word came down to Visalia, and Jake brought it home after a drink in the saloon downtown. He burst in the door and immediately announced, "Chris escaped!"

Eva squealed, jumped up and said, "I knew it. That Ed Morrell, sure enough. He broke him out."

Molly clapped her hands and all the children were jumping up and down cheering. Jake looked over at Mary Jane, who looked back at him as if to say, now what?

A month later Jake had an idea. From the scene at the jail in Fresno when he was there and from all the talk of admiration of their father in the Evans home Jake thought he might be able to lure Evans out of the mountains with a report to him of a dying child. He had Mary Jane come out to the barn and he told her about the idea. "What do ya think?" he said with a curious look.

"I think it would work, but how do you keep him from finding out you betrayed him? He'd kill you, sure, especially if he found out you are a detective working undercover right in his own home."

"I know. Lot a folks gonna think I'm sneaky and underhanded, but if it works, then that's all that matters. I think I got an idea on how to keep him from finding out. I heard Bill Downing say that he has to go up to Sonora on some business. If anybody knows where Chris Evans is holed up, it's Bill. I think Chris loves his children so much that if he thought one was dying, he'd be here in a flash. So, I let the word drop and Downing picks it up and runs up to Chris with it on his way to Sonora. By the time he gets back, it should be all over."

"Okay. Give it a whirl. See what we can do." She smiled weakly at Jake and he at her.

Late the next afternoon, Jake stepped into the saloon and saw that Bill Downing was there, along with a few other fellers he knew. He walked over to them to say howdy, then ordered a drink.

One of the men said, "Wal, J.V., how's things going over at the Evans nursery?"

They all chuckled, but Jake remained serious and downcast.

"Not so well, I'm afraid." He spoke loud enough to be sure that Bill Downing heard. "I'm afraid little Carl's in a bad way. I think he's got the pneumonia. Coughing all the time. Fever's real high. I don't know if he's gonna make it. Doc's been over to see him. Says there's nuthin' he can do. Just keep him iced up good. But I don't know. The poor little guy's probably gonna die." All the men grumbled and shifted around looking at the floor and the ceiling.

"Somebody needs to get word to Chris. But nobody knows where he is," one of the fellers said. Jake kept a covert eye on Downing, who was quiet but had a determined look come over his face.

Less than a week later everyone except Eva and Molly were gathered at the Brighton home in the evening after the children were in bed. Jake heard horses ride by and looked out the window to see two riders enter the barn. He caught Mary Jane's eye and gave her the high sign. Chris and Ed were there.

The two men burst through the door, and Chris stood for a moment to survey the room.

"Where's Carl?" Evans demanded.

Mary Jane jumped up and said, "Why, he's in his bed asleep."

"And who are you?"

"Mary Jane Brighton. J.V.'s wife."

"Oh, yeah. Okay. Well, I got word that Carl is in a bad way. I want to see him."

He went into the children's bedroom and put his hand on Carl's forehead. It was cool.

In a temper boiling just below the surface he came back out, pulled his pistol and pointed it at George Byrd. "What'd you do this for, George? I ain't never done nuthin' to you," he said in an icy tone.

"Done what? What're you talkin' 'bout?"

"Talkin' 'bout betrayin' me with a lie 'bout Carl 'bout ready to die so's I come down outta the mountains. Douse the lights and watch the winders, Ed."

"No. No. I never. How would I do it? I been here for the last two weeks, never left."

"That's right, Mister Evans. He's been chopping fire wood for two weeks," Mary Jane said.

"Don't matter. He could a sneaked off anytime."

"But I didn't," George almost wailed. "You know I can't go into town with that warrant they got on me."

"Please, Chris, I know my George didn't do it. He wouldn't betray you," Isabelle Byrd pleaded.

"Yeah, he would. So he could get the loot. He knows where it's stashed. Ain't that right, George?" He scowled at George as if he dared him to deny it.

"Well, Mister Evans, if George is innocent, and you shoot him, then you've done an injustice, and you don't seem to be an unjust man to me," Mary Jane said sober like.

He stood in the middle of the room with his revolver still pointed at George and looked as if he were contemplating the situation. No one spoke for a long minute. Then Mary Jane spoke up again. "Also, as the loving father you seem to be, I don't think you would want to kill a man right in your own home with your children here." He relented and holstered his pistol.

"He looked toward Morrell and said, "We'll stay 'til Sunday mornin'. I'll send the children off to Sunday School. Then we'll go. Anybody get the mail today?" He said as he sat in one of the kitchen chairs. Nobody had, so he said, "J.V., could you go into town and get the mail and a bottle a whiskey? Here's a fiver. That ought to cover it."

"Sure." Jake took his hat off the rack and went out the door. He fairly trotted, as best he was able, the whole quarter-mile to the telegraph office downtown. He was pleased with himself on how well the trap worked but still remained cautious. He sent the wire to Marshall Gard, who departed on the next train from Los Angeles to Visalia and arrived there on Saturday. He and Sheriff Kay organized a posse and before daybreak on Sunday morning had the house completely surrounded.

Jake went out to the barn to feed the horses and when he stepped inside, he froze. He was confronted by an armed officer who held his revolver pointed at Jake. Jake instinctively raised his hands and stepped into the shadow of the corner. Neither he nor the officer said anything and Jake calmly walked back to the house. He realized that the house was surrounded and everybody inside was at risk of being caught in the middle of a gunfight. He whispered to Mary Jane what was going on and gave her a serious look as he said, "Stay calm."

Luck fell again when a few minutes later Chris said, "J.V., can you go into town and fetch some sinus medicine for me? My head feels like it is 'bout to explode. Check around while you're there and see if you see any new officers in town. Give us a report when you git back."

Jake discreetly neglected to remind him that it was Sunday and the stores were closed. He got out of there before it dawned on Evans and went directly to the sheriff's office. He told Gard and Kay and anyone else who was there, "It's a ticklish situation. There's women and children in the house, and you don't want to start blasting away, cuz sure enough one or more a them'd get shot."

"Yeah. We better try diplomacy first," Gard said. "Got a give you some cover so I'm gonna arrest you and hold you in the hotel. We'll deliver a note to your wife that'll tell her we got you and we know Evans, Morrell, and Byrd are in there, so she better get out with the children cuz we're comin' in."

Marshall Gard wrote up the note and gave it to a boy to deliver. Mary Jane read the note out loud and as soon as she finished, Morrell jumped up and snatched it out of her hand. "I knew it," he said loudly. "You bitch." And he shoved her to the floor. He was about to kick her when Evans stepped in and said, "Leave her alone."

"But she and that lying husband a hers betrayed us."

"Not so sure a that."

"They've got my husband under arrest, you blockhead," Mary Jane screamed at Morrell. "How could he be a betrayer?"

"'Sides, it's no never mind now. They got us surrounded. We ain't gonna git outta this one," Evans said grimly as he flopped into a chair.

"Let's just blast our way out. Use the women and children as cover."

Evans shot Morrell a hot look and said, "You know better than that."

They waited and tried to figure out if there was any way they could get out. A crowd had gathered around their house and were screaming and yelling, some for Evans and some against him. Finally, Sheriff Kay sent in a note with surrender terms on it. Evans sent a note back demanding that Kay disperse the crowd, and he and Morrell would meet Kay and Undersheriff Will Hall at the gate of the garden fence in front of the house.

With the crowd dispersed, Kay and Hall waited at the gate. Evans and Morrell came out onto the porch and walked down the steps to the fence. There, the four men shook hands and the outlaws were taken into custody.

The next day about high noon, Jake shuffled into the sheriff's office with his hands in his pockets and a big smile on his face. The sheriff and Marshal Gard were out to midday dinner. The deputy on duty said, "Well, looks like your buttons are gonna pop."

"Yep. Want a cigar Virg?"

"You bet. Thanks. So, tell me how'd it all happen?"

"Sure." Jake pulled up a chair and gave Deputy Virgil the whole story from his perspective. When he was done, he said, "You know I didn't see much a that Morrell feller. Think I could get a peep at him? Just to make sure I got his face locked in my memory and all."

"You betcha. Just go through the jail door over there. I gotta git this report finished. You can visit through the bars."

"Okay. You better keep this, just in case." He pulled the thirty-two from his vest pocket and set it on the desk.

"Oh, sure."

Jake went into the cellblock and saw Chris Evans standing at his cell window with his back to the door.

"Hello, Chris," Jake said.

Evans turned, looked over his shoulder, said, "Hello, J.V," and turned back to his window.

Jake stepped down to Morrell's cell. Morrell was lying on his bunk with his face to the wall. Jake said, "Howdy, Ed. Got some info for you." That roused Morrell, and Jake motioned for him to come over. Ed hesitated for a minute, then threw his legs off the side and stood. He looked at Jake suspiciously and walked over to about two feet away from Jake, stopped and said, "What?"

Jake motioned for him to come closer so he could whisper without Chris Evans hearing. Jake had his hands on the crossbar, and Morrell slowly came forward with his arms folded across his chest. When he was about six inches away, Jake launched his strong hands and arms, grabbed Morrell by the shoulders, pulled him face-first into the bars and held him there so that his arms were pinned.

"I heard you assaulted my wife, Mister Morrell."

A wicked slit of a smile creased Morrell's face. "What if I did?"

"Well, that is just plain bad, and bad men get what they deserve."

Jake grabbed his head in both hands and bounced Morrell's face off the bars back forth, time after time, at least ten times. Teeth and blood were flying. Jake started breathing heavy and grunting but kept at it so that Morell's face was a swollen mass of bruises and bleeding cuts when he passed out, and Jake let him drop to the floor. He stared down at Morrell and said, "Never. Never, assault a woman." When he bent over to pick up his hat, he saw Evans's boots and looked up into his solemn face.

Deputy Vergil hurried in and said, "What the—?"

"You are right," Evans said to Jake. "Ol' Ed took after J.V., tripped and fell into the bars." And a small ironic smile briefly crossed his face.

A correspondent came down from the San Francisco Examiner expressly to interview Jake and Mary Jane. She stayed mostly in the background, but Jake was right out there in front and having a good old time telling the reporter about it all. All the papers picked up the story and once again Jonas V. Brighton was in the headlines. But, noticing a bit of a chill from the formerly warm folks of Visalia, Jake thought it best for them to get of town. So, they hopped the train for Bakersfield and rented a house while Jake figured out what he was going to do next.

———————————

IN THE SPRING, Marshal Gard came to their door again. Jake was napping on the sofa and snapped awake when Gard rapped on the screen door. He rubbed his eyes and could see through the screen that it was Gard. He shuffled to the door in his stocking feet and said, "Howdy, Marshal Gard." And he held out his hand as held the screen door open. "Come on in."

"Hello, J.V. Hello, Mary Jane," he said to Mary Jane as she came from the back of the house. "How you folks doing?"

"Fine. Fine. 'Course that might change dependin' on whether you got good news or bad news," Jake said with a grin."

"Hah, hah. Yeah, I reckon so. Well, it ain't bad or good news. Got another proposal for you."

"Would you like a glass of sweet tea?" Mary Jane said.

"Sure. That'd be fine."

"What's on your mind now, Marshal?" Jake asked with a smile.

"Well, while we were working the Evans case there were a couple train robberies at the Roscoe Station in the San Fernando Valley. We think we know who did them but, of course, we can't prove it. So, to help us, who comes to mind?" He grinned halfway.

Jake smiled back.

———————————

JAKE HELPED MARY Jane and Nellie Bly down to the meager platform of the Roscoe train station. They collected their bags and, first-off, got directions to a boardinghouse in Monte Vista where the train station was located. Jake settled everybody in and then went to nose around the train station. Marshal Gard told him that in the first heist the robbers got away in a wagon, so he was inspecting wagon tracks and came upon a track that showed a deep diagonal cut across the tire, and the hoofprints of one of the horses showed two cracks in the shoe of the left forefoot. The trail led away from the site of the robbery off in the direction of the Little Tujunga Canyon, where the suspects lived. Jake stared down the trail for a couple of minutes. Then he went to the general store where he procured a bag of plaster of Paris and a bucket. He found a well pump and mixed up a solution that he poured into the wagon tracks and hoofprints. Then he stood back, looked around at the nearly deserted station, leaned against a stack of railroad ties, and lit a cigar. He didn't know if the casts would be useful, but at least he had them if need be. When the cigar was smoked down to a stub, he tested the casts. They were dry and rigid, so he picked them up and carried them to the boardinghouse. There he marked them with charcoal for identification.

Two days later Jake hailed the mailman as he drove his buckboard out of town. Jake hobbled up to the driver and said, "Howdy. Name's J.V. Brighton. Wonder if I could hitch a ride with you into the Little Tujunga Valley? I'm lookin' for work. Ain't got a horse, and you can see I ain't too good at walkin'."

"What happened to your leg?"

"Horse fell on me in ninety-two. Snapped my leg clean in two."

"Sorry to hear that. I got a bum leg too. Against the rules to take on riders, but ain't nobody out here to report me to, so hop on board."

Jake climbed up next to the mailman and said, "Obliged. You know if any a the folk in the canyon are lookin' for hired help?"

"Matter a fact, the Comstocks are lookin' for help. I'll drop you at their gate. Think they got a little laborer's house that goes with the job."

"Obliged again."

"I'll pick you up on the way back to Tujunga 'bout two this afternoon. Okay?"

Jake got the job, and a week later he was painting a fence when John Comstock came up and said, "You play poker?"

"Sure do," Jake said with a modest grin.

"We got a game every Saturday night over at Fitzsimmons. Penny-ante. You want in?"

"Sure."

"Okay. I'll pick you up in the buckboard 'bout five."

"Thank you, Mister Comstock."

"Call me John." He tipped his hat and walked away.

After about four weeks the three suspects were getting loose around Jake and started to let things slip here and there. One morning Comstock told Jake to hitch the team to the wagon, gave him a list of provisions and told him to drive to the San Fernando Grange and fill the order on his account. Jake bought more plaster of Paris and on the way back pulled the wagon off the road on a level spot and poured casts of the wheel track and the horse's hoofprint. They were a match to the casts he had from the Roscoe Station.

After two months Jake, Gard, and the deputy district attorney met in San Fernando. Jake turned over the casts and affidavits of the self-incriminating information he gathered.

"I don't know about you fellows, but I don't think this is enough for a conviction," Marshal Gard said.

"I don't, either," Jake said.

"Oh, I think we got all we need. Let's go ahead and make the arrests." The deputy district attorney was nearly adamant.

The trial was in June and all three suspects, Comstock, Fitzsimmons, and Horne were acquitted. Jake said to Marshal Gard as they walked out of the courtroom, "You know, I always wondered why they would've done the heist. They are all doing pretty well. Don't seem to need the money."

"Yeah, I'm not convinced they did it. I'm going to start investigating a couple a friends of theirs who could be suspects. You want in on it?"

"Thanks, but no thanks. I think I am done with criminal investigation. I just can't git around like I used to before I busted my leg, and I don't feel secure... like I can handle myself. Make sense?"

"Yeah, it does. I don't envy you. Well, best a luck to you," Gard said as he held his hand out for a shake. They shook hands and parted ways.

"So, I'm thinkin' we move in closer to town. Rent a nice place to live in a nice neighborhood with nice schools for Nellie, and I just hang out my shingle and do noncriminal investigations to cover the bills. What a you think a that?" Jake said to Mary Jane as they sat at the kitchen table after supper.

Mary Jane beamed a big smile and said, "I'm ridin' that horse, pardner." She rose and went to the cupboard and took down the bottle of Kessler and two glasses. She poured the whiskey, handed Jake a glass, held hers up and said, "Here's how."

Jake clinked her glass. "Here's how."

They each threw back a shot, banged their empty glasses on the tabletop and embraced in a smoky kiss.

FOUR
THE SETTING SUN • 1894-1928

NO MORE HEADLINES for Jonas V. Brighton. With the Roscoe Train Robberies case, the public life of he and Mary Jane ceased to be. They moved to East Los Angeles and bought a small but nice Victorian in a good school district and life rolled on without incident for the Brightons. Nellie Bly was growing up and enjoying school. Mary Jane was busy with her domestic duties and volunteer church work. Jake confined most of his work to investigations for lawyers in civil cases and therefore avoided conflict. Six days a week he rode the horse trolley to his office downtown and back home. In 1901 the electric yellow cars were put in service and the *clip-clop* of the trolley horses was heard no more. He rode the yellow cars every day. Funny, but they seemed to be fuller with every passing year.

ON JUNE 5, 1908, Jake and Mary Jane sat and clapped with the other proud parents and relatives of the first graduating class of the girls' Sacred Heart High School as the girls processed to their seats in the auditorium. They located Nellie Bly and waved vigorously so she could see them. She did and waved back.

After the commencement, Jake and Mary Jane finally got Nellie Bly away from her girlfriends. They got her in a bear hug, Jake on one side and Mary Jane on the other. "We're so proud of you!"

"I have a special graduation present for you," Jake said.

Nellie Bly was every bit as pretty as her mother and looked up at her dad with anxious slate-blue eyes. "What is it, Papa?"

"How about your mom and me, you, and one of your girlfriends spend a few days at Laguna Beach? I have a cottage reserved."

Nellie Bly hopped up and down and exclaimed, "That would be wonderful. I better find Judy to tell her."

"Plus this." He pressed a fifty-dollar bill into her hand.

Before she recovered from her surprise, they heard someone call, "Hello, Nellie."

"Oh, hello, Sister Claire," Nellie Bly said to the nun in black and white habit who approached her.

"Are these your grandparents? Hello, I am Sister Claire. I teach English here. Wonderful girl, Nellie. Hah, I see someone. Excuse me. Nice to meet you." She held out her hand for a shake to them both, which she quickly did and whisked away. The three Brightons looked at each other and burst out laughing. "Grandparents, hah, hah."

———————

JAKE CAME UP out of the water and crossed the sand to their beach blanket and umbrella. He grabbed a towel and while he was drying off, from underneath her wide-brimmed beach hat, Mary Jane said, "How's the water?"

"Wonderful. You should go in."

"Maybe later."

Jake stretched out on his side on the blanket beside Mary Jane, propped his head in one hand and said, "You know, I been thinkin'. We got money saved up. I think I'll retire and spend the rest of my days at the beach." He grinned at Mary Jane.

"I don't know about the beach," she grinned back at him. "But, I don't see why you couldn't retire."

"Yeah. L.A.'s gettin' kinda crowded. What'd you think about movin' down here, say Buena Park or Anaheim?"

"See what Nellie Bly thinks. She may have other plans she hasn't told us about. Speaking of whom, here they come." She held her hand up to block the sun and looked across the sand. "Yep. That's them."

———————

TWO MONTHS LATER Jake retired. They sold the house and relocat-
ed to Buena Park in Orange County. Nellie Bly came right along with
them and in no time had a job as a secretary to the terminal manager
of the Red Car Line in Santa Ana. "Mama," she said one evening as
she came up behind Mary Jane, who was at the sink. "Mind if I invite
a fella over for supper?"

Mary Jane turned around and grinned at her daughter. "You got
some boy sparkin' you?"

"Yeah. I met him on the train. He owns his own farm already."

"He owns a farm? How old is he?"

"Well, he's twenty-two. The farm is a citrus ranch that his pa sold
to him from his inheritance. He still owes on it, but he owns it." She
smiled big. "They raise oranges."

"Uh-huh. What's his name?"

"Walter… Schroeder." She said quietly with much anxiousness.

"Oh?"

"He's Catholic."

"I see. Well, I think we should meet this young man, by all means."

That evening in the sitting room, Mary Jane said to Jake, "Nellie
Bly wants to have a young man over for supper."

Jake pushed his newspaper into his lap and looked at Nellie Bly
who held her head high. "Who might that be?" he said.

"His name is Walter Schroeder."

"From the German camp in Anaheim?"

"He is twenty-two years old and owns a citrus ranch between here
and Anaheim."

"Lutheran?"

Mary Jane smiled covertly. She could tell Jake was getting up for a
debate. He was paying more attention to religion these days. But won't
he be surprised?

"Catholic."

"Oh! Oh. Say he owns his own ranch? Never owned a ranch, have
we, Mary Jane? Well, by all means. Have him over. Let's meet this
young feller."

Six months later, Jake and Mary Jane sat at the kitchen table with pencil and paper and a pile of estimates. "Well, that should do it. Let's go down the list one more time to be sure," Jake said.

Mary Jane read from her list and Jake checked off his list as she went to be sure they had all the costs accounted for. "I think that's it. Schroeders have the alcohol."

"Carriage," Jake said. "Forgot the carriage." Then he looked up and said, "Yeah. John Zeigler is going to open the back door of the saloon to the garden at the hotel so folks can meander between the food, dancin', and saloon. There'll be tables in the garden and in the lobby of the hotel."

"You think many of the folks will just walk the few blocks from the chapel at St. Catherine's to the Commercial Hotel?"

"That's what we are encouraging. But some won't be up to the walk, especially keeping up with the carriage. So, they'll fall in line and there'll be a procession of buggies. But I hear old Albert Kearns is planning to drive his Ford Touring Car and offered to carry the bridesmaids. Ralph Kroeger is driving his roadster. There'll probably be others too. Seems like everybody has to have a motor car these days. I hope we don't get backfires and scare the horses. It'd be a Texas stampede." He looked concerned but smiled at the same time as Mary Jane did. "Okay, let's see." He took a moment and added up his figures. "Comes to just under five hundred." He stared steadily at Mary Jane.

"You sure you want to spend that kind of money?" Mary Jane said with a frown. "I want her to have the wedding we didn't have but... this is really puttin' on the dog. Not that I mind, of course." She grinned.

Jake grinned back and said, "It's a big chunk of our savings, but who better to spend it on, eh?" He leaned across the table and gave her a kiss.

JAKE BEAMED HIS love and admiration at Nellie Bly. She was so beautiful in her wedding dress and a fine person on top of that. He took her hands in his and noted that she was shaking just a little. "Nervous?" he said. She smiled up at him and shook her head yes. "Don't be, honey. You are Nellie Bly Brighton of Texas stock. One of the finest." He flashed a grin on her and she grinned back.

"You're right," she said and took a deep breath.

"Ready?"

"Yes."

Jake nodded to an attendant, and the wedding march music began and off they went down the aisle. After he gave the bride away, Jake sat next to Mary Jane and try as he would, he could not staunch the emotional weeping that followed. Mary Jane handed him her hanky.

The wedding and reception were a grand success and even made the front page of the Santa Ana Daily Register, even though there was no Texas Stampede. Another thing it did was to start Jake thinking about things.

He and Mary Jane had just finished a sandwich for dinner and he was still at the table staring into his coffee cup. "What are you so pent up about?" Mary Jane said with a hint of challenge.

"Well, you know, I been thinkin'. Nellie Bly's weddin' got me to thinkin' about a lot of things. You remember that when Chris Evans went to prison he asked me to adopt his children. That always bothered me. Still does. And it always bothered me that I betrayed his friendship so he could be captured. He never knew. He always thought I was one of his best friends. I was duty bound, but it still was an act of betrayal. I think I'll write a letter to the governor askin' him to pardon Chris. What a you think?"

"I think that would be a nice act of mercy. You should do it. Probably ease your conscious a bit too."

Well, there was one more headline for J.V. Brighton that broke in May 1908 and read: *Seeks Release Of Man He Betrayed To Prison.* It was published in Santa Monica and picked up by newspapers as far away as Spokane, Washington.

———————

JAKE AND MARY Jane continued to spend their days wiling away the time playing rummy or sitting on the front porch. Every Sunday Nellie Bly and Walter would pick them up in their new motor car and drive to the main ranch for early supper at the Schroeders'.

One quiet and warm afternoon Jake and Mary Jane were sitting on the porch watching the birds flit around, in, and out of the birdbath. Jake said, "You know I was looking at the paper last night and saw an ad for the Nickelodeon in Anaheim. They're playin' *The Cowboy Millionaire* with Tom Mix. I hear it's pretty funny. You wanna go see it? See how real it is?"

"Sure. Tomorrow afternoon?"

After the first few scenes, Jake and Mary Jane were chuckling. By the end of the movie were having a good laugh. As they walked out of the theatre, Jake said, "C'mon. I'll buy you a drink. I need one after that."

They walked down to the Commercial Hotel and stepped through the lobby to the saloon. John Zeigler was tending the bar. It still being early in the afternoon there were no other patrons in the saloon. "Howdy, John," Jake said with a friendly grin as did Mary Jane.

"Hello, Mary Jane, Jake," he said with a smile. "What can I get you?" he stared at them suspiciously. "You two look like you're sitting in the catbird's seat."

"Oh, no," Jake said. "We were just down at the Nickelodeon and saw the Tom Mix picture show called The Cowboy Millionaire. We're still chucklin' over it. Give us a couple of Overholts."

"Yeah. I saw it, too. You used to be a cowboy, didn't you?"

"Sort of." He looked to Mary Jane and she was smiling big right at him. "What's so funny?" She turned away.

"Was it like they were showin' with all that shootin' every time they got excited?" John asked as he poured two glasses.

Jake grinned and Mary Jane grinned. "Heck no. If those pistols were loaded with real bullets, there would a been a few bodies lying around, that's for sure. Cowboys used to get rowdy like that on the drives and hurrah a town, shootin' their pistols in the air. But not no more."

"I thought it was really funny when they started shootin' up the house in Chicago where Tom Mix's new sweetheart lived."

"Yeah and ridin' down the street when they first came to Chicago to visit their old pard. Hah, hah, hah," Jake laughed, as did Mary Jane and John who joined in.

John, still laughing said, "You ever shoot up a town like that?"

"Naw," Jake said still smiling big. "I never was on a cattle drive."

"Well, what'd you do then?"

Jake's smile faded a little and he took down half the whiskey. "I was in law enforcement."

"You were a sheriff or a marshal?"

Then Jake's smile disappeared and he looked over at Mary Jane. She was still smiling. She shrugged her shoulders, finished her whiskey and said, "John, you're lookin' at Rawhide Jake Brighton, the most feared stock detective in all of northwest Texas. He don't like to talk 'bout it."

Zeigler's eyes widened, he intensified and said, "Well, I'll be. Ever shoot anybody like in the dime novels? I still read 'em."

Mary Jane immediately turned serious and said, "John, there are some things you just don't ask a man. That's one of 'em."

Zeigler's smile vanished and he turned away from Mary Jane's icy stare to look at Jake only to be met by Jake's black death stare. He gulped and Mary Jane bailed him out by saying with her resumed smile, "Give us two more, John."

"Sure. Sure. Didn't mean any offense."

"None taken." Jake smiled, raised his glass and said, "Here's how."

Mary Jane raised hers and said, "Here's how."

Zeigler got the idea, poured himself a glass and said, "Here's how."

As they walked arm in arm to catch the Red Car back to Buena Park Jake pulled his hat down to shade his eyes from the dying sun. "You know, I don't know why people get so worked up about shootin' someone. They got no idea what it's like, but they all wanna know."

"Maybe it's the mystery of the thing."

"Yeah. And they act like you're some kind a hero. I ain't at all proud a the killin's I did. They were all justified, but that don't make them anything to be proud of."

"Yeah."

Then he looked at her with a funny smile. "We sure did freeze ol' John's guts, though, didn't we?" They had a good laugh over that one.

IN 1913, MISTER Schroeder died suddenly and Missus Schroeder wanted to move into town, so Nellie Bly and Walter moved to the main ranch and rented their house to his brother. So far there were no grandchildren for Jake and Mary Jane, and Nellie Bly was quite active in public affairs and the politics of Orange County. All was well until late in 1917 when Mary Jane started doubling over in pain. A year later she was in the nursing home becoming increasingly more emaciated with the passing of every month. Jake spent four hours a day with her every day. He met a woman there who visited her dying husband every day and when her husband died, she volunteered to sit with Mary Jane when Jake was there and when he wasn't. Her name was Minerva Springer. Jake was at the point now where he had to use a crutch to get around as the cane did not provide enough support. Both Mary Jane and Jake were thankful for Minerva's frequent company. And day by day they passed the time away.

On a balmy June day in 1918, Jake made his regular visit to the nursing home. He wobbled on his crutch up to the reception desk and said, "Hello, Arlene." He gave Mary Jane's name and patient number.

"Hello, Mister Brighton. How are you today?" the clerk asked.

"Doin' as well as can be expected, I suppose."

She gave him his pass. Jake tipped his hat and turned to go down the hall where he limped away on the crutch. He came to Mary Jane's ward, opened one of the double swinging doors and went through. Five beds down on the right. She was sleeping. He sat in the chair like he did every day and unfolded his newspaper. One last glance at her, and he started reading.

About an hour later someone dropped a bedpan and the crash made Jake jump as well as awakened Mary Jane. Jake looked at her and she turned her head slightly toward him. "Oh, good, you made it," she said weakly with a just as weak a smile.

"Just like every day, Mary Jane," Jake said as he stood, leaned over her, smiled, and kissed her on the forehead.

"Today's kind of special, though," she said in a voice barely above a whisper.

Jake smiled and said, "How's that?"

"I'm goin' home."

The smile immediately disappeared from Jake's face and was replaced by a deep furrow of concern. "What do you mean?"

"You know what I mean. It's time."

"No. Mary Jane, don't leave me. *Please.*"

"Minerva will take care of you. I want you to marry her."

"No. No. No. Please, Mary Jane. Don't go," he sobbed.

She raised her hand and Jake took it. Her grip was weak but still a grip. "C'mon now, Rawhide Jake. Be tough. I'll see you on the other side, pard." A slight smile. Her eyes closed. Her grip relaxed. And she was still.

Jake fell on her and sobbed for a good five minutes. Then he rose up wiped his eyes with his coat sleeves and stared at her face. A vision of Mary Jane when he first met her came to him. She laughed with him and loved him with her sparkling glacier-blue eyes as they twirled around the dance floor. He loved her back and his heart began to throb the more he looked into her eyes. It was but a few minutes and... he came back. The vision faded.

His forever love was gone.

He stared at her face and little memories came to him that were associated with her various expressions. Gently, he moved a wisp of her hair off her forehead and folded her hands on her chest. "You were too good to me," he whispered. "You were my rock. See you on the other side, pard." He kissed her forehead, picked up his crutch and stumped away. Nellie Bly came hurrying down the corridor. With one look at him, she gasped and started sobbing as she ran to the ward doors and pushed through.

All the arrangements had been made some time before, and Mary Jane was buried at a cemetery near the National Cemetery in Los Angeles. From then on it was mostly a slow downhill slide for Jake. He and Minerva were married in November of the same year and she cared for him magnificently for years. She was much younger at fifty-five years old, and could pretty easily help him around as he became more sickly. She fed him, helped him bathe, and kept their house. She nursed him quite well enough until his old war ailments caught up with him and his stomach, bladder, and kidney problems became too much for her. Then he had to enter the Old Soldiers Home at Sawtelle, where he lasted until September 13, 1928, when he succumbed to a massive stroke. He was eighty-one years old and was buried with full military honor on the same day he died. His gravestone stands to this day at the Los Angeles National Cemetery in Section 34, Row B, Grave Number 27. It reads: *CORPL. JONAS V. BRIGHTON CO. A 21 ILL. INF.* Mary Jane is interred close by.

LAST WORD

THE REAL-LIFE J.V. Brighton—allegedly aka Rawhide Jake—was in this author's opinion, a man of varied experience, including hardship, who could be relied upon to get the job done by various means available to him. Those jobs were dangerous and his life was often in peril. Nevertheless, in piecing together the available information on Brighton a central theme seems to surface.

There are long gaps in time between the headlines on Brighton's most notorious events. For example, after a barrage of publicity stemming from his work on the Dr. Perry Talbott murder and his arrests in Missouri in 1881 and 1882, except for his marriage to Mary Jane Whitaker, May 16, 1884, in Wichita Falls, TX, there is no known record of his doings and whereabouts until he appears in Springerville, AZ in September of 1885 when and where he is appointed Constable of the Springerville District. So, in this case, not only is there a gap but he also is un-trackable. To maintain continuity, I had to fill in the gap for which Volume II, *Lonestar Fame,* was devised as a purely fictional account of what could have been his undertakings then and is driven by his marriage to Mary Jane in Wichita Falls, Texas from which questions arise that needed to be answered, if not historically then fictitiously. For example, what was he doing in Texas two years after his troubles in Missouri? Why did they relocate to Arizona? Why in Springerville was he allegedly known as a stock detective? Where did he learn that trade?

But where he can be tracked during those intermediate periods, he seems to have devoted much of his time to community and/or tranquil family life in common labor. For example, he and his wife Mary Jane lived in Springerville, Arizona for nearly five years during which time they were homeowners, business owners, and J.V. was Constable of the Springerville District and sat on several juries. They lived in the San Juaquin Valley for six years where he worked as a farm laborer and managed to incur a serious fracture of his leg but, nothing more. Then after the Roscoe train robbery arrests in 1894 up to his last day in 1928 there is nothing remarkable about his life whatsoever. Therefore, it seems that fame came in short bursts and he grabbed the limelight to use to his best advantage when it was shining. Otherwise, he and Mary Jane seem to have been pretty regular folks. And that is the light in which I cast them. Although, admittedly, I attribute to J.V. a deep-seated rage at perceived injustice that flashes in instances of lost temper and a defiant ice-cold fearless glare at death.

Controversy to this day surrounds the killing of Ike Clanton. In this series of the life and times of Detective Jonas V. Brighton that story is covered in Volume II, *Westward Ho!* I think the controversy is fueled by a few factors. First, reports of the event were carried in many, many newspapers throughout the West and not long after found their way east. The articles are a cobweb of distortion to the point of presenting different locations, persons and circumstances. For example, *The Fall River Daily Herald,* Fall River Massachusetts, in its April 12, 1888, issue (see Newspapers.com) apparently re-prints a story from the *St. Louis Republican,* speaking of Ike Clanton: *"About a year and a half ago Clanton went to Phoenix, A.T. There he met Virgil and Wyatt Earp. The moment the old enemies saw each other they began to shoot. Clanton was killed, and Wyatt Earp was so badly wounded that he is no longer numbered among the desperados of the west."* Fabrications such as this from reputable newspapers cause all kinds of suspicion and controversy develops among historians and other writers about what actually happened.

Second, although Neal Du Shane and his colleagues believe they located Ike Clanton's unnamed grave in 2012, it is not beyond a doubt until DNA testing is conducted. A relative of the Clanton clan, Terry Ike Clanton, is working on that with the city of Tombstone to exhume the bones, identify them, and move them to Boot Hill in Tombstone next to other members of the Clanton clan. The location Du Shane identified is adjacent to the remains of Peg Leg Wilson's cabin, pinpointed at coordinates N33 26 44.06 W109 29 38 57, and marked by a natural X in a stone believed to be set at the head of the grave. However, the fact remains that Ike Clanton's corpse never received a proper Coroner's Inquest, has never been produced and only according to the word of a few people, who are now deceased, was buried at Peg Leg Wilson's cabin. Maybe he wasn't in actual fact, killed? But then, he was never heard of or seen again.

Third, some historians think there are clues in the print archives that could point to Wyatt Earp as the shooter and not Brighton—or at least as the man who Ike recognized and ran from at the door of Wilson's cabin. You never know what forgotten historical record could show up and prove them right. It is possible but not likely that Brighton and Miller gave a false story to cover for Wyatt Earp.

As for me, I say this. The Arizona Historical Society has in its file a copy (it may be the original) of the original hand-written article by probably J.F. Wallace who was the manager of the *St. Johns Herald* at the time of the printing of the article in the June 9, 1887, edition. It purports to be a report given on June 6 by Albert Miller, A.[sic]V. Brighton and Geo. Powell to the *St. Johns Herald* of the killing of Ike Clanton by J.V. Brighton. It is generally accepted as the record of the actual event and I stand by it for the reasons set forth below.

Although Powell was there for the report, he was not involved in the incident and can therefore be discounted. However, Miller and Brighton along with Peg Leg James Wilson are the alleged eye-witnesses. Why would they lie about it? Wilson either agreed with the story or stayed away from any public denial because he was wanted in New Mexico for murder. But, why would Miller support the story if it wasn't true? As far as is known there is no hint of refutation by him. The Apache County Stock Growers Association offered a two hundred-fifty-dollar reward for the capture and conviction of rustlers. However, there is no indication that a reward was offered specifically for Clanton's capture or killing. Brighton and Miller were both deputized and theoretically doing their duty. In that regard, it appears that Brighton in accepting a deputization might have simply responded to a request for help. There was a lot of chatter about Brighton working undercover for the Apache County Stock Grower's Association but, the association publicly denied it. Both Brighton and Miller were known to Clanton but he did not know that Brighton had been deputized whereas he knew that Miller was the law. That is probably why he lit out like they said when he saw Miller. He knew there was a warrant out on him. No, I think the detail supports the Brighton/Miller story as the accurate report of the event and to this day has not been successfully refuted.

The peculiar mystery in my mind focuses on the question: why didn't Brighton and Miller bring Clanton's body to the sheriff at Solomonville or St. Johns? Even Clifton could have been a place to take it. Granted, there would have been some transit time and St. Johns, the seat of Apache County where Clanton was wanted, was a stretch. But, Solomonville, the county seat of Graham County and the county in which Ike Clanton was killed, was probably not more than a two-day ride with a pack horse. Of course, we'll most likely never know the answer to the question because there is no known contemporary record of the question either asked or answered.

BACK IN THE day, when Jeff Arnold was a kid, he watched plenty of westerns on TV, read a few books and always wanted to be a rancher. As it turned out, he never got there. Instead, he is a veteran combat Army aviator, former deputy sheriff and death investigator, and long-time CPA. Now he sort of lives a rancher's life vicariously through the books he writes. After the Rawhide Jake trilogy, there is more to come with the novels *Paradise Creek, Sticker Joe Spurlock,* and a family saga set north of the Mogollon Rim in Arizona.

Jeff lives by the polo fields in Indio, California, with Diane, his wife of half a century, and Sofie, their canine love. His children and grandchildren reside in the next county over to the west. He wishes peace to everyone, everywhere.